The Swing of Things

SEAN O'REILLY

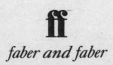

faber and faber

First published in 2004
by Faber and Faber Limited
3 Queen Square London WC1N 3AU
This paperback edition first published in 2005

Typeset by Faber and Faber Ltd
Printed in England by Mackays of Chatham plc, Chatham, Kent

A CIP record for this book
is available from the British Library

ISBN 0–571–22132–7

2 4 6 8 10 9 7 5 3 1

For Billy Ó hAnluain
. . . who came back laughing

O madam, bend over, I want to tell you something.

J. P. Donleavy, *The Ginger Man*

My whirling wings are the doors through which she enters the swan's neck, on the great deserted square that is the heart of the bird of night.

A. Breton and P. Eluard, *The Immaculate Conception*

Be it enacted by the Queen's most Excellent Majesty, by and with the advice and consent of the Lords Spiritual and Temporal, and Commons, in this present Parliament assembled, and by the authority of the same, as follows . . .

Northern Ireland (Sentences) Bill, AD 1998

The author apologises on behalf of his characters
for any unacknowledged (mis)quotations.

PART ONE

<u>Call him Boyle.</u>

He wiped the rain off the bridge parapet with his sleeve and leaned over for a look at the drop to the water. The river was low and stagnant in its wheaten stone trough. Angular shadows from buildings and spires were under the surface coloured by greens and browns and brief zones of blue from the sky, the moving sky. The green was the reflection from the age-old tapestry of weeds and moss hung on the walls all the royal way through the city to the sea.

Call him Noel Boyle.

Under the murky reflections, he would have been able to see the apocalyptic objects submerged in the mulch bed of the river: a shopping trolley, a metal window frame, a tractor tyre, a long crooked leafy bough, an armchair, a beer keg. Platonic outcasts, he mused and then a snarl appeared on his face, either from distaste with his own mind or because all these things were made invisible by a glare on the water from the sun set free from a nut-squad of cloud. Boyle raised his eyes and watched a train leaving the station.

Say this is Dublin. A man on the bridge watches a train leaving Heuston Station and the windows parry back the light of the Free State morning sun.

Someone passing across the bridge in a car might have noticed him check on either side before his hand moved quickly towards the bouquet inserted into the ironwork curls of the balustrade.

The flowers were white roses, wrapped in white paper. There was no card of In Memoriam.

Boyle seemed to be trying to nip the head off one of the stalks without crushing the petals. None of them would come loose for him. Using both hands, he began to twist the flower more roughly, too roughly because the whole bouquet was dislodged and dropped to the pavement.

Say a woman was walking over the bridge at the same time. She sees a man staring at a bouquet of flowers on the ground between his feet. What would she think? That they have fallen from the sky? That he has dropped them and is appalled by what it might mean?

The man has a thin build, and a smallish face under a tight brown beard although there is a touch of white like a feather in the hair at his throat. He wears denim, new and washed out. The woman is alarmed suddenly by the idea that the man is about to trample on the flowers. She would hate to see that. Violence of that sort would cast a shadow across the rest of her day.

Although the man doesn't look threatening, the woman decides that it would be safer to step into the road to avoid him, making sure to look the other way as though she is engrossed in counting the number of bridges to the sea. It is a lovely morning in Dublin, she repeats to herself. Yes, a lovely summer morning in Dublin. She has always chanted to herself when she feels afraid. Once safely past him, she risks a glance back only to see that he is standing in the same position.

After she was out of sight, Boyle picked up the bouquet and fitted the stems into a sturdier position in the metalwork. Moving slowly along the bridge, he scattered the rain with his hand from the balustrade and leaned out to see the drops falling and sprinkling the disgruntled water. Maybe as he did this he thought of himself as a boy and was unsurprised that his memories were bandy and trivial and sentimental; the heat from a flaming bonfire that tightened the skin and gave them all the eyes of squinting old men, the nettles grown tall and yellow from piss where he used to hide his warrior stick when he was called in for the night, the lonely summer day he went for a walk out the back roads and got lost but the dark didn't and came down around him in the fields and he prayed to God to bring him home and a woman appeared, a tall pale woman who walked beside him in silence, the imprint of pebbledash in the skin of the first girl he ever pressed hard against a wall and the puddle trembling between her flip-flops a second before the explosion, his mother and father dancing drunk in the kitchen late at night, the last drag on a filter butt from the scarred black fingers of the older boys at the corner.

Boyle stopped; he leaned out further over the bridge. The wind made tyre tracks across the water. Invisible golden chariots, no, tanks of sunlight, caterpillar wheel marks.

A car horn went off and a voice shouted: Jump. Do it now. Don't listen to them.

Boyle did not turn round. It was time to get off the bridge: he was looking suspicious. At the lights, with a bar of damp across his stomach and a bag over his shoulder, he waited, abiding by the law. Away from the city centre, the traffic all came towards him, big lorries carrying disaster from the docks out into the west. The long brewery wall might have reminded him of something else, an old jail, say, but he was tired of thinking about the past.

Yes, say he is a man who has had enough of the past.

Up in the wind, a bright new tricolour furling and lapping over the green dome of the Four Courts failed to disperse a complaining pack of gulls.

Say he decides to go in somewhere for a cup of coffee. Say he does this every morning; it is part of the routine that he has built up since arriving in this city. Yes, he is not long on these streets. In fact, he would be annoyed at whoever might have the nerve to tell him he had already established a routine.

He would feel intimidated, watched.

The café was a small place, one room with half a dozen tables and prints of racehorses on the papered walls. The radio was usually on loud but not this morning. No familiar faces either like the man with his tape who had been kept waiting for years it seemed for the right moment to put it on.

5

A young couple with faces that had not seen a pillow studied him as he took his usual chair by the window and after he had taken the newspaper out of his bag they were whispering about him. Pitying him, the way lovers think the world is for them alone, that they have found the exquisite secret, the happiness without wisdom, and the rest are lost in explanations and random lusts.

What would he know about lovers? When was the last time he had even . . .

The waitress arrived at the table with his coffee.

Say she has spoken to him before.

Arms folded under big well-used breasts, she looked out at the street where a truck was reversing, filling the café with its electronic warning bleatings.

I hate that bloody noise, she said. All day and all night you hear that. This whole place is going backwards.

She wouldn't have been bad looking if it wasn't for her mouth, the bitter tension in it, down-turned.

A fat man with a wet face came out of the toilet and made his way to the door. Keeping her back to him, the waitress blocked his exit. She started to clap her hands.

Bravo, she said. Encore.

The fat man wiped his hands on his trousers and looked at Boyle humbly.

This one's been in there for half an hour heaving up his guts. Tell me he's cleaned up after himself.

The fat man nodded to Boyle, fixing his tie.

He has, Boyle said.

Tell him I'm going to close my eyes and count to ten.

The fat man went out by her. When she had finished counting, she remained in the same position and Boyle turned a page of the newspaper and began to make himself a cigarette.

You have small hands, she said. You don't work with them either.

Boyle ignored her.

I used to go out with a Northerner, she went on. Some

town or other up there. I was only a young woman. I didn't have time for all that nonsense. I wanted to enjoy myself.

She made a sound in her throat that suggested she had failed utterly.

Where's your man? Boyle asked. The man with the tape.

She rolled her eyes. Hospital. Took a heart attack on the street I hear. No better place for him if you ask me.

Boyle smiled at the way she tapped the side of her head and the woman gave him a broad smile back, the bitterness erased from her lips and her eyes fluttering nervously.

So what's on the tape?

Songs. I put them on for him once in a while. German I think they are. Old ones now like. He must have lived over there or something. I made the mistake of feeling sorry for him once years ago and he's pestered me ever since. But he has no one. He's on his own.

Look at that, Boyle said, stabbing a photograph in the paper with his lighter.

Holding her hair away from her face, the waitress bent over him like she was looking into a pram at unwelcome progeny.

One of those foreigners probably, she said. Drowned was she? We'll probably have to pay for the funeral now as well. Who knows what she was involved in? What about that man found stuffed in the suitcase in the canal? They put a picture of his shoes in the paper to see if anybody knew him. They were an old pair of trainers only, real cheap ones now. You'd be ashamed to say you knew him. Always wear a clean pair of knickers that's what they say. Just in case. You never know do you? You never know what's going to happen when you walk out that door in the morning.

Boyle took stock of her ankles and her own shoes, platformed trainers, as she went towards the doorway, and then up across the weak belted hips to the sharp blade bones almost touching on her narrow back, and the huge gold hoops like ripples lodged in her ears. She looked both ways along the street like the rain was pouring down.

Passing him again, she said, When I woke up this morning, if you can call it that, waking up I mean, I don't know any more but anyway I had a feeling that something was going to happen, a strong feeling. Do you know what I mean? This was going to be an important day I said to myself.

Boyle nodded.

Probably kidding myself as per usual.

When he approached the counter to pay, she was talking on a mobile, telling someone about her presentiments, what her stars had said at the weekend. She waved away his money.

Say, after a short distance, he turned his back on the river and made for Dame Street. His pace was unhurried. He had eyes for the different windows, the people out in the open, the old buildings, he did his best to remain interested. It was necessary to stay connected to the world, to rouse the senses continually or else he would fade out of existence, fail to exist, like so many times before. There, for example, through one window was a man in a barber's chair, tucked up to the neck in a white gown and smiling at the barber who was acting out some story in the mirror for him, the scissors upheld in his hand like a puppet master. Or over on the other side of the street, passing the dirty statues that were supposed to be the Three Graces, which he reminded himself again to find out about, a man and a woman had stopped to talk together and it was obvious they hadn't seen each other in a long time and they were delighted to run into each other and it might have been years and even another country or friends from school or cousins. Or there was the extraordinary colour of the metal roof on the building at the corner with South Great George's Street, the colonial city, which was purple and blue in the sun up there like grapes or crabs or heather or that word amethyst maybe. The point was to stay awake, no, engaged, to pick out the details so that there was some feeling of control, the empirical hallucination.

At the end of Dame Street he stopped before the university gates. That waitress wanted things to change in her life but if this day was no different than the others Boyle thought he would be happy. This was a time for reflection, days of taking stock. Some kind of clearing away. Distillation. The blue clock said ten and a bit. The wooden doors were legally open to him: he had a right to enter. The holy trinity: life; death; rebirth. He held his breath as he passed through the sour air in the dark porch, no, archway. Once out again in the light his eyes took in the grandeur of the columns, the students on the broad steps, the old trees, the lawns cordoned by heavy black chains. The buildings of the past bred a healthy humility in the disciples of knowledge. A girl in a yellow dress was leading a group of tourists around the main quadrangle, pointing, explaining, turning it all into anecdote. She turned and smiled at Boyle as though they knew each other. Embarrassed, Boyle gave her a bad look. He saw the tourists sniggering. The girl laughed it off expertly. Boyle knew they were all watching him, and they were right to, and he deserved it for his lack of general communion, goodwill, a girl smiles a casual hello, maybe embarrassed herself at what she has to do to pay the rent, and he shuns it, humiliates her, one of them should be shouting after him to go back into his hole and stay there out of sight of the rest of the world just trying to get through the day with fairness and a touch of humour when possible, as he made his awkward way across the slippery freshly hosed cobbles towards the library.

Boyle had his choice of desks this early in the morning. A librarian pushed a squeaking trolley of books in front of him. He took up a position with a view of the grass square outside the building where they kept the Book of Kells on show. Threads of blood sewn into the margins. Viking sails on the horizon. War paint and holy wells. He found himself imagining a conversation where he was telling somebody his reasons for not having been in to see the book although he passed the building every day: I don't need to see it, he told her and she smiled back at him with her blue eyes, or something stops me when I go near the door, a revulsion, a resis-

9

tance, I don't need to consume everything immediately I see it, and she leaned forward and kissed him lightly on his lips.

Through the window, Boyle watched a girl jogging across the cobbles in a red baseball cap, a blond ponytail come-hithering out behind her, long Lycra-clad legs, a small optimistic arse.

Not a chance in hell.

He was meant to be working on an essay for his continental philosophy class which had to be submitted by noon the next day. Part of the job was to formulate his own question to answer. For the past month he had been reading whatever he wanted or found left behind on the tables by other students, books on music, archaeology, law, the start of a few novels which never held his attention for long. Boyle had lost his way and he knew it. The other essays, on Berkeley, Edmund Burke, Plato's Dialogues, Hume had all come out easily enough and the grades were decent despite the complaint that the writing was laboured and strangely inconclusive. Most days now Boyle sat in the library reading books indiscriminately and spying out the window at the life of the students sitting around the sunken grass square like children at a paddling pool, the spring duped again by the lies of summer.

He flicked to the back of Being and Nothingness and read down through the definitions of special terminology:

Actaeon complex: Totality of images which suggest that 'knowing' is a form of appropriative violation with sexual overtones.

Bad Faith: A lie to oneself within the unity of a single consciousness.

Négatité (néantir): Sartre's word for types of human activity which while not obviously involving a negative judgement nevertheless contain negativity as an integral part of their structure; e.g., experiences involving absence, change, interrogation, destruction.

Pushing the book away, Boyle took out the newspaper again and spread it across the table. He had heard the story the night before on the radio, which he often kept on while he slept, that a woman had been found drowned in the Liffey. The Guards believed she had been dead no longer than twenty-four hours but they were having trouble identifying her. Although she did not appear to have been the victim of any physical attack, they were keeping an open mind until the results of the autopsy were finalised. The article also hinted the woman was not Irish. Alongside was printed a photograph which showed a mask of a woman's face, a death mask in smooth white plaster. The mask was eyeless and stopped squarely at the hairline and narrowed sharply along the jaw to the chin. The ears were missing also but it was a good bet they were in proportion to the face which had strong sloping cheekbones and large oval eye sockets. Boyle imagined she would have been tall and broad across the shoulders, with a heavy chest, what might be called statuesque. Her hair would have been bountiful and long. The mouth was big, the thick lips caught for ever in a smile of serene fulfilment.

A happy death, he thought.

Say he stared at the smile until his eyes grew heavy.

Say he put his face in his hands and stayed that way for a long time, wondering at the nausea in his guts.

A few hours later, Boyle was outside having a smoke. The sun was comically alone in a blue wilderness sky, blazing panic-stricken over the heraldic slates and cricket players and the students seated shoulder-to-shoulder around the edge of the grass square, slugging on youth-inducing water and exchanging the latest theories on the nature of happiness. The sun made them brave, painted their faces and filled their eyes with trance. An army resting, waiting for orders on their mobile phones that would never come. For the enemy had moved inside, within, that's what their tutors gave them to believe, back into the heart and the mind, the savage dark soul, and there was nothing to fear among the stones and the holes but themselves. Standing next to the noticeboard Boyle was seething with the notion that all the philosophy he had been reading could be reduced to the single idea that every effect has a cause, that nothing happens without a reason, and therefore the world and all creation have a purpose. Ergo: I am and I will thrive and I will trample you underfoot if you get in my way. He picked a tobacco pube from his lip and scanned the announcements for open auditions for a play supposedly written by Wolfe Tone, bikes for sale, a martial arts demonstration by a visiting master, cheap drink in the bar on intercultural night and a debate around the question of whether Unionism had any future in modern Ireland.

A tap on the shoulder sent all this into oblivion and sucked Boyle after it. He heard her saying she was sorry and felt her hand touch his shoulder again and the back of his neck but it was a few seconds before he was able to put his feet on the ground and breathe again.

She continued to apologise but her eyes were alight, gleaming with delight, no, another word, amusement, or something in between that also involved curiosity, like a child with a strange animal.

She wanted to know why he wasn't at the lecture. Boyle's urge was to ask her what business was it of hers, that because he had spoken to her a few times didn't give her any rights over him. But when he looked at her all the words were a scatter of deranged birds flying into windows that reflected either a glorious sunrise or a city on fire.

You always used to come to everything, she said.

Boyle laughed and took out his tobacco pouch, leather, hand-sewn by Volunteer Keith 'Mildew' Madden, RIP, murdered by British imperialist forces, April 1995, a flag over his grave in a cemetery next to a new petrol station on the road to Greencastle.

Did you get your essays in?

He shrugged and squinted into the distance as though she had asked him to say what was wrong with Utilitarianism, or the use of violence, this young soft-faced girl with the safari-blue eyes who was only being friendly, facing him squarely, open and frank and showing concern with her shallow freckled cleavage, a lilac vest, the strap of an old school satchel biting into her tanned smooth shoulder, her wrists wrapped with coloured strings.

Her name was Emer. He had met her for the first time in the queue on enrolment day. They were both doing the same course, and were soaked by the rain. Because of the rain, and maybe the porthole windows in the domed hall, they began to joke about the ark and what she might bring back in her soft pink chapped beak. Privately he called her the Dove. In the weeks that followed, he spoke to her briefly outside classes but it wasn't until an introductory drinks party for the department that he heard about her year out in Asia and Tibet and began to feel uncomfortable with her permanent state of inspiration. It seemed that everything she had ever seen or done or thought about doing remained as fresh and feverish in her mind as the strawberries she had had for breakfast or the glorious sights on the journey in on the Dart that morning, from her childhood holidays on the Amalfi coast to the ancient faces she knelt before in the smoke on a lush Tibetan mountainside. The taste of one sip of wine on her young healthy tongue was enough to ponder for a week.

She began to surprise him in the library and in the canteen, pulling up a chair beside him, smiling, and looking into his eyes, a list of questions ready in her mind. Her earnestness had the effect of making him feel despondent, miserable, mute. Her soft monkey-nut curls were as disheartening as barbed wire. He would laugh to escape the paralysis and then she would frown and ask why he always laughed at her. Biting her sun-chapped lips in the January wind as though there were no harm in it, she stared into his eyes, the same way she probably did with the binman, or the Tibetan children, or the Chinese woman in her local shop whom she was always talking about: Oh her wit, her courage, she is so daunting like. It had reached the stage now when he was afraid of her; he had dreamed about strangling her one night after he had confessed everything.

The Dove persuaded him to have a cup of coffee with her. At the counter she changed her mind however and went for the apple juice. He asked her about the lecture that morning which he had missed, listened to her talk about Kierkegaard and their lesbian lecturer because it saved him from having to speak.

But the questions came eventually: So where have you been? Tell me. Is something happening?

Nothing at all.

So you're all right then?

The Dove had that face of concern and restrained annoyance.

You think I'm too young to understand don't you? Her obvious relief in finally saying this to him made Boyle want to touch the hand on the table in front of him.

He shook his head.

Are you thinking of dropping out?

Boyle had not put that question to himself. He suddenly felt very sorry for himself. He thought of what Dainty would say, the slagging he would get for being so pathetic and failing to take advantage of this girl's interest in him.

Don't let them ruin it for you, she said. Forget about them. You're right; it is a privilege being here and it's wasted on most of us. They're only kids. I agree with you. People shouldn't go to university until they've had some life experience.

I'm ok, Boyle heard himself say and it had a sinister ring to it.

Are you really?

He nodded, afraid to say another word.

It's just that I like talking to you. You make me think. Most of the people my age are only interested in what they're doing at the weekend. Tell me you're not going to drop out, she demanded and now she put her hand on his.

With his other hand he scratched the beard on his chin.

I don't see . . .

What? Go on.

He didn't know what he was trying to say.

Two other girls appeared beside the table at that moment. The Dove did not withdraw her hand before he did. Boyle studied the smile on her face as she introduced him and discovered nothing that was certain. The next thing he knew all three of them were laughing. Three sets of young impulsive laughing eyes communing briefly and then waged against his bewildered own. The reason for it must surely be him, he was the joke, the cause of mirth. His confusion sharpened the whole effect, of course. Maybe they thought he was doing it on purpose, playing the fool. He tried to shrug and made a mess of it. A spasm you would have called it. The laughter was like an X-ray and showed him up as a twitching skeleton sucking hungrily on a fag butt in an open-plan student leisure area.

There it was again, in full bloom: paranoia. The brain inhaling its lethal scent. Flora convictus extremicus. The advice leaflets said it could last years. You're walking down the street and suddenly you are convinced somebody is following you. Or a car. A helicopter, new silent ones they haven't announced yet. The smile on that woman at the corner is a fake, a professional tail.

Paranoia. Paratrooper. Paramilitary. Paramour.

Quickly, probably ridiculously, Boyle made his excuses and left. The Dove came after him. As if nothing had happened, she made him promise that they would have a proper talk soon, maybe even have a drink together. He went back to the library, gathered his books and headed for the side gate.

Between the steep cliffs of glass and brick, the crowds on Grafton Street were moving slowly. Security guards radioed from nook to nook, door to door; bank, shoe shop, chemist's, jeweller's, multinational, chocolate shop, multinational. They're on their way up towards you Jamesy, three of them, white tracksuits, watch out for the girl, she'll take the eye out of your head. Cameras buzzed high on the lampposts as Boyle moved through the sweating glut and the gulls cried out their bin-day song in the narrow bridge of sky. There was an Arabic theme to the display in a department-store window, turbans and floors of furs and sand. At an intersection with a side street Boyle stopped to watch a street-performer, a man sprayed in gold who stood to attention on a pedestal with an old rifle on his shoulder and a gold balloon on a string over his head which he would take aim at when a coin was put in the slot at his feet. A few yards further on a trio of sad-faced Romanian men begged for joy with their accordions.

Boyle bought a sandwich and decided to make towards St Stephen's Green and sit himself down on the grass in the sun, like others did, like he had the right to do, and to go so far as to roll up his sleeves and take off his shoes if he found the right place and nobody was near. As he passed the flower-seller's stall he spotted a character he had listened to on a few occasions before, who was making a meal out of the struggle with his sandwich board. Boyle watched him wipe the sweat from his head, cross his arms Egyptian style and raise his face to the sun. The girl from the flower stall cut a stem with her scalpel and inserted the bloom in the buttonhole of his filthy shirt. Another minute must have passed, and at least a hundred sluggish people, before this character opened his eyes and his arms and cried out to the summer throng:

Poetry on tap, the great classics of Irish literature. Joyce and his chamber pots. Wilde and his twilight balconies. Yeats and his randy ghosts. I'll take you turf cutting with Heaney or onion eating with Jonathan Swift, lamenting the earls with O' Leary, into the monasteries and out on the misty hills, I've got ballads of the Easter Rising and odes to autumnal hussies, Sam the merciless, and brawling Behan, poets from the North and the South, Bobby Sands and Lady Gregory, bohemians and rednecks, dreamers and believers, wasters and wantnotters, scavengers and squanderers, a poem for everybody alive and dead, for the yawning refugees and pale-faced gunmen, the new Spanish armada and the Russian angsters, your mammy in heaven and your daddy in bed all the livelong day. Ah now, ah now, sure we'll all get there in the end, we're all headed the same way but there's nothing like a poem to hit the spot on the way, you can't beat a poet to scratch your back on a bright sweaty day like today, or lower down there, a bit lower, right down, down in the pit, in your damp mossy bog, and further down, down as far as you dare to go . . .

He went after two women in the crowd, dancing at their backs, heckling with poems – Your narrow brows, your hair like gold, lady with the swanlike body, I was reared by cunning hand – until one relented and span round in a swish of hair to face her seducer in open-mouthed delight. What she saw was the yellow eyes of the wolf, the leer, the slight frame, the torn green shirt and she screamed, a loud shriek of warning down the centuries of women.

In the commotion, Boyle lost sight of the ragged proclaimer. The two women held on to each other like they had seen a ghost. A security guard pushed his way towards them. People were laughing. Then, there he was again at the sandwich board: I am the lad of ceaseless hum, it's enough to make you broken hearted, thousands of legs and none of them parted.

The flower-stall girl rushed over and gave him a piece of her mind. The chanter flapped his arms like a starving carrion bird. Shortly after, some tourists stopped, Italians, then a few Americans, and he fired words at them, sometimes putting on actions: pleading, slapstick fury, starving peasant, man against the wind, dying warrior, and hunting around the sandwich board where the names were written in gold paint on a white background scrolled with green Celtic snakes and birds.

Then there was an old woman who appeared out of nowhere. She stood quietly in front of the reciter while he seemed to be explaining something to her, joining his hands with promises. He delivered another speech to the street and yet she was still there, in an old tweed coat in the heat, small, slight, dusty with years of loneliness, no, poverty, clasping her handbag. The reciter made more promises to her, wringing his hands desperately until he covered his face and went down on his knees behind the board, a penitent on the street even after she had gone her quiet way.

Up again he cried out, flapping his wings: Myself unto myself will give, this name Katharsis-Purgative. Name your poison. One from the forest smoke of the ancient bothy or a moan in the rickety air of the bedsit still. I was a listener at the street corner. I was wild with frolic in the mead-hall.

The flower girl threw a coin high in the air, a livelier one come on please, a funnier thing, lighten it up, and the reciter went after it, wings a-flapping, skinny pinions, his tongue hanging out, but he made a mess of the catch and the coin disappeared under the feet of the crowd. Shocked, fascinated too, Boyle watched the lunatic go after it, a dog now on his hands and knees scuttling between the legs. He seemed immune to any type of shame. Some of the passers-by found it funny but most wanted to kick him out of the way. The barking grew more desperate and was broken by howls; going round in circles, sniffing, the reciter was licking at the feet of those who had stopped to watch. Meanwhile, the flower girl was calling to him, Leave it, leave it, a bucket in her hand. The street was choking up. Boyle spotted the Guard making a beeline for the commotion.

A drenched reciter snoring skyward beside him, Boyle sat under a tree in St Stephen's Green, his back against the wrinkled trunk, watching the strollers along the paths and the sprawlers on the grass among the votive mounds of clothes and shoes. Two ducks flew down and disappeared into the trees on the island in the lake of mealy green water. On the other bank, a barechested man danced slow nirvana steps with a sword, bend, slow swipe, elbow turn, parry, full minutes between each move, pitted against the sun whose exorbitance seemed more serious now, violent in a hard new blueness direct in from the Tropics; jungle stench, giant turtles, yachts drifting for days, dolphin bursts, horizons of the immortals.

Without preamble, the reciter shot up awake, a panic mask on his face. He took one look at Boyle and bolted off across the grass. He didn't get very far; the run ended suddenly like he had forgotten why and he came back in stages, jerkily disputing with himself, the clothes sticking to him.

Do I know you? he went.

Boyle said, You were in a bit of trouble there on the street. The Guards nearly had you. So I took you for a walk.

The reciter grinned, wiped his mouth. Did I lose it?

He had a gaunt look, a long neck and harassed yellow eyes. There was grey in his short stiff hair and on his chest under the threadbare bright green shirt. Boyle shrugged and spread his gaze around the sun-hacked park while the reciter kept wiping his mouth nervously. Then he sat down, no, quicker, he jumped into a sitting position on the ground.

Was it bad?

You were barking like a dog, Boyle told him. Some girl

from that flower stall threw a bucket of water over you. She said she would look after the board thing. I brought you up here and you conked out.

The reciter grinned, a sleazy, long-lipped grimace, pulling at his damp shirt and the stained trousers.

And you were talking to some old woman, Boyle said.

The reciter shuddered and the face changed to an ugly sneer.

Listen to this, he said. Can I tell you this?

Boyle shrugged again, eyes on the distant sword dance, blade tip to the sun from the chest plate.

I'll tell you and see what happens. A few months ago that old woman came up to me on the street. I have some poems, she says. They're all I have left of him. Poor sweet Walter. Day after day, this happens. Some days she would show up and stand on the other side of the street, in that depressing old coat of hers, eating her way through a bag of pears. Staring at me, just staring, not a word. So one day I agreed to have a look at them. Maybe they're good, I thought to myself, maybe he's an undiscovered lyric genius and I could make a bit of money. Can I tell you this? Do you think it will do me any good?

You might start to believe it, Boyle said, and turned to his tobacco.

You're right. It's perilous. These could be the last sane words I speak. Or perhaps you've been sent to listen. Tell me to go on.

Boyle shook his head as a refusal and drew his lip along the gum strip in tandem with the passage of two women in the sunglare, mothers with prams, wealth in their hair and clothes, well-fed married quietus, exiting stage left.

The reciter clapped his hands. A sign. The suburban muse. Milk-laden. They dream of writhing naked in the compost heap at the bottom of the garden. They want –

Boyle looked at him, squinting, stern.

The reciter went straight on: So one afternoon I went back with the old woman to her house. Up beyond the canal bridge at Harold's Cross. We took the bus together and she told me all about poor sweet Walter, how he'd courted her, the poems he'd written her, how he knew all the big bohemian names of the day. And then he died one day for no apparent reason and everyone immediately forgot all about him. Poor sweet sensitive Walter. The old women on the bus were weeping all around me, passing around tissues and mints. I thought she was going to invite them back with us. A Dublin chorus of wailing as she opened the box where she kept the poems. It was like a jewellery box decorated with blue sand and tiny red shells and lined inside with white silk like a coffin. So she hands me the first poem and surprise surprise, it's drivel. Ode to a rose. Your long and slender reach, your dewtipped thorns, your blush of carnal pleasures. Dire stuff. What was I supposed to do? I said I would need some time to study them. They were written in long hand, beautiful writing though. I told her I would type them up for her and she gave me some money towards expenses. So I was feeling all right. I'd type them up on the cheap and give them back to her. So away I went with them in a plastic bag. And that's the last I remember of them.

How do you mean? You sold them?

The reciter sniggered.

You lost them or what?

I don't know. That's the truth. It's more than a month ago now and every day there she is on the street. I've tried everywhere I normally hang out but there's no sign. Every pub, every place I can think. But I get around a bit if you know what I mean. Some nights I don't even know where I ended up. A party in some house in the Liberties or some flat in Ranelagh or both. You know what I mean? Nights that are a furious blank.

Boyle said nothing.

But she's starting to get suspicious now. There's a different look in her eye and it's not pleasant. I'm having nightmares about her where she's standing at every corner pointing at me. Then I have these thoughts that there were no poems and it's all in my mind. Or I'll get hauled into a lane by her sons or three of her cousins up from the country. I swear to you she's put a curse on me. A hex. Ever since I touched those poems my whole life's fallen apart. It wasn't much of a life anyway like but now it won't stick together any more. She's probably sitting in her front room watching me now talking to you here in her crystal ball. I swear it's a spell or –

Boyle raised his hand to say enough.

But you saw her there talking to me didn't you? I'm not making it up am I? You saw her?

I saw an old woman just.

Let me tell you what happened last night to show you what I mean. Now I'm homeless as well. Everything's –

Boyle raised his hand again for quiet. The reciter giggled and jumped to his feet.

Close one eye and be king, close both and be god, he said. You're from the North aren't you? Do you live in Dublin?

Boyle nodded. The reciter dropped over into a bow, like a man winded.

Fada he said his name was. They shook hands in the sharp island light.

Let me tell you about last night, he tried again, his hands joined on top of his head. Boyle put him at around thirty although he looked older. As he moved around, the sun came through his clothes and showed up a skeletal body, a length of knotted rope, a hairy gnarled root stick scarecrow man. The story was that he had been staying for a while in somebody's house and they had come back the night before from a long trip and threw him out on the street, and a binliner of clothes a few minutes later.

He came through the door, took one look at me and told me to get out. I'd spent the whole day cleaning the place. I'd bought food in and a bottle of wine. He wouldn't say a word, just kept pointing at the door. He's a musician and he goes away a lot and likes to have somebody in the house. What do you think? Something must have happened. Should I leave it for a while to cool off? He doesn't –

·The reciter went down on his hunkers and motioned with his eyes at the view over Boyle's shoulder.

Boyle turned and saw the silk trunk of a teenage girl on the grass reading a book.

What do you think the word is? The reciter grinned. She's looking up a word in her precious little dictionary that she carries everywhere, that she flicks through when she's lonely. What do you think? Braless and bellydown on the grass. She can feel the grass points against her furry Spanish nipples. I was out with an au pair last week, an Italian, oh there's thousands of them drifting around Dublin, and she sneaked me up to her room. In the morning the woman of the house made me come down for breakfast and she sent the au pair off with the children. I'm sitting eating my bacon and eggs and she's interrogating me, circling the table in her loose pink dressing-gown, wants to know exactly what we did, if the girl was any good, every detail, and she's getting more and more excited, strident, banging pots and pans. I have to know that word.

The reciter flashed out of sight. Boyle wouldn't let himself observe; instead he looked out across the green park and the people and the convict trees and the dogs in the flower beds and the cobwebbed island in the lake and the bright noose of the sun and cursed what-ever it was that kept him quarantined from it all, as though he wasn't even sitting there, and even his gaze was coming from somewhere outside of the daylight. He was bored of himself, worse, he was terrified that it would never change. Eight months before he had come to Dublin with a new hope in him, that was the simple truth, he was going to try his best to change his life. From the bus window he had seen the giant plastic wrapped tablets of hay scattered in the field like a food drop on either side of the smooth newly tarmacked road where the checkpoint used to be . . . and he had said to the Monaghan girl beside him that it felt right, he had a good feeling and she had smiled with her freckled face and nodded and said she thought it was great that someone his age wanted to go back to university to educate himself as she scribbled on her knee through a slash in her jeans. While he was helping her on with her rucksack in the station, she had offered her number: We should meet up some night and slag everybody off. The next night he called her and she agreed to a drink after some persuasion. Boyle was nervous, it had been a long time since he was out with a girl, he was alone in a strange city, the drink went to his head and he told her everything, blabbered his whole life story out in a way that brought tears to his eyes, but not hers, because it had never been a story before, that's what choked him, and how was she to know he hadn't told it a hundred times to a hundred other freckled farm girls, sharpened it up in pubs and bathroom mirrors. Later that same night, he was woken on a doorstep by a cop, gave a false name and address and ran until the shame was shaken out of him, and for a few days at least, every memory, every word.

When Fada returned, strolling, hands in pockets, winking at the sun, Boyle was looking at his paper again. The word she searched for was platitude. Fada spoofed he had got the girl's number also but Boyle did not seek the proof. He pointed to the photograph.

What do you make of that? Some wee shite of an artist who works in the morgue makes a mask of her face on the sly. This dead woman lying in a drawer. It's an insult. A fucken invasion of privacy. Then they take a photo of it and put it in the paper. Imagine it was somebody you knew.

Fada was staring at him, like he was gloating on his anger with that bad black-lipped sated grin on his face.

Maybe he did more to her than that, you mean? In the quiet of the morgue?

Boyle could have hit him at that moment, that sneering repugnant face, but he let the urge die in him and the reciter was back up on his feet, pacing the grass, looking in all directions for a sign, a call to the next move of the day. Then he seemed to go still as he watched a lost maxim of two swans float across the listless water.

I'll run into you on the street, he said vacantly. You know where to find me if . . . Thanks for earlier by the way. The mad stuff.

Away he went then, across the grass, the shadows, leaping over the bodies of lone sunward women, some of whom sat up in fright. Almost out of range, he stopped and waved wildly until Boyle surrendered and responded with a sharply executed salute. The reciter performed a belly laugh from a distance; Boyle too found himself smiling. He lay back on the grass and closed his eyes, held them shut, staring into the redness, although he could have easily been attacked or something happened or a snake came down from the tree or a bomb was falling silently . . . journeying in behind the red pulsing swarm to the deeper darkness which flashed sporadically with images, a girl's face, a broad street, a bouquet of flowers, a rioting crowd, a castle until the darkness was vast and sealed, no, not his.

When he got out that time, he went back to Derry, and the back room of Dainty's flat. Dainty had left his wife and two children a few years previously and set himself up in a new apartment building along the river, electric gates, lifts, pictures on corridor walls. There was a party waiting on him on the rooftop balcony which had a clear view down into the lighted car park of the Strand Road police station, an inhuman gloom of inscrutable and fastidious experiments. From the other side of the balcony the river was more alive, no, vital, potent, than anything he could remember seeing. In the past, on the rare occasions he noticed, the river had been a stretch of dead water, a flooded road that went nowhere anyway. Now it seemed to hold the power to start life from within itself at its own gross whim.

Boyle trembled like a man who was being celebrated for his luck, a windfall, a shift in fortune, cowering under the gaze of the gods. As the time had approached for his release from jail, he had refused to allow himself to imagine how he would feel or what he would actually do on his first day out; superstitiously, he had put it out of his mind like so much else down the years. Or maybe it was what they called Gate Fever. The advice booklets provided by the jail counsellors mentioned extreme paranoia, hyperventilation and depression, a nostalgia for the comforts of penitence. As it turned out, when Boyle stepped through the gate into the cheering crowds he knew immediately that his sentence had only begun: jail had been the training, the way Prince Siddhārtha had fasted and starved for years before the night of his great enlightenment, and he suddenly and painfully understood that he had failed in that as well, to make himself ready, to renounce himself completely. He had wasted another tract of years, dabbling with false enlightenment. Imprisonment and austerity had taught him nothing. He remained blinded by anger, no, revenge, no, some kind of grief. The people at the rooftop party were there to celebrate the return of the prodigal, the stories of lessons learned, the discovery of clarity and humility but Boyle would not give it to them, or he couldn't. It was this that would set him apart, keep him at agonising bay from every kind face, every drunken embrace and toast.

Dainty took him out into the corridor and told him to fucken spit it out.

What? I'm all right, Boyle said.

Are you fuck. There's your family in there, people who know you and look at the bake on you. Why do you think they bothered their arses to come? It's not a fucken wake. I promised them a party. You fucken survived it so you did. Eight years. Now forget it. Those people in there are all you've got. And do you have any idea what I had to do to get Amanda Mc Devitt to come along?

Give me a laugh.

You don't want to know. She's a single woman now you know. You see that dress on her?

I'll be all right.

When's that going to happen? How many years have you been saying that? And it just gets worse. But you better hurry up about it or you're out on your ear. You can find a bunk bed for yourself in some wee hostel with the other fucken heroes.

Watch your mouth Dainty.

Or fucken what?

Just watch your mouth.

They did the staring routine, void against void. There was no real threat in it, at least after a few seconds, because the vacuum quickly began to fill up with pictures, flashes of times together down the years, and voices, secrets, betrayals, moments when their solidarity was almost visible to them and made them sweat. Dainty's eyes were the same as ten

28

years earlier, twenty, the dopey sceptical gaze, the soft brown of meat about to go off. They could have been arguing over some girl in a campsite in the Downings or whose turn it was at the wheel when Boyle's father was teaching them both to drive. Or it was the same pair of eyes that had looked at him uncomprehendingly that day they heard Dainty's brother had been shot dead when the soldiers raided a house, no, murdered, assassinated by the Brits, martyred.

Dainty broke the stare. Jesus, he said, just try and get into the fucken swing of it will you for fuck's sake? Just for me. Just this once. There's enough big faces in this town without you joining the ranks. And get rid of that beard for a start.

Boyle laughed a bit. They don't know what to say to me.

They bloody well do. They want to tell you they hope you've wised up. They want to tell you to get on with your bloody life now. Do you expect them all to get down on their knees in fucken thanks? Do you think they feel beholden to you or something? Catch yourself on Boylo.

Dainty left it at that and went back in to the party. Boyle followed a minute later. He stood with Kevin his younger brother, married and separated in the time he'd been away, and two children, a niece and a nephew whom he'd never seen and that's what Boyle felt they were talking about, the wains, what was ahead for them, the city they were inheriting, although somebody listening in would have believed their conversation was to do with football and whether Jason Knight would resume his career as a striker now that he was out again. Patricia turned up a while later, flown in from London with her new man in tow. Every Christmas he had received a letter from her giving the comical account of her year, month by month, man by man, job by job. His sister threw herself completely into whatever she was doing, whatever man she was with, she loved to lose herself she said, but then she would wake up one morning and panic that it was all in her mind and drive herself and everybody else mad with her anxieties and doubts until she found herself on her own again, dreaming of the next thing that would come along. For a good ten minutes she cried her eyes out on his shoulder and then she went off to do something else and he barely spoke to her again the rest of the evening. Of course, the ma and da were there also, drunk as usual and eager to get the dancing started, pulling ones out of their chairs and throwing them back again just as violently when they proved too static or clumsy and finally falling into each other's arms with a curse on the rest of the world.

Dainty and Amanda Mc Devitt joined in. Dainty's finger slyly at her back signalling to Boyle to step in slowly grew into a pointed order and then a fist of revenge as Boyle continued to stand firm out on the balcony with the smell of the fermenting river in his nostrils.

Derry. A year and a bit more he had lasted back there. They had been right about the paranoia: he rarely went out, the city was too loud and unpredictable. Anything might be round the next corner. There were so many cars now that it was impossible to keep an eye on every one of them, for the shadow in the back seat, the window going down. People hurried about at a pace that suggested they had got wind of something or a minute later they had all stopped and were pretending it was a false alarm. Some days he didn't know a being but on his next outing he was assailed by the faces of everyone he had ever known, and their sons and daughters, and their cousins. The city had grown, no, it had new areas, names, blank spots in his mind, this park and that park, speed-bumped hectares of identical homes with driveways and patios for the workers in the union-free American technology companies. The pubs were full of red herrings, hoaxes, jibes, jokes he couldn't get. In the cinema one afternoon, he had smelled gas and ran out without telling the security man, none other than wee G. G. Carlin who used to beg for coppers in William Street. Behind the polished order of the new shopping centre he sensed a cute devoted chaos. It amazed him

that the city continued to function: on a bad day the amazement could turn into a terrifying notion that some kind of
deal had been done, a gory, no, a sinister pact that one night
he would be dragged from his bed and expected to sign his
name to in sacrificial blood and then drink from the goblet
before the assembled populace.

Dainty persuaded him to enrol in a night class to get him
out of the flat. He decided on philosophy and after a few
weeks he started going for a pint with the group. He talked
mainly to a woman, Patsy Lloyd, and before long they
began to meet separately, in secret, no, just to be away from
the others they would have said. It was Patsy who encouraged him to make the application to university. Boyle had
taken a lot of courses while in jail, an untidy mixture of
Open University courses over the eight years. Then one
night Patsy kissed him on the street outside a bar which did
salsa dancing. They went back to Boyle's place. Patsy took
off her clothes and lay beside him on the bed. He couldn't
make up his mind whether he was expected to undress as
well or if she was supposed to do it. In the end, he lay for a
long time with his head on her breasts. She spoke his name
but he didn't answer. His tears ran down and collected
against the single stretch mark across her belly. He felt
heavy, like a tree or an old wardrobe stuffed with worthless
clothes. They listened to Dainty come in and stumble
around the flat. Neither of them spoke when she got up and
put on her clothes and went back to her husband.

Now as he sat in the lotus position, one hand touching the
blue carpet under his left knee, the other palm exposed in his
lap, in his own flat in Dublin, this was as much as he could be
bothered to recall. Another year or so of perfecting the man-
dala of failure for his private contemplation. Other than his
leaving do in the drizzle on the same rooftop and the collection of stoned faces who were all Dainty's friends and of
course his ma and da dancing again. Saying he was going out
for fags, and meaning it, he had found himself walking with

nowhere in mind. There were fake golden fossils embedded in the new pavements, bits of seaweed and children's footprints. He headed towards the Brandywell by way of Bishop Street, past the courthouse and the gates of his old grammar school, and on until he saw an old woman calling her dog in for the night at her doorstep who spoke to him and invited him in for a cup of tea out of the rain. On a floor of newspapers, the old woman sat in a torn armchair and they talked for an hour about her life, her boys' deaths, her husband's death, what it was like to be left alone. As he was about to leave, the old woman caught a grip on her dog, a slow-moving shivering terrier, and set it upon her knee. Sunny here's all I've got left now, she said and hugged the dog to her. Boyle watched, smiling sadly as was right. The old woman brought the dog's muzzle to her lips and began to kiss it, lightly at first, pecking it, then pressing it harder to her mouth. The dog began to wriggle but she kept a firm hold, running her tongue around its teeth in the open jaw while the piss dribbled into her lap. Boyle laughed; he went over and took the dog and held it up in front of him like a child and kissed it too, even feeling some of its piss on his face. Then he kissed the old woman and went back outside into the fresh universe of darkness. He was free, he told himself.

Boyle had taken up the principles of meditation on the advice of the counsellor in the jail, a man by the name of Bernard whose accent was unidentifiable, to help with his recurring nightmares. The worst of these dealt with a beautiful woman and her dog. The dream began in a market place, an ancient bazaar of tents and spice baskets and caged unknown animals. Between the stalls there were corpses, hundreds of them, melting into one another. Boyle realised he was wading barefoot through blood. As his horror grew, and his teeth ached, Boyle noticed a woman in robes waving to him from the door of a tent. Inside, the tent spars were made of bone, she took his hand and told him not to worry, that this wasn't real, it was only backstage. Profoundly relieved, Boyle followed her through a door and found himself in another market place, this one set in a different century, where people wore high wigs and the women showed their breasts and painted nipples and carriages decapitated the beggars crawling at his feet. Again the woman led him out of the multitude and tried to soothe him by saying it was only backstage. Boyle pleaded with her that he couldn't take any more. Tell me how to escape this, do you know? he asked and noticed her dog for the first time, nodding at him, and its voice speaking in his head: Give me your soul and I will show you how to escape. Boyle thought before he replied, he thought for a long time, a million deaths, using everything he had ever seen or heard, every caution and every tale of adventure, and he nodded back and said to the woman and her dog: Ok, take it, for I am not the type of man who needs a soul anyway.

Boyle leapt screaming from his sleep, the fire. He was in the prison hospital on sedatives for three days.

I am not the type of man who needs a soul.

Bernard gave him books on meditation and oversaw his progress. First he learned the lotus, the practice of sitting still and hanging from the spine. Then for months he let his mind wander back over his own life until he grew bored and began to lie to himself, to make things up. Next he tried imagining the different parts of his body relaxing – the hand, the foot, the eye – and after that he experimented with breathing techniques. Bernard gave him chants, mantras, but Boyle remained stranded with his arse on the cell floor. The most successful approach for Boyle was choosing an object and focusing his attention on it: he stuck his eyes on the three broad white bars across the window. He spent hours on these bars, contemplating their number, their separateness from him, the history of metal making, the small differences between each bar and the space between them, the way the paint covered the surface, the bumps and fissures, the men who had built the prison, waiting for the moment they would vanish. The nightmares stopped, he was more relaxed and needed to eat less but the bars would not budge. Eventually he was resigned to staring into the darkness behind his eyes, the darkness itself a failure of some kind he strained to understand.

This was what he was doing now on the floor of his flat, the books scattered around him, thinking of his growing disappointment with the university, the students and teachers, and telling himself that he had been a fool to expect anything else. Jail had been the loss of freedom, his cowardice was the failure of his courage, bad was a starvation of good, dark was weak light, ugliness merely a deprivation of beauty, and nothing was the pipe-dream of something (reason was built up on a structure of opposites, chaos and order, Apollo and Dionysus, heaven and hell). It was like two beautiful mirrors facing each other. Erected on either side of a pit, a grave, no, a man trap. The mirrors drew you into their mystery, right into their false heart, and the ground broke under your feet and down you went into the hole.

Old fucken hat. Even thinking was an illusion, the possibility of it, clarity, just the wailing human ego. How many years with books and internal inspection and what had he come up with, what new thought? Nothing. There was nothing else for it but a no-holds-barred hedonism. Boyle scoffed at the thought, a loud laugh; he had about as much hope of being a hedonist as he did of a woman knocking on his door that evening, a woman in a light summer dress, a bit drunk, fire in her unholy eyes.

He kicked the books away from him around the room. The books lay still where they landed. The light was still, thick, pearly. For a second the city was silent. He waited. Straight ahead was the bed flush with the narrow bedroom doorway like the camel at the eye of the needle it could not conceivably get through. Where he was standing was both living room and kitchen; patchily carpeted with bare white walls, it had a burgundy patterned armchair and two windows which gaped down on a paved backyard and a lone wooden chair, buckled and weather-striped, against the wall, interrogation style. He could pass an entire day watching the rain falling on that chair. During the winter nights he listened to it being blown around the yard. He had seen crows and seagulls try to fly off with it and a cat shelter under the seat during a fall of snow. In the basement of the house there was a door to the yard that the landlord kept locked. Once a month when he came to collect the rent, cash only, Boyle would watch him sweep the yard clean with a redhaired brush he took away with him, a coughing eyeless man in a suit and tie, a dentist Victor had told him, his pockets sagging obscenely with the coins from the payphone in the hall and the washing-machine under the stairs.

Later, Boyle went out to buy some chips which he brought back to eat on the front steps of his building, fourteen broad steps from the lipstick-red front door to the gate and a bus stop under a tree. Each person passing moved timelessly in the soft yellow light; a man with a boy, a woman hurrying, two men with tattooed arms sharing a can, the lone mongrels, even the cars seemed to be part of something bigger, more solemn, lauded with shadow and the rich light. A chain gang of trees on either side of the road formed a colonnade all the way to the gates of Phoenix Park where the sun was going down. From that direction he watched a bus approaching and at the same time he spotted a woman running with folded arms and head down across the road to the stop. She was dressed up for the night, going into town to meet somebody. Like an animal charging through a forest, the bus was whipped by branches and leaves which continued to shake and wave from their mute captivity after the woman had been taken away and her perfume made it up the steps and threw itself into the arms of a vinegar stranger.

Boyle finished his chips. He had phoned in earlier to work to say he was sick, the first time in five months he had missed a shift. He wasn't sure why, he thought he wanted to be alone, that there was something on his mind. Now he couldn't remember what it was and he hoped Victor might come back early, and maybe they could go for a pint locally. Victor, a big Russian man well into his thirties like Boyle, rented a flat on the ground floor and claimed he had paid a friend to cut his ear off so he could claim asylum. Boyle and him drank vodka together in Victor's flat or out on the steps some nights and then avoided each other for the next month.

Since the weather had turned in the last few months, Boyle would often bring a book down to the steps and read or watch the ones out on their own steps, like the crew of black lads, sprawled and sullen and always barefooted, who made passes at the women and rarely spoke among themselves. Usually, at some point each night, the girls from the estate went by, tracksuits and ponytails and huge gold hoops in their ears, and there was a brief opera of abuse and flirtation echoing under the trees.

There was no sign that evening of anyone. The cloying light was full of unkeepable promises. The cranes were stuck in the city like acupuncture pins in secret stress points. He wasn't going to get any work done; he wanted to forget about himself, listen to the turmoil of somebody else's life. Boyle pointed out to himself that he had been in Dublin for eight or nine months and he didn't know a person he could call and talk into a pint. He made himself another fag and wondered if he could drum up the interest in himself to go for a walk. But what was there to see? A house with all its windows open, a busy street in a summer evening, a lovely woman on a park bench, the drinkers outside a pub? These things he already knew and his heart recoiled at them as though it were full. Or too starved to eat. As he continued to sit there, unable to make up his mind what to do, he heard with a strange relief the rigged notes of a siren lassooing out across the city, the widening gyre of awe, comfort music, then the gulls flew up and cried out for revenge.

A few hours later he was standing in a local pub near the old horse market. He had left a note for Victor to join him if he got in. He had been to this place before but never for very long because he found it difficult to drink alone without succumbing to self-pity or paranoid imaginings, as if the loneliness and desperation were smells off him, from his clothes, his hair, under his fingernails. The floor was wood, the windows coloured glass. The barman with his thin doctor's face nodded and that was all. The trick was to keep the eyes mute, the neck bent and humbled; a bar was always somebody else's territory. It was mainly men on one side, three loners drinking at the bar and a group who stood looking up at the TV above the doorway which led into the lounge where couples sat at tables and felt carpet under their feet. Discreetly, Boyle studied the men in the mirrors behind the optics, Dublin men at their ease, proud to survey the things their fathers had passed down to them, men with a past they were glad to talk about, with wives and children at home, men who slept in the same bed decade after decade and got up for work the next day grateful to know the world would continue on without them whatever happened.

The news was on. After the adverts, they started with a shot of the bridge where he had been standing that morning, then a close-up of the bouquet. The voiceover said that no one had come forward with information and the scientists were carrying out more tests. The reporter stood on the bridge with the flowers behind her and talked blankly into the camera about suicide and unsolved murders and illegal immigrants. Then they cut to the mask, lying on a black velvet background, the camera slowly moving in like a kiss was imminent. They said the Guards had named her Catriona until her true identity was known.

Boyle snorted loudly.

Poor girl, said a man standing next to him. He was in his late fifties, he wore a blazer and a cravat. A drinker's scalded face, the hair combed and greased back.

You can't even die in peace any more, Boyle said, without the Guards standing over your corpse making up names.

How'd they come up with Catriona I wonder? Some red-neck's mother. Some wee teacher from the Gaelteacht.

We all deserve a decent hearing.

She was smiling, Boyle went on. She went over that bridge happily. A pure happy death. Leave her alone.

You've a bad attitude.

Is that right? Boyle laughed.

I could see when you walked in.

Really? And who are you with your cravat and sage insights?

That'd be telling. The man winked at nobody.

Boyle looked at him, thinking. You a Guard?

The man shrugged and emptied his glass of brandy.

Nowhere's safe, said Boyle.

Not for the likes of you.

You're scaring me now. You away off now to watch the hurling with the priest?

The man got off his stool and buttoned his blazer. He was small, short arms and a pigeon's waist.

Keep an eye on this one here Jimmy, he called to the bar-man. He can't take a joke at all. He winked at Boyle and left.

Who's the comedian? Boyle asked but the barman turned away. A while later, he counted his change and ordered another pint. He had given up on Victor by this stage. In the toilet two lads asked him for a skin and offered him a twig of grass which he took. Back at the bar, his eyes were drawn back again and again to the postcards along the top shelf. One showed a woman who had just been pushed back against the wall of a bamboo hut. Her shirt was wet and ripped away to expose one heavy brown breast with a dark thick nipple like a dog's nose. She was looking with contempt at whoever had done the pushing but at the same time her hands were pulling apart the grass skirt across her thighs, strong bronzed thighs. Boyle's eyes went up and down between her face and her breast until his guts grew heavy with a sickening gravity.

He walked home soon afterwards and thought the stars

were like claw marks inside a coffin lid. What would he write if it were him trapped like that? Not a word, he decided. No message to anybody. It was silent behind Victor's door. He went upstairs and smoked a joint and stared at the chair. The last time he had smoked was three years before in a cell with Harry Giveny who had got in a bag of oranges injected with vodka. Boyle started to have bad thoughts after Harry fell asleep, that it was all a trick, the whole prison system, all the prisoners, the guards, the armed struggle, and it was there to fool him, to prevent him from finding out something. He paced the floor until dawn with the truth on the tip of his tongue and the window bars were all that were saving him. Harry got out soon after and blew his hands off in a cave in the Mourne Mountains.

Boyle worked in a telephone-call shop in Temple Bar, a pedestrian zone of restaurants and bars for tourists in the centre of the city. The shop, Talk Tonic, had eight glass-fronted cubicles along one wall where people could make cheap calls around the world. Boyle sat at his own desk near the door and handed out wooden tablets branded with a number corresponding to each cubicle. When the phone call was finished Boyle checked the cost on the screen and took their money. Somebody arrived every hour to pick up the cash, Boyle would know them only by a password, not by their face. The password changed every week. Boyle did nights mainly, closing at 2 a.m., before the streets were flooded by the moonless nightclub tides.

He had found the job by accident when he went in to phone Dainty, just before Christmas time when he was trying to decide whether to go back or stay where he was for the holiday. While he was at the desk waiting to pay, an argument started between the black man on the till and another man, Eastern European maybe, Finnish maybe, who didn't have enough money and was complaining the price was too high. The black man stood up and took out his mobile phone, threatening to call the Guards. Boyle offered to pay the extra; it didn't amount to much anyway. The response he got was a mouthful of what had to be abuse from the Eastern European. He saw the void opening in the man's eyes before the punch came and was well clear in time. Then he kicked the man in the balls. There followed a few seconds of tired slack in which Boyle thought he could see something ancient and lonely in all the watching faces and even the rain and lights on the street outside had it, or it was the feeling that he was about to remember what he was doing there, not only in the shop, but on the planet, why he was in existence and those other people were all waiting on him, hoping, part of the performance, and it would free them like it would free him . . . just a few seconds of that before the man straightened up again, laughed and slapped Boyle on the shoulder, and put down the full amount on the counter. The black man, Leo, who turned out to be one of the shop's owners, gave Boyle his call for free and told him to come back if he ever wanted a job. Boyle returned the following night. He spent his Christmas working there.

It was nearly midnight. Boyle was at the door of the shop, smoking. The cloud was low and unbroken and under it the denizens were out looking for amusement, packs of lads in short sleeves, girls staggering along the cobbles in high heels, the greed hard on the eyes. Music came out of the bright tunnel behind the three doormen on the other side of the street. It had been a busy night in the shop, one of the good nights when he heard laughter coming from the cubicles instead of the usual morbid grumbling or fury and then the stunned plaintive eyes of some refugee counting out the coins into Boyle's hands. All night the aching voices went out to the tundra and the mountain, harbour and slum, to the deserted and the waiting in the frozen tower blocks or merciless shanty noon and Boyle, their priest, their shaman, pressed the buttons and stacked the coins. Yet, at the same time, there were others who were simply making a quick call to friends to see how they were doing, like the two American girls that night who had stayed around for an hour to talk to him and ask for advice about their upcoming trip to the North. Or the young Basque couple who were hard at each other in the cubicle long after they'd hung up. Or Tierney, the old Dublin man, who came in regularly to use the sex lines, a well-read man who before he went in always liked to have a discussion with Boyle about whatever he was reading but who never said a word when he came out, his face gone sour, slapped down his money and hurried out of the door.

Boyle was watching a character down the street who was leaning against a lamppost. He'd been there for a while and Boyle was sure he knew the face, a hard man's low sunburned forehead, the whole stocky look of him with the new tight jeans and polished boots, the big watch, every stitch on him fresh out of the shop. A bright brand-new cement mixer. He had a bad instinct about it. The bastard was careful not to look in Boyle's direction. He was wondering what to do when another familiar rose up in front of him.

Martin? How's the form? You been fighting?

Martin was wearing his sleeping bag over his shoulders like a cape. He had a hat on his head like a traffic warden or a park keeper. One side of his face was badly bruised.

You the captain bud?

The number doesn't work Martin.

I'm going home man. I've got leave man, do you hear me?

Martin rummaged inside the sleeping bag and produced a limp piece of cardboard which he handed to Boyle.

I know all about it Martin. But we tried it a fucken hundred times haven't we? There's eight digits here so it's not Dublin. Did you find out where it might be then?

Let me ring her bud. I have to tell her I'm coming. Just let me fucken ring her man. Please man. I want to tell her I'm coming.

Boyle usually let him in and tried to calm him while he tapped in the number again and again. The week before, however, Martin had shattered the handset against the wall.

Look what happened the last time? Who the fuck do you think had to pay for it? You broke the fucken phone.

Martin seemed frightened by the idea, disbelieving, but then it faded mysteriously.

I have to phone her man. I've got leave. I've got leave.

The character by the lamppost had vanished.

I'm warning you, Boyle said to Martin and turned back into the shop. Martin followed him to the furthest cubicle. After watching him dial the number once, Boyle had to go back to the desk where a queue was forming. It was ten minutes before he went back to check on the cubicle; he found Martin sitting on the floor and the strip of cardboard on fire between his feet. Shouting, Boyle stamped it out. People came out of the cubicles for a look and news of what was happening went down the wires to bombed-out villages, African bars and apartments in suburban Korea. Martin wasn't reacting: Boyle put him in a chair. Then he noticed the phone was hanging at the end of its lead.

Hello, is anyone there?

Martin? I'll murder you, you cunt. You watch me.

This isn't Martin. I work in the shop he's calling from. Who are you?

His brother. Listen whoever you are. Tell that useless cunt if he ever phones her again I'll cut him in two. She's with me now. Do you get me?

The brother hung up.

Boyle went back to Martin and gave him his sleeping bag. I was talking to your brother, he said.

Martin wouldn't speak. He sat staring towards the door, elbows on his knees. For the next hour, Boyle was kept busy at the counter. One of the customers was a woman from Argentina who came in almost every night after her shift in a restaurant down the street. Boyle put her in her forties, a small woman under a stiff cloud of coloured hair, painted lips and her wrinkling bust always on display. They had spoken only briefly before about the weather, how she was enjoying Dublin.

This night she said to him, You are good I think . . .

No.

I think. Too good. That man is crazy.

She meant Martin.

He's upset, Boyle said.

The woman laughed hoarsely, loudly. We are all upset, no? Call the police.

No.

43

She made a gesture of hopelessness. Then, angrily: Every night I come here to talk with my daughter. She is ten.

How is she?

The woman made another gesture.

I come here to learn English, to make money. I have a job. What is he? Your friend?

He's ok.

You are sad, the woman said, and leaned over the counter.

Am I?

And sweet, she said and smiled, not a bad smile, a garish lipstick but genuine. Am I embarrassing you?

I have to work, Boyle said.

The woman nodded, still smiling, her eyes fixed on him.

I do, Boyle said and didn't know what to do with his own eyes.

The woman continued to nod, waiting, that unashamed open plump sticky mouth. Ok, but I see you again. She laughed, finally letting him off the hook.

In her short skirt and heels Boyle saw her stride towards Martin. She stood directly in front of him with her hands on her hips. Martin's gaze did not shift from the exposed line of her stomach. She spoke to him in Spanish; then she sat down beside him and began to talk to him in a whisper.

It must have been a long story but Boyle couldn't find out any details when he questioned Martin later while closing up. Martin wasn't saying a word about anything. He had gone beyond words, and his eyes seemed blind. Boyle helped him to the door and put a few notes in the sleeping bag for a hostel or a bottle. One of the bouncers from the pub opposite was too quick in coming over to ask if Boyle needed any help. Martin sat down on the edge of the pavement and Boyle went back into the shop to turn off the lights and set the alarm. Through the window he saw Martin get up on his feet, pull the sleeping bag down over his hat and head, down as far as his waist, and wander away into the night like a half-hatched insect.

The streets were hectic even at this time. The swills of ablaze faces were like masks for an emotion Boyle didn't know the name of: desire, glut, need, revulsion, bliss, rage? Nothing fitted. It was impossible to tell what was real. The darkness was all tangled with umbilical strings of light, an inexhaustible electrical birth. Some eyes seemed to identify him as traitor and others grinned in wanton conspiracy. He walked aimlessly, looking into the doors of pubs past the sphinx-like bouncers where they could have been celebrating the end of hope for all he knew.

Boyle went into a kebab shop and ordered a plate of food from a singing coven of Turks who were cutting and chopping and slicing around a huge table. He took the tray to a ledge by the window on to the street. He ate slowly, holding the crumbling parcel of meat in his hands. Outside, a girl stopped in passing and curled a green pointed finger at him and when he shook his head she disgorged a shower of curses at him and spat on the window, thrice. The couples went through the crowds with their heads down as if they wanted forgiving. He didn't eat much; the meat jammed up in his gullet. He smoked a fag, then another. Out of nowhere, a face slammed against the window, slid down the pane, yellowed fangs, taking the girl's spit with it.

The chanter character appeared beside him and began to devour the remains of the meat on the plate. Two lads, bouncing from their knees, knocked on the window for him to hurry up but he waved them away; they went but not without throwing back signs of hate. The chanter seemed to be using every muscle in his gaunt face to keep his eyes open. He was deep in conversation with Boyle but there were no words.

You're in flying form, Boyle said. What's your name again?

The chanter took this as a joke by the silent grimace of laughter and tried to tap Boyle on the head and fell forwards off his stool instead. Boyle grabbed him. The chanter pushed him away and announced for all to hear: I am Fada of the frolics. Fada of the sweet frenzy. Twelve score joys have I experienced tonight. The heifers of heaven shelter under my tongue. A blink of my sour eye is a virgin's ruin.

This was all Boyle heard because he left the restaurant and had gone well along the street before Fada caught him up, wing-beating his arms.

We're going to a party. Me and you.

Boyle kept up his pace. The river was straight ahead, the three-eyed bridges floodlit in green.

I knew we'd meet again, cried the chanter and climbed on the bonnet of a car and on up to the roof where he stayed still for a minute on his hands and knees before he flared up.

I come to your country from my own country across mountains and wild seas in a big box and there was three hundred of my family in the big box and we sang and dancing all night and many died, my poor mother and my ten brothers and we buried them there in the big box and made crosses from the leather in our shoes sewn with our long hair and we danced on and build homes and go to work and the children were born, many, many children, so many children that . . . For it is written, cried the chanter, switching voice now, In ze room ze women come and go, talking of ze decommissioning. Hear me all ye who talk without talking, who love without loving, there is that which creates and that which loathes all creation. We are playing on the slopes of Cithaeraon. Oh they call me the fugee in the oozy and they robbed me off my face, oh they make me feel so cheap and woozy when they stick their cameras up my lacy bum dede bum bum bum.

Boyle alone had stopped to watch the performance on the car roof. Most ones didn't deign to notice or there were bits of applause or heckling and the occasional handful of chips thrown at the gesticulating busker who seemed to be only warming up, the voices taking him over, fighting against each other. Very soon, it wouldn't even be funny, Boyle thought and decided to get out of there.

He turned a corner and saw two Guards. They noticed him

freeze and turn back; he was pulling the Fada character off the car when they came into view, two pale country boys, the hats too big for their shaved heads. One had birthmarked hands. Boyle was holding Fada up against a wall. He admitted his friend was drunk and he was looking for a taxi. Fada asked the Guards over and over again if they could smell the eucalyptus trees while Boyle tried to laugh it off: Don't mind him, I'll look after him. After a few tense minutes, the Guards told them to get lost and Boyle had to wish them a good night and put his arm around Fada and pull him along the street.

He wanted to see what they knew that he didn't. They all had a serious, no, a proud, disdainful look that they knew something. But they had to pretend and be blasé about it. They knew why they were: none of the faces showed any doubt about the reason they were all together. Maybe the point was to give up on a reason; they had assembled to create the reason, then destroy it, or humiliate it. Or somebody was watching, there were secret cameras, or they were following orders to be there and were worried about why they had been commanded.

This was paranoid thinking, Boyle advised himself. He was sitting on a stacked pile of scaffolding poles in some room. The walls, one of them still to be plastered, went up out of sight beyond the standing lights in the corners. He counted fifty people in the room before he gave up. They were all moving around, most of them, roaming, searching, exchanging secret information, but some had taken up positions around the walls like himself and nodded away sagely to one another like they had made it to the end of a long dangerous journey. Music, bassline and drums stuff, was coming from the next room where ones were dancing under the manic control of a barechested DJ with his face painted red and an old bath was filled with ice and cans and bottles. The Fada boy was in there somewhere; Boyle was sipping from a can which Fada returned at intervals to replenish with a different drink – rum, vodka, beer, gin – whatever he could pilfer. Like he was on reconnaissance, he might sit down for a while and describe some incident next door, or a girl's figure, or some conversation but then he was away again, prowling, sniffing, passing so close to people, the girls, and a fair few lads, like he was inspecting their eyes for a sign of – the word was beyond Boyle, corruption, no, he was forcing himself into their vision to see if they showed any recognition, a momentary response to whatever it was he was offering.

There he was again now, grazing past them, eye to eye. He sat down beside Boyle.

What do you think of it?

You ask me that every time you sit down.

I'm looking after you like I said I would.

I'm a big boy now.

I told you I could show you things didn't I? Anything you want. I know every corner of this town. The rich kids and down to the sleaze, the real hardcore sleaze. Whatever you want I can get it. Do you know what I mean?

I'm not looking for anything.

Fada made a sceptical grimace. He showed Boyle two pills, dissolving already in the sweat on his palm. Boyle shook his head. Fada placed one on his tongue and took a swig from Boyle's can.

I heard you give a false name to the Guards.

Boyle looked at him: Maybe the name I gave you was false.

The chanter grinned. A minute later he was up and away again.

Boyle had just enough time to decide that he was going to slip out soon and head home when this slick lad in black knelt before him and offered him a smoke of a joint. He said it was a present and pointed to a girl on a sofa across the other side of the room.

Do you like her?

Boyle took the joint and told the lad to fuck off. He tried not to watch as the lad went back to the sofa to report in the girl's ear. She was smiling. There was a couple next to her, mouth to mouth, wrapped in each other, and she was stroking the girl's hair. Boyle thought she must be only twenty. Bleached messy hair and a dirty thick mouth she must have sensed him looking at for she showed him the length of her tongue. Boyle turned away.

He looked again and she had her mouth open wider, edging her tongue around her lips.

Boyle inhaled, pollen, and tried to concentrate on the tip of the joint, blowing on it, turning it in his nicotined fingers.

Through the smoke, the legs were being opened, bare young legs from a short skirt, opened a touch and brought together again, and the tongue loose in her crude mouth at the next glance.

He wanted to go over to her, the cramp in his guts was his witness. Then he told himself it was a trick, somehow she knew the type of him and she would make a show of him if he went near her. Meanwhile, she was growing more extravagant; a flaring spread of her thighs and then she sat forward, staring at him, a challenge with that swollen bleak grin. Her breasts fell loose under her vest. No one else in the room seemed to notice her behaviour.

Boyle stared back now, freely. Play her at her own game, see how far she'll go. The girl sat back and now her hand went across her breasts, trailing the fingers. The other hand settled on her thigh and inch by inch she was sliding the skirt up. Her tongue was now at full stretch.

You're a coward. Boyle heard the words in his own head.

A shadow appeared behind her and put its hands across her eyes. Some other fella was whispering into her ear and all during it she continued with her hands on herself, massaging her breasts and down to her hips. The thighs fell open completely for a second. The shadow brought her to her feet and as he led her out of the room by the hand the girl's eyes stayed on Boyle and she gave him one last sight of her tongue.

He sat in a daze until Fada returned.

So what do you think of it? His eyes were high in his head.

I'm too old for this carry on.

Fada wasn't listening.

So where you been sleeping? Boyle asked to put the image of her hungry mouth out of his mind.

I met this German one. Not the prettiest thing but dying for a bit of action. Crazy stuff. A screamer. She goes completely mad when you blow on her asshole. And in the other bed her friend lying there reading a book. Any action yourself?

There she was again, stumbling back. She took her place again on the sofa and leaned towards him. The hair was messier, the eyes lazier. Then she smiled, wiped the back of her hand across her rude mouth and performed a long slow gulp.

Boyle was terrified. He couldn't breathe.

Fada went on, And who did I meet in the other room? This'll interest you. He put his arm round Boyle's shoulder.

Boyle smelled sweat – a fume of solitude so rich it heightened his fear. He had to get out of there: he was out of his depth.

The artist who made the mask of that woman you knew.

Fuck off. I didn't know her, Boyle said.

Fada grinned.

I didn't. No fucken way.

You can tell me you know. Seriously, Fada said, trying to pull him closer. You can tell me anything. Doesn't matter how bad. You know that don't you?

What was that look on his face? That bad mouldy grin. He was dying to hear something. The eyes were blinking. Boyle pushed him away.

Away and fuck. I didn't touch her.

Boyle stood up, too quickly, and the room dipped sharply to one side. The girl still had her eye on him over the shoulder of another girl who was crouched down talking to her, hand in hand. Boyle staggered into the centre of the room. As he passed the sofa, he saw the girl lay back her head and reach out a hand to him that he refused to touch. She was crying.

Boyle staggered into the other room. Only music, pulsing lights, there was no air. People screamed. They were dancing like they were all stuck together, like they believed it was possible. Fada had come in behind him and he was going from face to face, whispering, insinuating, like there was some pleasure in it for him being spurned, wriggling his arms above his head. One girl pushed him away with violence and he stumbled into some fellas who pushed him about also.

He's over there, said Fada, winking. The corner by the window.

Fada went dancing over in that direction.

A few seconds later Boyle saw him falling backwards across the room. Two lads charged after him. Fada went down at their feet, made a ball of himself, squirming, begging for mercy, sickening. Boyle hit one from behind and the other took a full kick in the balls and collapsed back against the amplifier. One more appeared with piercings and a Celtic tattoo on a shaved head. He was only a youngster and no threat to Boyle he realised too late but he was on his feet in front of his friends.

Think. What are you going to do? Boyle said to him. He pulled the chanter back on his feet.

That's him, said Fada. The mask maker.

You're dead, said the youngster.

I know worse than that.

The youngster made a move and Boyle kicked him in the stomach. People were circling him now to calm him down, waving their hands like he was on fire. The music had stopped. Boyle nodded to Fada to get out of there and followed him through the rooms. At the top of the stairs the girl with the mouth was smiling at him now, but a different smile, the eyes dried, it was like triumph he saw in her face.

Outside he put the chanter against a wall and said, You fucken brought that on yourself. Now fuck off and leave me alone. I don't need any trouble around me.

I know worse than that, Fada called after him, no, sang.

The smoke came down the chimney, oh I know worse than that.

The fingers went round the neck, oh I know worse than that.

It was trying to get light. Boyle couldn't tell where he was in the city but after a few minutes he saw the river and began to follow it. A taxi stopped finally. The man turned round in his seat and nodded towards the back window.

Look at the state of that one, he said. Bird-brain.

Boyle looked through the window and saw the chanter running down the centre of the street, arms wide and a-flapping.

Beating the air, he flew towards the light on tumultuous wings. Only the lost and injured were left on the streets, the broken streets, blinded stragglers across the battlefield. Him there on the corner come to a final stop at the edge of his own precipice. Or that one laid out on the bench, face down, singing, punching the ground. Or another way ahead stumbling along the middle of the street, his shirt off, arguing with the Georgian silence. They had thrown themselves completely into the battle. Now they couldn't remember where home was or who had taught them the meaning of the word. A great effort had been made, the terrifying expenditure. The hordes retreated and sadness looted the dawn streets. Rubbish blew about like love letters fallen from the hands of the dying. The walls showed the last SOS piss messages, hardening pools of vomit like ditched shrivelling flags. Some had broken through, there were tales of triumph, heroism, and gone beyond catharsis at last. The morning was a door hanging only by a buckled hinge. Squander everything shall be the whole of the law. The poets were sleeping in their beds, moaning, unable to find a dream. Fada halted with a gasp before a ravaged bus shelter; the shattered glass had fallen on the pavement in the shape of a bird glistening with the first sun, a thousand uncut diamonds, a mirage of burst sun grains, hot on his eyes. Beauty is in the wallet of the beholder, he sighed, down on his knees before the sparkling bird, and noticed two approaching, young lovers hand in hand, freshly minted in the night furnace. They were silent and stunned, walking through an unknown landscape. Fada stayed on his knees as they passed and gave thanks and they smiled at him benignly and he was one of the blessed. Waste all, want not, he cried after them. Behind the curtains and the shutters and the painted doors the cocks were hardening against the maternal thighs. Hurry, Fada called to the lovers. Speak to nobody. Only the rats love the truth.

Fada had met two lads on the street who were coming from a party only a few streets away so he had gone there and knocked and talked his way in. The party was long over but a circle of people had formed on the floor among the cans and bottles earnestly debating some social topic like water pollution or the price of condoms. Fada dropped into an empty chair, smoked a joint and was about to contribute his own opinion on the condom question, why the price should be kept as high as possible, but fell asleep in an instant. An ugly girl woke him a few hours later and told him to get out. Then on the street right outside the house he had met Molly, the ravishing Molly with her slender ankles and green eyes and the sleepless lament of her thick red hair. She let him take her arm, such a fragile wrist, and they walked together for a while as though she were taking a turn in the streets in a diaphanous hour. People looked at her helplessly, men and women, and the sniggering greasy slur at her side.

Years before Fada had managed to take her home one night; Molly had just broken off her engagement to a young heir from Carlow because she could not believe he loved her enough. Fada had done his best to remain gentle and compassionate while she sipped her wine in a hotel bar but as soon as they were inside her flat he was gripped by the idea that Molly wanted him to take her roughly, that she was tired of listless embraces, and he had stripped off his clothes and tried to start on her. It took him much too long to accept that he had frightened her and she was never coming out of the bathroom. So he performed a poem for her at the door and left. But that was all in the past now and Molly was able to see the funny side of it. That's what she liked about him, she told him as she let him kiss her goodbye, you make me laugh, a different kind of laugh, a strange laugh, and her green eyes darkened.

Tell me that poem again, she said and Fada obliged, whispering it close in her ear, Swift sniffing in the lady's dressing room, a paste of composition rare, the alum flower to stop the steams, puppy water and soiled petticoats, the magnifying glass for her nose worms, such order from confusion sprung, such gaudy tulips from the dung.

It was a good start to the day, Fada told himself as he watched her glide away, her hair crying out for devotion. Women and poetry and not even lunchtime. After counting the change in his pocket he decided he would treat himself to some breakfast. He needed to have a think about a number of things.

He sat by the window in a regular spot of his, a café with an eye to the street and another eye to an indoor market, and in particular a jewellery and piercing stall which Fada watched with keen interest. A group of Spanish teenagers were gathered round the display cases of rings and studs and hoops. The coloured hair extensions hanging from the wall were like the scalps of outlandish tribes. This thought had never occurred to him before although he often sat observing the stall; it was something else that boded well for the day. Ear, navel, eyebrow, nose, labret, he intoned quietly. Gold. Niobium. Blackvine. Surgical steel. Titanium. UV glow. All those young Spanish girls going back to their barrios and tower blocks on the white shores after a month of English in Dublin, with pierced nipples and a small cold seed between their legs that they have to keep secret at all costs, young swollen-eyed girls, taking their virginity in their own hands, their dark fingernails tapping at night against the stub, a semaphore of wantonness. Fada grinned: what man would take that small silver fruit seed between his teeth and pull gently, the philosopher's pip?

Your tongue is hanging out.

Con Greene pulled up a chair and sat himself down with a long glass of coffee and a slice of chocolate cake. Both of them watched the luxurious stretchings and thickenings of soft plump waist flesh as the girls leaned and straightened and nudged for position in their torn jeans.

It's too early in the day for that, Con said.

Fada sighed: All those tiny punctures. They're letting the air out of themselves. They're afraid they'll float away with all their naughty thoughts and steamy dreams. Did you ever think how many holes Dublin has made in the Catholic youth of Europe? Since I've been sitting there I've seen five. It must be a hundred at least every day. And there's another ten shops around Dublin. It's like a big sieve. The children have to filter out something from the air. Or like a strainer for gold. Panning. No, maybe it's a necklace, a rosary, a garland of children for sacrifice to be draped round the neck of the beast or –

Good night? Con asked, pressing the lip of the spoon into the chocolate.

Great one. One of the best. Absolutely. Feel on top of the world this morning. So what were you up to yourself?

Con's face was annoyed incomprehension.

What's the problem? You can tell me, Fada said, admiring his own sensitivity.

Just forget it.

You can tell me.

Con used the spoon to make his point more clearly: You. And me. Drinking pints. Together. Hours. Early evening. Remember the American woman?

Nothing stirred in Fada's memory. He looked in terror at Con.

You'd need to watch yourself Fada my boy. You're overdoing it. Anyone'll tell you the same. Did you go on to that party in the end in the docks?

Fada said yes and then no.

Con swallowed another mouthful of chocolate. Take this

the right way, he went on. I'm a friend of yours and all that jazz but you're becoming a laughing stock to people.

Things aren't going well for me at the moment, Fada said.

They never are. You never let them. It's one calamity after another. I ran into Brian yesterday and he told me he threw you out.

What did he say?

He'd just had enough of you. He said he came in and couldn't bear the sight of you.

The house was clean.

Where've you been staying?

A girl's house, Fada told him.

What are you going to do?

Fada stood up but realised he wasn't going anywhere. He looked into the eyes of a serial killer on a film poster on the wall and for a moment thought he understood the call. To save his skin he went up to the counter and chastely ordered another coffee from Valerie, the New Zealand girl with her blond hair in dreadlocks and her blue eyes that had seen vastness and her boyfriend with his moped who had once put Fada against a wall and accused him of depravity or something like it, some feeling his moped and his stylish clothes couldn't help him articulate, so he took hold of Fada's throat instead and warned him never to speak to his girlfriend again, hence the chastity with which Fada requested his second cup of coffee. In his mind, however, far back out of sight, he was taking her for a walk in the woods and he would lie her down in the ruins of an old chapel and show her another kind of vastness.

We all go through bad patches, he said sitting down again. Remember that time you broke up with Orla and the state you were in? Remember that week you went on the mushies.

Don't fucken mention that, Con told him straight.

Fada had known Con for years now. He was one of the few who had stayed put during the lean decades when everyone else was clearing out to the States and Germany. There had been some attempt at an escape to London but it went seriously wrong for reasons Con refused to talk about. Con preferred silence on many aspects of his life. Facing into his forties, he sold a bit of blow and tried to make a living out of whatever came along. He was stocky and indifferent but he could talk eloquently about the different porn shops around town when he was drunk enough.

I'm on a bit of bender at the moment, that's all, said Fada. It'll all work out. Change is good.

Your life's a bender. Standing on Grafton Street all day eyeing up the young ones and the foreigners. Where you going to be in ten years' time? A dirty old man.

Fada had to laugh. How many nights had he brought Con a woman out of the last dregs of some club, warmed her up for him, paved the way for him to her bedroom?

Worry about your own future. I'm not sticking needles into my arm or beating up old women, Fada said and then had a fit of laughter.

Con was watching him suspiciously.

Have you got a bit of dope? Fada asked him.

You owe me for a quarter already.

Even so, Con slipped him enough for a joint when he came back from the toilet where he had obviously been thinking more about what he wanted to say.

Put it this way, he said, whatever happens, I wouldn't like to be you if you carry on. I'm not getting at you. I didn't sit down with the intention of saying this to you. It's just the look of you at the minute. You're shaking. You look anxious. Not in control.

Control?

Whatever word you want. I'm no poet.

Neither am I.

I'm a lazy bastard but you're a waster. If you wrote down half the things that come out of your mouth I –

What?

Take that fucken grin off your face. Did you hear from Jess?

Fada shook his head violently.

She's back in town you know.

What, some hippy flower-smelling straw-house credit-card self-help find-your-inner-child claptrap?

She's back in town, Con said, with a shrug, and licked his spoon. Fada tore open a sachet of sugar and swallowed it, then another.

Jess was a girl Fada had been with for more than three years. They met in a hospital ward where they were both being treated for nervous disorders. Fada was nineteen and Jess was twenty-five. She had been committed after a series of spectacular suicide attempts, one of which involved seducing a young homeless boy, showering him with money and luxury and deranging his mind with her pagan sensuality and then dumping him, in the hope that he would come after her, kidnap her, torture her and finally kill her. The poor boy took a syringe to himself in the hermit's cave in Glendalough.

In a few hours of meeting each other in the hospital, Fada and Jess were shagging in every corner of the ward and around the grounds. She was the first woman he had ever pissed on. He was the first man who had ever stood naked above her, beating his chest, covered in muck and reciting the poetry he had learned by heart that day.

After eight months they were both free and they went on the road together around Ireland in her white van. Jess was the one with the money. Fada managed to stay fed and drunk and stoned for longer than he ever thought was possible. They rented cottages all along the west coast, staying for a few months at a time in villages and small towns, seeing who else was around, for there was always somebody who would join in with them, Dublin drop-outs, hippy gulags, American painters, suave Czech poets, hysterical mystics, and the odd bored corny paramilitary, until they moved on again without a word to anybody, usually on Jess's whim, after she had slept with most of the men in the vicinity and it was dangerous to go into the pub. On one occasion Fada had not wanted to leave. He had been sick for days, exhausted. Jess left him alone in the bed for a week before she arrived back, her hair cut short and her face badly bruised. Then there had been a long period of calm, in a house overlooking Galway Bay. When the mist cleared in the mornings they could see the Aran Islands like lumps of madness in the foaming bile. Fada thought he could hear screaming at night from across the water. Jess roamed the limestone Burren Hills collecting flowers and herbs for a devilish perfume of her own design. Fada continued learning poems and spent most of his time in the local bar with the rich young Americans who were over to learn how to paint at the art school. The night came when Jess and Fada were making love on the small stony beach. After a while, she tapped him on the shoulder and told him in a quiet trembling voice that he had better get off her because there was something standing behind him; something horrible, he could tell from her face. She shook her head at him not to look but how could he resist?

A heavy-arsed Spaniard burst into the café and hobbled towards the counter. Another waitress with a Maori face understood the danger instantly and fetched a jug of water, a cloth and a glass; one of the Spaniards had fainted at the stall, a plump nipple between the jaws of the stud gun.

What am I going to do? Fada was suddenly afraid.

Jess'll find you if she wants. When she wants.

She's the least of my worries. About everything? I'm homeless.

My place is full. Sorry.

You live with your father.

My father lives with me.

Did I tell you there's a spell on me?

Con said it wouldn't surprise him, slapped Fada roughly on the back and stood up to leave.

Everything's going mad, Fada said. I have a bad feeling I can't stop it. Can you not sit down for a bit longer? There's a jinx on me. The evil eye.

The fool's path is not for everyone, Con said sadly.

A light rain was falling when Fada stepped out on the street not long afterwards. He had been trying to think but sometimes there was nothing to be achieved by that activity. The important issues as he saw them were: homelessness, a shortage of cash, some lost poems and a spell, a sense of doom, and now Jess haunting the streets again. He had to address them one at a time. First was to find somewhere to stay. Michael Gibbon was an option there so he took himself up along Aungier Street to the green cupola of Rathmines, and a second-hand bookshop with an old bedsit above where Fada had stayed once or twice. Michael was down the country at auctions, Sylvia told him and made them both a pot of tea. Fada began to tell her the story of the last few days. Sylvia laughed along, and groaned with sympathy at all the right moments, but as soon as Fada finished she moved the conversation on to something else entirely as though he had been only trying to entertain her and it wasn't important. In a huff, Fada went into the toilet and rolled himself a joint. He smoked half of it and found himself proudly recalling the funeral of Michael's lover the year before when he had talked and hypnotised and tempted that fifty-year-old woman all the way up in a lift to her hotel bedroom, and beyond. She wanted him to pretend to be her son's best friend and the son might walk in at any time. He considered having a wank to settle his nerves but the worries of the day destroyed the triumphant images before he could really get going.

There was a young woman in the shop when he came out of the toilet.

May I be of some assistance?

I don't know, she said, French, slim, no make-up, embarrassed.

Ah, I see, we should sit down and discuss this carefully. Une tête-à-tête non? Confusion is a dangerous maladie, mais oui? Follow me. Andiamo. He bowed.

The young woman gamely followed him out of the shop

and into the café next door. Ten minutes later Fada was back.

Sylvia said, In my opinion you need a bath, a shave and a change of clothes. You look like you've just escaped from prison.

I'm homeless. All my belongings are in a bin-liner in the back room of a porn shop in town. This is a difficult time for me. When's Michael back?

Sylvia laughed heartily again as though he was joking and returned her attention to her book on the history of gardens, fully illustrated, indexed, only one owner.

Fada set off again, the joint in his mouth, the rain heavier and darkening the street like it was being rolled up under his feet. Like the ground recoiled before him. Was he a ghost already? Did he walk among the shades? A man passed him in an old-fashioned suit and hat, striding along with a cane. A woman was looking in the window of a shop but he had already walked by her when he realised he had seen neither her nor his own reflection. Maybe he had passed over into the city of the dead, a parallel universe where life seemed to go on as normal. Lindub. Budnil. Even that dog there coming towards him had the look of a drenched mongrel from another century. Fada stopped on the bridge and sneered at the swans patrolling the canal beyond the weir. Guarding against what? Always the suggestion of aloof waiting, always circling and gliding and stretching their wings in preparation for the wondrous moment. How could people control their rage at the sight of them, the revolting dignity, the decadent grace? Why didn't people attack them with hammers? Pour petrol in and set the water aflame. The rats farting and clapping in the rushes. See then the tumultuous fiery wings outspread. A swansong fit for the realms of self-born music.

He pressed on into the rain. Why was there no rest? Why was peace denied him? Only a few weeks ago he remembered himself talking to Tanya at the flower stall, telling her he was feeling good, that he was up, that he wasn't afraid, that he was seeing a woman, Lorraine, an Englishwoman, and he was sure she liked him because she had told him and he couldn't see what could go wrong. What went wrong then? He wasn't sure. He had gone out one night without her: that was as far as he could trace it back. Then some days were missing, silent, blank. And a queasy blighted feeling whenever he thought of her or looked at a telephone. There was always the chance she was still waiting on his call but he was too much of a coward or he knew too much about himself and his own instincts to ignore the bad air that fogged over the blankness. Something must have happened, an incident too traumatic to keep in his mind. Or maybe she had met somebody else and changed her number. Or she was dead, like he was. He might never know.

It had been a good spring. He was on a roll. The energy emanated from him. Everybody commented how well he was looking. There must have been at least ten women during April alone. Which did he cherish most? Liz, the married businesswoman. They had met three or four times in hotels around the city. It wasn't her first affair and she laughed in the face of guilt or she stuck her arse up and farted in its face. Her thing was rope and blindfolds. Tie me up and leave me here. Go out and get drunk. Here's some money. She often complained how few hotels in Dublin offered a good four-poster bed. How had that one ended? Do things ever really end? She announced she was going away on a trip and would contact him when she got back. He wasn't allowed to question her. She left him a handsome sum of money on top of the hotel TV which Fada had used to fund a three-day binge. There were people who owed him for that. When he had money he prided himself on being generous with it. Where was everybody now? They called on him for entertainment and then sneaked guiltily back to their girlfriends and wives and their mysterious jobs. Now he was without a corner, condemned to walking the streets. He would have to put in a few hours with the sandwich board to drum up some cash. Contrary to what people thought, the rain was a boon to the street entertainer; not only did people feel pity for and even envy of the lone performer on the wet street but the rain trickled through the make-up and the shirt collars and the security codes and drip fed the old regrets and passions of lives that had lost their shape somewhere down the line. Fada had taken his highest booty in a storm that blew the sandwich board through the window of a shop on Grafton Street.

Passing the vegetable stalls on Camden Street, he began to think about the old woman Doreen and her poems. The advice-givers were unanimous in their instruction to take one thing at a time. Deal with each issue singly in terms of urgency. The poems he suspected were the root of all his troubles. They were the stranger who had arrived and upset the town. The barter system of give and take, desire and excess, was clogged up. They had to be found and returned. Fada's heart sank, or was it a rising sensation, at the thought he would have to visit every dirty pub and themed drinking emporium and illegal club and hotel bar in the city. A man in the best of health, a poet with an itchy arse, a sacked teacher, a disgraced politician, a gambler on a wave of luck might not survive such a dangerous excursion. Or were they right when they said the culprit will always find some excuse to return to the scene of the crime. Not true; they didn't know what they were talking about. Take for example the case of –

Now look who it was. On her bicycle.

Fada waved her down.

Marion. How's it going with you? I like the bicycle. And the hat and the rain. Where are you off to?

Home, Marion said wearily.

What's the matter?

Are you as bored as I am?

You're bored? Fada laughed. The last time I saw you, you were in great form. How's Declan?

He's fine, Marion said with a helpless air. What's going on with you? Tell me something interesting. Anything.

Struggling on you know? I –

66

I can't get this feeling to lift, Marion cut across him. This morning I got up early, cycled into town and got the Dart out to Dun Laoghaire for a walk on the beach. To see if the wind could blow it out of me. But I feel worse now. And frozen to the bone. I don't know what's the matter with me.

Maybe there's nothing the matter with you, Fada said. Maybe it's just how you feel.

Do you want to have a cup of coffee or something?

I'd prefer a pint. Fada grinned.

And you're bloody right too, Marion agreed and swung her leg over the bike.

Gleeful, Fada watched her lock it to a railing.

Let's go and get drunk. Fuck them all, she said.

Every last one of them and their sisters too. Fada rubbed his hands.

Victor's voice sounded the same whether he was telling a joke or was angry about something he had seen on the street. Toneless was the word. His head was shaved tight to the skin, the eyes dark and unreflective of his mood. Boyle thought that it would be a bad thing to cross him and his mangled ear. Yet it was strangely moving to sit there and listen to a big man unafraid of embarrassing himself in another language, the same as watching him pounding about in the small bedsit, emptying ashtrays or rummaging in the miniature fridge or refilling their glasses, the tiny thimble spirit glasses that always reminded Boyle of those Russian dolls, one inside another, that had frightened him as a child. Boyle wanted to ask about the exact significance of those dolls but it would mean opening up the subject of home and country and why Victor had left and come to Ireland, or who had forced him to leave. Both men seemed to have agreed to leave those topics alone; the past was something they couldn't share or pretend to understand about each other in any language. Boyle had come to believe this was the foundation of their friendship, the silence, no, it could be called humility.

It was a relief not to have to explain yourself, Boyle thought as he watched the big Russian fumbling with a tape. The tapes were mainly Irish traditional music made by people who worked with Victor in the kitchen of a Russian restaurant in town. Victor had once asked Boyle about the words of one of these songs and was shocked, no, dismayed that Boyle couldn't help him. Boyle had never heard most of the songs himself. Victor moved a table and standing in the middle of the room he delivered a song in Russian at the top of his voice. He sat down and gestured to Boyle that it was his turn.

They were drunk. Boyle insisted he didn't know any songs but Victor pointed to the spot under the light. Boyle had no choice; he gave in and stepped on to the stage; he racked his brains for a tune, for words. There was nothing there. Inside him was empty, mute. He thought he could forget his own name. The emptiness drew him in, lured him. It was spreading through him coldly, but soft, clean. He was vanishing, particle by particle. If Victor hadn't started clapping his hands to wake him up, Boyle might not have ever been seen again. Strange Disappearance Of Man In Dublin Bedsit. He stood up there to sing a song and the next thing he's vanished, says Russian neighbour. Victor was looking at him strangely, ashamed maybe, thinking hard, but he didn't ask, he kept the silence.

Other than in one of their flats, or on the street steps as was happening with the better weather, they had been out only as far as the local pub and once during that terrible Christmas, to a party in a house miles out in the suburbs, a gathering of Russians. Victor warned him before they went in not to believe a word anyone said and not to show more interest in one over another. The evening quickly became raucously drunken. One after another, the Russians seized the opportunity to talk to him, to tell him their tragic stories of brutality, executions, rape, while at the same time maligning the other people in the room as though they were all informers. Victor explained that a lot of them were still waiting on their papers and were terrified that they would be informed on by the very people they were spending the evening with if it could help the informer secure their own papers. Boyle wanted to ask if Victor had his own papers but decided it was none of his business; if Victor wanted to talk about it he could bring it up himself.

Later in the evening a lot of younger people arrived. The girls were black-eyed and sullen and loud and harshly decorated with make-up and tight cheap clothes. The boys gathered sourly in a corner and watched the girls come at Boyle one by one, wanting to know what he did for a living, what kind of car he drove. They wouldn't believe him when he said he was a student; they were annoyed by it. Boyle told them to ask Victor which they all did and then seemed to tell him off. Following any one of those girls in the act of crossing a room and putting food on a plate was like witnessing a display of every extremity of emotion, disdain, hatred, adoration, joy, wretched disappointment, all for no reason that Boyle could identify. One girl however was calmer, depressed he guessed. Boyle stood beside her at the sink. Her name was Rebecca she said. Boyle made the comment that it wasn't a very Russian name and the girl looked at him sharply and said that was the reason she chose it when she came here. She was small with strict black hair and violent dark paint on her eyes. The clothes she was wearing disfigured her large bust. Boyle was stuck in a silence again. She seemed to have nothing but scorn for everybody in the room. You don't look too happy to be here was the best he could do. She turned her furious panda eyes on him then. Boyle's beard prickled from ear to ear. He must have insulted her, said the wrong thing. He was about to call on Victor for help when he saw her powdered face relax and a smile take shape that, while it lasted, just a few seconds, freed him from the loneliness and desperation of the last few days by himself in the flat. They began to talk. Boyle tried to make her understand that he was not from Dublin but the difference didn't register with her. Instead of the bit about being a student, he claimed he was training to be a teacher; he softened the outline of himself, made himself easy to imagine as an honest, careful man. Rebecca said she was in Dublin only to study English and then she would go back home to look for a job in accountancy. I do not like it here, she said. The Russian people . . . you can't even imagine. She went out of the back door when two women broke into song, and Boyle sneaked after her. An icy path went out to an oil tank like a bomb on stilts at the far wall.

So have you met many boys here? Boyle asked her, trying to

be funny but realising how creepy it sounded. He was useless in these situations, out of practice, no, just bloody clueless.

I have an Irish boyfriend. He works at the airport, she said with some pride. But he is very jealous. You can't even imagine.

So where's he tonight then?

She shrugged, a long one, the shoulders held up, eyes closed. Boyle wondered if this was the moment to step in closer to her. The chance was lost anyway, if it really was one, when Victor came out looking for him. He spoke in Russian to Rebecca who responded with what sounded like a vicious outburst that Victor nodded calmly to. Victor sent Boyle back inside with a jerk of his head. They were on their way home in a taxi before he had the chance to ask about her.

You like her?

I was just curious. Interested.

What is your question?

I don't know, said Boyle. She's not happy anyway.

Are you asking me if she is happy?

After a while Boyle said, She was saying she can't wait to go home. Victor's face was reflected in the side window.

I told you not to talk to one person only. The others think stupid things. Everyone fighting and arguing.

Have I got her into trouble?

Victor said nothing more and Boyle decided he was better keeping his nose out. Not another word was mentioned about the girl or about the party.

So, bearing all this in mind, Boyle was surprised when Victor sat back in his chair in the bedsit months later and broke all the rules by demanding to know about Northern Ireland. I want to hear the truth, he said.

The truth? It's just politics now Victor. Compromise. Times change. Maybe that's the only truth.

I hear people talk about it. On the television and the radio. It is your home?

Was. I don't know any more.

Most people like to talk about their home. Life is not so easy there maybe?

Not for some.

Not for you?

It got difficult just. For me.

Difficult? A woman?

Boyle laughed but not Victor.

Government?

Boyle looked at his hands, balanced the shot glass on his palm, moved the hand around. Then he nodded.

It doesn't matter a fuck now, he said after a while. He had never said that before. The words carried nothing with them.

It doesn't matter a fuck, he said again. I got dragged into something. The suits run the show now. Like everywhere else. Business as usual.

Victor gave them both a refill.

And you? Boyle raised his eyes to Victor.

I was a Russian soldier.

Later Boyle was upstairs in his own flat, lying on his bed. He couldn't sleep, probably because of the vodka. Victor must have gone AWOL or changed sides, sick of the slaughter. He thought of that Russian girl's smile and how it had lifted him for the briefest moment, or turned over a stone in him. Where was she now, back home among the palaces of Vladivostok or a Moscow tower block? If he was to take Victor's word, she could be living in a flat round the corner, working in a chip shop. The subterfuge was worse than the Provos. Moles and double agents and grasses and counter-intelligence. Why was it at that moment that the busker character jumped into his mind again? Boyle saw him clearly, walking away down a cobbled street where the lights were coming on with the gait of a man who just got away by the skin of his teeth. Boyle flipped over on his stomach to smother a sharp qualm of fear or dread or some uneasiness about that fight at the party. He had to be more careful than that. It had been a long time since he had gone for somebody without a good reason. That meant he was wound up. He couldn't lose control of himself in public. One thoughtless reaction and he would be back inside. He had to keep a grip, a focus, submerge himself in the books, and wait. That's what he had come down here for. To take his life into his own hands and make something. Revival was a word he liked for it: he wanted to revive himself. A clear determined focus. With this in mind, he pushed himself off the bed, gathered the books he wanted and sat down to write that essay. He was going to use the line from Sartre about perception, that it was never neutral, that values spring out on people like partridges from the bushes. Partridges were beautiful birds it had to be said. He would link it somehow with the Platonic Dialogues, maybe all the stuff about the transmigration of souls and memory. He was sure he had it.

The chair stood in the backyard in the moonlight.

He worked for an hour and then abandoned it.

. . . Rocket of bloom flare flower of night wilt for me.

Fada had some people around him, perspiring Americans, oversized people in shorts, four of them, bed-spine snappers, inflated by married sloth.

. . . on the breasts of the water it has closed it has made, an act of floral presence on the water, the tranquil act of its cycle on the waste.

He could say whatever he wanted and they would swallow it.

Muggers of rare dark, alas the beached inanities, the xylophone thighs in the secret mausoleum, Venus dances around the blood drenched pasquinade of truth, he declaimed in a classical pose, one hand on his heart.

Over their corpulent tea-towel shoulders, Tanya was making bundles of mixed blooms, a scalpel between her teeth, shaking her head disapprovingly at his antic carry-on. Tanya with her black girl's tight weave of threaded hair and her cabbalistic sun tattoo at the base of her spine, the jeans low around her hipless waist. He had known her for years now, since the out-of-focus days of her puberty when her mother started bringing her to the stall. Now she was hardening, sharpening, exfoliating. An hour earlier the old boyfriend had turned up at the stall to plead with her to have him back. His name was Higso but he didn't need a name. He was a vicious bastard and that was all. Tanya told him she had dumped him because she found out something about him, she wouldn't say any more than it was a house burglary that Fada guessed had turned ugly. Higso denied it and wanted to know who was grassing him up. Moreover, Fada was sure that Higso was part of a crowd who had chased him around the streets of Dun Laoghaire one night in a car. Fada had knocked on the doors and windows of twenty houses and cried for help at the top of his voice, a voice in himself he had never known, that seemed to come from long before he ever existed. In the end he had hidden in a garden in a child's play tent where he had prayed and wept and was found still babbling in the morning by a woman who called the police.

Higso came over to him and said: How's life treating you sleazebag?

Fada understood that a crowded street wouldn't protect him.

He ran.

An hour later when he came back, Tanya wouldn't look at him. She was not impressed by his survival instincts.

... Charred curtains in a Liberties whore-house. Staircase of bones. Her black lips first opened long before the gates of hell ... Hey, excuse me, this is a business arrangement, he shouted after the Americans who were walking away without having made an offering.

He took a few steps after them and stopped. Amid the bare legs and hair and parcelled arseflesh and loose-hanging breasts on Grafton Street, he noticed a familiar face. He skipped over to Tanya.

You haven't seen me. I'm begging you. It's an emergency.

I'm not lying for you or anybody, Tanya informed him.

Look I know you're poor and still have moral fibre but if a girl asks for me don't say a word. Tell her I've left the country. I've always been there for you haven't I?

Tanya looked at him in disbelief, then sarcasm, then pity at his gutless, shyster frame receding down a side street.

Fada went straight into a café and started telling Oisín Mc Cormack about it.

He said, I saw her just now on Grafton Street. What's she want? She swore she would never set foot in Dublin again. Not until it won back its soul. How does it do that? I asked her. Only a few know the answer, Jess says. A chosen few.

Now she's back. What's she want? I don't need to see her. It's not good for me. My head's wrecked as it is Oisín. I told you what happened didn't I? About the swan business. We were lying on the beach together one night on the coast of Clare. Jess taps me on the shoulder and says, Don't look around. But you have to when a woman says that don't you? You have to know what it is that frightens her. I told you this one night at Bradley's party didn't I? I looked around and there it was standing over us, the wings outspread, the beak open wide, right over us. So Jess got out from under me and she grabs her clothes and runs along the beach. I keep slipping on the sand and falling over. We'd had a few drinks as well. And it's coming after me. I can hear Jess screaming. And the big white neck straightens up and bends and it snaps at me and I roll out of the way and I'm trying to get up off my knees again and then it gets me by the back of the neck and pushes my face down in the sand.

We're busy. I have to take your order, Oisín said.

It got me by the back of the neck in its jaws. I was pinned down. Blinded, couldn't breathe. Have you ever smelled a swan's breath? It's like burned skin. Scorched flesh. Like you're being branded. I couldn't do anything. It was stronger than me, Fada persisted, his hands gripping the table.

I'll come back in a few minutes, Oisín promised but he never did.

That afternoon, Fada decided to phone around to see if he could find a sofa for a couple of nights, Just a few nights until I work out what to do next, he said to the people down the phone, some of whom he had been avoiding for months, some of whom were still trying to forget him and then those whom he was chancing his arm with, people he'd had a night out with and not seen again, women, men, girls. He went into a cabin in a call shop and inhaled the smell of top-shelf misery, the bitter saliva on the mouthpiece, hardcore, adults only, the reek of pagan genitals, spices and cheap leather and hairspray. He made about twenty calls without much luck other than a horny conversation with the mother of Orla from Cork. When he came out of the booth, Boyle was there behind the counter.

They looked at each other.

Should have known sugar you'd get your kicks in a place like this, Fada said in some kind of American accent.

And in a different voice: Babel FM, tune in to-night to the weeping and the wailing and gnashing of the gold-filled teeth. Pure quality feedback from the myriad stringed lyre of human suffering. Give it up for DJ Boyle. People power. Ah the lost and downtrodden, such sweet heart-swelling cadence. Poor wee exiled loves. Wouldn't it make you want to give a donation? Where's my purse? Hi, my name's Tabatha and I'll be your waitress for this evening? How do you like your keening sir? Blood raw or charred to the bone? With coleslaw? Do you take plastic young man?

Boyle stood squarely, bleakly, and watched him.

Is that supposed to be funny?

So we meet again. Fada laughed nervously. This Northerner wasn't intimidating but there was tension around him, a consternation in the air. He was serious, slow to banter, maybe humourless. Working-class Northern Irish, well into his thirties and studying with the Trinity scholars. There was some story behind it. He reminded Fada of a bar after closing time, stools knocked over. The words came out of him sparsely, reluctantly like he didn't trust them or he knew they'd be back to haunt him. But there was also naivety, a fear of all before his eyes, and it could turn quickly into violence. He was uncomfortable in the world, ashamed, sullen like somebody forced up on a stage at an audience-participation community-theatre fundraiser stop-the-rot benefit.

Fada said, I've never seen you here before. I come in here all the time. Well there's another one I use on Nassau Street more often. You work here then?

Boyle said nothing. Standing behind his counter he flicked

through the pages of a book. Fada was trying to remember the events of that last night, the party, the fight, if he had done or said anything for which he needed to make amends. Nothing much had stuck in his mind. Fada felt he had been attacked for no reason.

Are you annoyed with me?

I wouldn't waste my energy.

That's good then, Fada said, seizing the chance to end conversation on the topic. He moved quickly towards the counter, extemporising.

Not a bad day. How's it been in here? I had a good steady crowd all afternoon. This hideous twenty-stone American woman who gave me her address. A toothless Dublin man who was coming from a funeral of his best friend. Then a couple who started arguing about which poems they wanted to hear and it developed into full-scale war between them. You had to hear the things they were shouting at each other. They're scaring off all my customers don't forget. Why do people like that stay together? What is it? Do they get addicted to the aggression do you think? Or is it just habit? The woman walks off eventually and I try to persuade the man to go after her. They're gone about fifteen minutes and then they're back arm in arm and I have to go for a pint with them as an apology. I'm trying to say I'm at work, trying to earn some money and then the man takes out a fifty and gives it to me. And then I'm stuck in the pub for an hour listening to the long story of their relationship, how they met, their first kiss, every detail, and waiting for the argument to start again. Which of course it does. I tell them I'm going to the toilet and sneak off. I can't even go back on the street because they'll find me. What about you? Any news?

News? said a bewildered Boyle.

Anything happening? Fada put an imaginary microphone to Boyle's bearded mouth. We're reporting today from the streets of –

Boyle interrupted him. No witches or old women on

broomsticks then?

Fada acted out a shiver down his back which he felt become real.

Money, Boyle said and told him the price of the calls. Fada emptied a pocket of coins on to the counter and began to count it out.

She's probably out in the Wicklow Hills searching for some herb to perfect her next spell. Eye of sparrow and all that shite. Listen to me joking about it but I'm scared, I really am. I have to find those poems. I met somebody who told me he saw me with some papers one night in the Shelbourne so I ran round there full of hope but there was nothing. Met a lovely girl in there though. A Norwegian waiting in the lobby for her daddy.

Boyle swept the coins into his hands and dropped them in the till.

I heard some people talking about your friend, the woman in the Liffey, Fada went on. They say she was definitely drowned. It wasn't murder. And something about the food in her stomach.

She wasn't my friend, Boyle said.

But didn't you know her or something?

I told you before I didn't know her.

Sorry, Fada said, stepping back from the counter. I was just asking. But she could have been pushed I was thinking.

Smiling like that? Have you thought about the smile on her face, Boyle almost shouted at him.

Fada followed Boyle's gaze towards the open door. People passing along the street that's all. Some of them looked in. Summer faces. Bare limbs. The light said it wasn't too late, to forgive everyone, to die of generosity. The beardy Northerner was thinking furiously about something; Fada sensed he was fighting to keep it in, away from words, out of reach of the tongue. It was bubbling to the surface, whatever it was, a new idea or a memory or maybe something to do with the woman and the mask, the hairy lips were twitching, and Fada waited

79

it out in silence. He was laying bets that his interest in the mask had to do with some women from his past. He would have put Boyle down as a married man, separated now, lost. Maybe the wife ran off with another man. Or maybe she died. Maybe the mask reminded him of her.

Or he might have known the woman from this very shop. That was another option. He used to listen to her lonesome homesick songs in one of those cubicles of disaster.

Fada was about to ask but the moment was scattered when two Italians tripped through the door together, two long-limbed girls, lean young unsnappable saplings, arm in brown arm, laughing of course, and came straight up to the counter. Fada tried to catch their shining identical opal eyes. He was about to declare a poem when Boyle pointed them towards the booth.

Fada stayed there for another while, trying to draw Boyle out of himself, teasing him, guiding people to their booths and holding the door open for them. Nothing was happening. Boyle listened to his stories but said nothing. Eventually, giving up, he told Boyle where he'd be later on if he fancied a pint and went off to change his clothes and see what there was to see.

Around eight, he went into the Gorge to meet Fiacra H. He had managed to have a shower and change his clothes in a flat in Ranelagh, and then the girl, Anna, silent Anna with the perfect ears, had been good enough to make him something to eat, the first time he'd eaten in a number of days. The Gorge was lively already; Fada scouted around and then approached the bar. The face of a new girl behind the bar gave him what he called the opposite of an out-of-body experience, opened up a hollowness inside him that must feel like a womb. The barmaid was Spanish, slothful Aztec eyes peering out from the doorway of her black tent of hair. As if she could read his turmoil, the girl kept her distance at the other end of the bar. Fada went off to the toilet without managing to get an order in, and began to wank. The images were of fires in the deserts at night, camels snorting, and men in robes guarding the door of a tent where she lay on a bed of furs, chained . . .

In a few minutes he was back at the bar, in control of himself again. Fiacra was there now, trouble on his face, the forehead cut by two deep scars of worry which pointed down towards the seat of wisdom. The Spaniard served him now without demur and they went to sit round a pillar plastered with film posters. There was a jazz outfit up on the stage, four bearded men led by a younger lad in front of a computer terminal. The stage was framed by a papier-mâché proscenium arch ridged with blood-red thorns the size of shark fins. Fada waited for Fiacra to speak first. He knew this from their history together; whatever way he chose to ask what the trouble was he would have it thrown back in his face.

Fiacra had come back from the States the year before and met Fada, whom he had known casually at school, one night at a party and then again the following weekend. Fada was quick to see that he had brought plenty of money back with him and he was at the mercy of reckless appetites only a vainglorious homecoming can bring to life. They went out everywhere together looking for women and whatever else might happen. Fiacra rented a flat in the city centre and it became the customary regrouping point for a diverse crowd of people after the clubs. Six months that had lasted and then Fiacra had met Lucy and retired to his bedroom. Lucy was plain, Fada thought, and highly strung. She didn't like crowds or bars and preferred to sit in a restaurant all night talking about house prices and the end of communal life in Dublin. Fada saw desperation in her eyes and wanted to fuck her neat gym-tightened arse.

She's pregnant, Fiacra told him eventually. The worry lines were like a divining rod over his forehead.

Is she?

She's gone down to her friends in Galway.

Did you know about it?

What kind of question is that? Did I know about what?

Don't take it out on me.

Did I know what?

Were you planning it?

Fiacra shook his head.

Was she?

Look at your face. You fucken hate her don't you?

She hates me.

Maybe if you didn't try to tell her every sick thought you've ever had whenever you see her. She calls you the sewer.

That they may dream their dreamy dreams, I carry off their filthy streams, Fada sang.

On the stage the double-bass player plucked out a hectic solo while the saxophonist blew down the scale into the depths of an accordion. A girl appeared on the dance floor and began a slow-motion pursuit of a butterfly.

You don't want her to like you. You enjoy that. That's the kind of thing you like. Your mad swan routine. Women who want to vomit while you whisper in their ear.

Fada laughed: he remembered one of his dreams where he is led into a classroom of schoolgirls by a stern headmistress who enjoins him to do his worst, teach these young madames the poetry of corruption, and goes out and locks the door behind her. The girls start to giggle as Fada pulls the blinds. But it wasn't the right time to draw Fiacra into a conversation about erotic dreams.

Is there any chance I can stay at yours tonight? he asked instead. She's not there sure.

Her name's Lucy. And I'm going home after this.

One more, said Fada, on his feet immediately.

I love her, Fiacra said. Can you understand that?

Fada looked at his friend's plump boyish face with the scythe-like sideburns and the wishbone anxiety lines. He saw anger in it, pain that a scream wouldn't heal. There were tears in his frightened eyes. Maybe he had been wrong about Fiacra and Lucy; maybe she wasn't suffocating him, keeping him in, maybe it wasn't so one-sided and Fiacra wanted to be with her.

Shaking, Fada stood at the bar. All of a sudden he was afraid to move, his hands, even his eyes were taut. The slightest movement would set off a chain of other movements, a sickening infinite litany of repercussions he didn't want to take part in. The blink of an eyelid catapulted him to the end of the world, the final spasm, the last laugh. Even the corpses carry on jerking and shuddering in their coffins. But what had this to do with the fear in Fiacra's eyes? Fiacra meets a girl who gets pregnant who detests Fada who orders another drink from an Aztec who takes his money which goes to the owner who likes to play golf where he meets a woman who is into bondage which she buys from a man who owns a shop in town which he wants to sell so he can afford a sex change to be with the husband of the woman who is into bondage and Fada buys another drink which he will carry to Fiacra who is going to be a father and the child will be sent to learn languages and geography and who is in control and the price of drink goes up and up and Fada has to stand on the street and recite poems from the twilight of the heroes and the woman takes out her whip and washes the blood off in the bath and through the window the neighbour is watching all because Fiacra is in love and Fada is standing at the bar catatonic and hoping his eyelids won't move and the show will stop just for second, just for a second . . . And the place was busy now, people on every side of him, people dancing. They were all parasites. They wanted blood. Applause and burned offerings. Then they went home and polished their shoes in front of the television. The barmaid opened her bottomless Inca eyes like they were a curse. Fada brought his eyes down cautiously to his shoes; Lisa-Ann had bought them to him, brogues she called them, brown, with black stitching. Lisa-Ann: he had forgotten about her. I have to phone Lisa-Ann, he told himself. Lisa-Ann would sort everything out, fix him up. The barmaid was taking steps away from him. She knew, yes, she saw it all coming apart inside him like his guts were spilling out over the bar. The tent door swayed in the desert night air. She had those eyes burned black by gazing into her own soul. His jaw was locking, the muscles stiffening. That's what was happening; he was going to lose it again and end up back in hospital, the Puzzle Factory. They were all waiting. Worse than that was the relief in the idea. His heart seized on it like a compliment. Really, do you mean it? Am I? Say it again. No don't. Hospital, a few pills, talk to the doctors and lie in bed for a while, crisp white sheets, regain his strength, just for a few months idling around the flower beds in the misty dawn.

He leaned his elbows on the bar for support. They were all pretending not to notice, carrying on with their wonderful conversations and taking bets under the table. Tonight Fada will crack? No tomorrow night? We all know it's coming. By midnight tomorrow it'll all fall on his head. He wanted to call out a name but his jaw was locked tight, twisted down to the left like he'd had a stroke. There was a thing coming down from over his head like a block of dark light, a colossal shining black ingot, that wanted him flat on the floor.

He gave in to it.

He was sure he did. He sank. But now he seemed to be dancing. Many people were dancing around him. The butterfly chaser was behaving like a snake coming out of her basket. He could see himself from a distance, down on the dance floor, amid the parrots and cockatoos of lights. Over in the corner he waved at Fiacra who had his arm round a girl, telling her everything, his entire life story, the way he did with all of them. There were other people there in the alcove: Alan, Cormac, JP in his high heels and his fluffy pink bag of pills, all watching him dancing, like a man in slow-motion pursuit through a jungle, scooping back the overhanging giant leaves, shooting snakes, beating his chest, where is she, I must find her, nothing will stop me . . .

*

They went back to Fiacra's place after the pub was closed,

about eight of them. Fada and the butterfly chaser arrived long after everyone else. She was a tall thin woman who liked to laugh. They kissed until it wasn't enough any more against the railings outside the courts. Fiacra opened the door and hugged both of them. Fada led the woman straight into the spare bedroom. She was one of those who was naked in a few seconds. She laughed when he went into her and wrapped her long cold legs around his back. He pitted himself against her, searching for their rhythm. She laughed and laughed.

Fada couldn't come and they fell asleep. Sometime later, he woke sweating and rolled her over. Her face was red from his stubble, a new dawn of redness, and two new suns around her nipples. Holding her legs spread across his arms like a precious garment, he found his way into her again. The rhythm was immediate this time. Her begging bowl overflowed. He watched her gasping for breath as though she might not succeed. Just in time he got out and shot himself across her stomach.

She was sucking on her gums, waving her hands around.

Water? Fada asked and she blinked her eyes twice.

Fada kissed her damp forehead. Naked, he went out into the kitchen. Fiacra was there in the dark.

Good time?

Great. You?

I couldn't do it, Fiacra said.

Fada sat his buttocks down on a wooden chair: I feel a lot better now. In the Gorge there I thought I was losing it. I saw this black thing like a sharpening block. You know for knives. Can I tell you something? I was thinking about hospital again. It's never crossed my mind before. Is there something the matter with me do you think? Tell me. Be honest.

I've other things on my mind, Fiacra said.

I need somebody to be honest with me.

You know when she told me the first thing we did was make love. Fiacra was talking now. We made love straight away. It was incredible. The heat of her skin. We were both crying. It didn't matter what would happen later. But just for that hour, I've never felt as strong or alive. Imagine how she must feel with it inside her. It was the nearest I've come to beauty. Living beauty.

I can't go back into hospital. They won't let me out again, Fada said. Fiacra stood up; he said he was going out for a drive. A minute later Fada heard the front door shut. He brought a glass of water into the bedroom, ice cubes' rattling that always reminded him of bringing his mother her whiskey in bed at night, and tried to rouse the girl. She looked out at him from deep in her dreams. Her face seemed much older now. Then he went into the other bedroom with the glass.

Fiacra sent me to see if you were ok, he said. Here's some water.

Up on one elbow, the Australian girl smiled and swallowed the water. The duvet fell away and showed one of her breasts which she covered again without haste.

He's a lot on his mind, Fada said. Let me lie beside you for a bit.

He was hard again as soon as he felt her arse against him. He kissed her shoulders and hair for a long time as though he were lulling her to sleep but pushing now and again with his pelvis against her buttocks to see if she would respond. Her breathing quickened when he moved his hand down along her hips and thighs. She was going to pretend that she was asleep he guessed. Pushing against her again he felt the pressure of her hips responding. He reached round and filled his hands with her breasts, heavy, smooth, soft. The girl stretched, threw an arm drowsily across the pillow. One last time to be sure, he pushed against her and this time she sighed.

Boyle had been standing at the corner for fifteen minutes. He was already late for a lecture. At his back, behind the hoardings, he was dimly aware of the voices of the men working on a new building. A crane shadow passed over him, a cement mixer at the end of a chain, and he counted eight, nine, ten, you are sleeping now. He could tell people noted his presence as they passed but not even his chronic fear of being conspicuous was enough to move him. The butts scraped out at his feet had made a many-pronged black star which might have intrigued him in another mood, but not this morning, not with what was going on in front of his very eyes, the sheer gall of it. Two young women were unloading a box out of a van. He had already seen how they had set up a table on the cobbles, folded open the metal legs and checked it for balance.

The two blondes in black berets carried the box to the table but changed their minds and put it carefully on the ground. Then they both ran, no, skipped back to the van and repeated the same procedure with an identical unmarked box. That done, one of them returned to the van, shut the doors and parked it while the other cut open the boxes with a Stanley knife. Both girls were wearing long black skirts, old fashioned ankle length, and T-shirts on which was printed a blurred white eyeless face.

The one who had shut the van returned with a bundle under her arm; she flapped out a square of black velvet over the table, perfect first time. Boyle saw the first mask come out of the box. The girls passed it among themselves and one put it almost against her face only to be stopped by the other with a superstitious shake of the head which sent her beret awry.

They laid out two rows of six masks on the black velvet.

Boyle's anger burned in his stomach, like his brain was down there, floating, eaten up in the basin of acids. After they were satisfied with the table display, the girls stood to attention with their hands behind their backs.

Don't forget her, one called out, a gentle plea.

Please don't forget her, the other chimed in.

Then they both broke down laughing.

The street remained empty for a few minutes. Two men in suits glanced at the stall as they passed and made an expression like forbearance. First to approach was a well-dressed woman who seemed to be in a hurry; the girls remained at attention while they answered her questions and the woman went on with what looked like a promise to buy one later. After that, the street filled up then went quiet again. The first buyer was a tall bearded man wheeling a bicycle who also wrote down something the girls had said on the back of his hand. The mask was handed over in a black paper bag. Straight away, a redheaded teenager took out her purse even before she had reached the stall. A couple were next up, a Chinese couple.

In another lull in the street, Boyle made his move.

Don't forget her.

Please don't forget her.

He looked from mask to mask. He could see no difference between them and the one in the newspaper, without eyes or ears. The smile was the same, the thick flared lips stretched to a swooning fulfilment. He was panting. Glancing at the girls he saw their eyes were fixed on a point over his shoulder.

So what's this about? His voice sounded hoarse, broken. Explain this to me.

This a face of an unknown woman, Blue Eyes said and showed her white teeth in a smile. She was discovered in the river, the Liffey.

Just behind those buildings, Brown Eyes informed him.

I know where it is, Boyle said too sharply and he caught the exchange of looks between the girls.

What happened to her? Was she murdered?

No one knows.

The point is we don't want her to be forgotten. No matter where she might come from. If you buy a mask, you will help to make sure she is remembered.

So are you selling the faces of all the victims of unsolved crimes? I heard on the radio last night that two junkies burned to death in a house.

We feel she should be remembered, Brown Eyes said, keeping her calm.

Where did you get the face? Did a relative give you permission for this? How many do you have?

We have no desire to upset anyone.

We merely want to give the people of this city a chance to remember her. To ask themselves why this happened.

And hopefully not allow it to happen again.

And where does the money go?

Look at her, Brown Eyes said, turning her face to Boyle.

Please.

Look at her. Don't you think there is something special in her face.

Something extraordinary.

Vivid.

Her beauty is striking.

Don't you think she is beautiful?

Boyle looked from the blue pair to the brown pair, then down to the empty eye sockets in the mask, searching for an end to this, an escape. When he found nothing, he put his hands on the table and taking a step backwards he turned the table over into the street. Some of the masks shattered in the fall and the others he started to stamp on or kicked across the street. The girls kept well back, stunned but silent. One of them was already typing on her mobile phone. Boyle cyed the two boxes at their feet, took a step forward, stopped. Two men from the building site ran out into the street wanting to act the hero.

Boyle began to run. At the start it was a sprint, head down, the knees high, concentrating on the breathing while the bag of books punched at his spine, fingered him. People looked over their shoulders as he went by or stepped out of the way. Without direction, he took whatever side streets came along, lanes, across a new shopping esplanade, through an un-opened office complex, the glass in the windows the colour of insect shells. The gradient began to rise as he hit his first wind; his mouth dried, his breathing out of sync with his legs. He slackened the pace when he got on to Thomas Street. It was more like jogging now, a man who had decided to hurry somewhere just in case. He couldn't remember the last time he had run like this, a long time anyway. Even in jail he was never one of those who did the laps of the pitch or the Frisbee throwing or the fitness regime although he occasionally went into goal in a football match to keep on the right side of some-body. He veered right across the main road, then downhill again steeply past dismal flat blocks with washing hanging out on the verandas and boarded windows and signs that said Drug Free Zone.

The memories began then: running the rises and crescents and porches and gardens and shattered padstones of the Creggan estate on its hill under a slanted overcrowded sky, the hop and leap over the white summer-softened man-size words painted on the tarmac, BRITS OUT FREE DERRY, that the dogs had pawed around into every backyard like snow tracks of hunter dogs and the birds speckled and scuffed across the slates and window sills and telephone wires. Always running in the midst of a gang of children, like water near boiling point, then cooling and bubbling over again into groundless races from one scorched pebbledashed gable to another, to that lamppost down there, first to the front door of the McIntyres'; to the shop with its permanent brace of metal grille, last to the barricade is an informer; or the sudden unanimous attacks with bricks and bottles on thin-air enemies while your mother natters with Mrs Grant at the door, then the screaming retreat down glass-mohicaned lanes to regroup at the cemetery gates where the girls were playing ball and singing and away again in another explosion of roars and curses because there was word of a fight two streets down or a fire in a bin or two dogs stuck together or a stolen crate of lemonade or a shot fired or just to see what's happening on Lisfannon Drive. Then the dark, and the shout to come in for the night that would set you running home, in the door and straight up the stairs to bed where you fell asleep in your clothes and dreamed of mounting kamikaze missions on a fortress of black ice.

Boyle ran on. Now he had a football scarf wrapped around his face and an armful of bricks. The dust on his hands was like the touch of his girlfriend's hair, the ache in his palms the same as when he fingered her. There she was sitting on a wall with her sister. She had once asked him to run across the bridge to the Waterside and bring her back something to prove it; he couldn't find anything that was different and came back empty handed to be called a coward, that he didn't love her enough, to be given a slap by her big brother. Smoke avalanches fell across his path like clouds of wisdom. Flames flew like joyful birds. One arm was twice the length of the other, stretched by the long slow swing of stone or bottle, the double step with the feet as the hands let go and the body stops, ducks low and turns to run back past the next wave, past Jimmy Caldwell RIP, past Liam Doherty RIP, past Patricia McDaid RIP, past Hector Coyle butcher millionaire, past Greg Johnstone actor and TV presenter, past Fat Vinny manic depressive child-molester until you reach the back and the gathered spectators and your ma is still standing there nattering in the doorway to Mrs Grant.

And Boyle ran on until he came to what must have been the last run, years later this, a man now, through a housing estate and out across the fields, through a farm where he tried to hide in a shed and then panicked and kept going through a field of wheat, a river, another field with sheep that didn't move, field after field that's all there was, and them coming after you, the sirens, the helicopter up and the murder of swallows heading off to fairer climes. He had left Sock Mc Kinney back there in the library van, shooting through the back doors. Get fucken back here you fucken lousy cunt. They're not getting it. They're not fucken getting it you chicken cunt. But Boyle had fled at the first sight of the checkpoint, turning the mobile library off the road into a field. They were transporting the most precious of all precious, an armour-piercing yoke, to a safe house on the Strabane Road. Sock had banged on his door first thing and told him the score. It's an easy run, Sock said, wee fucken buns. He sat in the back of the van, reading out passages from the big-print books and rolling joints while Boyle took his usual route through the town. But the checkpoint was waiting for them. They'd been grassed up. Boyle saw in the mirrors that they were coming out from behind as well, materialising out of the grass and trees. They're not fucken getting it, Sock was screaming, laughing, and kicked open the back doors. Boyle span the van off the road and jumped – You fucken chicken cunt, you're a dead man for this Boylo – and he ran as the shooting started towards what he thought was a forest that soon showed itself to be less than a grove, a fucken measly copse, a soggy glade . . . and now there was the helicopter coming down over his head and they were knocking out the window to him, waving, blowing kisses, the camouflaged faces, they could piss down on him running across another field ploughed with a fairy circle in the middle, waiting for the shot that would bring him down, the finger in the back, the knock on the nut, running towards it, ready for it, and it never came, there was no mercy, there was no fucken mercy and he slipped and went down and got up again and way up ahead he saw two old women leaning over a gate nattering.

That same afternoon Boyle was hiding from the world in the university library. His usual place was occupied by a restless poser in cricket whites with grass on his back, fair haired, floundering in idleness. Due to the rain that had blown in across the city with oracular haste the library had the sodden chaotic atmosphere of an emergency flood evacuation. Ones moved freely from table to table, chatting as they called it; packs of them sat around on the floor loudly flouting the attempts of the pale-faced library staff to keep order. Boyle was forced to browse among the shelves for a long while before he foresaw the departure of a morbid young lad with disfiguring acne and being first to the seat found himself sitting opposite two callous-mouthed stuck-up right-wingers-to-be, who looked him up and down and raised their eyes to a banal heaven.

Instead of the black denim shirt he had put on that morning, Boyle was decked out in a soaked yellow T-shirt emblazoned with a smiling green crab while on his head he wore a red baseball cap carrying the number 57. It was a laughable get-up, he was well aware of it, but he wanted to punish himself for what he had done to that stall earlier, for losing his law-abiding equilibrium, and it was in his nature to chastise himself publicly. He also had two pairs of shorts in his bag.

The great run had come to a stop at the window of a charity shop on the main street of Phibsborough. On going inside, the elderly woman sorting clothes at the counter raised her hands feebly in the air while her sister volunteer had other ideas and tightened her grip on the hoover ready to wield it bravely in the defence of the aid to crumbling orphanages in Romania. Boyle had to think quickly; it was clear to him that

93

if he turned round and left the shop the old women, emboldened by their victory of sorts over a criminal degenerate, might pick up the phone and enlighten the police to his whereabouts. With this in mind, he decided it was wiser to convince the crones that he meant no harm and uttered the words, I'm looking for something to wear on my holidays, and throw himself on their mercy.

They stood him in front of a huge cracked mirror in the dressing room, a curtained-off corner of the shop filled with unsorted boxes and bags of clothes, shoes and ornaments, and limped off. When they returned, each with an armful of holiday wear, Boyle found himself in another merciless position; he was obliged to try on the things, they wouldn't hear of selling him anything that might not be right, they couldn't live with themselves. The ladies withdrew reluctantly, but only a few steps to just outside the curtain which Boyle tried to pull closed, an action which could never been have been completed successfully because the curtains were hung on a rail balanced between two boxes, and lo and behold the whole thing came down on top of Boyle's head. The gravity of this accident was almost too much for the two biddies and served to increase their administrations to the point where one of them went off to make Boyle a cup of tea while the other helped him out of his denim shirt and into a range of colourful beach clothes.

An hour he was in there before he could make his escape.

Back in the library, oppressed by the preening and itching and fingernail picking, the bored slander in the eyes he met over the page edge of the total night of postwar authenticity – Birth as an ekstatic relation of being to the In-Itself which it is not and as the a priori constitution of pastness is a law of being for the For-itself – Boyle wondered if he was overreacting. Obviously, the safest place for him after his antics on the street was home in the flat with a cup of tea but he simply couldn't go back there and face the walls or that interrogation chair in the backyard. At the same time he guessed the berets probably didn't have legal permission to set up a stall for their obscene wares and so it was unlikely the cops were keeping an eye out for him. Even so it was another example of his failing grip on himself. He had to keep out of bother. He wasn't going back to jail for anybody. All of these thoughts were there in his head at the same time and they wearied him and Sartre was wrestling with the demons of irony around the bonfire of non-being when the book was snatched out of his hands.

I've been watching you, the Dove said and instead of snapping the book shut and disposing of it like anyone else in their right mind, she brought it close to her face and was probably paying special attention to the sentences he had underlined, smiling, smiling eyes.

The two misery-bound stylish young things tutted their well-brought-up suburban garden lips – some wee flowsey first-year doting and fawning all over this older weirdo mature beardy student type.

You missed the lecture again.

I didn't miss it, he said. I didn't want to go.

The Dove seemed to lose her breath for a second. Boyle was trapped again; he didn't know what to do with his eyes. He brought these things on himself, that was the story of his life, moments like this when he was unable to act, to make a move, to know what he wanted. He was a coward; the Dove was waiting for him to take control, to show her what he wanted and those other two were waiting thirstily for a glimpse of humiliation.

Boyle stood up.

I want to get out of here, he said and met the Dove's crystal-blue eyes. They were asking him if that meant he wanted to go alone. She was strong, braver than him; she wasn't intimidated by the whispering of the other two.

She risked another smile, cracked safari lips, small white teeth, and Boyle found himself smiling back at her.

Imagine you are lying on a hospital trolley. Go on. Imagine it. Please. Close your eyes.

They were sitting in the bar of a small hotel near the university. She had wanted to go walking in the rain but Boyle was wary of being seen on the street. The Dove brought his eyelids down with the tips of two fingers cold from her glass of beer.

Imagine it. Close your eyes. You are lying on a hospital trolley. There is another empty trolley next to you.

Immediately she removed her fingers his eyelids sprung open again. They both laughed, then tried again. As he listened, her thumb and index finger pressed lightly against his eyeball.

A surgeon is going to come into the room and wants to move you to the other trolley. Bit by bit but completely painlessly of course. You have to concentrate. Imagine it. First she chops off your feet and puts them down on the other trolley. Ok?

Boyle nodded. She?

She, confirmed the Dove. Then she cuts off up to your knees and moves them over.

Are they connected up again?

Yes. Then she cuts from the knee to the hip and moves them over. Then the hip to chest. Then the chest to the neck. Ok? Are you still lying in the same position on the first trolley?

Where else would I go? said Boyle.

Ok. You haven't moved. So she has cut off most of your body. Only your head is lying there on the first trolley. Then she begins to cut away your head, slice by slice. The chin to the bottom lip. The top lip to under the nose. Have you moved yet?

How can I? She's taken away my body.

You have to say when you feel you have moved to the other trolley. She keeps cutting. The nose goes, then the eyes. All that's left now is your brain.

Boyle pushed away her hand.

That would wreck your head.

You're afraid, she mocked him. It's only a thought experiment. You've no imagination.

I sold it.

There's more you see. She cuts away your brain, bit by bit, sliver by sliver. The point is: try to figure out when you think you'll change over to the second trolley. When you've actually moved. Think about it: she cuts away your whole body and you feel you're in the same place. Some people feel they are in the same place even when there's only a morsel of brain left on the first trolley. The mind–body problem you see. We think we're more than the sum of our parts.

And what do you think? Boyle asked her.

Do I believe in a soul?

She was able to talk about these things without cynicism.

Yes, I do, she said scrupulously, looking him full in the face.

Boyle was the first to turn away.

Do you?

If you accept that there is a soul, then you have to ask where it came from and then that leads you down another road entirely into religion and God and destiny and transmigration and reincarnation and hell and –

I didn't ask you what the problems are. I asked you if you thought of yourself as a soul.

Boyle found himself laughing. He filled his mouth with stout.

Do you? she insisted, smiling, her hand on his other arm.

I don't know was all he could say. How can you know?

That's not what I asked you.

She took away her hand and sat back in her seat so that they were shoulder to shoulder again, facing towards the door which never opened. The bar was dark and quiet; most of the tables were old sewing-machines with movable black pedals. The barman was refilling the mixer shelves from a crate. The only other customer was a fidgeter, a young lad, on his feet near the taps who kept taking sips of his beer and then setting the glass back down again as though he had made up his mind about something, that was it, the plan was decided, no more indecision.

Boyle and the Dove were quiet for the space of time it took him to roll a fag and light it. Boyle was thinking that it wasn't too bad, this sitting with her, that he shouldn't have been so careful with her. She was light-hearted and profound. She could smile like a child while telling you that your body chained you to death. Her skin – her face, her neck, her bare shoulders, her legs, her feet in sandals – she was covered in skin that seemed wise to the light of day.

What was the news you were going to tell me? he asked her to stave off the flashes he was getting off her belly, the inner thighs.

Again, she turned round towards him, suddenly alive again: I'm not going away this summer. Remember I told you I was going to Australia. Well, I've changed my mind. I've got a volunteer job teaching English to refugees. That's what I'm going to do. I want to get involved in something. I feel like I'm always on the outside. I've no experience of the world. Do you know what I mean?

Boyle nodded sagely.

You think it's a good idea?

Might be, he said. If that's what you want.

I do, she said, and again she looked directly at him. What about you? What kind of work did you do before Trinity?

Various things. Anything to pay the bills. Labouring jobs. Driving jobs. Worked in a library, driving a mobile van. But you've done a lot of travelling don't forget, he said to take the pressure off himself. I've never been out of Ireland. Ever. Nope.

What do you want to do when you finish?

He shrugged. Teach maybe.

In the North.

Who knows?

Do you go home much?

He shrugged again and she sighed and dropped back in her seat.

It's like blood from a stone, she said and then suddenly sat up again and asked him what his saddest memory was, no, his happiest, she changed her mind. I'll tell you mine first. It's to do with my father. After my mother left him he got very sick. Depression. It was terrible for about a year. Then one day – he always liked hats you see – I brought him home a new hat. He was asleep in bed and I laid it on his chest. He came downstairs a few hours later in his best suit and the hat on. He looked wonderful. He was laughing. I said something about how handsome the hat was and do you know what he said? It was magical. He said, I've been dreaming about this hat for a long time. And today I woke up and there it was.

You mean he didn't know it was you.

It didn't occur to him, she said. My father's a dreamer you see.

The fidgeter across the bar slapped the counter hard at that moment and then began to perform a pantomime apology to the barman and to the empty bar, seeing Boyle and the Dove only at the last minute and coming towards them seeking their pardon. Boyle made a gesture to show it was no problem and the man backtracked to his spot, shaking his head.

And speaking of hats? the Dove said, and pulled the baseball cap off his head. You look different today.

Long story.

Tell me. I've got all day.

Boyle shook his head.

Tell me, she insisted, trying to be firm.

Forget it.

Ok. Your happiest memory. You've got to give me something.

Boyle thought but nothing came to him.

Tell me something. Why are you trying to be so mysterious? Do you think girls find it attractive?

She was making fun of him.

I was at this play once, he began to tell her. Well, it was after the play. I watched these two men taking down the scenery. That's a moment that's really stayed with me.

The Dove was thinking hard. What really stayed with you?

Watching them taking down the scenery.

Had you never seen it happen before.

I don't know. It just struck me. It's one of those moments where I think my life went off in a different direction. This living-room wall falling backwards and then it was just the canteen again, darkness, banging. And me sweeping up.

It was in a canteen? the Dove asked.

That's what I said. Boyle glared at her, irritated, trying to cover his tracks. It was in a canteen and I was sweeping up, he told her again roughly so that she would have no chance to question him more.

As though he had sensed the pause between them, the silence that seemed to be deepening with every second, the fidgeter flew across the bar like a saviour and sat himself down on a stool at their table. In his early twenties, he had short flattened-down hair and a very pale face, an almost girlish face maybe due to the black scarf wrapped copiously round his neck. His blinking eyes moved all around the bar. With a confidential air, he said he had a story for them, something to think about, you can take it or leave it.

Boyle nodded for him to continue.

This happened about a year ago, he began out of the corner of his mouth. Bear with me. I was living with my fiancée Denise and our little girl, Saiorse. We had to live at her mother's place because the money was tight. We were just starting off, you know what I mean? It wasn't easy, space-wise, but it could have been worse. We were getting on with it anyway. Then a few things came together and we got a bit of luck and I landed a job in a kitchen in town there, a big kitchen in a government building. I was just washing up and all that. I was the only man. But the women were great gas. So I was happy enough. And at the end of the first month I got my first wage,

I was on top of the world. I remember it, getting out of the work in the afternoon and walking through town with some money in my pocket. I was proud and I was thinking everything would work out for the best. I stopped in and bought some flowers for Denise, a big bunch. So I went back home anyway. Walking on air. I was planning to take her out for something to eat later, and a few beers. We hadn't had a night out in months together. In I go to the house and there's Den and Saiorse and I give her the flowers and everything's great and then I play with Saiorse for a bit. It couldn't have been better, you know what I mean? So next it's time for the kid's nap and Den takes her upstairs and she shouts down to me would I hang the washing out that's finished. I empty the clothes out into the plastic yoke and carry it out to the garden, well, a yard really. Now, I remember looking at the sky and thinking the weather was good and the clothes would dry in no time. And there was a radio on in the neighbours' kitchen that I was wondering might keep the kid awake. And I remember there was some rope lying by the door of the shed and I was wondering who might have been using that and there were a few snails stuck on the wall and I was thinking about putting down some salt against them. At the same time I was hanging up the clothes. It was all Saiorse's things. And that's about all I remember. My name's Kev by the way, he said and Boyle and the Dove shook hands with him before he continued.

You know where they found me? I had climbed up into the attic and put the rope round my neck. I was hanging there when Den and her mother found me. It couldn't have been too long. I didn't even finish hanging out the clothes. I must have taken that bit of rope and went straight up there. Do you see what I mean? An old bit of rope lying on the ground. It catches your eye and the next thing you're at the end of it. And do you know what I'm doing today? I'm up in the court to try to get access to see my daughter. Den and her mother wouldn't let me back in the house. Mental illness issues. I'm a bad influence. All that kind of stuff.

He was sitting with face averted now, finishing off the pint he had kept in his hand. Under the scarf there must be a scar, Boyle thought. Beside him the Dove was absolutely still, like she had stopped breathing. Boyle reached out his hand and put it down on hers. She gripped him suddenly, tightly.

I don't know, I'm not sure I believed him, Boyle said later, much later that evening in another part of the city. The Dove had taken him north on the train to Malahide. Proudly, she showed him the village, a crossroads of shops and pubs, and then they walked downhill to the marina and the floating runic markings of yacht masts against a pink and yellow sunset. She took him home to her father's house and they ate a meal on a wooden veranda in a high-walled garden with ivy and palm trees and mist forming and failing and a dog, an old Labrador called Milo that lay at her feet.

So what do you believe in then? was the Dove's shocked reply.

Boyle laughed. You can't go round asking questions like that.

You have so many laws don't you? I can do whatever I want. What do you believe in? You don't seem to believe in what you're doing at university. Why not?

It just seems to be about giving answers to questions that nobody is asking. Or questions that are out of date. It's like a dead language. Hermetically sealed.

What should the new questions be then?

Boyle shook his head and shrugged.

What should the questions be then?

I reserve the right to silence.

So you must have something to hide. She was playing the part.

That's for you to prove.

So you believe in the process of proof.

I'm at its mercy. That's not belief.

She withdrew from the game now: You're not doing anything to help me. It's not fair. I'm doing all the work here. You constantly patronise me because I'm younger than you and yet you won't tell me anything to help me understand. Do you think I can't? Am I too middle class, too closeted and sub-urban?

It's not that, he said lamely.

You sure? Are you really sure? Because it's sad if that's what you believe and you're a lot stupider and more trapped than I thought.

Barefooted, she went inside, followed by the padding drowsy Labrador.

Boyle looked at the night sky, black, a few weak stars, no sense of vast spaces. She was right: he was trapped. Infinite paths inside him that led nowhere, back to the skin surface and touch and cravings and eyes that vomited it all out instead of seeing. He couldn't move beyond himself for an instant, even with a gun to his head, a pair of young lips raised to his own. He had come down to Dublin and nothing had happened. The same eyes, the same lonely hypocritical insignificant tongue. I wanted to change my life, he mouthed to the darkness. But nothing had happened. He sniffed the same staleness around him as in every cell he had moved between. The books that had once opened like windows into new places were all an illusion, moral fables against getting above yourself, stepping out of line, fighting back, wanting more, changing yourself. There was a price for every syllable of discontent. No escape was possible outside of dying. Prison is not the seat of clarity. Nothing had happened despite the debates that could last for days. The great dia-logue and enlightenments he had hoped for at university were simply not part of the deal. It was a training in obedi-ence that's all. I failed to change myself, he mouthed then to the dark garden. Another failure. He was more alone now than at any time before because he had lost hope.

The Dove, her with the unsettling blue eyes – he realised she was standing behind his chair.

I could almost hear you thinking, she said.

Talking in my sleep just.

She put her hand on his shoulders and said, What would you do if I kissed you?

Typically, Boyle remained silent. Her face came down in front of him – her face that seemed as naked as a breast, and as warm. He was a stain on an old wall. This young face would be poisoned and burned out by his despair. She didn't have the slightest idea who he was. Whatever it was she was seeing in front of her, the face she was craning forward to kiss wasn't his own. She wanted him to pretend to be something, to put on another face, a mask for her.

Sit down, he told her. Sit down there and listen to me.

Say Boyle was at home the next day thinking about what he had said to the Dove. He felt depressed as if he had lied to her although he knew he hadn't.

Say he had told her it was like stones, his life was like a pocketful of stones.

The stones were markers or counters on a board game that you move around but you don't know the rules, he told her.

Or worry stones twiddled and smoothed between the fingers.

One stone was the getting-out-of-jail stone. The homecoming stone he also called it now. That was one of the more recent ones. He didn't even know it was a stone until lately when he realised with dread, no, anger that the move to Dublin was already doing its best to turn into a stone.

Things were turning into stone before they were even over. It was a bad sign. Ossification.

Say he had told her that the homecoming stone was a big one, a halfer with a cavity on the top, coarse redbrick. He pointed to the brick base of the barbecue in the garden. Half of one of those, he said, with scabs of cement on it.

He was a ghost on the streets of his own city. The ground under his feet was as tender as skin, many skins. The sky was as raw as a sore eye. One of those ghosts who's always whining that something's been left undone, that they haven't been buried properly, that the truth is different, that it's all wrong – people saw him like that, they saw it in his own humiliated eyes, in the way he was continually getting in their way on the shopping streets, like a man with a hangover who can't bear the noise of an ordinary day, out of sync, easily startled.

He feared for his own safety for the first time in his life. He wouldn't answer the door unless Dainty was in the flat. He set up a tripwire in the hall every night after Dainty fell into bed. But he knew they would do it in broad daylight anyway. It was all out in the open now, showy, glamorous. They would walk up to you and give it to you in the face, then take a bow, a round of applause. One day he began making notes of the cars passing the window. Just to see for a laugh, he told himself but he knew it was more than that. Dainty found the paper with all the registrations and took it into his work: he came home with a hundred photocopies and tried to pull Boyle out on the street with him to distribute them.

Dainty was shouting: Come on. Enough's enough. We'll fucken show them we know who they are. They're not getting away with this kind of harassment. Driving about in their fucken cars like they own the place and hounding poor mentally unstable ex-convicts. Out into the streets with us. We'll take the war to them.

And: And who the fuck's they? Nobody gives a fuck any more. It's just gangland stuff now. Drugs and protection rackets. Everybody knows that. They can't even remember what they fucken did last week never mind eight years ago. You're fucken paranoid. The only person after you is yourself for being such a stupid wanker in the first place. I came up to see you there every month remember. That's a lot of time when you add it up. Every fucken month.

And: You need a good shag, that's all that's the matter with you. You were always useless with women anyway. Mind Veronica? She would have done anything for you. And you trying to give her books to fucken read.

And: Get this into your head Boylo. You were fucken small-fry. What did you do anyway? A few fucken taxiing jobs. They wouldn't let you near a gun. Moving things around. One post office job which was a fucken fiasco. And then that balls-up with the mobile. Sock was a nutcase anyway and you shouldn't have allowed yourself to be pushed into it. I would have run too. Only a fucken idiot would hang around to be shot to bits. You were had. Fucken cannon fodder just.

This last was said to Boyle after he went missing for a week. Boyle had been stopped on the street one day by a man named Doe-Hoe, another ex-prisoner. He told Boyle that himself and a few others had got into the habit of escaping from it all every other month, the wife, the wains, the TV, and heading for a weekend away in a caravan over the border in Donegal. Only ones that had been inside were welcome. They called it the Pow-Wow; it was a chance to cleanse the mind, Doe-Hoe said, to talk about all those fears and anxieties that nobody else could appreciate. We've had some great talks. Seen some great things. Higher things you know what I'm talking about?

Boyle mentioned the meeting to Dainty and heard that Doe-Hoe was a certified junkie and that the crowd around him were all the same. They go down there and get out of their heads that's all. They got into that shite in jail. Stay well clear.

Boyle was at a low point. He was on the verge of going to a doctor to ask for help. He couldn't shake the lethargy, the indifference, the sudden attacks of panic. He borrowed his father's car and drove down late in the night, further into a darkness that seemed to be moving backwards in time, from the distant future into the past, from the fires at the end to the original flame, with the news that nothing changes.

There were seven men in the mobile home and they welcomed him warmly. He had come across a few of them before. Doe-Hoe offered him things from different bags: powder, pills, a suitcase of grass. They were all on mushrooms as well. Boyle had a lot of catching up to do. He sat on the floor with a bottle of whiskey and a plastic basin of defrosting mushrooms, and listened.

Say Boyle told the Dove that it had felt good to be among them. They seemed to know a lot about him already, what he was in for, the reputation for books, but it seemed natural and right and saved Boyle from an interrogation. One of them said he knew Boyle's parents: That's some couple all right. Dancing about everywhere and don't give a fuck what anyone thinks. Now and again they would ask if he knew so-and-so or if he had been there when such a thing happened – arguments about dates went on for what seemed like hours. The curtains were closed on the silent caravan site. The smoke grew heavier and settled down among them solemnly like people who had been sent for, one over there sitting on the fridge, another in the bedroom doorway, listening, until he thought there were people moving constantly around him. They had all been married, those men, but only one had lasted on after their release. The lucky man was asked the reason for his success and replied that she was usually too stoned even to make it to the shop for a pint of milk. Another told the story of how his wife had refused to visit him in jail and on the day he got out there she was waiting in the car; when he went to get in she said, Where do you think you're going? I only came along to see the look on your face when I drive off and leave you. Just like you did to me and your children ten years ago.

None of them was working. Sometimes one would fall asleep, no, the body would go limp like their spirit had been carried off somewhere for a while. Boyle began to see people moving behind the curtain, like actors checking on the audience. There was a conversation about the smell of canteen cutlery compared to their own kitchens. The noise of the crows was recalled and volleyball matches and the female screws and the mammoth debating sessions. The talk was lazy and senseless one minute and then something would explode in unison in each of them, an urgency, a vehement disagreement, and they would all be arguing before the thing had even been said.

Doe-Hoe was responsible for bringing up the stuff about the blessing of the cells one year. It seemed that this character called Nixon had a dream one night about a woman at the bottom of his bed, taking off her clothes and trying to get in with him. He told somebody about it and this person said they had a dream like it as well and the more they discussed it they realised they were describing the same woman. Then the word went round and a lot of the men said they had been subject to the same temptations. Hysteria set in on the blocks, Doe-Hoe was saying, the place went out of control, the men weren't sleeping and they had to call the priest to bless the cells.

Somebody opened the caravan door and it was like being sucked out through a pinhole into a ravenous void. Boyle flipped and squirming on the lino floor with his hands around his head he was laughing that hard. He hung on to the yellow canister under the cooker until he heard tapping and scratching inside and it was an egg about to crack open.

It was a man called Hill who brought out the Ouija board.

Boyle started screaming.

The men pulled him outside and left him lying on the grass. Under the stars which were clearly spelling out words.

He got up on his feet and made himself walk. Everything he saw in the dark, pyramids, a rowing boat, men in robes, keys dangling from bushes, he knew was coming from his own mind.

He saw himself standing in the muck by the outdoor water tap.

He reached a concrete hut and became so afraid of what was inside that he had to go in. Squatting in the grass, he believed his past selves were gathered inside awaiting their liberation from the world of suffering. He prayed to Gautama for courage and charged in. It was a toilet.

Sock was lapping piss water out of the trough like a dog.

Coward. Traitor. You'll get yours.

Boyle staggered back outside. The stars were falling to the ground all around him. One of them had hit the caravan.

He ran towards it.

Then he thought it was a trick. Maya. It was an illusion of his own making. And right enough, two Guards were dragging Doe-Hoe out of the caravan. The boots were going in.

Boyle crawled underneath the body of a caravan, got up and lay along the axle above the ground.

Here the Dove broke her silence and asked him was it real or not and Boyle said he wasn't sure until the morning, he wasn't sure if he was actually lying under a caravan at all, not until he saw the dawn appearing.

The light showed him some hills and he decided to get to the top of the highest one.

He spent the day up there, with fields and a road and a village for the eyes, the wind for the ears and the odd hovering hawk, and a blue bay of water for the heart. It got dark again. And then the day was born again.

What were you thinking about up there? she asked.

I felt like I was waiting. Then the light started to come and it was these giant curtains. I'd never seen anything as beautiful. These colossal curtains. Pure light. Moving towards me. And I knew they were dangerous. That if they opened I would be wiped out. But I couldn't move. There was this incredible sadness.

I don't understand Noel. What happened?

I started praying. I begged everything. I swore I'd do anything if it left me alone. These curtains were flowing towards me.

And what happened?

They left me alone. And I had this feeling of shame and failure that I knew I would never get rid of; like I was tainted.

That was when she got out of her chair and came towards him and he put out his hand to stop her.

Maybe I know how to get rid of it, she said.

Say he said it was like stones.

But they did not make a path back.

There was the growing-up stone, the Hunger Strike stone, the joining-up stone, the first-arrest stone, the sentence stone; some of them had worn out, maybe he had lost some, or they'd been stolen.

They didn't make a track back.

You see when you're in it, there are no words for what you're doing. You're pushed outside words. Take words away and you get an emptiness that fills up with blood, he told her.

God's blood if necessary.

Sacrifices.

Death died one day you see.

Saviours appeared at every corner, shivering with legendary duty. They covered their mouths and ran into the smoke. Skeletons swept the streets each night after the riot. So many bull-beam moons the waters tore themselves to shreds. The lights exploded in the houses. So many drums the blood broke through the skin of the streets.

The day came, and he ran into the smoke, screaming no words.

He used to dream of finding a new dictionary buried in the forest and the run home with it under his jumper, the new language, the spell that would bring back death.

Say he told her that he was arrested first when he was twenty-five but got off with it.

Then the next year he was caught running across a field after a shoot-out. Sock had survived long enough to take two of them with him and from his hospital bed to brand him a coward. The papers reported it all in detail with quotes from the soldiers in the helicopter.

That he was charged with attempted murder and conspiracy and membership of the IRA and sent to the H Blocks.

That he was moved to Maghaberry Prison after a year because he had turned his back on the war. That immediately he was caught it was all over for him. The whole thing vanished from his mind before he had changed his clothes.

There was silence.

Death was reborn.

Those weren't the right words either.

He had done eight years and got out and realised he had died, no, he had been left behind, no, he had never started.

When death dies, the memory takes over.

He went back to Derry and tended to his own grave for a while.

I'm a coward for telling you any of this.

Once a pocketful of stones used to take the weight off the heart. The people tore up the streets in the search for death.

All this he told her and every word of it was a lie and it wasn't. The things that had shaped him could not be put into words and that was a lie.

That was the torment – no words for it.

Lie.

That was the exhilaration.

Lie.

Or there was a language that could be spoken only in secret, in the backs of cars, in the dining rooms of sympathetic businessmen, priests' kitchens, in caravans by the sea. A language coughed up in prison cells.

Lie, lie, lie –

The truth was in the lie.

Lights fade. Exeunt. New scene.

Say he rushed out into the street looking for a phone box. Dainty was in.

Hello stranger.

Dainty, I'm losing it.

Join the club. What's the matter with you now?

I don't think I should be down here. I can't talk to anyone.

You never could. Did they kick you out of the university? You'd start a fight in an empty room you know that?

They're all wankers. Rich kids.

Stop press. Rich kids found to be in majority at educational institution. Feckless paramilitary quits in protest. What the fuck did you expect? Catch yourself on. You sound like our Gerald and he's only ten.

Is Gerry ten?

Next week. Life goes on boyo. Why don't you come up for

it? We'll have a wee party. Met a new woman as well. Her name's Maureen.

I mightn't leave again.

So what? Fucken pack it in if you want. It didn't work out. Change your mind. Who cares? But did you hear me? I met a new woman. This one is important.

What would I do?

The same as the rest of us. You see that's your problem Noel. I've told you before. You think you're different but your not. You're panicking now at being part of the state. There you are right at the heart of it. They've welcomed you in. They let you into the libraries and classrooms and give you a wee identity card. You've never had to face that before. You can't cope with it. You're just the same as everybody else now. Biting your lip, waiting for pay day.

Boyle put down the phone. That was Dainty and his relentless sarcasm. It never broke these days. He claimed it was marriage did it to him but Boyle could remember Dainty's lazy scathing humour as far back as the days when there were ten or more of them in a gang with their customised sticks, brush poles decorated with paints and wrapped in coloured tapes for grip that they took everywhere and hid in a clump of nettles at night. By the time they were teenagers Dainty and Boyle had plans to escape to the States where Dainty had some family. They dreamed together of the girls they'd seduce with their tales of the battle-scarred streets. It all came to a stop when Dainty's brother was shot dead. Dainty was sent away to the States a lot sooner than he had expected. The family were trying to keep him out of it. Boyle was left without his best friend. They wrote letters to each other; Dainty said he hated it over there on the outskirts of Boston. One night a car pulled in beside Boyle and a man said he knew his name and asked him to run a message. Boyle was given a bag of crisps and told where to take it. By the time Dainty came back two years later he had run a lot more messages. He couldn't say a word to Dainty. He was glad to leave the deceit behind him when he went up to start university in Belfast. Dainty was the one left in Derry now. Within a year he had met a girl and was planning to get married. Meanwhile Boyle was attending meetings in houses where he learned how to put together a gun. The only book he was interested in was the IRA rule book, the Green Book. When Boyle was arrested for the first time in a hijacked car, Dainty was on his honeymoon. It was a year before he would speak to Boyle again. Boyle lied and promised he was done.

Say this is what was going through Boyle's mind as he stood in the telephone box on Manor Street, looking up at the flat roof of a convent building where a Jesus statue looked all set with arms outspread for a suicide plummet. The symbolism was stomach-turning, perfect, crass, suffocating.

Say it was at that moment when Boyle decided he was a fool to think there was anything more than these moments of illumination, brief aching glimpses into his own freedom, or the loss of it. That he was only fighting against himself. That he couldn't escape from his past just by packing his bag and getting on a bus.

So he told himself that a trip back up the road to Derry might be what he needed to clear his head. To realign himself. To get back into the rhythm.

Everything else could wait.

He would get drunk with Dainty around the pubs and ask him finally if he had grassed up the Pow-Wow. Then he would call in to his ma and da and have a dance.

He wanted to be among his own.

The rat has his cold eye on the truth at the corner of a street. Horsemen dismount and gather round for Fada has a tale to tell of the rat swimming deep in the sewers of blood. Only an angel can understand the foul lure of his mouth. See her, there! She is one of six or more, teenagers of sun-born ilk, but a full vestal bandanna-ed head above the rest, and shoulders beach-bowered by soft brown fleece. Fada's tail goes straight as she sways her hips absentmindedly, easterly, westerly, for you, for me, hands in her back pockets that pull the denim down further over a taut white band, the watertight drum of her brown belly, the downy knuckle at the bottom of her spine. And as her hips move one way, her head turns the other way, enjoying her own ample elasticity, dreaming of who she will one day offer it to, she is dancing for him, her eyes wafting the street scene more fully into life, stronger, harder, brighter, busier, louder. Meanwhile her friends have formed a treasure-hunt party around a map and there is pointing and disagreement and huffing and giggling all of which she seems blind to in her secret incantation. See those breasts now, the way they judder and quake with each twist of her well-fed torso. Is it their weight, their Latin black-ringed burden, their ache, their bondaged softness that entrances her? The rat imagines her undressing at night, the few seconds of nakedness in front of the mirror she permits herself . . . and the time she let her hand go down there into the uncombed hair and the limp wordless lips and the warm juice drooled over her fingers and she peeked a look in the glass with one brown eye only.

But there's more to this, horsemen. Listen hard. This unplumbed puella in her swinging motion is constantly returning in her sweep to the spectacle of a lad on his arse in a doorway, a dozing junky, a deadbeat, a snoring skanger with a traffic warden's hat on his unwanted head. Between his legs he still manages to hold tight to a fastfood Styrofoam cup nibbled down around the edges as if by rats. This is where it's at: Fada is fired up by this vision. This is one to save and ponder. Bear witness for she is slowly edging the queenly fullness of her arse backwards to the slumped downtrodden denizen of filth. This is parable material; this is epiphany time.

Why is the question? Does she hope he will wake and look on her beauty and suffer? Does this young thing already understand the chastisement of her form? Or is she lost in the drama of transgressing so near to the dirt and failure and violence and all those words she only reads in books? Now she smiles innocently, oh so patiently at one of the map group who still have to make up their minds which direction to take. Is it the old prison they are looking for or the brewery or the cathedrals with their unavailing bells?

But there is more to this than meets the jaundiced ludicrous eye. As he watches, the extent of her sway is steadily increasing, breast wobble and hair whip, and finally she follows through and turns full circle. Then she is down on one knee, fixing her sandal, long painted toes, and a long brown arm stretches out and drops something into the beggar's gnawed cup. Up she rises again in her unawakened voluptuous stealth and skips back to her friends but not before she has caught sight of Fada at the corner and his sordid transfixed gaze, the ugly rapture of him.

Oh the horror in her tender eyes put the light back on him that he thought had gone out for ever. The light he peddled around the night swamp of the city.

She had been caught and there begins her corruption – her liberation. Blushing, confused, she tries to hide herself away among her friends, seizes a corner of the map and begins to talk and point wildly. Her friends fall silent and lower their eyes instinctively.

The questions make his skin itch. What debt was she repaying with that money in the beggar's cup? What games had she been playing with her own hair-lipped beggar's bowl in the gooey dark? Or in the back row of the classroom in daylight? Was it simply an act of charity, a good young deed? No, the subterfuge was too considered, the manner in which she hid it from her friends. She's giving alms, she's buying indulgences. Señorita Penitentzia and the shameful mystery of her carpet-burned arse. She was disgraced by being seen, it was in her horizon-drunk eyes. Sweet Lord, when shall he come for me and save me from myself?

Fada creeps slowly closer. She is hurrying her friends along, trying to take control and they acquiesce to her without argument. There is alarm in her eyes now, like she is about to cry, or tear off her clothes. She knows precisely who he is, what he wants; she has dreamed of him, almost, smelled him. Passing the beggar, Fada sees the notes in the cup, two, maybe three, twenties.

But he is too much of a coward to chance robbing it, superstition he blames. Instead he peers towards her victoriously: I have travelled far. Here you are at last. What was your golden crime juicy daughter? Tell me what you did. I can forgive you. Only me.

The girl links an arm with two friends and checks back over her shoulder.

Fada unfurls a bow.

As soon as they are out of sight, he scurries after them.

Fada woke, gagging, sweating. His feet were on the floor before his eyes had taken in his surroundings. He was naked. White curtains were blowing in an open doorway revealing moments of blue waveless water. He had jumped out of a huge white bed which was in a room with lemony walls patch-worked oppressively with paintings of different sizes. All of this was somehow familiar but for the moment it was beyond his grasp, tempting but not convincing. A wooden xylophone rippling from beyond the curtain made him freeze like a fan-fare for some angel approaching. He lay down again and tried to think: Last night, last night where were you? How many times had he woken to the day in strangers' beds? Handmade sea-shipped altars to filth-loving deities, department-store marriage slabs, bunk-bed au pair miseries and mattress shows of terrifying excess in windowless bedsits. Who was outside this morning waiting for him to show his face? What pair of eyes that he had seen split open and sucked the stale life out of was making him coffee and bacon sandwiches? What mouth that he had shat in would call his name from the sunny balcony where the kids keep their bicycles and . . .

Even now he knew where he was, this was Lisa-Ann's place, he could tell from the paintings, and yet there was a part of him still pretending that it was a new corner, he had done it again, broken through into the unknown, unleashed a sound or a look or a thought that made sure the world was different than it was the day before. The eyes would smile more darkly from then on. A new recruit, a bruised acolyte. The knowing tensed glance on the street.

This thought made him hard immediately and he threw off the satin covers. The reek from him filled the room immediately like the breath of a sick animal, an ailing cloud. Vent the pent, he intoned to himself, inhaling, and remembered the girl from yesterday and her solar porno largesse. Another spell of fluted tinkling from outside was the tumbrils and jingling accompanying a dusty Roman litter and reclining inside on unicorn-skin cushions and wine-red robes was the dissolute queen whom everyone knew was deranged by her search for arcane pleasures . . .

But her face wouldn't appear; he couldn't get inside the veils. The hot desert dust blew into his eyes. Then he saw the laughing face of the old woman and the urge was lost. He needed a smoke, that usually brought the tiniest seediest thought to life. Still toying with himself, the curtain blowing and being sucked out, the music fading, he tried to piece together the night before.

He was sure he had been with Fiacra. Yes, Fiacra took him for a pizza and started ordering wine. Fada tried to be a good friend and listened to Fiacra's fears of turning into his own father if he had a child. Then they got in a taxi to Kilmainham and picked up some coke. Another taxi back into town with a driver playing American Indian chanting music and Fiacra making comments about reformed junkies. Fiacra was on a bender; he couldn't get the drink into him fast enough; he would keep going for a few days like that. Until there was no one left to fight with. So there must have been a universe of many-doored pubs, cramped constellations of chewing faces, sudden black holes of lust but Fada didn't have it in his memory.

His bones went cold. He was a skeleton of dread. For a single pure second he saw the dreadful prospect of forgetting who he was. The sheer will that kept everything going inside him gave up, fell silent and everything collapsed. He couldn't move. He saw himself lying on the bed and people coming through the door and asking themselves who he was and what he was doing there. No one knew. Then they gave him an injection and carried him off.

One moment of doubt could open the flood gates and wash him away. He knew this fear: he told himself that he had been through worse. Lie still and it will pass. Try to think of wholesome benefits. A time you were happy. But there were only fears in his head. And then he remembered something, was it last night, had it even happened? He was on the streets, late again, by himself; he was scouring the streets for a straggler, some drunk, some girl waiting on a cab, word of a party, a prossie, a brazzer and he was suddenly very afraid that there was a badness in the air and he waved down a Guard car and tried to tell them about it, that he was being followed. What if they had taken him seriously? He would have been locked up and sent away again. They would throw away the key this time. He knew if he started talking he wouldn't be able to stop. His guts were squirming now like there was something gestating in there.

The bedroom door opened and he jumped up to defend himself.

You're still here, Lisa-Ann said, with a sad stoned perplexity.

What time is it?

Lisa-Ann took a drink from her glass; vodka and pineapple as usual. Why? Then a laugh came up out of her, the shallow giggle of a solitary woman.

Where am I? Fada demanded.

Staring at the floor, sunlight on wood, she seemed about to speak but then her face closed over, shrank back, the sharp lines appeared either side of her debauched puppet mouth. She was a small woman, somewhere at the end of her thirties, who looked much older than she was sometimes, especially when she had been drinking. Mainly, it was the eyes that aged her; they were green and sealed and rarely surprised by the world around her.

In the silence Fada stood up on the bed and beat his greying chest with his fists, leaping around like a monkey.

Lisa-Ann turned and left the room.

I came to you for help, he shouted after her, and waited, listening.

All he heard was the cracking of ice-hymens, the bottle-top tambourine rattle on the floor, glass kissing glass.

Still naked, he went after her, and found her out on the veranda in the deckchair under the hanging jingling skeletons of wind-chimes. She had put on a pair of sunglasses. On the table beside her was a bowl of fruit – oranges, bananas, pears – which Fada found himself detesting wholeheartedly.

Fruit, he said as though he had never heard the word before.

You're still here? she said, wearily ironic.

I'm sorry.

She rattled the ice around in her glass and held it up to the horizon – buildings all around, other blocks of flats, spent clouds, pre-packaged trees, a retirement-home courtyard below.

What for exactly?

She hissed at him when he put his foot beyond the door on to the balcony. He wasn't allowed out there; probably to do with the neighbours but she said it was her private refuge, that it soothed her. Fada didn't argue; he wasn't keen on having his nerves torn to shreds by the expectation of voodoo apparitions every time the wind changed its mind.

The foot he retracted was filthy, black smears between the toes, nails like old claws. He covered his crotch with his hands.

I'm sorry, Fada tried again. Can you hear me? What do you want me to say? Can you hear me?

The wind-chimes gently heralded a soft-footed angel.

Don't raise your voice to me please, Lisa-Ann said.

Well stop punishing me.

I have no interest in punishing you. That's what you can't understand. I don't care what you do. Outside of here that is. What I do care about is you hammering on my door at five in the morning.

I came to you for help.

She sipped and beat a hiccup out of her chest. Don't lie to me. You came here because you had nowhere else to go. This is my home. It's all I've got. You wouldn't understand that. I won't allow it to become some joint for you to crash in when nobody else will have you.

Fada wanted to laugh at the way she used the word joint. There was often an irritating formality about the way she spoke, a fear of saying the wrong thing, or keeping everything at a distance. But it wasn't the right moment to share these thoughts with her.

I wanted to talk to you. What's wrong with that? he tried again.

I won't allow it. No more. Leda can flap her wings and fly off somewhere else, she said and illustrated his airborne departure with the use of her free hand.

I thought we were friends.

What do you want?

I'm afraid, Lisa-Ann. Afraid. Afraid. Afraid. I've never felt so afraid. I can't stop thinking about hospital. You said you were interested in me.

I must have been drunk.

You're always drunk, Fada shot back at her.

Lisa-Ann put down her glass carefully. Holding her sunglasses in place, she bent forward and slid her hash box out from under the deckchair. It had an image of an crocodile on the end of a spear burned into the lid. Bought in Africa she had told him.

I didn't mean that, Fada said. Now the bells were ringing from some spire. He listened to the twelve tones before he asked her if she wanted him to go.

Your shirt and trousers are in the hot press, she said, licking the edge of a paper. I washed them. But they should be dry by now. I took the liberty of disposing of some of your other . . . things. You left some shorts behind and socks the last time. Remember?

122

She looked towards him now. How much do you remember I wonder? Fada found himself running towards her. Trailing and beating his hands against the wind-chimes, he shouted down at her in the chair: Help me. Can you hear me? Help me. Please.

Then he locked himself in the bathroom. He turned on the taps and sat on the toilet, waiting to hear her harangue him through the door. Help me: he wondered if he had ever said those words before. Did saying them mean they were true? He was shaking. Indifferently, the steam began to dance the seven veils in the windowless bathroom. They would have his head on a plate. Fada sings while Dublin burns. In the hospital there would be no locks on the doors. Privacy was forbidden. The windows are big and don't open. They pull the curtains around your bed and ask questions about the world as if you've come from somewhere else. The corridors are washed and buffed every night to erase the footprints. Spending too much time alone meant you were not getting better. Doing anything too much would land you in trouble. The golden mean they called it, the search for balance, equilibrium, moderation. Ah, such refined longevity. Seasonal and temperate and long live the gentle joys of endurance. Build your cities on the slopes of Vesuvius, the Northerner said that night at the party. Yes, let us suckle on the horn of plenty and vomit up all over your golden mean. Shove it up your fanny where you wiggle your wedded fingers while he's out washing the car. Help me. The toilet air was as hot as a morning kiss. Fuck me. Suck me. Hit me. Ruin me. Cut me. She was dancing around him in clouds of sullied muslin. Ah what would your daddy think of you now? A tremor went stretching through his cock. Fada spat on his hand and set to work on himself.

A short while later, buoyant in the bathwater, he was thinking about Lisa-Ann, trying to tease out of himself what might have happened the night before, if he had done bad things or said them or . . . but it was probably something else upsetting her. The way she got when she drank. She was on another private binge, a solitary wake for the past. Lisa-Ann was a woman who drank by herself, sometimes for days on end, never leaving the flat. With each glass she became more morose and defensive and embittered. Any attempt to ask her what was the matter was met with rage: You lowlife self-indulgent travesty. Or perhaps her mood this morning had to do with his absence over the last few weeks, no, longer, nearly two months it must have been. When what happened was that he had arrived late for a dinner and found her already drunk. He had sat in the living room for ten minutes listening to why he was such a hopeless bastard and a selfish user and then left without saying a word in his own defence. Generally, because they never went out together, the plan for an evening involved a meal and plenty of wine and a few sniffs of poppers which she liked or some E crumbled in a joint. They often read to each other from the books on her shelves or Fada would perform his lewd oratorial office, manically extemporising from lines of poetry across a range of voices, Dublin lads selling gear, Estonian men looking to sell their daughters to pervert priests, Spanish tourists complaining about the weather to farmers to Northern politicians to bored horny housewives. Or Lisa-Ann would question him in detail about his adventures as she called them since their last meeting. She told him she often wrote about him in her diary, tried to keep some record of the things he said, his moments of filthy perilous illumination.

They had an agreement that Fada would not ask about her past; she would talk about it one day, when she was ready, when she was sure he was capable of understanding. All he knew was that she had been away a long time, probably Paris because she had mentioned it occasionally and now and again a few French phrases had been spat at him. Lisa-Ann had come back to Ireland for some reason, which, remembered, could set her off on another binge.

Fada took it for granted that she had a job of some sort but he couldn't be sure and didn't think much about it anyway. Sometimes she would mention a film she had seen or a play but he often wondered if she was making it up to pretend she had some friends other than him, that she had another life. Something about her told him that he might very well be the only person she talked to in the city of Dublin.

He had known her now about eight months. Some months he saw a lot of her, at least once a week, then it might be weeks before he was eating at her table again. He enjoyed coming to see her; he was fed and drank well and all for nothing but he also felt able to say anything to her, to try to put into words the experiences he had, even to draw conclusions from them. He ran his life by her to see if it was comprehensible. He could tell he made her laugh. She was particularly interested in the swan story. Leda the Louche she often called him. It was rare to meet somebody who took him seriously, who wanted to hear what he had to say and wasn't simply looking for amusement. He was always refreshed the next day when he left, striding up the street back into the world, knowing that somewhere on his person she had slipped him some money to go and enjoy himself. Bring me back news of the truth, she would say.

But then that last night she had told him about the man she brought back. He listened to her and found himself doubting all she said, what he looked like, what they had done, how awful it was when he got on top of her. Fada didn't believe her. But why was she making it up? It was difficult for them to talk about sex because ever since the first night they had met there had never been any physical contact between them. Fada accepted it was his own fault, that for some inexplicable reason he was unable to make love to her. He couldn't stay hard enough to get a condom on. This had never happened to him before – with anybody, even the ugly mean-faced ones he picked on in a corner of a nightclub at the end of an unsuccessful night, the last-ditchers, or the shy ones who went tense when he put a hand around their neck. Did he not fancy her, was it just that simple? This kind of question was usually irrelevant to Fada; when he was given the opportunity he took it. The fact that he didn't fancy a woman was often a turn on for him, the uglier he found her the more exciting it could be. But Lisa-Ann wasn't ugly but neither was she touched with beauty. Her breasts were small, her mouth sometimes as small and hurt as her eyes. She was lonely and angry and depressed but there had been numerous women like that, ones who threw themselves at him in the hope of a good fuck and those whom he had to tempt into his lair with talk of reawakening desire and changing your life, I'm discreet, I don't want anything, we could just meet once a week and have some fun, all those women he had met through the lonely hearts columns, and the ones he might just walk up to on the street. He had been over it in his head obsessively that first time he failed with her; it had sent him off the rails for a few weeks, drinking, needing to fuck everything in sight to prove he was still virile and now he was afraid somehow of her making a move on him and at the same time he wanted to make a move himself and would have loved nothing better than to grab her from behind, whip up her skirt and go into her before she had swallowed her mouthful of vodka and pineapple.

Maybe that's what happened, he wondered in the bath; maybe he had come in last night and tried to go to bed with her. Maybe he had treated her badly, pushed her too far. Have you ever gone too far, sweetmeat? That is the true question. Help me: who else could he say that to? The answer came to him in the form of a face – the Northerner's face, the beard, Boyle. Fada was shocked at this idea and sat up quickly in the bath, spilling water over the edge.

Then he heard a step at the door, a knock: I'm making some lunch, Lisa-Ann announced.

Fada said nothing. What was the Northerner's face doing in his head at a time like this? Who was he? Some working-class book-sniffer from the black North, chasing the spoiled bitches in Trinity, a bit of classy tennis-skirt thigh, using the guilt card? He wasn't the usual type of drifter; he was too uptight, too humourless. He lacked ease with people, acceptance. The solitude was a stink around him. It got into Fada's eyes and drove him mad. A kind of arrogance from the habit of looking down his nose at his firebreathing brethren. Then there was his interest in the drowned woman and the mask. A man with a streak of violence in him also, who knew how to fight. There must be a story behind him, some desolate misdeed, some smoking brand of truth.

Clean, dressed, still confused, Fada sat at the kitchen table. He had made up his mind to talk to Lisa-Ann about Boyle; it would be a good way of calming the situation, flattering her by asking for advice. She was cooking a pasta dish with cream, maybe with bacon. There was a wooden bowl of salad on the table that Fada took a leaf from and tore along the spine.

Never leave animals that are real in the gutter, she said before he was ready.

She said the same line again: Never leave animals that are real in the gutter.

Am I supposed to understand that? Fada asked and noted that he was already irritated.

You were chanting that last night at my door, shouting it through the letter box. Another of your epiphanies?

The moment's gone, Fada said. Was I out of it?

What does it mean? Tell me. Where did you come across it? What happened?

I don't remember.

Yes you do, she insisted. Does it mean that you should only leave animals that are unreal in the gutter? Did you see something unreal in the gutter? Like a thought or something? A bit of a dream? A swan maybe?

You're mocking me now.

No I'm not. She laughed and turned round to face him.

Can I have a smoke?

Wait. Tell me first. What does it mean?

What does it mean? What does it mean? Fada was on his feet now throwing the salad in the air. What does it mean? So you can write it down in your diary? The journal of a depressed alco. Le journal d'une femme voyeur or whatever. You tell me something for a change. The clown here isn't laughing any more.

He had never spoken like this to her before. In her hands a wooden spoon was trembling, a girl afraid to light a candle. He looked up at her eyes, low over the glazed green source, at the I-knew-you'd-let-me-down smile, the puppet jaw. She seemed to be disappearing before his eyes, into the mist from the frying pan.

It's not what I think, he called after her. I tried to tell you. I'm not thinking straight. Everything's going wrong. I'm on the streets, I'm broke. There's a curse on me. Remember those poems? The old woman I –

So you think I only take from you, she said from the obscurity of her anger. You're not the first to say that but I thought you knew better. Another illusion shattered. Not to worry. I'll survive.

I won't, Fada said, approaching her now.

She kept him at a distance with the wooden spoon, dripping cream.

I'm scared, Lisa-Ann. That's what I've been saying. I'm scared I won't survive much longer. I don't feel safe. I feel danger all around me. Let me stay here for a while.

She turned back to the cooker and turned off the gas. Our dialogue is finished, she said.

Why? Because of last night? What did I do?

It doesn't matter. It's time for you to go now.

We've only started. I don't want to go.

Fada dropped to his knees on the floor and raised his joined hands.

She looked down at him and said: Do you remember the night I met you? Well of course you don't. But I do. It was late. You were standing on the street, leaning against a wall. The rain was heavy. I thought you were a tramp or a junkie or I don't know what. Your mouth was open like you were screaming but there was no sound. Then as I went past you, you spoke. It was a hiss. I am the new Leda, you said – you hissed it at me. And what did I do? Did I run home screaming and lock the door? No, I took you home and fed you and gave you somewhere to sleep. That's what I'm like. That's how selfish I am. Did I laugh in your face when you told me about a swan raping you? Did I say it wasn't true?

You said whether it was true didn't matter, Fada said. The tears were unstoppable now.

I said it sometimes didn't. Now you're talking to me about curses. I thought I was doing some good. Talking to you. Being interested in you. I thought it was a good thing. Good, she shouted at him.

There's an old woman and these poems –

I've gone as far as I can.

This is because of last night isn't it? What happened? Tell me. I'm sorry.

It doesn't matter. You were talking about those poems. They're yours. Stop telling me about the old woman. I know they're yours.

No, Fada said getting back on his feet. No. No. That's all wrong.

They are, she insisted. Admit it. This is getting out of control and I don't like it. I won't have it.

Control, Fada sneered.

Don't look at me like that, she warned him. Don't you dare.

They're not my poems, he screamed at her.

This is my home, she shouted back.

Control. Home. Friend. Poems. Fuck. Shit. Fucken windchimes. Control. Fuck, Fada stammered into her repelled face.

She went by him and out of the kitchen. Fada looked around the kitchen as if it were closing in on him. He took a plate, white, round, from the table but couldn't bring himself to smash it. Holding it in front of him like a window into paradise, he started stuttering again in a different voice, his devil's cast-out voice, a low smeared growl against the glass: Connnntroool. Contrrrol. Varrrmmn niice. So perrfectn cleannn. So lovelovelly. Hoommme.

Lisa-Ann threw the bundle of poems at him across the floor and the trampled lettuce leafs.

She said he had better be gone by the time she got back.

Boyle had sat up late drinking with Victor the night before. He was still drunk as he took a place in the lecture hall; it must have been obvious he was the way he had a word for the young people who wouldn't normally be granted the music of his voice, the faulty rigour of his eyes. Even the fact that the Dove was absent made him grin; the mystery of it, the rightness of it was obvious. She wasn't there purely and simply and necessarily because he had come looking for her. Her absence was a priori. He had wanted to tell her he was going home for a few days to see the expression on her face, the modest glad health in her smile. Good, she would say and touch him, that's good. She knew what goodness was and could look it straight in the eye.

The lecture was given by a man called Drummond who was already up to his neck in an incomprehensible monologue by the time he stumbled on to the stage. According to the timetable, the topic was supposed to be Hegel but the name was never said. Drummond never took questions and rarely gave the students a sign that he was aware of their presence or his own slowly vanishing existence at the base of the sloping tiers of seats: it was as if Drummond was gradually disappearing, no, he was moment by moment being consumed by a sentence he could never reach the end of. There was mention of Kant's categorical imperative, the courtship of the sign and the signifier, the Narcissus myth, Feyerabend, pantheism, Santayana, and even Leibniz was dragged out and it was all a laugh to begin with and the students covered their mouths but after half an hour of it the heads were down with some kind of shame as Drummond, stringy dirty black hair and a shirt burst open at his belly-button, hung forlornly over the lectern or paced the stage in anguish, scratching, picking, correcting himself, stopping suddenly to stare into space, an exterior space that did not contain him, while down at the very front some girl held a tape-recorder aloft at the end of an anorexic arm.

By the time it was over, Boyle was depressed. His hangover had set in and his mouth was too dry even to chance a smoke. The students left in silence. Outside, he walked straight into his tutor, O' Leary, and the essay was demanded. Boyle explained that he had not found anything worth saying on the subject of Sartre. O' Leary laughed up his sleeve as was only to be expected from his type, a younger man, lazily suave, good looking, who hid his self-confidence and ambition behind the façade of gleeful lassitude. As always, Boyle wanted to ask him if he never got sick of it, all the words, the old books, the young faces, totally sick of it, the transfer of knowledge, the reproduction machine, the walls of books. O' Leary winked at him however and now it was Boyle's turn to laugh and he actually enjoyed some relief in it for the briefest of moments during which O' Leary put his hand on his shoulder. He wanted some advice, it was delicate, he wanted to test the water and would appreciate Boyle's honesty. The matter was Drummond: Did Boyle think the lecture was useful? Informative? Was it pitched in the right way? Had any of the other students mentioned how they felt? Did they feel ready to take an examination on the subject? Anything he said would be treated confidentially.

At that moment Boyle saw the Dove. She was talking to another girl; she had her back to him.

What was that pain he had at the sight of her? Stunning, cold, familiar yet not exactly his own, an ache that had been practised and developed down the centuries and still wasn't perfect. Many more would have to suffer it first. She was talking at length to somebody else, arms folded, being listened to, that's all, her bare neck, the hair carelessly pinned up, red elbows. It was the enormity of what she was doing, the heartfelt urge to communicate, to understand other people, to share her own thoughts, she believed it was possible, no, a duty, she wouldn't be able to turn out the light at night otherwise. All the while Boyle had O' Leary in his ear with his box ticking and assessments and polished teeth.

I know how you feel man. I had some night myself. That last tequila blew the hat off the house. It's amazing what a woman can find to do with a pinch of salt. I'm sure you know what I mean, a man like yourself.

I think you're asking me to grass up Drummond, Boyle said.

O' Leary changed his tone immediately: I'm asking you as one of the more mature students if you think the class is being taught properly. I'm asking for your help. Complaints have already been made. There is nothing underhand in my question.

You're barking up the wrong tree. Boyle watched the Dove and her friend walk out of sight, down the steps to the cafeteria to continue their conversation among the bottled water and tassled bookmarks handmade in Guatemala.

I don't think I'm the one who is barking here, said O' Leary irritably.

Boyle barked, no, he howled, weakly but enough to surprise O' Leary never mind himself. Two lads passing took it up more passionately. O' Leary handled it well of course; he laughed and winked and shook his head like he should have seen it coming.

I'm going back up home today, Boyle heard himself say, unsure whether this was meant to take the joke further.

O' Leary took it differently; it seemed to explain Boyle's strange behaviour and he put on a sympathetic face.

Is that right? So how does that feel? It's not easy is it?

Boyle dried up. There wasn't a word inside him. Embarrassed, he stood there staring at the buffed tiles. If O' Leary spoke again he thought he might cry like a boy, no, worse, ask for his help, ask him for a drink, apologise, do something drastic. He started walking; he stopped and looked back; O' Leary waved to him, a frank commiseration.

Heading across the cobbles, Boyle swore blind to himself that every word he could conceivably speak, every blink of his eye, the sucking in of air, every lift and press down of the feet was a betrayal, no, a corruption, including the domes and porticoes of the university, the statues the same colour as the sky, those manacled trees, a swindle, a profoundly humourless deception that he couldn't figure out.

Crossing the river, he was revolted by the lurches and bubbles and swells of the water that day, and directed himself straight for the bus station.

A bus had left a few minutes earlier which meant he had an hour to kill. He bought two newspapers and took a seat in the waiting area, no, the public hall, no, the main body of the building, whatever it was called, the concourse, a municipal hangar with glass walls out to the buses on two sides, an administration tier on the upper level. Between the glass and the tiled floor the human noise was exaggerated and harsh and ricocheted back so that he often heard the same thing twice, a voice, a suitcase being opened, the cups and plates in the cafeteria, a woman's heels or things that were already over and done with from another point of view.

Two men were sat opposite him, country men he thought, farmers: it was their clothes, the bloated hangmen's faces, which said nothing to each other. Facing the same way was a younger man and a child eating crisps together, father and son, a trip down to the grandparents' maybe, then a woman reading a magazine, a boyfriend trip maybe, then an old woman, a pensioner – where was she going? – then a teenager who might only be sitting there to kill time, nowhere to go, homeless. Boyle also had his eye on a woman behind the row who was dipping her fingers in the returned coin font of all the telephones, bless me father for I have sinned. A bus began reversing into position at the glass doors, the Cork bus, sending its high-pitched hazard pulse deep into every human heart, laser fucken surgery, the air thickened with alarms for the public's safety, the overproduction of awe again.

Big ideas again Boylo, he smirked at himself and began to read down the digital red names of places he had never visited. Ballina. Kells. Ennis. Ennistymon. Tralee. Wexford Town. Doire it said. Dundalk. Dun Laoghaire for the ferry across the water. He didn't know Ireland at all, the hills, Mac-Gillicuddy's Reeks, the coasts, the islands, all the talk of the melancholy beauty of the west. He didn't know anywhere. He had been to London twice and that was the extent of his travels. The second time he stayed in Crouch End with a girl – what was her name? – short hair, elfin – the face and name were gone. He tried to remember . . .

His mind wouldn't focus. He rubbed his eyes and turned to the newspapers, moving quickly through the pages, saving the good stories for the journey. Both papers had the picture of the mask face and a few paragraphs. Boyle had managed to put the whole thing out of his mind since the stall incident. He decided not to read any more about it, then changed his mind. It was better to know, he told himself without conviction. The Guards still didn't have a clue it seemed; they were planning an advertising campaign; they would not be drawn on the notion that the woman was in Dublin illegally; they had not made up their minds what to do with the body if it could not be identified.

Boyle looked hard at the mask photo: he was sure they had made changes to it. There were small differences; it was cropped closer; the cheekbones had been softened, and the rapt smile had definitely been tamed. The woman looked less foreign, less disturbingly blissful, more of a victim. Perhaps, he wondered, the whole thing was invented, a hoax, a distraction; it happened all the time in the media. But what would be the reason behind this? A message; laying the ground for something? It could be anything. You had to dig behind a story, why it was happening at that particular time, who was communicating with whom. The best form of secrecy was often the public domain, the so-called surface.

Boyle went outside the building to have a smoke and think about it, no, not think about it, escape himself. The day was windless and grey, like it had no faith in itself. This part of town was bleak and rundown, and even that seemed deliberate. A Dart train was stalled between two buildings high above his head. Taxi-men sat in their cars, a Romanian woman and child begged below the broken cash machine, and barrels were being dropped into the cellar of a bar across the road. Green dome of power to the left, verdigris or lime, what he knew now to be the old port authority building, cop shop to the right. The day he had arrived in Dublin off the bus he had stood in almost the same spot and had a smoke, more frightened than he had ever been before. Now he argued with himself that he had achieved something, the panic had subsided, the fear of attack, he had found a place to live and nearly completed the first year of university and he had met some interesting people – Victor was sound, the Dove, the people in the call shop and even that headcase Fada was somebody whom he wouldn't have encountered in Derry. This was a new experience, what he had wanted. A character like Fada was part of Dublin, he would not have been created in the North, he wouldn't have survived anywhere else. Dublin. Beware the risen people. He was standing on a Dublin street having a cigarette. This was a real moment. So were those men kicking the blackened cushion around that the kegs landed on off the lorry. So was that taxi-driver loading his boot with the suitcases of two Chinese. He was sure he would remember this moment in years to come; that day I waited on the bus up to Derry, the rest of my days ahead of me.

The voice came up behind him, right at his back: Buddha Boyle.

Boyle didn't have to turn round.

You got a light there Buddha? You ignoring me?

It was a man they called Snowy. Boyle was thinking that it

was possible this was his own mind working against him again, a delusion, a hallucination.

He turned round, registered the face. Still the same. He dug out his lighter.

Buddha Boyle. The most boring fucker I ever shared a cell with, Snowy said.

Helpless, Boyle kept his eyes on the street, following any sign of movement: the men at the lorry, some pigeons, the train moving on again, a taxi-driver with a lapful of tapes. Nothing lasted; this would be over soon like everything else.

Fuck I was glad to see the back of you so I was. Mind you used to sit for hours dead still. Couldn't get a word out of you. Then who do I get? Slim Mc Cara. The biggest smelliest cunt you ever saw. And so here we are. How's the form?

It just gets better every minute, Boyle said. For distraction he started rolling another cigarette.

No need for the sarcasm, he heard Snowy say.

Boyle glanced at him and saw the same gentle eyes.

Seriously. How's the form?

Grand, Boyle said.

What has you in Dublin then? You working down here?

Just visiting.

I'm down here a while now myself. The wife's from down here. You know I got married again? She's in there picking up her sister off the bus. That's all I do these days. Chauffeuring her around. When's the last time I saw you anyway?

Boyle made no attempt to remember.

Not so long ago you wouldn't think we'd be standing down here would you? You never know what's going to happen.

Boyle licked the paper and said: Some people always know a lot more than other people.

Don't start me Buddha.

I'm just saying what's true.

Wasn't I behind you all the way? Who was the one encouraged you to move out of the blocks? What was I always saying? Most of the men who were put away had done their bit and that was them done. Who fucken helped organise the move for you? Wasn't I the one told you to stick to the books and get on with your life? Don't you fucken forget it.

Boyle had to assent. This was true. He gave up his associations with the IRA and requested a transfer out of the H Blocks to the new Maghaberry Prison where there was no segregation of prisoners and he would be able to work and study. Snowy was his OC at the time in the Blocks.

So don't fucken start me, Snowy said again. Then, like he was known for, his mood changed suddenly: I heard a good one the other day. Mind Donald Duck? Funny voice. Aye you do. I heard there he married some filthy rich German woman and lives in a big house on the lough with a boat. That's the way it goes though. Did you hear about Apple Hegarty? Strabane man. No? Where you been hiding? Fucken shame. But he was another one who couldn't take it. They say he started strangling dogs. He was passing this old woman on the street with her dog and he jumps on it, some wee lapdog type of one. Then he moved up to German shepherds. Guard-dog types. They got him anyway and took him to the hospital and he jumped through a window. So we may count ourselves lucky.

Boyle laughed.

Dublin's not too bad, Snowy went off on another track. They've torn the heart out of it true but you have to ask if that heart wasn't sick anyway. It's a place for the young ones now anyway. Pleasure land. Instant gratification.

I could do with some of that.

Mind some of those tricks on the new arrivals? The confession one? Did you get that done on you? One of us dressed up as a priest and all the lads hiding behind the curtain listening. Did you ever have thoughts about other men my son? Then mind the one we did on Knoxy about his wife? We set this young lad up to tell the priest he had been having an affair with a married woman. And Knoxy's behind the curtain with the rest of us and he hears a description of his wife. He went mad. Or what about the tunnel? They got you there I remember.

Boyle nodded. On his second night in he was taken aside and told confidentially there was going to be a breakout through a tunnel. They wanted to take a new arrival for propaganda purposes. He was to be outside the canteen at eleven. The hole was under one of the tables. Boyle was sent in with three others, into the darkness, crawling on their bellies under the tables. They couldn't find the hole but they were trained not to give up. A man at the door was whispering frantically to them to get a move on. It lasted about ten minutes and then the lights came on and there were two screws shouting and screaming. Boyle and the other two ran around the room, passing one another, still looking desperately for the hole. Boyle was the last to realise that there was a crowd of men at the door laughing their heads off at the headless chickens. What was worse: Boyle had pissed himself from fright.

I'd better be going anyway, Boyle said. I have to meet somebody.

Do you want a lift? She'll be only a few minutes.

I'll walk. Have a look around.

Well enjoy the visit, Snowy said and Boyle could detect nothing in it of doubt.

He watched Snowy reach into his jacket and take out a notebook. He was thinking of what address to give. The pages were covered in writing.

I'm writing my memoirs. Snowy laughed. The story of my life. Keeps me focused. I keep it handy. Mind those flocks of crows? And Charlie Ramsey with his matchstick sculpture things? It's amazing the things that just jump into your mind.

The things that go out are just as bad.

This was said by none other than Fada who had come up behind Boyle.

Guess what? he said to Boyle, shaking his fists in delight on either side of his face. I found the poems. The poems I was telling you about. He patted the breast pocket of the corduroy jacket he was wearing.

It was the cleanest Boyle had ever seen on Fada. Snowy was looking at him, measuring him swiftly from head to toe.

Fada put out his hand. My name's Fada. I'm a friend, he said ludicrously.

Are you now? Snowy looked at Boyle who could not tell what his own face might be saying. He was trapped; all he could do was wait to see how bad this might become.

He saved my life a few weeks ago on Grafton Street. Fada put his arm around Boyle's shoulder.

Saved your life?

A slight exaggeration, Fada laughed, but he helped me out of some trouble. Then he turned to Boyle: I was looking for you the other night at your job. It must have been your night off. Anyway, I found the poems, just this morning. So we've something to celebrate tonight. You on for it?

Boyle couldn't move. His eyes had gone out of focus, the muscles on his face were aching. He knew he should take control of the situation, play it casual, but it was beyond him.

Well you think about it, Fada said. I have to rush now but I'll be in the Two Mists later on. Hope to see you later then.

Fada waved his fist in victory in front of Boyle's face and then shook Snowy's hand, adding that it was a pleasure to meet another friend of Boyle's.

All Boyle could do was wait.

He was aware of Snowy turning the pages of his notebook, the quick scratches of the pen, then the paper being torn sharply. Boyle expected to hear the hammer coming down. You have been found guilty of . . .

Here's my number, Snowy said.

Boyle took the paper in his hand.

In case you need anything. Give me a ring.

I won't, Boyle said.

I know you're only down for a visit. But you never know. Just in case like.

Boyle looked at Snowy closely for the first time.

Don't turn too sly, he was told. It doesn't suit you Buddha.

Snowy had taken a few steps away before Boyle called after him: Did you hear about that woman they found in the Liffey?

The Russian? Why?

She was Russian?

That's what I heard. Why?

Just wondering, said Boyle.

Stay fucken well clear of the Russians.

I was just wondering.

Don't.

Right.

Boyle had gone a few streets' distance before he remembered he was supposed to be catching a bus. Dainty had a get-together planned. He had also talked to his ma on the phone; she was drunk and made him laugh. He came to the river again, leaned over the wall, smoking. It was one of the few places left you could stand on your own without evoking pity or suspicion in the hurrying legions of the populace. Standing still would bring the force of the law down on your head in the guise of some red-cheeked boy from the hills in a hat he stuffed with paper to make it fit. He took out the page Snowy had given him and read the name and number. The brown water churned and slapped, no wider than a good stone's throw. A strong arm could probably make it across with a hatchet. A woman had gone into it smiling like a bride. Enough bodies jumping in would bring the level up to the street. He watched the racket of another Dart cross the overhead bridge. Most of the buildings opposite were only façades, splints in the windows, wooden braces propping them up like defences. Preservation orders. Land awaiting development. He checked his watch and saw he had five minutes to get back to the bus station. Snowy and his wife would be gone. He imagined Dainty wheeling a trolley around the supermarket, the trays of cans. The wind was trying to tear the scrap of paper from his fingers, the eager tugging of it. Was it a force for good or bad? If he parted his fingers and let the paper fly would he ever know the consequences? Or was it arrogance, no, vanity, to assume that one small decision could make a dent in the chaos?

He shut his eyes. There was nothing there to help him.

The wind died suddenly, no, he had moved off before, no, he moved, he was moving and the paper scrap was still in his hand, going against the river tide back into the city centre and that was the end of it, no, the end was another vanity, it just went on and on, decision avoided, no, rejected, vanquished, non-utilised, he was walking back into town, he wasn't getting the bus, he was walking that was all, they meant nothing, these pseudo moments of choice, just another man in another city, it was happening all over the world, man walks along the street by river wall, hopelessly, the heart could feel as sick as it wanted, vertigo, futility, yearning, he was nothing more than a male pedestrian in a small European city, the broader context was the main thing, he folded the paper and put it in his back pocket, a man who had set out to do one thing and found himself doing something different and it was of absolutely no significance.

I have a confession to make.

Keep it to yourself that's my advice.

I can't. I want everybody to know. This was a character called Fiacra, a fat-lipped friend of Fada's. He was drunk, and stoned as well. They all were around that table. Fiacra stood up and aggressively demanded quiet. I am ugly, he said. Ugly. I have ugliness in my blood.

Some laughed. Fada seemed to grin with pleasure. The Dove kept her eyes lowered.

Feel better? Boyle asked when he sat down again.

That was not my intention. I am ugly on the inside. On the outside however I am –

An obnoxious bastard. The sentence was finished by a quieter lad called Con a few people along.

The point being, as I'm talking to a philosopher here, that my progeny will also be ugly. If my veins are running with ugly bile then what chance does the little creature have? I'm right. None of you has ever had to face it. But where does my ugliness come from? From my own parents? Then from theirs. And back and back we go until we reach the numero uno, the big chief.

What is there of any value in me that I want to pass on? Any one of you swear to me you aren't a total hypocrite and a sell-out. Go on convince me. Not fucken one of you. Hypocrites and fuckheads. Afraid to take anything seriously in case it shows you what you really are. Am I right? This man here understands what I'm talking about.

Boyle shrugged. He was tired of listening to this character's obstreperous self-loathing. The story seemed to be that he had been drinking for the past week, unable to come to terms with the fact that his girlfriend was pregnant. Boyle had sat through a good half-hour of the reasons why it was selfish and sadistic to bring a child into the world. Here was a young man with his looks and his freedom and his money and his girlfriend who wanted to carry his child overshadowed by –

Fiacra stood up again, knocking the table, and announced that he had another confession to make.

Boyle used the opportunity to escape to the toilet, careful to avoid the Dove's eyes. With the bad wind of Fada at her ear, she was seeking him with her perfume-bottle blue eyes. In them he would see a complaint, a tensed instruction to rescue her, to get her out of the foul atmosphere of this place. But Boyle was drunk himself now, and he was enjoying himself for the first time in ages, amused by the malignant humour, the satire, the absurd bragging, the forked tongue of failure flailing in every flooded stale mouth.

The crowd, they were nearly all on benders, each with their own excuse or disdaining the notion they needed one for a summer afternoon drinking session in the septic twilight of an old pub. Boyle counted twelve of them around the low table although the faces changed every hour. Fada recounted the story of the rediscovery of the poems to each one that arrived like it was a spell that left them helpless and stunned and uneasy and begging for the next drink. Ones Boyle had been talking to earlier had disappeared without a word, some couple from Belfast, an old Dublin man with a white beard and an American who told him about a gathering of people in the desert. Then there was some who left and returned bringing new characters with them, new anecdotes, new energy. The floor carpet had a faded biscuit-tin design and there were paintings around the walls for sale, bits of shadows in pigeon-shit mist all called Unfinished. Long ago, the dusty black blades of a massive fan had come to a meaningless halt up in the carpeted ceiling.

When Boyle arrived back at the table, Fada was on his jester feet, reading from the newspaper in an old woman's voice, a posh Dublin suburban accent: Letter to the Editor. Sounds of Summer. Sir – On my walk to the bus stop these bright summer mornings I enjoy the sound of the birds singing. There are beautiful gardens on my route which have been lovingly cared for by their owners. But, Fada raised a palsied hand, but none of these give me the same pleasure as the garden littered with the remains of yesterday's playthings – a discarded book, a doll's blanket, a chalk-marked driveway. The birdsong is momentarily replaced by the happy echo of children's playtime. Yours Margaret Murphy.

The Dove was the only one not to laugh.

There's ugliness for you, Fada hissed across to Fiacra. Can't you smell that womb rot my boy. The muggy menopausal hot-water-bottle taint in the sunshiny air. The sun is as cold to me as a politician's smile.

Boyle had found the Dove in the library earlier in the day and it had come as a surprise to him that he immediately began to tell her about the aborted trip to Derry. He had never made fun of himself in front of her before; he had always been locked inside some fruitless seriousness. There he sat mocking himself gladly, laughing at the world and the preposterous situations which could develop in a quiet hour in a blighted part of the city. The fact that he was lying, no, keeping some of the truth from her, namely meeting Snowy, might even have added to his new-found pleasure, he wondered, but it was a short wonder, a briefly held hypothesis, because he suddenly realised that she was not laughing along with him. She was smiling all right, but only around the mouth; her eyes were occupied by a different emotion, a strained emptiness like she had forgotten something important. Boyle asked her if she wanted to go for a walk, maybe have a pint somewhere. He wanted to talk to her, not about himself, he was a fool for the day at least. They could walk around the streets, look in shop windows, or they could go to that gallery she had mentioned once with her favourite painting in it.

To whatever he suggested the Dove shook her head. He asked if something had happened, told her she looked sad.

I am sad, she said. And I want to talk to you too. But later. I need to get my thoughts straight first.

Boyle went over it all in his mind as they stared at each other. His nerves fizzed with each flick of her blond-tipped lashes. What he had told her that night in her house was stuck inside her, undigested, a poisonous mush. He lifted a book from the table, went blindly through some pages, sweat creeping out in his beard, then told her he would be in the Two Mists if she wanted him.

She said she wasn't fond of that pub and Boyle stopped himself asking why.

When she did appear a few hours later, he had already managed to put her out of his mind. He bought her a drink and sat her down on a stool and went back to his conversation with Fada who was telling him about an old girlfriend who always liked to pretend her mother was watching.

Boyle now moved in beside Con and Tanya, the flower-seller girl.

He's sick in the head, Tanya said.

I don't really know him, Boyle told her.

You're the lucky one then. Is that your girlfriend he's talking to? She doesn't look too happy if you ask me. And who would blame her with him crawling all over you? I think she's trying to catch your eye.

Boyle turned in the Dove's direction and saw her eyes cast towards the door. He frowned as though not understanding. She could without doubt be described as fresh-faced, he thought, young, lovely, calm, softly charged with well-being. He had noticed that some around the table found it hard to raise their eyes to her and some began to laugh when they were introduced to her. Fada couldn't leave her side. Earlier he had been touching one of her blameless tanned feet. His eyes had swollen and bulged; he was trembling. Her presence seemed to make some kind of demand on him. For her part, the Dove was trapped by politeness.

Boyle swallowed the dirty meniscus of foam and smiled at her. He was making her wait, he realised.

He listened to Tanya relate some of the incidents she had seen on the street involving Fada. Con joined in with his own opinion. Neither of them had anything good to say.

So why sit here drinking with him? Boyle asked.

We've known him a long time, Con said. He keeps the bad spirits away like a gargoyle. He needs to get things out of him that's all. It's like letting blood. Sewer-rat psalms, he calls them. But don't trust him. Don't believe a word he tells you. I learned that lesson years ago. We broke into a shop one night: we were going to run away to London. We made it as well. But then he gets it into his head that everybody is after him, MI5, CIA. We were staying in this bed-and-breakfast and one morning the cops knock on my door. What had he done? He'd gone and given himself up. All we'd got was one hundred quid from the cash till.

There she's going now, Tanya said.

Boyle followed the Dove out into the street. The light was harsh, coming down like rain.

Why you going?

I only came to talk to you Noel, she replied sharply, the first sign of temper he had seen in her.

Well let's go in and sit down again. I was caught up with those other people. They're ones I've never met before. They're a good laugh.

Are they? she asked.

Boyle couldn't think what to say. Then: Why what's wrong with them? They're doing their best.

Who is that person Fada? she said with a put-on shudder. He wouldn't leave me alone. You should have heard the things he was saying to me.

Boyle knew he was smiling: Like what?

It's not what he says exactly it's the way he says it. I didn't imagine you had friends like that.

He's only winding you up. You just laugh him off.

He's a creep, she said firmly. He's a lech. I was trying to catch your attention and you were ignoring me. Are you angry with me?

Why would I be?

Why were you ignoring me then?

Boyle didn't argue with her. He was drunk. People were passing along the street. The working day wasn't over yet.

Maybe you're angry at me for what you told me at my house, she said.

Boyle responded too quickly: Maybe you're angry at me for having to hear them. For having to acknowledge the world's not the happy wee place you like to believe. Let's all hold hands will we?

Stop it, Noel.

Well don't ask me to talk and then throw it back in my face because you don't like it.

Ok. I am angry, she said. Ok I didn't like what you told me. Who would? It scared me. The thought of prison and violence scares me. Or perhaps like your friend in there you thought I might find it exciting. Is that it? Did you think it would turn me on? Prisoners' fantasies at night?

Those words in her young clean mouth made him want to laugh but there was a more important issue that took the light out of the sky.

Say that again. Did he mention to you about me being in jail?

We talked about it, she said. We were talking about you. What else would we have to talk about?

And you told him?

She was silent, confused; her hand went out towards his chest and he stepped out of its reach.

Did you tell him?

I don't know, she said. I might have. I don't remember.

Doesn't he know already? I thought he was a friend of yours. Watching the way you were talking together when I came in.

Nobody knows about that stuff, Boyle said.

I'm sorry, she said. You see how confused I am. I don't know what to think about any of this.

I shouldn't have told you. I should have kept my fucken mouth shut.

Maybe you're right, she said.

Boyle looked at her. The skin, the blue eyes, the sandy curls of hair.

No maybe about it.

I talked to my father about it, the Dove said.

You what?

I talk to him about everything. I told you that. I needed somebody to talk to.

And so did I.

Maybe you chose the wrong person, she said then. I don't know. I just need some time to think about it. I don't want violence in my life. It's so ugly.

Boyle leaned back against the wall. This was turning out to be some day and there was nothing funny about it any more. Dainty waiting on him up in Derry, Snowy knowing he was in Dublin, Fada who was probably halfway through a slapstick paramilitary funeral oration in the pub that very minute and the Dove petrified of gunmen wanking all over her from their moonlit cells.

Ugliness. Boyle laughed, the sun in his eyes.

The Dove moved towards him; she wanted to kiss his jail-grown beard goodbye. He turned his face away and saw a camera moving on a lamppost towards the door of a sex shop where a man was throwing bread to the swooping screaming gulls.

Noel I just need some time to think.

Leaving her, Boyle went back inside the pub. What he saw there was entirely right and in keeping with the day. The truth was ludicrous, misshapen, overflowing, heavy-handed.

They were passing around a white mask, measuring it, putting it against their faces, giving their theories on the dead woman. Boyle sat down on a stool. He was in danger of losing control. Fada was sitting back quietly on the sofa, eyeing him calmly, no, in anticipation.

Boyle went off to the toilet again and this time Fada followed him.

That's a lovely girl, Fada said with his blind man's grin. Very sweet. A summer flower.

Boyle washed his hands and then leaned against the door.

One word of what she said to you gets out and I'll kill you, he said.

Fada backed away. She started it, he said. I didn't have to try. She told me that –

One word. Do you hear me?

I hear you. Don't hit me. Fada cowered like a dog.

I'm not joking.

I know you're not.

With dread Boyle realised the fear in Fada's eyes wasn't enough; it didn't go deep enough below the sleaze and the smell and debauched mouth. Boyle heard the useless wish sound in himself that he had never helped the wanker that day on Grafton Street and left him to the cops.

Boyle went on drinking. He moved around now, from stool to stool among different groups of people. He talked to anybody who caught his eye: other students who gave him lists of books to read, a woman who was learning Polish, two men who had plundered a salmon farm one night, an alcoholic filmmaker, a couple who had moved back to Dublin from Amsterdam, some more with Fiacra who was looking for an argument with everybody, Con briefly about the girl he was kissing and Tanya who told him she wanted to set up her own business before she disappeared for a while with Fada and they both returned flushed and exuberant. The mask lay forgotten on a table, black and crumbling at the chin where it had been soaked with stout.

Fada came up to him again with the eyes of somebody watching a cheat in action.

You enjoying yourself? The voice was slurred, defiant.

Getting near it.

I want only the best for you, Fada said. I want to show you things.

Like what?

We're going all the way tonight. There's no stopping us. Vive nous. I know what you're looking for you see bud.

The accents and voices changed continually.

You see I know you. Fada wagged his finger. You stick with me. I know what you're looking for. I have the recipe madame.

He tapped the stained finger on Boyle's lips.

You see there are many paths. Different roads to the light. Back doors, secret corridors. Underground tunnels. Sewers. Sliding walls. We don't need the priests do we? We don't want to be numbered among the slaves to happiness do we? Free the slaves, free the slaves, he started shouting.

The faces were all people who had survived some disaster. When he went outside for some air he was followed by an older woman with a rose in her cleavage and she wanted him to kiss her. Boyle obliged. I thought so, she said and went off down the street with a glass in her hand, singing.

Back inside Fada was down on his knees. I crawled till I reached the House of Sin, the door was locked and nobody was in.

Boyle took a pill from somebody who had visited Sartre's apartment. He was transformed into water, soft warm water moving through soft warm water.

A look from a girl sent a wave of delight lifting through him, unbreaking, unbreaking. When she sat down beside him and took hold of his hand, he was water that had reached an exquisite impassable barrier.

It was so simple. Rapture was a word for it. He told her that just the touch of her hand was the way forward in himself he had been searching for. Desire. Rapture, endlessly. She hugged him tightly, profoundly. They went to a club, at least twenty of them. He danced with the girl. Fada was thrown out and then somehow reappeared. There were others there who understood exactly what Boyle was trying to tell them. People's eyes filled over with pleasure, unbearable joy, tears. He was staggered, breathless. Solitude was over; it was another lie.

I can't believe this, she said. I've never met you before and I would let you drink my blood.

She would walk off and come back to him like she had seen things beyond words at last, and was sated.

Boyle brushed his tongue along the velvet choker around her neck and his mind emptied completely, radically, no, it filled him, so that there wasn't even room for the touch of her lips when she offered them.

Say a group of them sat in a circle on the open grass plain and watched the soft ectopic sun low behind the bloody swabs of cloud.

Fada slithered and squirmed in the long grass in the centre of the circle. He had ripped off his clothes. He was talking to his mother, pointing, spitting, to his father, the old girlfriend Jess, someone called Hilary, Lisa-Ann and a pack of others who were not there, a swan included.

Another girl undressed and went running towards the trees, then another girl, then Con, no, was Con there?

A crowd of them had climbed over the gates of the Phoenix Park.

None of you ever believed me about what that swan did to me.

Boyle stayed put to keep an eye on Fada. And the girl was sleeping with her head in his lap.

So who am I now? Boyle said.

Fada was crawling towards him, his face streaked with muck, grass welts across his scrawny body. He was hissing, seething, snarling: You and that bicycle. I hated that bicycle. I hated seeing you spinning down the street with your legs out. The wind in your hair like a big rat. The pettiness of it. The smallness of it. Your liberation. Oh I feel like a young girl again. You were an embarrassment. It was me who stole it. Me. And you knew it didn't you? And you still went to the Guards. Oh hello Sergeant. Oh please come in. I'm distraught. It was so precious to me. And I saw you take his hairy hand and put it against your saggy tit in the living room. It's in the sea. I rode it off the end of the pier. The pier my dear. And the green dress. Remember your favourite green dress which meant you were angry and we were going to have soup for a week? Green. Green. No wonder he left you. He was right. You made everyone unhappy my precious dear.

Fada stuck his face hard into the ground and was screaming. When he came up it was another target; some nurse it sounded like with a Northern accent. He rolled over and kicked his legs in the air, his cock standing up, a long cock all right.

Say this was one of the images that returned to Boyle over the next few days.

Every blade of grass was in sharp focus. The hills to the south were tantalising and elemental and soft and naked enough to give Boyle a hard-on.

The girl's face in his lap. Hair sucked in her mouth.

Then she was up in the tree. He had helped her get a hold, supporting her foot with his hand, shoulder under rump. She stepped out along a heavy low bough in the stalemate light. Wistfully, no, it was darker than that, fanatic longing, she began to take off her clothes, the few that she was wearing, a vest, a short denim skirt, then her black knickers and bra, dropping each piece down to him where he was lying on the grass under orders not to move, strict orders.

Look at me.

As she began to masturbate, he saw the dying moon between her legs.

Do you see? Can you see me? See it.

She had a Gaelic name he couldn't pronounce or call out to comfort her.

Look at me.

Other screams, incantations, came back through the trees to meet hers. Boyle tried to wank but she was too powerful, beyond him, prodigious, the energy, wonder, the hunger.

Look.

She was coming convulsively, piss in it as well, weeping.

Fada was singing somewhere.

What would the world do with this power?
Conceal it. Destroy it.
Look at me.

And what was the remorse in the days afterwards? Over and over again as he lay about the flat, Boyle reminded himself that he hadn't done anything. There seemed to be a price for beholding that torrent, the abundance. When he tried to meditate in an effort to cleanse his mind, he saw a thousand pairs of open legs, breasts painted with muck, cocks in foaming mouths, men with horns.

He had woken up out in the open in the grass. He thought he was alone, excruciatingly alone, in a beautiful white morning mist. His feet were bare and his jacket was missing. For a long time he looked at the line of trees and they were ancient and bored with cryptic meanings he was not far from understanding. His heart was choking with voices that brought the saddest news. He sat up; something moved near the trees. His first thought was that it was the police and he was almost relieved to have the company.

A few minutes later when he struggled to his feet, ready to give himself up, he saw the company he had was a herd of deer on the outskirts of the trees. They were resting most of them, folded up in the grass, breathing, browns and whites, except a young one and the big male, the stag, with its growing burden of velvet horn. He began to move towards them as slowly and unthreateningly as he could; he begged them quietly not to move, just to let him sit down among them, breathe with them, stroke their hides. The stag wasn't bothered by him although some of the smaller ones hefted to their feet, hind legs first. He stumbled over a thing and went down on his hands.

It was a body he had just time to see before the body jumped up and ran moaning towards the deer. It was Fada. The deer moved lazily back into the trees, no, unmistakably with tenderness. Fada was wearing a shirt and nothing else.

Eventually he ran back towards Boyle and fell on the ground at his feet and curled up.

It wasn't me, he whined over and over.

Say Boyle had to take control. He hid Fada in the undergrowth and went off looking for clothes. Most things were soon found except one of Fada's shoes. They headed back in silence under a violently new blue sky to Boyle's flat. Fada lay down on the sofa. Boyle got into his bed and fell fast into a bottomless hole. He slept until the evening. When he came out into the living room, he found Fada asleep on the sofa with his trousers round his ankles, the cock still in his hands.

Boyle stood at the door of the shop watching the two girls at the stall on the corner of the cobbled street. It was a different pair from the day he had done his Jesus routine sacking the temple of Mammon but they were dressed identically in their berets and T-shirts. They had little opportunity to stand at attention with the constant crowd of purchasers at the table, touching and lifting the masks; trade was good and the rain failed to fall. He had heard a report on the radio that the mask gimmick was beginning to catch on. The people of Dublin were buying them in droves. A craze for the stolen face of a nameless dead woman. That artist lad was making a fortune. Boyle told himself he didn't care any more; there was nothing he could do about it. He had as little chance of persuading them to boycott the exploitation of a woman's death as he had of . . . what? Feeding the whole city with wingers and setting them loose to run wild and naked in the park? People didn't want to know the highs and lows, the bursting and the depletion. What did they want then, the languid crowds on the city streets that evening? What were they looking for? What was the secret that held it all together and kept them working and building and sleeping on buses and worrying and marrying and spending and abiding by the law? They had struggled and saved and pushed themselves on while he lay in bed in jail reading books about religious visions and existential bohemians. Who was he to claim he knew anything about people? They weren't looking, that was the answer. They were out and about in their own city trying to forget, happy to have won a few hours of idle enjoyment. What did they want? Maybe it was the question itself that was the problem. It had too many airs about it. A person can't stand outside of life and ask questions like that, what is there to do, what is the point, why do they behave themselves day after day after day? The question must always start with the questioner. Any question that doesn't include yourself is a bad question. Boyle could see it now clearly for the first time; this was what Sartre had meant. Why that young couple passing the door of the shop with the bags of things they had bought had decided to spend the day shopping rather than lying in bed together was connected somehow with this ex-paramilitary, ex-POW, ex-combatant standing at the door of a low-cost telephone shop in a peacetime city smoking a roll-up that wasn't sticking properly and kidding himself he was detached from it all by asking pointless snooty questions.

Boyle flicked the butt into the street and hurried in behind his counter to write down some of these thoughts. He was excited, no, go further, he was surging with ideas. This was the way into the Sartre essay he had been waiting on. The partridges were exploding out of the bushes like peacocks.

Excuse me. Is there a phone free?

The woman before him was familiar. Irish, somewhere in her forties he guessed, she might have been lovely once but now she was overweight and depressed and never stopped blinking. The hands she rested on the counter had not been washed in a long time.

I don't think so, Boyle said.

Of course, as soon as he spoke a Romanian woman came out of a booth with a child around her in a sling fashioned out of a scarf. Boyle checked the screen and wrote down the price on a piece of paper.

What about that one? the woman asked, the money exchange complete.

I'll have to see. A few of them aren't working properly. Boyle stared at the computer screen again, clicking away grumpily with the mouse and asking himself why he was preventing this sorry woman from having a booth, why he was letting it annoy him today that she would sit in there as she had done how many times before and hold a conversation with nobody for ten minutes or more and come out and try to pay. It was his own fault. The first time it had happened he had taken pity on her because there was a queue of people in the shop and charged her for a call to England. The woman had paid happily. This had gone on now for a couple of months, twice sometimes three times a week. Boyle usually gave the money to the same beggar on Capel Street bridge, a Northern lad he had once stopped to talk to.

Where is it you want to phone to? Boyle asked her although it was none of his business.

Again they were interrupted, this time by an Australian lad. The woman waited, picking at her nails.

Where is it you're trying to phone?

Her silence forced him to look into her face. The eyes were closed; she couldn't handle what he was asking her to think about. Why was he being cruel to her? What the fuck did it matter anyway? Let her sit in a booth all day talking gibberish to the wall if she wanted.

Number three, he said.

The eyes opened. She looked straight at him and in the few seconds before the blinking resumed he thought he saw a room filling with smoke.

He put this down as well in his essay notes. Everything seemed connected, every idea joined up to another one, like frogspawn, a vast sea of it. Since he had woken that morning, his mind was bursting with notions on all sorts of things, stuff from the past even, with a freshness. Walking along the river he wondered if he had come out the other end of a phase of lousy self-recrimination he hadn't been aware he was in. He felt good enough to believe he was ready to throw himself into the university work again. He was going to get this fucken degree and show himself he could complete something, try to feel a bit of pride for a change. Skipping his customary read of the paper in the café, he had rushed on to the library. There he found himself for the first time in ages accepting what he had in common with the other students at their books, money troubles, worries about their future, trying to get through it as best they could. They had their own lives and their own problems, stories and secrets, and surely among them there had to be somebody all for him, yes, a woman he had to make himself ready to meet.

It was a relief after the depression of the last few days, since the night in the park and the following night with Fada in the flat. They drank tea and smoked cigarettes and said very little other than when some kind of fear drove them to make another attempt to piece together what had happened in the trees, who was there, who the girls were. Fada was badly shaken; his skin was grey, his eyes clogged with anxieties. He lay on the sofa staring up at the ceiling as if he could see his life re-enacted there. Boyle threw a blanket over him. The silence gave him goosebumps. Fada could pass out right there or die in his flat and the Guards would have to be called along with the ambulance. It wouldn't look good: Ex-Republican prisoner in drug orgy with dead street entertainer. They would throw the book at him. He pulled Fada up on his feet and walked him around the flat. Fada began to slip off into stories about being in some hospital. One of them was about how he was forced to attend art therapy classes. Some woman was the teacher. The patients sat at their desks and the woman told them what they were going to draw: a windmill in a field of flowers. As the woman walked among the desks she talked them through every line and brushstroke and the colours they could use. Fada found himself beginning to enjoy it, the picture was coming alive in front of him. When the time was up he was very pleased with himself; it wasn't a bad effort at all. He was going to pin it up by his bed. He would join this class every day. Maybe a painter was what he should be, an artist. Then the woman asked the patients to hold up their paintings so everyone could see. Fada held his proudly aloft and looked at the other ones.

You wouldn't want to have been there, Fada said, holding

on to Boyle tightly. You wouldn't want to imagine it. Every one of those paintings was exactly the same as mine. Identical. It was horrible.

Boyle went downstairs and knocked on Victor's door but there was no answer; he wanted Victor to sit with Fada while he went to the shop; he had run out of tobacco and milk. In the end he had to risk it and ran across to the corner shop. Some food would be a good idea also so he stopped in for some chips. He hurried back. He could not have been gone more than fifteen minutes. Fada was gone, one-shoed, delirious.

Boyle fell asleep in the chair and dreamed about wandering through a devastated city until a woman took his hand and led him through burning streets to a metal door which she kicked open and pushed him through and he was falling . . . falling . . . falling . . .

After the episode with the blinking woman, who spent thirty-seven minutes whispering into the phone, the shop was quiet for most of the day, leaving Boyle plenty of time to get on with his essay which he had decided to start without any more preparation. Leo stepped in unexpectedly to collect the cash but there was little else happened to distract him, a few more Romanians, Africans, a beautiful Scottish girl, who all made their phone calls and left without incident. It was dark when he took a break, five pages done, and found himself on a whim dialling Dainty's number in Derry, expecting to get a mouthful about failing to show over the weekend. A woman answered, an unknown voice, loud music in the background and Dainty shouting, trashed, incoherent. The woman said her name was Maureen; she had an English accent.

Who the fuck is it? If it's any of those cunts that call themselves my family tell them to fuck off, Dainty was railing.

What's happened? Boyle asked the woman. This is Noel, I'm a friend of his.

The woman made a sound of recognition. He's extremely upset, she said. Do you want to risk it? There was a memorial today for his brother in the cemetery. We all went back to his sister's house afterwards. Things got a bit out of hand if you know what I mean. He's very angry.

Who the fuck is it?

Do you want to talk to him? Maureen said to Boyle.

Put him on.

Long pause. Muffled voices.

Dainty came on: What the fuck do you want?

I'm sorry about Greg. I didn't know it was today.

Don't make me fucken laugh. You did your fucken best to end up under a flagpole as well. I'm not going to stand around singing Fenian songs that nobody knows the words of and think it was all fucken great and up the united Ireland. It's a fucken waste. He was my fucken brother and it was a fucken waste of a life. For what eh? Is this what it was all about? Is this the glorious freedom now? It's a fucken sick joke. And where the fuck were you at the weekend?

I know, I'm sorry. Things just happened. I got stuck.

You got fucken stuck? Change the fucken record will you? You annoy the fuck out of me sometimes so you do.

Why?

Fucken listen to you with your whys. Don't fucken patronise me. You know what I'm talking about all right. Don't fucken patronise me.

Maybe I'd better go.

Go and fuck yourself for all I care. They might all think you're great down there in Dublin with your big fucken sob story but don't try it on fucken me. And mind those fucken sticks? The sticks? Well I took them out there the other day and fucked them in the Foyle. That's the way I'm fucken feeling. And you'd go in straight after them if you were here. I'd dump this whole place in there if I could. Do you get me Mad-dog fucken Boyle?

Dainty was the one who put down the phone. Boyle didn't know what to think; he had heard Dainty in a rage before, it was in his blood from no age, but this time Boyle felt responsible in some way, guilty about failing to show at the weekend. When they were young, Dainty with his stick was unbeatable, and fearless, and prone to losing his head. He took on Nixon one day, a ruthless hard bastard a lot older than them, and had to be pulled off him by many hands and Nixon came back the following week with a knife and Dainty battered him with the stick like he was fire to be put out, the zebra-striped stick he could send high into the air for five cartwheeling Catherine-wheel spins and catch behind his back with a fag in his mouth at the age of ten. Or the time during a visit to Boyle in jail when he attacked – who was it? – Sizzle, no – who was it? – Flipflaps for acting the mick and spoiling the photograph of the two of them by flashing his arse and the screws nearly arrested him, and to calm him down this screw volunteered to take the snap and now it hangs on the wall above the toilet, the two of them, sitting at a table, shoulder to shoulder, a grim skinny Boyle with a heavy beard and a flushed Dainty with a look that warned the camera to get it fucken right or there'd be big trouble, above the toilet Dainty hung it of all places in a frame Boyle made himself out of bamboo cane in the arts room of Maghaberry Prison, where else would I fucken hang it, it's the only place I can think what I fucken like.

Typical of the way things were going for him, a woman entered the shop, the exotic Argentinian woman. She announced she was ready to have a drink with him as though she had kept him waiting long enough. Boyle, of course, pointed out that he was at work only to hear her say that she would wait, that nothing was going to get in her way. She was dressed up for the occasion: a very short skirt which showed off her brown muscular legs and her breasts stuffed into a leather corset thing. Boyle thought she looked like someone his father wouldn't have minded dancing with, or a woman in an ice-skating tournament from some country he had never heard of. She patted his ear, ran a long purple nail through his beard and sat down on a chair at the back of the shop. Boyle looked at the pages on his counter; it seemed like days since he had written them.

I'm going to be a while. Why don't you go off and do something and come back later?

What would I do? A woman like me? Alone? Where would I go? It's my day off tomorrow.

Go for a walk.

She snorted and took out her lipstick.

You'll be bored, Boyle said.

How was he going to get rid of her? Or maybe he should loosen up a bit and go with her? What would they talk about in a crowded bar, everyone in the place looking at the two of them, the shifty bearded one and the overpainted kitsch Salsa dancing around him?

I don't know your name, she called over to him.

Before he could answer, none other than Fada slid across the floor towards him in a new pair of shoes and a creamy suit jacket and grabbed hold of the counter as if he were on ice. There was genuine panic on his face. Boyle sighed, put his face in his hands. This day was doomed for sure. Wearily, he went towards the door and locked it, thinking it was probably to do with somebody in hot pursuit. Salsa crossed her hard legs, a wry smile on her big cherry lips.

Fada was mouthing words.

What the fuck's the matter? I've had enough to deal with today. Just leave me out of it.

Dead was a word Boyle heard from Fada's havoc mouth.

Who? The first name to appear in Boyle's mind was Tanya but Fada shook his head at it.

Fucken who? What have you done?

Fada pulled out a package from his pocket, a brown envelope.

The old woman? What the fuck did you do?

Came here first, Fada said.

Boyle pointed him into a cubicle while he got rid of another customer. He counted and there were still three more on the phones. Fada had hunkered down under the ledge in the booth. Every time he tried to speak Boyle told him to shut up; he couldn't decide whether he wanted to know, if it was the right thing to do, listen, get roped in, involved. Pacing the shop he was cursing himself for not being able to make up his mind. Never hesitate. Delay is death.

Spit it out, he said.

I borrowed some clothes and went round to her house, Fada began. To give back the poems. I showed you them with your friend outside the bus station didn't I?

He's not my friend, Boyle pointed out. Just forget it. Go fucken on.

I knocked but there was no answer. I rang the bell over and over again. I wanted to get rid of them. I thought of you and told myself not to give up.

What?

I thought of you and told myself not to give up.

Boyle held his head again. And then what?

I kept ringing the bell. Nobody came out. Then I got worried about attracting the neighbours' attention. So I decided to put them through the letter box. That was ok wasn't it?

Just get on with it?

Well before I dropped them through the letter box I bent down and had a quick look in case she was coming down the stairs from the toilet. That's when I saw her, lying in the hall.

Boyle watched in disbelief as Fada came out of the booth and lay on his back on the floor.

What are you fucking doing?

Showing you. How she was lying. Doreen.

Boyle wanted to kick him.

I panicked. I ran straight here. Did I do the right thing? Fada asked sitting on the floor.

A Russian-looking man came out of a booth and stepped over him indifferently. Boyle took the money, and opened the door for him. Two Chinese girls tried to come in and Boyle had to tell them he was closed. He knocked on the other cubicles, telling the three customers there was an emergency and if they left immediately they wouldn't be charged for their calls. Fada remained on the floor.

The shop cleared, Boyle lost his temper: What the fuck do you want me to do? Eh? What?

Do you think it was me? he said.

What?

Salsa, he had forgotten about her, said something in her own language and blessed herself. She came over on her heels, and getting down on her knees put her arms around Fada.

You are frightening him, she scolded Boyle. He looks for your help.

Boyle made himself ignore her. Look at me, he was shouting at Fada. Fucken look at me. What do you mean, was it you? Why the fuck are you telling me, no, fucken asking me? Did you or didn't you? What the hell am I going to do about it?

Salsa tutted at him, said that he was being too hard.

I don't know, said Fada.

Did you hit her?

Salsa blessed herself again with her free hand. Fada's head had slid down to her bosom.

Did you fucken hit her?

I don't think so, Fada said.

So what did you do? Scare her? Piss against her windows?

Salsa now gave him a mouthful in Spanish maybe which was probably about being disgusting. Boyle vented a hopeless laugh at the ceiling.

What the fuck am I doing in this situation? he moaned.

Fada shouted back suddenly: I was going round to see her a few days ago. Before I found the poems again. I was going to tell her the truth.

Poems, Salsa sighed as though it explained everything.

And?

I turned back. I thought I did. I really thought I did.

Talk sense to me now or I'm done with you and this fucken

nonsense, Boyle warned him. There's the fucken door. Right?

Salsa now stood up and aimed her body directly at Boyle.

You have no children, it is clear, she said.

Boyle wanted to tell her that she wouldn't be having any more either if she didn't shut up but Fada jumped up instead: Why did I turn back? Because I was afraid. And why was I was afraid? Why? Because I thought something bad was going to happen. Maybe I wasn't going round to tell her the truth. What if I had something else in mind? To get that curse off my back. Maybe I had something else in mind.

Boyle and Salsa watched him pacing the room. When he made a dive for a booth Boyle saw what was happening and pulled the phone easily out of his hand.

I have to phone the Guards. I might have done it. I might have gone round there and done it. Then blanked it out. I feel like I did it.

Boyle slapped him with the back of his hand and Fada collapsed on the floor as if he had been shot. Salsa screamed, swiped at Boyle and knelt down beside the chanter, no, the gargoyle was right.

Boyle rolled himself a cigarette, trying to get a grip on his breathing. He had to think clearly. Through the window, the three bouncers on the pub door across the street were laughing their heads off.

Salsa wouldn't give up on her drink no matter who was dead or who had done it. The drama had passed for her after ten minutes of holding the shivering Fada against her loose, no, her crooked cleavage. Her blood cooled and it was time again to think about enjoying herself. Boyle didn't have any better ideas; he locked the shop, ignored the jibes and whistles of the bouncers and followed Salsa who had her arm around Fada into the glittering cave of some disco in Temple Bar. Salsa even bought the drinks herself. She wanted to dance. It was the only reason to go out at night. What else could a woman do? Boyle and Fada sat in uncomfortable chairs and watched her wriggling and stamping and stretching around their table. It didn't take long before she was being approached by men from all sides. To her credit, Salsa wasn't intimidated by any of them, she knew how to handle them but it began to annoy Boyle that after every couple of songs she would sit on his knee and sip her drink as a sign that she had a guardian, that if there was any trouble, any rough stuff, she had her man to defend her. With a sinking heart, Boyle observed the growing number of drunken characters who were gathering in the shadows, men who spoke different languages, sizing him up and waiting for the slightest excuse to start a row. One trip to the toilet and he was finished. He couldn't afford any more trouble. Salsa would have to look after herself. She was at the bar again, a young black lad on her. He leaned over and told Fada he was going.

Where? You can't leave me.

Boyle despised him at that moment, the weakness, the helplessness. He should get this bad-luck character out of his life, leave him to his own demons, walk away. He would drag Boyle down with him, down a slope that was all his own invention.

I'm going right now, he said.

He had reached the crowded street and gone a few yards when he heard his name being called, no, moaned, an intoning, wailed.

People stopped to watch and snigger at Fada stumbling behind him.

. . . And there he was now on the sofa again. The eyes were closed and the mouth ready for the last delicious drop. He gripped the package of poems against his chest. Boyle sat by the window, with a view of the yard and the chair against the wall in moonlight. A tape was playing, one that he had made himself in jail, taped off the radio, mainly old blues numbers and some classical stuff he never caught the name of, discordant modernist stuff, Bartók maybe. Other than a candle lodged on a saucer on the floor, the room was dark; the bulb in the ceiling light had blown when they came in which caused both of them to make a run for it, the place full of cops, drop your weapons, hands on your heads.

Should I tell the Guards? Fada had asked him earlier.

Boyle told him not to get involved.

She's probably lying there now in that hall. What if no one finds her and weeks go by, I couldn't cope with that.

Somebody will find her.

How do you know? You can't be sure.

Look if you go to the Guards they'll drag you into it. Somehow or other. You'll regret it. Or some journalist will get wind of it. Old Woman Dies Broken Hearted Over Poems. They'll take one look at you and rip you apart.

That's very paranoid, Fada said. I could just ring anonymously. From a phone box.

Then what? The Guards are thinking they get an anonymous call to tell them some old woman died so they're going to think something's up aren't they?

I could get someone else to call. A girl's voice, throw them off the track.

What track? You're talking nonsense. Don't give them a track. You didn't do anything for fuck's sake. And you call me fucken paranoid?

What if I did it?

You couldn't hurt a fly.

After a long pause, Fada said, Don't you think so?

You're a born coward.

Boyle was certain he could smell Fada's feet. Howlin' Wolf was stamping about at the crossroads.

Fada started laughing. This is weird isn't it? He switched to an American accent and said, Hey man let's pretend we're like Republican prisoners. Ok? I've just come in like and you're the old timer. Hey old timer? Why the long face? What do you say? What will I be in for? Something stylish. A sniper with his own –

Boyle told him to shut up. Fada launched straight into the chorus of some Nationalist song Boyle had never heard.

I'm warning you. Shut up, Boyle said. Leave it.

Fada then approached with an imaginary microphone.

Go on tell the viewers at home how it really was. Tell them. Give them all the gory details, they love that. Were the nights lonely? Tell them, were there female prison officers? There must have been one. With a cute backside and a leather belt. Ah remember that night she caught you looking at her and the wee snide smile on her. Or the day she found the porn mags stuffed in your shoes. They love all that. Tell the viewers back home.

To his own surprise, Boyle let him away with it. He was laughing eventually himself. Fada picked up the candle and put it close to his face.

Let's pretend we're trying to escape. We go down under the prison and we find tunnels and catacombs. We hear the screaming of many women. There's a young virgin tied to a table and we have to untie her before the men in the masks arrive. Hear them coming down the tunnel. Hear them humming. A labyrinth of evil under the prison. Black Mass shit brother. We can't get her free. We find some masks ourselves. See the torches now. We have to join in. We –

He put the candle back down on the floor and said: Thanks for looking after me tonight. If you ever need anything then I'm your man.

Boyle couldn't keep a straight face: Is that right?

I'm serious, Fada insisted.

The day I have to depend on you is the day I'm fucked, Boyle said. But what are you going to do anyway? You have to find somewhere to live. Get off the streets or they'll swallow you up.

Fada put on a droning Russian accent next: I am called Serge. I come to this place to find my woman. She drank my vodka and left me in Vladivostok. I come here many years ago. Day and night I walk the streets of your city. I will kill her. I think you know her. You have her picture on your wall. Tell me or I will kill you also. Nothing will stop me.

Fada had the candle over at the mask picture Boyle had cut from the newspaper and stuck above his table.

This is my wife. Her name is Betty.

Fada fell down laughing.

That's not funny, Boyle said.

Fada stopped immediately: Why won't you tell me about her? I promise I won't say a word to anyone. I tell you everything.

Boyle remained quiet, like he was under interrogation. Fada kept at him for a while, asking questions to tempt him into speaking, changing voices, accents, trying to make him laugh. Boyle knew he was playing the game as well and his silence would only add to the suspicion in Fada's mind.

Eventually, Fada ran out of steam and collapsed on the sofa like his strings had been cut. A few minutes later, he was asleep. Boyle stayed up in the chair. The tape clicked off and the room went quiet, no, seemed relieved, no – push the words away. Just be in it. Just breathe. This moment was an origin. The world was being born before him in the flickering room every second. More words again: let them melt away. The clown character snoring lightly at the nativity. Clutching a package of poems that could well be his own. He lived in a fantasy. And so what? Leave the questions. Total acceptance. Embrace everything. Open yourself. The snake devours its own tail. Down in the yard the chair was old, a long-ago thing, a broken cradle in the moonlight. Somehow, in that room, with Fada sleeping and the candle about to flutter out, Boyle thought that nothing would ever stop, there could be no possible end to things, not enough deaths, like a girl rubbing herself in the branches of a tree, never sufficient, never complete, always too much, like the feel of his tongue along a girl's velvet choker.

Boyle laughed to himself.

The two of them arrived late at the chapel, Boyle and Fada, out of a downpour. They came through the doors together wiping the rain out of their eyes and plucking at their trousers, new black trousers on Boyle's part, Fada's borrowed from Con and held up by a belt with an extra hole made by a nail that morning in Boyle's flat, and were met by a tall expressionless man, one of the undertakers, who looked them up and down and seemed about to block their way until Boyle chose to bless himself and Fada did the same and the man dipped his head slightly and made a fuss of looking for the right seat for them. Other than the six people at the very front, and the priest who was praying with his hands aloft, and the two elderly women kneeling at the back, the chapel was painfully empty. Having decided on where to squeeze them in with the least disruption, the undertaker indicated that they should follow him up the wide silent aisle. Boyle and Fada, drenched heads bowed, hands joined across their rain-darkened groins, walked slowly after him the space of four rows and then slid into a seat all the way to the middle where they got down on their knees, covered their faces and looked through their fingers for the moment when the under-taker would stop and turn round and realise he had walked the lonely aisle in vain.

Boyle watched the heads of the mourners over the tilled field of empty pews. Four were male, brothers maybe; one of the women wore a hat, the other had long straight black hair which fell over the back of the seat. The priest was a short man with a monk's beard and sandals under the cassock. Fada was unusually still beside him, gazing towards the altar, hypnotised, or perhaps it was the coffin on its trestles, the unimaginable body inside, the screwed-down darkness. For the first time, Boyle wanted to ask Fada about the old woman, where she came from, what sort of person she was, if she went to Mass. What was left of her, blazing for a few days in the mourners' minds, then slowly fading? Is memory all that is left behind, Boyle asked himself, fragments of moments in other people's minds, misremembered joys, warped by each person's own pain, anger? The thought made him feel sick and was worsened by the pains in his legs from the damp trousers, early rheumatism the prison doctor had told him, too long spent in damp rooms and fields at night. Sick and depressed: all the years of struggle and anguish and defeat and regret for the sake of just staying alive, enduring, just another day, dreaming of meaning and consolation. What kept her going each day, Boyle wanted to know. What kept him going, Fada, anybody? What were people looking for? They all knew that this was the eye of the needle, that nothing lasted, the silence will win. The animal driven to survive and the human reason knowing it is futile – was that it? People knew it was pointless and dwelling on it changed nothing. What did all the books in the world add up to in the face of the death of an old woman in her hall in Dublin? The great stale void sucked everything into it whether you were aware of it or not. You could laugh or put a gun in your mouth. Or in somebody else's mouth. Or you could go to work, marry the woman, bring up the kids and keep it out of your mind. Her love of life, Boyle heard the priest say and looked at Fada who was still transfixed. Was Fada another one who loved life? Did he himself love life, Boyle wondered uneasily. There were moments but they were soon lost. Lying on the ground, looking up at the girl in the tree was one of them, and already fading. The time he had seen Charlie Enright give up his own life to protect a child was another. Moments of triumph over chaos. But did he love life? Existence was tenuous, arduous, shameful, cowardly. Why did people think of it as a good thing to say about somebody? She loved life. I love life. As

173

though it is something that we are not lost in, drowning in, pretending it is necessary that we are here. Catharsis, synthesis, illumination, understanding: did they not delude people into thinking there was something else possible, a richer, passionate, exuberant way of being. Then they display your box on the altar and try to make a story out of you, a story of courage and compassion and forbearance, stamp your name on it and lower you into the ground. Placate the moaning soul with ritual. We used to love life, somewhere, some time, way back in the darkness, we danced and sang. Nostalgia. All those who do not love life please speak now or for ever hold your peace. Would he speak up?

I'm going outside, Boyle whispered to the gaping Fada.

Why?

I can't take this.

What will I do? Fada was horrified.

Give them the poems and get out of here.

Will you do it?

I came here with you; that's enough.

Boyle slid his wet arse along to the end of the bench. As he took a last look towards the altar to check he was unnoticed, he realised he was being watched. It was the one with the long shining hair. She was too far away to see her features but her gaze held him, tore him apart like the priest was doing to the Eucharist behind her. The void he had been feeling a few moments earlier seemed to have its source in her face, no, its refutation. A huge rage echoed through his body. He was trapped, surrounded, helicopters circling him, spotlights. Was she smiling? He wanted to separate himself from her gaze, detach himself, but he was afraid there was nothing outside of it, absolutely nothing, not even madness. Seconds went by like open graves under him. Was she smiling or scowling? What did she want? His body, his entire history hardened into a moment, no. He was being broken up into a golden goblet. Then he was feet above himself in the pews, looking down at himself, a vegetable man planted in the

174

wooden rills. Then he was looking out of the window from his cell at the crows on the football pitch and turning round suddenly, instinctively, seeing her behind him. Did she know him? Don't you know me? He couldn't move. What was happening? His heart was frantic, pursued.

She let him go, dropped him, turned away, back to the altar. Astonished, Boyle looked across at Fada and saw the blind man's grin on him.

Outside in the porch he smoked a fag, pacing up and down, for all the world a man facing an urgent decision. What was the question, the stake, what was the substance of it? The rain had stopped. Dead leaves blew around but it wasn't autumn. A bleak sky and leaves and the Daimler hearse parked at the bottom of the steps. What was the point of all these things? He considered taking a walk until the service was over but there was no sign of anyone on the streets, it seemed too lonely, the image of himself walking the soaked streets. No, there were too many things he would have to look at: windows, lamp-posts, more sky, fucken cars, bits of pavement, grass, front doors, sky, seagulls, too many things. He was full up. He was famished.

Something had happened in the chapel. Like somebody had pointed him out in a crowd and accused him of being a coward or a grass. But it was merely a woman turning round to look at the chapel and catching his eye, and smiling maybe. It was entirely arbitrary, chance. Did she know him? Or thought he was somebody else? Why did he think she was smiling; she was too far away? He thought he should just go home, walk off. Nothing was stopping him.

The priest came out first, then the coffin on the shoulders of some of the men from the front seat. At the top of the steps the undertakers took over. Boyle stood off to the side and watched her. She was tall, long limbs; she stood alone, arms folded tightly around herself, slightly stooped from the waist. She was wearing a kind of shawl, a black shiny dress and black biker boots. The wind battered her. She was cold. She stood apart; she preferred it that way. No, it was just a woman, in her thirties. Until she looked at him again and there wasn't enough room or space left in him for anything else. He thought he was going to throw up, spew or cry. She had a crooked smile that enraged him – he couldn't fight against it, no, the words were wrong. It was a place without words when she looked at him. Words were rusty and blunt. She stood at the top of the steps in the wind and showed him her crooked smile. Then behind her he saw Fada, scratching himself, hopping from foot to foot, trying to find the courage to approach her with the poems.

No, Boyle said.

He shouted the word and this time the people really did stop and stare at him. Fada jumped back against a pillar in a panic.

The woman scraped the hair away from her face, twice, three times. Her expression was quizzical, but not stern. He took a step towards her and stopped, sick with some kind of fear. Then he stepped back to where he was. Someone called her name. Eleanor. The place she left when she descended the steps was lonelier than any prison cell or any stage.

I was going to do it, Fada was saying to him. Why did you stop me?

Calm fucken down, Boyle said.

Are we going to the grave?

Boyle couldn't decide. The coffin was loaded now and the cars ready.

I'll ask one of them which cemetery it is, Fada said.

No leave it. Give me the poems.

Why?

Give me them. I'll sort it out.

Who do you think the woman is? I saw you looking at her. She gave a reading. You missed it. She was funny. She kept making mistakes but it didn't faze her. It was like she was giggling to herself. There's something funny about her.

They watched her hold her hair and climb into another car.

Just give me the poems.

You sure?

Boyle pocketed the envelope. They watched the flower-capped cars drive off. A woman with a wonky smile. Boyle and Fada were alone on the steps with the wind.

What do you want to do now then? You feeling all right?

Boyle took a taxi to the house the next day in search of her. He had managed to get the address from Fada by asking questions about the old woman, hinting that he might just put the poems in the post. Eleanor might not be there but it was the only move he could think to make. He didn't want Fada to know he was going, he was clear about that, although he wasn't sure why, lack of trust maybe, or a fear of losing control, or possessiveness already borne in him. The two of them spent the day after the funeral in the Two Mists, and then the evening. Boyle wasn't good company; he ended up at the bar by himself while Fada chatted up some tourists. He left the pub without a word to anyone and walked home. He was exhausted. He got straight into bed.

It was a fine morning. He knocked on the door and she answered.

Eleanor, he said.

Smiling, she nodded and held the door open for him.

She was alone in the house. He sat on the sofa and she went out into the scullery to make some tea. A coal fire was set in the grate behind an old buckled guard. There were ornaments along the tiled shelf above it, some photographs. Opposite him was a window out to a small backyard and plants in big pots. The carpet was like one in an old pub. Boyle had no idea what he was going to say; he couldn't believe what he was doing; he had never acted like this in his life. It was a new side to him he was delighted to discover. He was a man without a name. I don't care who I am, he announced serenely to himself at regular intervals. The worst that could happen was she would tell him to leave.

She came back in carrying a tray which she put down on the table by the window. There was only one cup and saucer on it.

I saw you at the funeral yesterday didn't I?

Did you? she said, smiling, blinking. Her accent was almost English.

I was . . . Boyle began and then stopped. They sat in silence until she poured the tea.

You not having one? I suppose you're tea-ed out over the last few days.

I don't drink tea, she said. Never liked it.

She sat in a chair opposite him, her hands clasped on her lap, looking directly at him. Her long arms were bare. She wore a plain black T-shirt and jeans. She smiled with her lips covering her teeth. Her eyes were blank, somewhere between grey and blue. He supposed the blankness had something to do with grief, crying, remembering.

You don't know me, he said and they both laughed.

You're funny, she said.

Am I? Not many people have said that now. But I feel funny sitting here.

Why? she said, gently.

Boyle shrugged. Eleanor shrugged in response and the question was soon forgotten by her.

My name's Noel, he said.

She nodded. She wasn't going to ask him what he was doing there.

I knew your . . . he stopped.

Eleanor did not offer any help.

Your mother?

Eleanor shook her head like a young girl playing a guessing game.

Your granny?

Yes, she said.

Do you live in Dublin?

Again she shook her head. Boyle understood that if he

didn't ask she would not feel the need to tell him. He decided not to ask, with half a thought of playing her at her own game, if it was a game.

So how are you keeping? he said. Did you have to travel far to come back?

I'm fine, she said. It's nice to be back. I haven't been back in a long time, she added and her eyes widened. Boyle thought she was trying not to laugh all the time. He had a grin on his own face that wouldn't shift.

Somewhere in England is it? London?

She nodded, her smile broadening. She had long lips and a strong face that could easily be elegant. But there seemed to be too much going on in her mind for elegance, something that was continually making her laugh.

I definitely saw you yesterday at the funeral, he tried again. And I wanted to call round and say hello. You see I have something of your granny's that you might like. It's a long story.

He took out the package and handed it to her. Eleanor sat back and emptied the pages on to her lap.

They're poems Boyle said. Somebody wrote them to your granny I think. A long time ago.

She started reading. Boyle watched her closely, no, in amazement. It was as if he weren't there suddenly. She was going to read every page and he could stay or go as he wanted. She didn't want an explanation either.

She read slowly, finishing one and starting another, licking her fingertips sometimes.

It's a long story but . . . his voice trailed off again. She sucked in her bottom lip as she read. The scale of her, the lengthy limbs, even sitting down, the strong knees, caused all types of doubt in him and yet he continued smiling, gazing. It was absurd and ridiculous and there was nothing else he ever wanted to do. He could laugh away anything.

Can I smoke do you think?

She nodded.

He thought about nothing for the hour it took her to read the poems. She read some twice. When she was done she folded the paper and replaced them back in the envelope which she then offered back to him.

No, you keep them, he said.

Thanks, she said.

Can I ask you something?

She nodded.

He didn't know what it was he wanted to know. Eventually he shook his head.

There's something I want to ask you but I don't know what it is. Did you ever have that feeling? Ever since I saw you yesterday? Am I making any sense?

She shrugged and laughed along with him.

They both looked into the fireplace.

I did see you yesterday, he heard her say. You were at the back of the church. I looked around. I thought I heard her voice. My grandmother's.

Boyle was afraid to take his eyes from the fireplace. Under the hill of coals he could see the screwed-up newspaper. He had been right; she had noticed him in the chapel. His heart was trying to digest some new kind of energy. Sweat came out under his arms, under his beard.

Both of them staring into the fireplace.

I wanted to . . . Boyle said and the words died again. He had nothing to say.

Now he willed himself and looked at her and she met his eyes at the same time, her whimsical and solitary gaze out from under her clear brow, and that strange ambiguous smile, either of knowing too much or too little, of having had her fill of life already or never having hoped.

Boyle was shaking. Then she did something. She put out her hand towards him and he took it, sliding his fingers between hers. Then he brought it to his mouth and kissed the back of her hand.

Boyle was up with the sun the next morning. He sat at his table, under the photo of the death mask, and wrote the essay on Sartre in one bout. He would type it up later at the university but it was done. He didn't know what it was about exactly; about living, thinking, about freedom, about God, about trying to write an essay. He thought it was good, confusing but real. It was what he wanted to say. And now that it was done he had to get ready to meet her – Eleanor. They were going to spend the day together. She said that she hadn't wandered about Dublin in years. He was meeting her at the gates of St Stephen's Green at midday. The weather for the day was already looking good, no clouds, no wind.

What was happening to him? It had already happened; it was too late and he wanted to laugh and laugh. The night before he had tried to explain it to Victor. That he couldn't stop thinking about her, the scuppered smile, the empty amused eyes. Victor told him he was in love. Boyle noted the absence of ridicule in himself, that he didn't disparage the words. He understood why people longed to use words like those. He was exuberant, thrilled, privileged, mad. He wanted to give himself away. With this feeling in him, a man could walk the streets without a home or food and keep the smile on his face.

He had got down on his knees between her long legs and kissed her. Then she put his head against her chest and they stayed that way until his knees went numb. The pins and needles attacked him. She had to help him back up on his feet; he couldn't walk, his legs folded under him. Their laughter was unashamed in the dead woman's house.

Boyle took a shower and put on his best clothes, a pair of

cotton trousers and a burgundy short-sleeved shirt. He had to get out of the flat. It was only nine o'clock; hours to get through before lunchtime. He set out on another long walk, over into the park and down towards the river and the bridge where he stopped beside the shrivelled wreath to the dead woman. The purple water had forgotten her already. The sun was on his back. He hadn't looked at a newspaper in a few days but there was nothing about her on the radio. He shut his eyes with some intention of saying a prayer for her but all he could do was offer her some of the warmth and excitement that were in his heart.

He followed the river into the city centre. It was going to be a warm day. His face was already itching in the heat; maybe he should go for a trim, or even have the beard shaved off altogether. He might duck into a barber's if the whim took him; anything was possible. Although it was still early, the streets were lively, that word bustling. He drifted around, Wicklow Street, Westmoreland Street, Nassau Street, South Great George's Street. The pubs weren't open yet. A man was hosing down the inside of a van out the front of a butcher's. Girls smoking outside a hairdresser's, the first coffee of the day. The sky was high, tantalising like a warm sea in the distance. The seagulls complaining, always the lamenting seagulls over Dublin, the lonely echoing accusations from above the narrow streets, adherents of a hardline sect. Lest we forget. Summoning his courage, Boyle stopped outside a café, a place he had never dared go into before at the edge of a covered market. The walls were layered heavily with posters for gigs and films. He sat at a big wooden table with a rake of people who all looked like they had been out on the tear the night before. Through the window young foreign ones were having piercings done.

He sipped at a coffee, and smoked, and warned himself to be careful. Eleanor was only visiting; she had another life elsewhere. When was the last time he had felt this kind of excitement about someone? His mind had always been on other things. He was entering new territory, breaking down walls in himself. That was the thing he had to hold on to; it was enough just to feel something for a change. It was proof he had it in him, the capacity.

As he was sitting there, Con came in with a girl, a new one. They had obviously just got out of bed together. Con sat down with him for a few minutes and they talked about Fada, then about Fiacra who had been kicked out by his girlfriend.

Boyle was at St Stephen's Green an hour later. He walked the paths, under the trees, over the footbridges and round the lakes. He stopped beside a man with his child who were feeding bread to the swans and ducks. The man spoke about the child as though Boyle had one himself. He sat on a bench and watched three winos having a laugh together. As the time approached, he began to worry about what he would talk about with Eleanor, how they would fill an afternoon together, whether he could make her laugh. Women liked that in a man he had heard, a sense of humour. He tried to sort through some topics in his mind – childhood, books, London – and then gave up. The city would feed them. They would talk about what they saw. No, don't go near the past, he warned himself. Try to keep the talk light. Be confident, optimistic. He wouldn't get moody or angry. He wouldn't try to tell her everything.

There she was, waiting at the crossing, a head above most of the women, smiling plaintively.

They went down Dawson Street, past Trinity and across the river to O' Connell Street. Boyle found that the pavements were too crowded for much conversation to develop. Then Eleanor happened to mention she had once lived in Drumcondra. Boyle asked if she wanted to go and have a look at the area again. Eleanor shrugged: If you want, she said. So they passed the statue of Larkin with his arms spread to the workers and under the portico of the GPO to the Parnell monument. He took her into the Garden of Remembrance for a break from the noise of the street. The birds of freedom broke free at the far end of the shallow tomb of water. Eleanor closed her eyes, unimpressed, no, simply uninterested. A young junkie lad came up, trembling, drooling and asked for some money. Boyle rolled a fag for him. Eleanor kept her eyes shut through that as well. To get her attention, he mentioned the university, that he was a student there. She said she had never been inside the gates.

And you a Dublin girl?

She shrugged. There was never any occasion to.

Do you want to have a look?

If you want, she said. I really don't care what we do.

What do you care about?

She stretched out her long legs. A simple pale blue skirt to above her knees, silk maybe. Sandals on her feet. She took out sunglasses and put them on. His question was forgotten, ignored. She was right; it was fucken stupid. He was being too serious. The way to get to know a woman wasn't to interrogate her about what she thought was important. The fact that she was walking around the city with him was her answer to every house-bound philosopher. Nevertheless, on he went with the questions he swore not to ask. What was her life like in London? Had Dublin changed much since she'd been away? What did she do?

I've done lots of different things, she sighed. What does it matter? It's work. I don't want to talk about it really. I don't want to spend my time thinking about work.

Again she was right.

I'm sorry. I'm just trying to get to know you. I'm floundering.

She took his hand as they went into Trinity.

What about the Book of Kells? Have you ever seen it?

She shook her head – was it proudly? No, freely, like she was enjoying it, the not knowing, or maybe the swing of her hair.

He told her about it as they stood in the queue with Americans mainly. It's one of the oldest books in the world.

The monks used their own blood to illustrate it. Hitler had wanted it, like the Spear of Destiny.

She smiled at him hazily while he spoke.

We don't have to see it if you don't want.

No it's ok, she said. Why not?

He wanted to kiss her; it would take away the nerves.

That's the library over there, he pointed to the row of windows. At the same time he saw the Dove coming out of the arts building: he had not even considered the possibility of running into her. She stopped when she saw him but he threw himself into another speel about the Book of Kells and some of the intellectual tramp characters that hung around the university, anything at all until the danger was passed. The Dove had gone on her way. Students were eating sandwiches around the grass square.

Are you hungry? We could go and get something to eat and come back later.

She nodded, too eagerly he thought.

You should have said if you didn't want to go in, Boyle told her.

You decide, she said.

They walked around in the lunchtime crowds and the heat in search of a café. Nowhere seemed right for them. He suggested a quiet pub but on the way he came up with the idea of a picnic. They could sit on the grass in Merrion Square. Eleanor agreed.

As they ate he told her the full story of the lost poems. He found himself talking a lot to her about Fada. It was one thing he could talk about without needing her help. He began to find a faint annoyance in himself against her that she didn't seem to be making much of an effort. It hadn't escaped his attention either that she seemed passive, no, indifferent, ready to do one thing and then switch to another. He was the one who was struggling to keep all the talk going. She didn't put a single question to him about himself.

Eventually he couldn't keep it to himself any longer.

Well what is it you want to talk about? she asked him.

It's just you're very quiet.

Am I? Is that wrong?

No, he said knowing he was making a mess of it.

I'm happy, she said.

So am I.

Well there you are then.

You haven't asked me a single question.

You've mentioned that.

You don't seem . . .

Even when he left a sentence unfinished she didn't enquire or push him. She kicked off her sandals and lay back on the grass. Boyle sat above her, his shadow blocking the sun from her face. Why couldn't he just keep his mouth shut? He lay down beside her on his stomach and touched her hair.

I'm sorry, he said.

Eleanor opened her eyes slightly and put her finger on his lips.

From there it got better, he thought. Hand in hand, they walked up past the government buildings to Baggot Street and turned left in the quieter direction towards the canal. They stopped to watch the police divers in the water at the bridge. Eleanor started to tell him a story about a storm when she was a child and how her father had taken her to see the damage, the broken trees fallen into the canal. She had never forgotten it, she said. Boyle fought with all his strength to resist asking where he was now, and her mother. She would tell him if she wanted, he repeated to himself. They took the canal path as far as Rathmines. The sun was hot, the light itself. Eleanor put on her sunglasses again. Boyle was tired; he was flagging. Then he had an idea. He took her towards Grafton Street.

Fada was on the street, performing for a middle-aged couple. The woman had laid her head on her man's shoulder while his hand was pushed into her back pocket. Fada held the woman's hand.

True tidings she revealed, most forlorn, tidings of one returning by royal right, tidings of the crew ruined who drove him out, and tidings I keep from my poem for sheer fear . . .

Boyle waved to Tanya who made an impressed face to show her estimation of Eleanor. They waited for Fada to finish; Eleanor seemed interested. As soon as he saw the look of horror on Fada's face, Boyle realised he could have played a good joke, and lamented his own lack of imagination. He could have made Eleanor pretend that she was angry about the poems, that her brothers would be coming to see him.

Fada wiped his hands on his trousers. He was sweating all over him.

This is Eleanor, Doreen's granddaughter.

Fada took a small step back from them. He was about to bolt, looking around him wildly.

Was it me? Fada asked. Did I do it?

Boyle took pity: It's ok, he said and put his arm round Eleanor's hips. Fada transformed in front of them, from cowering into snide lechery.

Each man kills the thing he loves my dark Rosaleen. Some love too little and some too strong, some sell and others buy, my dark Rosaleen, do not sigh do not weep, oh there was lightning in my blood, I lost the battle of the belly. See the darkness shining in the brightness that the brightness can't comprehend.

Fada put his face close to hers, almost lip to lip and said: I gave a love that I can't conceal to her hooded hair, her shy intent, my cloud-hid love for her body bright, her languid laugh, her timid hand. Alas it is a fearful thing to feel another's guilt. The vilest deeds like poison weeds bloom well in prison air, it is only what is good in man that wastes and withers there. O the grip, O the grip of irregular fields. O try to love me still a moment's space for –

Ok, she gets the picture, Boyle said and pushed himself

187

between them. Fada was panting, laughing, hopping, spilling out more words. Eleanor stood motionless, her hand still in the air where Fada had left it.

Enough. Boyle had to raise his voice. Quit it now.

Fada snarled back at him like a dog.

Boyle pushed him, both hands into that weak chest, and Fada fell backwards over the sandwich board; he lay on the ground, wriggling his arms and legs in the air, ranting on to himself. Tanya ran to him.

He gets carried away, Boyle was saying to Eleanor later. He can't stop himself. I don't even know what I'm doing hanging around with him. It just happened. It's one thing after another with him.

They were in a café.

I liked him, Eleanor said.

Did you?

She nodded, looking away, past him, into something else.

What are you thinking?

Nothing, she said.

I shouldn't have pushed him. But did you see that look on his face? There are just times when you have to stop him.

He reminds me of a friend of mine, she said then.

Boyle showed that he was curious to hear more. Even so he had to ask who she was talking about.

He reminds me of somebody that's all, she said. Maybe you should go back to see if he's all right.

Boyle was angry enough at himself for showing his temper on a first day out with a girl. He couldn't shake that vicious snarl out of his mind.

Forget about it, he said.

I have to go soon anyway. Stuff to do.

Boyle looked at her and asked what he needed to know: How long are you staying?

She shrugged, smiling at him, her bottom lip folded in over her teeth. The smile either meant I know you want me to stay longer and I'm thinking about it or it meant Don't pressure me – I have to go or it meant Ask me and anything might happen.

Before he could decide she took hold of his hand.

Maybe we could see each other later. Tonight. I could come round to your place.

Boyle's first thought was she was only saying this to escape from the situation; he would be pacing the flat all night and she wouldn't arrive. He wanted to say something to show he could see through her but he couldn't find the words. He was no good at talking to women, he decided.

He shrugged. Sounds great, he said, trying to be casual.

He wrote down his address on a napkin and watched her leaving the café. She stopped in the doorway and blew him a kiss. There wasn't even any sky behind her or background, only her hair-cloaked face, the confusing shyness, or a clandestine cheek, and seagulls fighting.

Boyle was reading when there was a quick harsh buzzer noise and the book flew out of his hands. Nearly a minute must have been lost to the panic before he realised it was somebody pressing his bell on the street door. No one had ever called for him at the front door before. Without turning on the light, he went down the stairs, slowly, as quietly as he could. It might not be her, he was telling himself. These were the moments when you could be taken unawares – expecting too much, assuming things, hoping, and suddenly it's too late.

He stood in the hall and listened. The dark smelled of damp and stale heat. He heard a bus gearing up away from the stop, children shouting. Hard-soled shoes scuffed the step, boots maybe, changing position. Still no way of knowing who it was. He let the silence grow like it might wash away what was unwelcome, counted his breaths. Why was he being so careful? This was the paranoia again. He told himself to open the door but did nothing. He listened. The children again, on bikes. A lone seagull. Maybe it was a mistake or the kids playing about. A sudden storm of muffled noise sent him back from the door in fright; bracelets tinkling, shoe soles on concrete. Somebody cleared their throat – was it irritably? – and the buzzer hissed up in his room like a patient calling for help.

It was her.

How many times would she ring before she gave up?

Freedom always smelled rotten, gone-off. All the waiting had turned her arrival into an event, an adventure that he was at the beginning of and as he stood there he began to feel the end of it somewhere in the future, its death. He was paralysed by the enormity of opening that door, the futility of it, the necessity.

She sighed.

He heard the boots reach the top step, wait, then go down.

Then he threw himself at the door, pulled it open, and called her name.

Eleanor.

She came back up the steps silently, no, unhurriedly, or regretfully, eyes lowered. Boyle led her up the stairs to his flat, offered her some wine – he had spent an hour trying to choose a bottle of red in the supermarket. She stood in the middle of the floor; she didn't even look around her. It was like she had been there a thousand times before. Or she expected never to be there again. Less seen, less remorse.

Did you get everything done? Your stuff?

Yes was all she said.

So wine then?

She shook her head like a child, enjoying the whip of her hair across her face, the jangle of earrings. She was wearing a longer skirt, green, with a design on it.

I've had enough, she said with a giggle.

Did you have visitors?

She used the space for her reply to come up close to him. The face made that smile again, full or empty. Then she raised her hands, long white hands, and placed them flat against his face, his beard. Watching her own hands quizzically, amused, she moved them down along his neck to the top button of his shirt. She whispered something soothing to the button as she opened it.

No wine then? Boyle said.

She closed her eyes now. The next button was undone. The smile was there, like somebody falling into a dream.

They lay on the bed, kissing for a long time, gentle ones only she made it clear by turning her face away whenever he pressed too hard. Bit by bit, Boyle pulled up her top and her skirt over her hips which were broader than his own and

191

powerful. Sometimes she would bury her face in his neck and they would hold each other for minutes on end, him kissing her hair. She didn't make a sound. In the dark bedroom he couldn't tell whether her eyes were open or closed. Once she put her hand on top of his and guided it from her face down across her shoulders to her belly. Boyle released one of her breasts from her bra and took her long nipple between his teeth.

Everything happened at the slowest possible pace, as though they had already been making love all night. They were sweating. Hours might have gone by when she slid down towards his groin and loosened his belt. She kissed the tip of his cock gently again and again before she took it into her mouth and with the same slowness and gentleness set about coaxing the life out of him.

Around the same time that night, Fada was lying on the tiles of a nightclub toilet, under a pall of tissue paper. The queen was downed on the black-and-white tiles. The pawns had risen up and lustily befouled her. He had managed to wedge his head behind the base of the toilet to prevent them damaging his face. But that had been after the headbutt and the kicks that caught him as he scrambled into the cubicle on his hands and knees.

You don't know me. You've never seen me before.

It wasn't porcelain any more. What was it made of this white featherless toilet neck that he was pressing his face against, this smooth icy substance he was trying to absorb into his skin to seep downwards into his chest and guts where the pain was worst, was alive, like there was a presence down there eating him, a nest of spiders, or rats or birds, pecking and stabbing and ripping, a white sun? Yet his body was bigger than any nightclub toilet, any corridor, any drink-splashed dance floor; the pain inflated him to mystical proportions. The holy OM of the baseline trembled through the toilet bowl; the filthy water would be gently a-tremble, a-gargle in its gullet, six of them in a row.

You don't know me, said redheaded Declan Moran, youngest son of Michael and Gloria who once had lunch with a former Taoiseach, and pushed Fada from the back against the tinkling metal trough, against the fine bifurcated waterfalls trilling down the burnished slopes – and Fada was stunned by a memory when his forehead struck the metal and his balls scraped across the trough edge: of his mother in the back garden hanging out the washing, wide white luminous sheets steaming among the trees on a summer morning, oh sweet nylon transparency, and how as he watched from his bedroom window he saw the sword of the sun come down and pierce her through the head and he could see deep into her brain, into the thought-carrying blood-filled corridors, sloshing and pouring under the faces painted on the cave walls, the films projected upside down and running backwards, the furniture of their old house spinning in the ceaseless floodwater along with cars and dresses and babies and a golden chalice and peeled potatoes and as he watched in horror she turned around and waved up to him serenely and lifted her hands to the sky in humble rejoicing . . . And Moran pushed him again while Fada hurried to get his cock out of sight, grabbed him by the hair and brought his forehead down squarely on Fada's nose.

You don't know me. You've never seen me. Don't even look in my direction again, said the cured, much matured, oh hasn't he blossomed after that awful adolescent episode, he's left all that behind him now and settled down into the swing of things, that's my boy Declan Moran who at the age of seventeen had been caught in his own front room with a sweet innocent from two doors along, the Mac Stiofains' no less, whom he had stripped and tied to a chair, and wearing his mother's Sunday morning lingerie, black silk purchased in Madrid, was whipping the child with the finest cuts of the rose bush from the back garden where he had also dug a shallow pit in which were found the family pets, two servile spaniels, and who thus detected was locked forthwith into a room with another young man who liked to draw many-headed swan-like shapes on the walls in excrement not necessarily his own, who heard voices that told him people weren't what they appeared to be and who had once attacked his mother with a coarse-whiskered sweeping brush in her own back garden while she was happily pegging out the sheets one fine summer morning. Bless me, she had told the doctor, I thought he was going to brush me all the way into the sea or (and she blessed herself here) up into the hills, a nuanced distinction, a personal differentiation that had caused such a revulsion in the young man's – Fada's – soul that he had fainted on the spot.

You don't know me, insisted the shameless amoral scoundrel as he kicked and spat at the spastic shape of Fada on the tiles whining for mercy. And after the nights they had shared together too under the stiff heavy sheets, sharing kisses and cocks, medication and fantasies, and the urine-scented breath of boredom – all of it seemed to mean nothing now as Fada slid and crawled towards the cubicle.

You've never seen me before you disgusting cunt. Don't ever come up to me again. You don't exist at all. You're slime. If you walk in somewhere and see me, you walk straight back out again. If you see me dying on the street you don't stop.

And Fada was screaming back, Ok I don't exist. Stop hurting me.

He had been upstairs in the club with Tanya and spotted redhaired Declan Moran with a girl on the edge of the dance floor. The urge took him over, he didn't think, he was going to say hello and that was all, smile, good to see you, a cheeky wink, leave it at that, it was well intentioned. Fada approached the couple with snaking limbs across the floor, danced around them once and bowed. Moran smiled and shrugged his big shoulders to the girl.

How's it going? How's the form? Having a good night?

Do I know you? Moran said, rolling his eyes for the girl.

Do you not know me?

I've never seen you before. What's your name?

Don't worry about that, Fada said. If you don't know me then you don't know me. No worries, and he slid back out among the dancers.

Tanya told him to stop bothering people. They had started drinking in the afternoon after Fada had been caught finally by Jess; it had been a busy day, a crowd around him for a couple of hours, non-stop performance, and there she was among a crowd of Italian teenagers, a ring in her nose, a new tattoo on her right shoulder, some abstract Mayan design, but otherwise exactly the same. Once she was sure he had seen her, she waited off to the side, sitting down in the street with her back against the wall of a bank, as if it were some field she had discovered where the hawthorn grew in a magical circle, and took out a book and started reading, and the crowds rolling past her.

Fada decided to get it over with. The old woman and the poems saga had reached its romantic resolution with Boyle and the dusky granddaughter with the deep-set eyes and now it was only Jess left and he could get back into the harmless circus of his days, find himself a room, and everything would be right again. Taking the sandwich board with him as a kind of shield, he went over and stood beside her. She put her head back against the wall and looked up at him.

I'm busy, he said. You can see it's a good day. I can't go anywhere.

I'll come back later shall I?

What do you want Jess? Is there something in particular?

I had a dream, she said. It told me to come and see you. That you needed help.

Fada tried to contain himself. Well I don't, he said. Things are going fine for me.

Jess shook her head even before he had finished.

Stop that, he told her. Just stop it right there. I don't need your help. In fact everything is just starting to work out. And I'm in love.

She stood up now beside him. Fada was shaking.

You called me, she said. In the dream. A man with a long beard spoke to me and pointed with a stick and said your name.

Jess don't wreck my head again, Fada said. I'm fine. I don't need you. What else do you want me to say? Do yourself a favour and believe me. Go and save somebody else.

Jess nodded. I see, she said. I should have expected this. Resistance.

Stop talking shite, Fada shouted at her. You're like white noise in my head.

Jess stayed calm; she put her book into her bag. I'm going to be around for a while, she said. If you want to talk, well –

I won't, he said. I'm fine. Don't poison my day with that shite. I'm fine. Thanks for coming to see me but I'm all right.

Well I'll be around for a while, she said again.

Fada stared after her as she passed into the throng. The years of silence between them were nothing to her. She would never let him escape. In ten years' time he would come out of his house and find her sitting on the front doorstep. Hello, you were calling me weren't you? The rain running down her face. She thought she was some kind of witch, some wicca slut, blood bonds and crystals in her bag to ward off the bad spirits. But what if she was right? The dread made him want to vomit. Something was sucked out of the world at that moment, the street seemed to fade and flatten to one flimsy dimension; the bricks were a smear of burned sienna, the glass was water, the faces were identical and bland, fragile, cartoons, bubbles, stains in the air, he could put his hand through them like smoke.

He ran across the street to Tanya and put his arms around her. Help me, he said.

Help me, he said again on the toilet floor. How many times in the last few weeks had he cried out for help? Declan Moran had made his point, the dance was over, the past kicked back into place behind the toilet. Now there was another person there.

Help me. Fada lifted up his hand blindly. One of his fingers must be broken; he screamed when another hand took hold of his.

Did I hurt you? Maybe it's broken. Is it this one? No. This one? No. Yes?

Fada screamed.

That's the culprit.

The finger was squeezed again.

What did I do on you? he moaned and opened one bloody heavy eye. For an answer a boot went in between his legs, making him retch.

Do you not remember me? Because I remember you. And your fucken nordy mate. Remember a party along the quays? Is he up there? Is he?

Fada said no and took another kick.

No I swear.

Well you give him this for me and tell him we're not done yet.

Fada braced himself for another kick but instead came a flow of piss into his face and then down his body.

You're lucky I don't shit all over you. Tell your Nordy mate to watch his back. Here's some bog roll to wipe your runny nose prick.

Fada lay quiet under the festoons of tissue paper. When some guy asked him if he needed a hand up he didn't reply. He was tired, extinguished. Why get up again? He was a clown. Eventually they'd come with a stretcher – there now was a mesmeric word of soothing and succour. The stretcher. Stretcher him out under the reeling lights. The girls kneeling in the dancing pit. The crowds on the street stare after the ambulance and bless themselves or rip off their clothes and fall upon one another with screams and obscene truths. The horn of plenty has run dry. They look at the night sky and realise it is wrong and so are the moon and the stars, all wrong, the bars, the river, the rabid eyes of their lover . . . where was Tanya? He had kissed her earlier and felt the hunger in her. A tight hard aggressive mouth. She used her teeth in a kiss. She had talked him through that flip-out after seeing Jess. She was the only one who knew him, how weak and scared he was, the coward he was, the depths he would go to to find the light. Darkness shining in the brightness. What light? What darkness? He danced and sang and found nothing. Where was the wisdom now under this corpse cloth of toilet roll? Where were the nights when he had shouted,

We don't care what we find? Boyle thought he had found something; he could see it in his hairy face. Prison beard. So that they all look the same. Confuse the Guards for the big breakout. See him now moaning in the damp air on the old woman's bed, locked between the long thighs of that strange one with the lank hair and haunted face, a chastised smile, like somebody who has been humbled, punished, who sees the world as empty for ever after. What did she want from Boyle the broken man? Mister Silence. Mr High-Security Nausea. The entertainment's over. The burlesque has lost its way. Fada the randy clown, the prurient pierrot, the sticky-groined stooge is curled up like a trampled turd on the toilet floor. Close the curtains and bring on the stretcher. They would all forget him in a week. Who would come to visit him in the hospital, bring him books, wheel him around the gardens? Con, Fiacra, Boyle? Lisa-Ann? In about a week's time he'd open his eyes and stretch his legs in his own fresh bed and yawn and boy-hipped Tanya would be sitting in the chair with a bunch of flowers. Sleep was what he wanted, weeks of it, dreamless sleep. A period of recuperation, food provided, no money worries. And a lonely dirty-minded nurse, plump yet prim, a country girl, glasses, raw and hairy, to relieve him now and again . . . yes, glasses she has to wipe clean when they're finished on the corner of the pillow, yes, with a touch of anger, fear of what she's done again, her fattening arse from hours of crisps and chocolate eating on buses home to the stony west at the weekends, dreaming of her sophisticated urban bedridden lover, his tender-throated poems, and all the things he asks her to do, yes, more, yes, harder, grip me harder, yes, yes . . .

She left before it was light and came back while Boyle was still in bed, took off her clothes quickly, no, it was as if she were throwing them away, even her underwear, like they were rags, and got back in beside him. They slept for a few hours more, Boyle curled up behind her, his bony knees sheltering behind hers, his arm like a lonely dead-end path across the mountain of her hips. The kissing started again slowly, time and time again, as though they kept reaching an unbearable impasse, a border that was impossible and dangerous to cross, and they would fall apart back on their separate pillows, gasping, awed by a sublime and unnamed courage.

Eleanor pulled him on top and put his cock inside her with her long pale hand. She closed her eyes.

Boyle saw her face more clearly than he had ever seen anything. It was almost excruciating, her existence, horrible then shockingly beautiful. Her hair, her nostrils, her ears filled him with questions that had no other answer than to thrust deeper into her, to dig down into the guts of her, until eventually he lost control of himself, and thought he saw a light, a door, some place where he had to get to, and it was all collapsing behind him, there was no going back, time, centuries of time, folding up behind him, crumbling, he had to hurry, get to the light . . .

But he came before he made it and lay down with his head on her breast. He heard gulls high in the sky. He remembered the chair down in the yard and laughed at it, fondly, sentimentally, now that it was harmless. It could have been raining or the city had gone up in flames.

Your beard. My face hurts, he heard her saying.

Tell me to shave.

Eleanor shook her head.

Tell me and I will, he said, delighted to hear himself saying these things. You could tell me to do anything.

She pulled his head close to her chest again and he wasn't sure whether she meant to stop talking or she was saying she understood.

That's what it was; he wanted to say things to her. It made no difference if they were exaggerations or pathetic. There were phrases he couldn't keep to himself: I've been waiting on you was one. He would order himself to be quiet and then a moment later hear himself telling her. He was disobeying himself, as if there were a child in him, running rings around the law, a cheeky bright-eyed trickster.

No, it wasn't saying; singing was the word. He would be lying still, content and then something would come surging up in him and come out of his mouth in the shape of: That first time I saw you, I'll never forget it; or You are so beautiful; or I don't want to move from this bed ever again. Somehow the words had nothing really to do with what he was feeling; he was singing the words of a song and making up the words, an old song that he had simply picked up without anyone ever teaching him, an air, a ballad.

But Eleanor did not speak. She simply pulled him closer to her.

He had never stood before an audience and sung a song, even during the mammoth music sessions inside, not even at Christmas time. It now seemed a terrible impoverishment, a sign of malaise that people should have taken more seriously. A man who will not sing is sick in his soul, Boyle concluded to himself and touched her nipple with his tongue. He would have gladly now stood in front of a room of strangers and sung to her.

He asked, Can you sing?

She said no and laughed at the idea.

Was there singing at the wake?

Never in our family, she said.

Tell me about them.

Not now. I don't want to.

You put everything off.

Do I?

You're afraid of something. Are you afraid of me?

No, she said and it didn't matter to him whether he believed her. It was all part of the song. He had been taking words too seriously for far too long. Freedom. Uprising. Pogroms. Jury. Revolution. History. He tried to nail the words on to big plaques and plant them in the world, big signposts: Imperialists Beware. Collaborators Will Be Prosecuted. Do Not Walk On The People. They were only words. He put too much pressure on them, demanding truth and honesty and a well-ordered path into the future. Tanks had taught him to dream of tanks. Guns were in love with bigger guns. He had to leave all that behind him, think in a different language, come up with new words. Sing himself clean. And sometimes the song was a lament or a call to arms or an expression of love and it would keep changing always and there were a million other songs being sung at the same time and it didn't matter if they were all being heard somewhere or they faded out for there would be another to pick up the melody and another. Change was the hardest thing.

Each stroke of his hand along the length of her was worth a shelf of books. Then he would meet her unguessable smile and it would be all wiped out and he had to start again. When he put his hand on her breast or inhaled the smell of her between her legs he fell back further into himself than the day he stood in the court whose jurisdiction he refused to recognise and listened for the verdict.

They got up towards the end of the afternoon. Both of them agreed they were starving but Boyle had no food in the flat to offer other than cheese and bread.

What about the chip shop?

Ok, she agreed but she couldn't decide what she wanted. I'll come with you.

Even so it was another hour before they were leaving the

flat. While Eleanor sat with her bare legs folded under her like a deer, Boyle put on one of his tapes, began to show her books, read some pieces aloud to her, told her about the landlord, and Victor downstairs, the chair in the backyard, and tearing the photograph of the death mask from the wall how he had overturned the stall . . . Eleanor sipped her tea and listened and put balm on her lips and asked nothing.

You're very quiet, he said, kneeling in front of her. I feel like I'm telling you things you already know. Like you've been in here a thousand times already.

I'm just hungry. She smiled and he thought it was with sadness.

You all right apart from that?

She said she was.

They got dressed quickly; Eleanor was ready before him, happy to go into the street without brushing her hair or a single glance in the mirror. On the stairs she said she had forgotten something. Boyle opened the door for her and watched how she found her knickers and pulled them on over her long leather boots and came out by him again without the slightest taint to her modesty.

In the chip shop Boyle discovered she was a vegetarian. Instead of bringing the chips back to the flat they hurried towards the park. Boyle was delighted with this new information about her; it seemed as important to him as if she had told him she had once been married or that she had trained to be a dancer. He questioned her about why, if there had been some incident that had put her off meat, but Eleanor insisted she couldn't really remember, it had been years ago.

They chose a bench on the main road that ran through the park lined with copper-hooded gas lamps. The sun was bleeding into the clouds. There were many people out walking: power-walking pairs of women in tracksuits, people with dogs, elderly couples, fathers with their young children on bicycles, the shadows fusing when they passed one another into momentary Rorschach shapes on the grass.

Do you miss Dublin? Boyle asked her, licking his fingers and wiping the grease off the hair around his mouth.

Not really, she said. I've been away a long time now.

Do you have any friends left here?

She shook her head and made a ball of the chip paper. He watched her take their rubbish across to a bin where she stood by herself for a while, oblivious to traffic and the ones going by, some of whom looked at her and then at him as though they were having an argument.

She sat down again. Boyle was making a cigarette; he thought about giving up on any attempt to talk to her and taking her back to the flat, and into bed again. But everything seemed to be falling, no, descending, as if every moment could be seen sinking out of sight, and him and her with it: the trees, the lamps, the ground under them, and then the next new moment after it, with all its movements and smells, and then the next, skins falling away, softly disappearing.

Boyle took her hand.

How long are you staying?

Don't, she said crossly.

I want to know.

You already know.

Do I? The day after tomorrow?

I told you.

Why are you angry?

She dropped her head on his shoulder and put her arm across his stomach.

What were the words for this? He wanted to say that it didn't feel right but what did that mean? How could it feel either right or wrong? The heart was arrogant and greedy. Eleanor had come back to Dublin to bury her granny, to stay a few days and see her family, and then she had to go back to her own life. It was neither right nor wrong; the heart concocted rights for itself that the world laughed at. Boyle imagined a court of rights for the heart where a person could make a plea that their life would be put in extreme jeopardy if their lover was allowed to depart. Who would be the judges? Or would it be a jury of ordinary people? Boyle saw himself in the dock representing himself, making an epic speech, based on utilitarian principles, that Eleanor should be prevented from leaving the country, that the store of pleasure in the world would be increased by her staying with him . . . and the tearful jury rose to its feet in applause when he was done.

Do you know what I was just thinking? he said to her, kissing her head.

I know, she said.

Boyle laughed. Do you?

You should come with me.

Boyle began to tremble; he couldn't breathe. You should come with me. He hadn't thought about that option. London. Pack his bags and go off to London with her. Leave Ireland. Cross the water to London. Live with Eleanor in London. There they were sitting side by side on the underground train.

That's what you want? he heard himself saying.

She shrugged and then gripped him tighter. His heart was pounding madly. Meanwhile all those people went about their walking, going nowhere but home in the end, to their husbands and wives, plates of food, reading stories to their children, the walls they painted themselves, the carpets, the beds they were still paying for. The lavish bloody sky had gone too far, no, overshot the mark.

He lifted her face up from his shoulder, held her so she would have to look at him. Is that what you want?

Her face was all confusion and fear and sadness and anger. He wondered what the last thing was that had made her cry: had he seen her crying at the funeral?

Yes . . . No . . . I don't know, she said.

Would you not stay here?

She shook her head.

Why not?

She gave him a look to say: Please don't ask me.

You have to talk to me, he said.

I can't. She pulled her face away from his hand.

For a brief moment he wanted to shout at her: You want me to give up everything here and run off to London with you and you won't even speak to me. I don't even bloody know who you are. I don't know a thing about you.

But it passed and vanished like every other moment they were sitting there together.

Eleanor stood up and held out her long arm. Let's walk.

I want to sit, Boyle said.

Please. Ok. I'll try to talk.

They went side by side in silence, under the trees, past the zoo, the polo grounds, the gates of the president's mansion at the crossroads opposite the gates of the American ambassador's place. At the centre of the crossroads was the miniature bronze phoenix which always annoyed Boyle because of its pathetic size, its humility, no, its servility. He wanted to ask Eleanor about it but he wasn't letting her off the hook; the longer he remained quiet the more pressure he put on her to speak.

Eventually it happened; they had already reached the Castleknock Gate and turned round again. She walked with her head down, her arms folded, stooped forward slightly so that her hair covered her face. People had to step out of her path.

So you want me to come to London to hold your hand? Boyle said, taking her arm and forcing her to stop. He had been listening to her for a long time.

No. I'm sorry. I don't know what's happening.

But I do. Sorry's no good Eleanor. That's what you accuse him of doing all the time. You're doing the bloody same thing.

No, she said. I met you. I've never done this before. I couldn't stop myself.

Just like you can't stop yourself going back to him?

I wasn't trying to hurt you. I thought you would –

What? Understand? Help?

I don't know.

Are you going to tell him when you get back?

Yes, she said. I promise. I told you. I can't go on with it.

Stay here then. Tell him from here. Phone him. Go back later.

She shook her head.

Why not?

Stop shouting at me. I've told you what you wanted.

What if I'd said yes? That I'd come with you. What would you have done then?

I wasn't thinking. I wanted to be with you. Can't that be enough?

She tried to take his hand but he threw up his arms.

You weren't going to tell me, Boyle said again. I had to force you. That's what I can't fucken believe. I'm not worth telling. I'm some sort of eejit. I had to force it out of you.

She went to walk away but he grabbed her by the arm again. He stared at her but it was only a face; there were no answers in it.

Stay here, he said, with a helpless laugh, at himself. I want you to stay here with me.

She was trying not to laugh too. Let me think, she said.

I tell you Eleanor I've tried it and it doesn't get you anywhere. Where has it got me? Into one fucken mess after another. And where's it got you in the past few years? Nowhere. Don't think, he said, amazed at himself.

She took the steps back towards him and kissed him.

I have to go, she said. Tomorrow evening.

He passed that night walking. He couldn't have said where he had been, only that he had gone northwards, along the motorways into the suburbs. He looked at nothing. The traffic roaring by him in different directions was a bitter comfort. When he got back to the house he knocked on Victor's door but it stayed shut. He went upstairs and threw himself on the bed. The blankets lay twisted under him like a dead body. He turned over and found the smell of her hair on one of the pillows, some shampoo. She wasn't the type for perfume. Even her underwear was plain, purely functional. She put colour in her hair and that was it. He saw her again carelessly pulling her knickers over her boots. But what did he know? In London she might look completely different. She could walk the streets in glamorous clothes, in hats and furs, with garter belts gripping her long hard thighs, a heaven of perfume around her. The conversation in the park was still clear in his head as though it had happened only a few minutes earlier. He doubted he had acted properly; maybe he shouldn't have pressed her; maybe he should have stopped her walking away. Did she want him to prevent her leaving?

He stayed in the bed for most of the next day. It was only the need for a smoke that moved him out from the covers. He was back out on the street before he had even smoked it. There was a fine misty rain falling but it barely managed to darken the pavement. He went downhill through the dirty terracotta rows of houses towards the river, high and muddy that day, and along its flank and the bridges into the city centre. He had a few hours to kill before work. It was too much time. A greasy futility hung in the air, like wave after wave of old curtains. People hurried about uneasily in and out of buildings; the streets weren't long enough, the shops were too small and humid, conversations trailed off without conclusion. He was sure he was seeing the same frightened faces wherever he went as if there were a small frantic coterie who had nowhere to go, who suddenly felt themselves exposed. Along Dame Street, he pushed himself towards the university gates; as usual a number of people were waiting there, leaning against the railings. It was a common meeting-place all through the day, particularly at lunchtime and around nine in the evening. Women felt safe there and the young foreigners had no difficulty finding it. Boyle stood between two girls. He would fit into the surroundings there. He was waiting on somebody like everybody else. All he had to do was occasionally lean out and look this way and that in search of the familiar face. The girl to his right, a Continental with skin like wet sand, held herself perfectly straight, gripping a small black bag. She was nervous, he thought, no other thought in her mind than who she was meeting and how the day would go for them, whether the rain would keep away. On his left was an older girl who slouched back against the railings smoking; she was plump and bored; her blond hair needed dying again but she probably couldn't afford it. Through the noise of the traffic parting fiercely into Dame Street Boyle heard her sighing frequently, sighs without any reason, purely to remind herself of her own existence. He put his head out into the street and saw a collection of people waiting in a public space, mainly women, arranged at polite distances from one another, and wondered whether any one of them was standing there like him, pretending, ashamed, hiding among the greater purposes. Just then the stylish Continental girl took off like a greyhound and threw her arms passionately around a young lad in a cheap suit, an Irish lad Boyle heard from the voice, his face pale and exhausted by some office job, hardly able to raise a smile or embrace the girl properly, merely lying against her while she chatted away and kissed him. The girl next to him put out her cigarette under an ugly shoe and blew her smoke and all the air in her joyless body exhaustively over her head and Boyle followed it with his eyes as it was caught by the wind and twisted and ripped . . . On the traffic island someone was pointing a video camera at the university gates while another one, it was two lads in those baggy military shorts, Americans, made hand gestures and gave advice. Boyle watched them come across the road when the lights changed and begin to discuss their next shot. They made up their minds to start from the blue clock, pull back to the statues and then do a pan along the people lined against the railings. Boyle saw ones change their position and turn away their faces. These two arrogant shits thought they could point their camera at the world and take it home with them back to some leafy university town in the States. Boyle went over and stood in front of them.

You point that camera at me and I'll break it over your head.

Both of them laughed.

Did you ask these people's permission?

The taller one who was a fair size seemed to realise that Boyle wasn't joking.

Come on man, it's a public place. We don't need permission.

I'm telling you that you do.

They looked at each other vacantly.

The big one said, You're not even Irish man.

Boyle held back on a response, kept his stare focused on the braver one.

Come on man. It'll only take a second. You don't have to be in it. Stand over there.

Boyle took a step nearer him. The lad was bigger than him, pony-tailed lazy health.

He said, I'm not fucken moving. You are. Do you think I like wasting my breath on you?

Ask that cop Rick, said the one holding the camera.

A Guard was giving directions to some people on the other side of the street. Boyle held the blue eyes of the big one for another moment, glaring into them, trying to make a mark there on what was only water and salt and muscle and blood. He saw only himself. He moved on.

A few minutes later he found himself on Grafton Street then took off in another direction to avoid Fada's spot. That was not the person whose face he wanted to look at, the grimace just under the yellow skin, the dead man's grin, the rolling eyes. He didn't want to walk any more, especially in that part of town where he had been strolling around with Eleanor only two days ago, holding her hand, being hard on himself for thinking she was too quiet. Not a single café or pub looked welcoming to a damp dispirited man with a thin bearded face. Finally he gave up and made his way to the call shop. While he was having a smoke at the door he spotted the same character leaning against a lamppost that he had seen before, the cement-mixer character, the new clothes, the shaved head. Boyle went inside to phone Dainty.

He had spent the night in the hospital with his son who had some kind of fever.

Is it not safe to talk? Boyle asked.

It's grand. I'm on my own. Maureen's coming round later.

But you know what I mean.

That is highly unlikely.

The phone I mean.

Jesus Christ what sort of state is your head in? Dainty shouted at him. You're a wreck. What are they doing to you down there for fuck's sake? Catch yourself on will you.

Boyle told him he had met a woman.

Big fucken deal, Dainty said. So have I.

It's a bit complicated.

I wouldn't expect any less.

She lives in London. With another man.

Dainty laughed at the other end of the phone. Boyle had a sudden flash of the flat, the old sofa with the leather arm patches, the white doors to the bedrooms, the photo under the cistern.

She wanted me to go back with her.

211

But you thought it was an MI6 set-up and . . .

Boyle tried to explain.

Dainty was adamant: Stay well clear. You're well rid. Let her go. Forget about her. Too much hassle. You take everything too seriously. You had some good sex finally. Leave it at that.

She's the first woman I've met in years, Boyle said.

And who's bloody fault is that? You'd drive anybody mad with all your moaning and paranoia. Just fucken relax and try to enjoy yourself. Tell you what: how's about I come down and we go out on the town?

Boyle said that would be great. Dainty had to make a few arrangements first and told Boyle to phone him the following week.

Hang on in there Boylo. The cavalry's arriving. But one word about people following you or strange cars or women with bugs in their bras and I'm calling for the men in the white coats myself do you hear me?

Everything's going great one minute and the next you can't remember why you were stupid enough even to bother.

That's the way it goes Boylo. Don't make things hard on yourself. And by the way the other night when I was talking to you, just forget what I said do you hear me?

I'm surprised you even remember.

Only the bad things. Give me a call in a day or two. Ok?

Boyle checked the street. The lamppost was untended. The shop was quiet other than a Romanian couple with their three children squeezed into one cubicle and a young black man with a lot of gold on him. He had forgotten to ask Dainty if he really dumped the sticks in the Foyle. Across the street next to the pub a new restaurant seemed to have opened; there was a large video screen attached to the main window that showed women in maids' outfits dancing and waiting on tables. He had brought nothing to read. There wasn't even a newspaper to be found in any of the cubicles. But time was moving quickly, almost too fast, as if it were powered by his own heartbeat whenever he thought of Eleanor and whether she would show up later at the flat. He hadn't given up on it happening. She knew he was working because in bed they had talked about their last night together, what they might do and Boyle had told her he would have to take the night off. She had another few hours to decide. But what would he do if she turned up with her suitcases still intent on going? Would it mean that he had a chance of persuading her to stay? He simply didn't know; he was useless at understanding what people wanted unless they told him outright. He didn't trust in appearances, he couldn't read them or was it the opposite and he took them too literally, at face value, too seriously as Dainty said. The thoughts went round and round to no avail. It was pointless and endless and frustrating. Maybe he should just stay out all night and forget the whole thing. He had told her what he wanted and she either disappeared for good or she stayed with him; he didn't want to play any games; he didn't know how anyway. Thesis and antithesis. Either/or. Eternal recurrence. Bad faith . . . Not so long ago he had been lying on her firm and simple breasts and thinking about songs and a limitless generosity. Now he was banging his fist on the table and making demands.

A few hours into the shift, Tanya appeared in the shop with some news about Fada. She told him about the hiding he'd been given in the club and that she had taken him to the hospital.

There's a lot of bruises and they put two of his fingers in a splint, she said. But then he wouldn't leave. He took off all his clothes. You know the way he can get? Well this was worse. He was screaming and crying. They had to sedate him, inject him. I had to promise I was responsible for him or they would have locked him up. I didn't know if I was doing the right thing. But I took him back home anyway and put him in my brother's room. He said they were after you.

Who is?

One of them was, he told me. One of them was after you.

Some student type, some kind of artist. And there was another one he used to know from the time he was in . . . hospital.

I know about that, Boyle reassured her. So one of them said he was looking for me?

Guess what the bastards did. They pissed on him.

You're fucken joking me. So where is he now?

That's what I'm trying to tell you. I'm worried sick. He climbed out of our back window and I haven't seen him since. It must have been last night some time. And the shyster took my brother's good trainers.

That's about typical. Boyle laughed.

He was talking a lot about you, mad stuff, babbling. And about swans. He's a nut sometimes.

Tanya's young confused face, the thick eyebrows, made Boyle laugh again. He wanted to give her a hug. They both smoked a cigarette at the door and swapped ideas of the places he might be.

I see him every day but I don't know much about him really, Tanya admitted. Where's he been sleeping lately?

He was in mine one night. Two nights.

But I thought you were a friend of his. And you don't know? You don't ask him like?

Boyle shook his head guiltily. Tanya said she had to go and Boyle promised he'd drop into Grafton Street the next day to see if she'd heard anything. Immediately after she'd gone, Boyle had the ugly thought that Fada was with Eleanor. He tried to push it out of his mind but something about the image of Fada knocking on Eleanor's door made sense. Eleanor would invite him in. Maybe she was alone. Fada would sit near the fire where Boyle himself had sat and watched her read through the poems. Boyle hadn't lied to her exactly but he hadn't told the full story either. What if Fada was sitting there at that very moment confessing to having murdered her granny, crying his eyes out, forcing Eleanor to come and sit beside him on the sofa, to comfort him in her arms, his head slowly, craftily making its way down her chest, his hand on her leg, whispering polluted poems into her ear?

The image was still with him like a sickness as he walked home after work and took a seat on the empty steps where he had been hoping he might see her waiting. She was vulnerable, she was desperate. She wasn't there. The road was quiet, occupied by a thin deceitful darkness. The parked cars were full of thoughts people didn't want to take to bed with them. The long tunnel of trees mocked the feeble street lights, the yellow windows. It would be unwise to go up to the flat; he would start kicking the walls, wrecking the place. He made cigarettes and smoked them and flicked the butts down the steps. The stars nursed vengeance. It was two in the morning and he couldn't leave the steps.

Big Victor's arrival brought him to his feet in applause.

You've no idea how good it is to see you Victor. Boyle hugged him.

You need a drink I think, Victor said.

I think so Victor.

They sat on the step together, knocking back vodka in toasts, and Boyle told him the story of Eleanor.

You cannot let him get away with it, Victor said.

But I'm not sure. I don't know. It's just in my head.

Victor spat down the steps and said, These things are usually true.

Not much later Boyle found himself alone on the step again with a few shots left in the bottom of the bottle. He threw one down his throat but spewed it out again. His mind went off in furious lucid tangents that left him constantly fighting for his breath. He tried to calm himself. Whatever thought came to him – the orgy night with Fada in the park, Dainty drinking cans on the sofa with some Peace Studies American student, the deer herd, Tanya's hairy eyebrows and dented silver hoops, whatever life he had left to live – all ended up back in the same image of Eleanor leading Fada up her granny's dark staircase and Fada with that simmering grin and his hand up her skirt.

Fada (a shop doorway late at night): The bastards are everywhere. Do you know what they did to me? They think they can keep me down. It's just you and me my hard little pale-faced sister. My precious pebble of delight. You're as tight as stone. I know what you dream about. Big Daddy Fada knows all your dirty secrets. What are you doing out so late? And all by yourself? Was your bed all warm and restless? The dreams are falling heavily tonight. I can smell them. Are you looking for trouble? 'Cause you've found it here baby. Come here to me. Look at the splints on my peace-making fingers. They beat me. You're a firm little thing. You're a cheeky randy little piece of stone. I saw you lying there and knew what you were after. Pick me up mister. Take me in your hands. I'm alone tonight like you. They've deserted me. Out on the streets like you. You want to look don't you? You want to see it don't you? Go on whisper it to me. Yes. I hear you; you've been waiting to say that haven't you? Look up there at the semen-splattered face of the starry heavens. That big hairy arsehole moon. Under the buttock night. Sit on me mother. Shit on my head sister. All the world a dream trapped in one of her farts. You like that kind of talk don't you little stone dreamer? It's ok. You can tell Daddy Fada all about it. Will I show it to you now? Here. What do you think of that? Look at the size of it. Come on nearer. Touch it. Rock fucken hard. I'm your big hungry man. Go on. Nearer. Rub yourself against it. You like that don't you my smooth street diamond. You're a greedy gem. Rub harder. At the tip. Harder. My filthy fossil. I'm glad I found you tonight. I'll put you in my pocket and carry you everywhere with me. I promise. On special nights like this I'll take you out. Rub harder. It's just you and me baby. I'm your big rock and you're my dirty street pebble. Harder. Harder . . .

Early the next morning Boyle was clinging to a desk in the university library, gazing in disgust at the sham maze of shelves arranged on the freshly hoovered carpet. Against the grey breezeblock walls, he counted five others at their bent measly labour, three female, who like himself were afraid to lift their heads and behold the soft glowing face of the day, no . . . the day wasn't new and the eyes were long out of use; it was a feeling, a constant drastic sense . . . the day pressed and lapped around them as if it were already lived out, complete, faint ripples returning across a conquered sea, a sea that could stop finally at any moment, cease to move, dormant, tideless, silent. All the winds had blown, all the words had been spoken, the kisses had all been given and accepted, the flowers were trampled into the muck on the overcrowded horizon. For some people there was nowhere to hide. It was impossible to find a corner, a doorway, a seat in the park. The costume shops were sold out. Not a dream or a smile was in need of an owner, every expression was taken, tears, fury, love, regret, even parody was out of stock. The confessions were all bagsied. The eyes full up to the limit like old wheelbarrows brimming over with rain, old rain. The shop windows were done revolving and glittering, the beds gone moist, the fires on the hills were lies and the light was shredded second-hand rags. The streets had forgotten where they were going, some kind of password was needed, clearance, maximum capacity had been achieved, the day was done and dusted, it was ten to a cell, they had bolted the heavy doors to the altars, and if you got down on your knees and put your nose against the crack you could smell . . .

Smell your own fucken self Boyle, he told himself and

dropped his head to the open book on the desk. Plato under his forehead. The sealed cave of the mind where the light never shines. To think that he had managed to get out of bed, do twenty press-ups and convince himself that there was nothing else to be done but make for the library and begin his revision. The exams were less than a month away. Everything else had to be put out of his mind. Learn to forget, our saving grace. Nietzsche and Plato and empirical Hume and Berkeley and the logic and the ethics and the hermeneutics and the metaphysics and the logocentrism and solipsistic decadence . . . and Eleanor might be on a plane that very moment above the non-unionised post-colonial city.

Suddenly there were automatic shiny bars slicing down noiselessly across the windows. Alarms started squealing, primed at an intolerable pitch. Never hesitate, never hesitate. He put his hands in the air, shouting: I'm unarmed . . . innocent. He ran for the exit through the smoke dancing sadly in the avenues of the maze. He tripped over a body, one of the desperately diligent students, who had been shot in the chest. Never hesitate. In the smoke he saw a hard white plastic face, then another. One of them jumped from a desk and brought a standing shelf of books to the ground. They were wearing white masks and academic gowns. They were shouting and carrying guns, handguns and Armalites. One of them appeared in front of him out of the smoke and jammed a pistol under his chin. Help us, she said. Show us fucken the way out of here you coward. Blood was trickling down her neck from under the mask. He shook his head, no, he nodded, he wasn't sure, he couldn't control them, his own movements. Help us, she screamed at him . . .

Boyle was up on his feet, startled, no, much worse, aghast, cornered, petrified like a moment before he had been enjoying a leisurely breakfast with his resplendent kimono-ed wife at their handmade kitchen table — this is what might have been going through the mind of the young library assistant who just then was wheeling a squeaky unwieldy trolley towards the archaeology section, Larry say his name was, which he hated, who stopped and watched the hassled young lecturer or beardy postgraduate or nervy mature student or whatever medicated care in the community sort he was who had sneaked in past Barney at the turnstile (Larry wasn't going to get involved, no chance, not after the pandemonium caused by that rumour of the hundreds of lottery cards slipped into the books by that sacked dean of students, when Larry had pushed some obnoxious skateboarder type over a computer terminal in an effort to protect the vast riches of literary culture, only to be reprimanded by the library head, Mrs I-am-from-Huguenot-stock for wanton use of force, that's right, the shithead was actually trying to sue the university for endangering his physical being, the same guy whom Larry had seen jumping four flights of steps on his skateboard to show off to the girls none of whom ever seemed to be interested in the library assistants, a fact often discussed after work in the pub with Eugene and Paul who . . .) stuff his books quickly into his rucksack and rush towards the desk and beyond that through the security barrier which was triggered and the shifty man had to empty everything out of his bag under the last-word-I-spoke-was-not-in-jest eyes of Barney and Eugene who had not closed his eyes the night before on account of, so he told Larry anyway, the cheeky young Russian in fishnets he met at . . .

A few minutes later Boyle was released from custody. The bag he dropped at his feet was now heavy with books that he would have to carry around with him for the rest of the day. He leaned against the wall of the bunker corridor that led out and up to the street and began to make himself a smoke. His fingers couldn't get a grip on the fag paper and his tongue was dry. He was trying to drum up some saliva from the back of his throat when the Dove fluttered down beside him. Before he knew what he was doing he threw his arms around her, held her, hugging her was the word people used, and she was laughing happily in the hairy crook of his neck.

Tell me you're not busy, he said. Tell me you're going to come for a walk with me. No heavy stuff I promise.

Her hair smelled of almonds. She pulled back from him so she could see his face.

You're pale. Are you ok? her chapped mouth said.

Just need to get out of here.

She folded her golden-haired bare arm in under his denim and led the way out towards the daylight. Boyle came running back not long after for the bag.

She filled his ears with talk and his eyes with her soft blue-eyed face. She told him all about the few days she had spent in Galway with her friend Miriam, the drive they had taken out into Connemara, the skies, the changing seas, how she felt rejuvenated, brighter, less anxious and caught up in myself were her words. I've been very selfish, she said. I can't wait to start working with the refugees.

No you haven't. Boyle laughed at the idea.

I have. I've seen it in myself before. I get disappointed easily and I don't know how to cope with it. So I get cross. I expect everything to be perfect, to be exactly what I want it to be and then when it isn't . . . You were trying to share something with me and I didn't like it so I threw it back at you. That wasn't right.

Boyle said, It doesn't matter. Maybe you were right and I was testing you. Or trying to shock you.

Well you did, she said, and pulled on his arm. But then I had another shock when I saw you with somebody else. In Trinity. Queuing for the Book of Kells. Who was she?

She forced Boyle to stop. He made a face to show he didn't want to talk about it.

Tell me, she said. I want to know this time. It's ok. I promise. Come on; let's go and sit down somewhere.

She was set against any kind of pub so Boyle let her choose a café. They sat on metal chairs by the window out to the crowded narrow street. It was a summer day in Dublin, the droving crowds had nothing of importance to say but he alone had managed to find another knife to put at his throat.

I'm sick of talking, he told her. Things happened that don't make any sense. Everything's retrospective and then it fades away.

You're avoiding the point I think.

The woman was called Eleanor. She's gone now. It's done.

How did you meet her?

Boyle laughed. It's funny when I think about it. But it's too complicated. You know that fella Fada you liked? He ended up in hospital there.

I'm not interested in him, she said and made a childish face of disgust that Boyle for a moment, a long moment, wanted to attack, no, chasten out of her.

There's no cure in talking about things, he said.

Is that how you feel? You want to be cured? Of what?

Me. That's why I came down here. To change myself. To find something. To fill myself up. To . . .

After a while she said, It takes time. You're doing that. You're making changes. You're studying, reading, thinking. You just can't see it yet.

Boyle shook his head vigorously. I don't think so. I have this bad feeling that nothing is changing at all. That this is me. Stuck. Jammed here. That I don't move from here. Finito.

That's because you lack faith in yourself.

Jargon, he said disparagingly.

Is this because of that woman maybe?

It just brought it home to me.

Well I think you're wrong. When I look at you I see all the things you can do with the rest of your life. After what you've been through. You have lots to say, to tell people. This society needs voices like yours.

Boyle threw back his head and laughed – he knew it was too loud for the café but he didn't care.

I mean it, the Dove said, full of determination.

I know you do. That's what's hilarious.

You're patronising me now.

Boyle couldn't stop himself laughing again.

Was she older than me this Eleanor? the Dove wanted to know. I'd bet she was. Well, any woman who cared about you would say the same thing. You might enjoy thinking you are worthless but I don't. And I don't see why I should be laughed at and made to feel a fool because of it.

There were tears in her eyes, and anger. Boyle took her hand. He turned the cloth and leather bracelets on her wrist with his thumb. This lovely young girl was showing him her feelings and he was mocking her. She let him watch the tears travelling down her freckled face. She was brave and clear. What was on his own face? He tried to smile. The blue in her eyes was an icy mountaintop colour. She was frightened and naive. The shadow of his life loomed over her. She didn't think in terms of secrets and suspicion. Spitting out words wasn't enough to cure him. Her fine pale eyebrows had their own natural shape, and somehow their own kind of silence. He looked at her desert mouth and remembered lying on Eleanor's breasts. She needed him to speak now, no, it was action she wanted.

Boyle leaned across the table and kissed her lips.

When he sat back in his seat again, he saw Fada pinned to the window, grinning from the bruised face. To Boyle's relief he moved off without coming in or banging on the window with his splinted thumb.

Boyle told the Dove he had to go. She didn't understand; she was dejected; she looked around the café but forgot to check the street. She demanded to know why and he had to promise to meet her later to explain. Even then the blue eyes were unforgiving.

I have to. It's important, he said.

She threw up her arms. I thought this was important.

He found himself smiling. There's just something I have to do.

He promised again he would explain later and arranged to

meet her outside the front gates of Trinity at six. He went out then after Fada, heading for Grafton Street.

At six Boyle was in the Two Mists with Fada. They had been there about an hour after spells in three other places or maybe four. Tanya had Fada pinned against the wall when Boyle showed up at the pitch on Grafton Street. Fada had this look on his face, as if he had been hanging upside down for too long. He wouldn't talk to Boyle at first, pretending he didn't hear him, looking the other way, laughing with a revolting smugness. Then he suddenly agreed to a pint. Tanya said she would meet them later and gave them each a giant daisy. Fada stuck the stem in his zip. His bandaged hand and his clothes were filthy. The barman in the first pub they went into refused to serve them; Fada started ranting and asking the other drinkers to take pity on his thirsty drooping flower. It took two more pubs before they could find someone to believe their story that Fada was out on his stag.

Boyle couldn't get a straight answer out of him about where he had been. The account of the kicking in the club took a long time and a number of rounds to come out of him with Boyle constantly having to rein Fada back to the point and keep the voices at bay that seemed to be on the verge of taking him over, some of them new voices that Boyle had never heard before: a London black voice in search of his Irish mother, a Frenchman just off the plane in the wrong city, a pantomime serial killer with a woman's hand in his inside pocket, a delusional Northern rent boy on the run from the forces that be not, and an old Dublin man who had forgotten where he lived – I've been foostering about these streets now for ten long miserable years what amid the multibunioned democrazy what.

Boyle grabbed him by the neck. Just tell me what the artist fucker said.

'Twas him who spavined my paddle. Do you want a suck of my stump? Fada held his bandage in Boyle's face.

Did he mention me or not?

It happened on the road from Gort. Near a foul festering puddle in the road. The hand was bitten clean through the bone and I heard a voice, a voice I never want to hear again and it said, Tell the Northerner not to close his eyes into the sweet sanctity of sleep.

I'm warning you. Did he mention me or not?

I stood up for you, Fada roared and beat his chest.

Boyle smelled a wet dog.

I stood up for you. Who else would?

What was said?

And I've this to prove it. He hit me when I was down. Do you know what he did? He pissed on me . . . Is a problem in Dublin no? This pissing on streets? Is no a problem in my country. Is here in Dublin is crazy is flood. Yesterday morning on the autobus I look down and see my feet in the water. Is the rain I think. So much rain here in Dublin. Is no a problem in my country. But rain is no hot is no steam. So I look back shoulder and is a woman and she smiling is – He's after you. He says he has people out looking for you. He told me what he's going to do to you. Tell that to the nordy bastard. He had a knife. A big knife.

They moved on to another pub when Fada began doing poems at the other tables. Nobody was amused. On the street he went up to people begging them for their purple secrets. Flapping his injured wing, he slipped inside a restaurant and acted laying an egg in the fireplace. Boyle pulled him out and warned him he was on his own if there was one more stunt. Con strolled up to them at that point; he swore a cryptic oath that he would join them within the hour and went off to buy some hash.

In the Two Mists Fada had fallen asleep by the time Boyle had come back from the bar. Two students were playing chess in the other corner – Boyle recognised one of them from Trinity's library. Out of the daylight men came in by themselves to the dark for a pint and a brave stare at the wall.

Some decided to stay. These men didn't speak to one another. They knew there was nothing anyone could tell them. They had wives and children, houses with their own front doors, a chair moulded to the shape of their backs, they had cars and an eye for the changes on the streets on their route to work. They could argue among themselves about what was good or bad for their city. Boyle tried to imagine himself in twenty years' time, with a job in some office, no, a teacher, taking books of homework back to the house to correct, stopping in for a quick pint on the way, not asking too much of the world, wagging his head in mild censure at every mention of – what? Youthful folly. Anything too extreme, excessive. Any wild notion or passion. Idealism. How would he look back on this moment sitting there out of sight of the bright summer afternoon with this deadbeat character slumped asleep beside him? How long ago was it he had stood outside the bus station and thought that his life had changed for the better? Maybe he should have had more courage with Eleanor; maybe he should have gone with her. He had waited like she had asked him to: had that been entirely the wrong thing to do? Fada woke up with a shout and immediately dipped his face into his glass and took a long drink. Then a man approached from the bar, fifties somewhere, congealed white hair, a face like a collapsed-in grave. He said he had a story to tell them.

Boyle and Fada listened to the story of how he had come back from work one day, feeling sound, not a bother on him, and found a piece of rope under the sink and took it out to the garden shed to hang himself.

Get lost, I'm warning you, Boyle told him.

The man winked and sat where he was.

Get away from me now.

He has no decency, the man informed Fada.

Show me your scar then.

The man seemed to take offence at this and went off with his pint to complain to the barman.

He told me the same story I heard from somebody else, Boyle said. He's a con man. He's looking for money or something.

Fada started laughing giddily and crossed himself with his injured hand. There's many a remedy in a good story. The chilblains, the cysts, the piles, the drink, the lack of money, the lack of love, even impotence, or the bad conscience. And there's many a curse.

I heard it with the Dove. I'm supposed to be meeting her. Around now.

Don't, Fada said, his face turning grey.

Con will be in.

I fought for you.

Wise up.

I need somewhere to stay.

She'll be waiting as we speak. I can't just stand her up.

Fada sneered. I know what you want with her. A nice bit of white cotton panty is that what you're into? Her name sewn in. Little flowers around the waistband. A wee bit of balaclava-ed daddydaddy on the bedsit carpet. Or a kidnapping virgin fantasy in a cow shed in Leitrim. Disobeying your superiors' orders. Sweet revenge on the soft unspanked unshaven moneyed ass is it? Hold on to those bars love till I tell you to stop. I'll get you another one. Fifty of them. There's a queue of them want a good spanking. They'd pay for a bit of border porn.

This was all done in a bad Northern accent. Boyle laughed it off like he was learning to do with so many things. The light-limbed Dove standing outside the big locked wooden door to Trinity, she would probably be sitting on the railing, reading or kindly gazing at the double kissing of couples meeting for the night or staring into the shadows of the archway through the smaller doorway – but these were only words. Boyle couldn't see her. There were no images. She had earnest blue eyes, freckles on her chest, a small clean tongue . . . and she was invisible, no, she was somewhere outside of his mind. Eleanor was the same; he tried to picture her with that troubled smile somewhere in a house in London talking to her junkie boyfriend but nothing moved in the darkness. For a horrifying moment even the pub he was sitting in, the different groups at the tables, Fada beside him were like things that had failed to come to life properly: they were stuck and frozen in a different kind of reality. His mind was dark, empty, a black river, no, just black, a place where nothing could grow, poisoned ground.

And where's Eleanor anyway?

I told you an hour ago. She's away back. What's the fucken matter with you tonight anyway? You took a kicking. Forget about it now. It's like you're coming apart at the seams.

Do you think so? Fada said and seemed to mean it.

Just calm fucken down. I've had a bad day as well.

I can't. Fada shook his head. He looked around the bar like he knew it might not be real also. I've done a terrible thing, he said.

What?

I don't know yet. But don't leave me alone. I stood up for you. I have some money. Let's get them in.

I'll go round and tell her. I can't just leave her standing there.

You won't come back. She won't let you. Her Daddy-don't-go eyes.

I have to tell her, Boyle said and went out of the door.

He was half an hour late and she had already flown home. He had messed it up again. He waited, smoking, in case she was late but he knew it wasn't possible. A Swiss girl appeared beside him and asked if his name was Sebastien. A better man might have made a joke, held her in conversation. Boyle simply shook his head grimly. When he arrived back at the pub, Con was there and another lad and Tanya waved from the bar and her eyes darted scornfully towards Fada who was doing his gallant slick-tongued tour-guide act to a hopelessly beautiful young Spanish girl.

Boyle got himself into a corner and decided he was going to drink until the names of things were washed out of him.

People sensed it. They didn't ask. Pints appeared in front of him. He drank them down like they tasted uniquely of himself, brewed from every failure in his life. That's what they meant when they said a man was drinking himself to death. Boyle knew he was no drinker, not like some of them he had seen, but he had been doing more of it in the last few months than ever before. Maybe that was Fada and the ones around him. Pubs like the Two Mists drew them in from all across the summer sundown city, the big scorched never-give-up sky over Dame Street he had seen coming back from Trinity. His thoughts went nowhere of interest even to himself, circling vindictively around the usual pile of shite, women, university, the point of it all, him getting older, what was going to happen to him. To brighten himself he tried to think about the night in Phoenix Park when the girl had slid out along that bough in the dark and spread her legs or Eleanor lightly picking the hairs off the tip of his cock before she took him into her mouth or what the Dove would be like under those scraps of clothes but they were another man's stories, a kiss from a nameless girl was as hard to imagine, no, remember, as the slamming of a prison-cell door. He couldn't have been said to be watching the burgeoning excitement with interest either, an excitement that had no grounds, or purpose, perhaps only its defeat. He was a man drinking sullenly by himself, glancing around now and again in search of some kind of threat, hostility, not communion. During these surveys of the bar, he would see Fada frozen in some other tasteless vignette, hands on the Spanish girl who was growing more languid and gentle as the rest of the bar raced once again towards some kind of euphoric bedlam it could never reach. Or he would see Con in some kind of clandestine conversation with two lads. Or Tanya, poor Tanya who must be in love with Fada, who sat mainly in silence or disappeared to some other table.

Fada returned only after the Spanish girl had left.

I'm in love, he said. One minute you think you've had it and then a girl like that sits down beside you.

Was that her boyfriend?

Not for long. Look at the size of the boner I have on me. She saw it. I couldn't keep it down. She's only in town a week. Staying three months and wants to have a good time. Had to bring the boyfriend with her. You having a good night?

Not really. Bad form.

Ah come on muckeroo. It's our night. Let's do some damage. If a girl like that can sit there and smile at my boner then who knows what's in store? Wasn't she gorgeous? Admit it.

Boyle nodded impatiently. Where've you been staying the last few nights? You know Tanya has a thing about you?

Tanya likes to sit close to the fire. But she's too afraid to touch. And I don't want her mother coming after me when it all goes wrong. That's my patch too. God's teeth man. Don't shit in your own pocket. Whiskey or tequila?

Tequila.

Fada saluted with his bandaged hand: Immediatamente compadre dolorosa.

It was much later, after countless rounds of all sorts, after they were put out on the street from the Two Mists because of a shouting match over some comment about the release of prisoners in the North, after another row on the street when Fada accosted a group of girls, after being turned away from two nightclubs, after giving up on a taxi to take them to a vampire party some lad who was with them knew about in Killiney, after chips and kebabs leaning over the Liffey wall, still about eight of them looking for something to do, drinking, music, drugs, a flat with a TV would do, after buying some poppers from some gay sauna down a lane, after appeals to the slow cavalcade of black hearse clouds dumping the broken hearts of the night into the burning moon hole, after various near-violent attempts to find out what others on the street were up to – this can't be it, there must be something on somewhere – and hearing about a secret club somewhere on the docks that they couldn't find, that the five who were left rolled back through the town and climbed over the fence into St Stephen's Green.

This is where I've been laying my horny head. Come my children of the black lake, Fada said and led them dancing along the dark pathways towards the bandstand.

Fada introduced Boyle and the rest of his company to the four homeless ones sitting at quarter-hour intervals around the stand. Con immediately started skinning up as an offering. Fada did most of the talking to begin with, jokes and impersonations, sniffing regularly from the poppers. He got the laughter going.

One of the homeless men interrupted: I'll tell you a good story if you pay me for it.

Everybody put their hands in their pockets without a second thought. He must have made more than a tenner on it. He held the poppers under his nose while he told it. It was a story about him and his wife and his two children. They had a house out in Finglas. He was working, a delivery driver; things weren't too bad, as good as could be expected. One day he was driving back from Drogheda and stopped for this woman by the side of the road. She said her car was broken down. She was the nervous type, she wouldn't stop talking. He drove her home and she invited him in. Here he skipped a bit, only saying they started to have an affair, seeing her almost every day. As the weeks went by, the guilt came to life in him, he grew sick of the deceit, and decided to finish it. When he tried to tell her it was over she called him a fool and said his wife had been having an affair for years and his children weren't his own. He thought it was rubbish of course; she couldn't have known anything about his life. He broke it off anyway. But he couldn't stop thinking about what the woman had said. He started to become suspicious. When his wife was happy he wondered why and when she was in bad humour he wondered why. He began to miss time at work because he was sitting in hired cars watching the house for visitors. He opened the bill for his wife's phone to see who she had been calling. One night he cracked: he went to the woman's house, demanding to know why she had said what she did. He ended up beating her. He waited for the Guards to knock on his door but they didn't come. He relaxed; it was fine for a month. But the suspicion returned, the distrust. He couldn't look at his children. It got worse and worse, he said and fell silent for a long time. They all waited, respectfully, that awe again, and a cop siren soothingly near.

Go on, a girl's voice said.

I can't, he said.

Everybody made noises of encouragement and support. He was no more than a shadow in the corner, lit up now and again when he took a pull on a reefer. He had a moustache.

Go on.

What happened?

Where're your wife and children now?

It'll be good for you to tell it.

Affairs wreck your fucken head man.

Ssh.

Tell us.

Fucken women.

You shut your face.

Go on for fuck's sake. The night'll be over.

The man jumped up at this point and started cursing them. He threw the money back at them – nobody moved other than to cover their faces from the flying coins. The man was raving, spitting. Then he ran off into the park.

Shortly afterwards, Boyle got up off his arse and said he was going for a piss. He knew he had no intention of returning. The rest of them were arguing about different things. The air was hard to breathe; it was thick and heavily scented and sour. He crossed the humped bridge; the last time he had stood there was the day he was waiting for Eleanor. He had been an idiot to think she would be interested in him and he would be grateful for ever to her for it. He was always too eager to sort out everything, plan it and order it, annihilate, understand. She had shown him her warmth and her easy sensuality and he had demanded a timetable of whys and whens. Why couldn't he have just said, Thanks Eleanor that was great and when you're next in Dublin . . .? No, Boyle had to lay down the law. Him or me. Here not there. Dainty would laugh in his face when he told him. Take what you can. Take your bit of pleasure and be thankful you're not sleeping out on the bandstand or in the bushes. The same with the Dove: Just take it easy on her. Don't rush it. She's trying her best, extending herself, touching something that frightens her. All he was doing was making rules people could never keep.

Do you want to chase the swans? Fada whispered in his ear.

Where the fuck did you come out of?

Smell the air. Swan's breath. Fanny fumes.

The conference there is a bit chaotic.

They're bringing out the overhead projector now. Then there's a break for lunch. We forgot the name tags. Let's go after a swan. There's a family of them over there. The Maguires. Northern stock. Did I ever tell you about the red-eyed one that attacked me?

It was more likely you jumped the poor animal.

When I have a child, people will believe me and rejoice. Her face will launch a thousand peace-keeping land-to-sea mobile units.

I'm going home.

Can I come? I've a bone to pick with your sofa. I need a shower mucker. I have to meet that Spanish one in the morning. After her English class. I'll tell you a wondrous story on the way. Look.

He showed Boyle a flat stone in the palm of his hand.

I picked her up the other night. She was calling to me from the gutter. We had some time together. She's ravenous. My rough diamond.

Fada kissed the stone. He offered it to Boyle.

Do you want a go? She's magic.

Fuck off, Boyle told him.

I'll tell you about it on the way. You got any cash? I know where we can pick up a late bottle.

Fada ripped the back of his shirt on the climb over the railings. He tore off the rest and walked, no, strode, bare-chested, no, without a shirt, alongside Boyle through the streets. Everyone they saw could have been coming from the same party which had been interrupted at its height. People saw the walls getting higher all around them. Boyle caught the violence in many sets of eyes and kept his head down. Fada didn't notice; he was talking away about sorting out his life. Boyle didn't say a word about the three lads who followed them for a couple of streets. Boyle wanted to get home as quickly as possible.

They crossed the river at the H'appeny Bridge. Further down the quays Boyle pulled Fada down to the ground behind a parked car. Two lads were on the other side of the road, one balancing along the river wall, drunk, singing.

Is that who I think it is?

Before Boyle could stop him Fada jumped on the bonnet of the car and began spouting: Beauty is what I'm talking about here tonight. Gather round. What is beauty and where can we find it? In the offices, in the bars or in the morgue and museums? There are some who say it can be found only in the morgue. Well I am here to say the beauty is on the streets.

Boyle thought, no, it was an attempt to pray: I didn't ask to be here. This is not my doing. There was no way out. He crossed the street at a run. Never hesitate. The first he took with a headbutt. The second was who he wanted, the artist fucker with his masks.

I hear you were looking for me.

Behind him, Fada was bouncing up and down on the bonnet: Behold in me the living beauty in my eyes, in the clench of my fist, behold the beauty in the taste of your own blood. Piss on him. What do we say? Piss on him. Drown him in it. What do we say?

Boyle had to throw a few dummy swings before he connected. The fucker went down against the wall, kicking his feet wildly. Boyle put in a few boots to his ribs. Then he called over Fada; he took it out and emptied an endless steamy gush over the mask-maker. He skipped away back to the bonnet and went on with his oration.

Stay away from me. And anybody I know. You hear me? Boyle said.

Fuck you.

You a hard man?

Boyle stamped on his guts. He left them there and walked away. He was waiting for Fada to catch up when he heard him shout and as he turned he took a fist in the face. Another one went by his ear. Boyle went back in straight away. He soon had the fucker by the neck with one hand, pounding the face with the other until he let him go and the arsehole lay draped across the river wall. Boyle looked across at the car where Fada was standing in silence on the bonnet, his hands in the air as if he were being searched. Then Boyle looked back at the sprawled figure and took hold of his ankles and tipped him up over the wall. He was already walking before there was a splash.

PART TWO

Say a week has passed now, a week gone by, it is a week later. Since the night of the . . .

Since the night beside the river.

Say he is in a different place, a room. He is hiding out in a room.

Describe it.

Rectangle. Eight by four. A single bed points his feet towards a window. One brown-stained pillow and a duvet without a cover. No sheet. A radiator. Walls painted off-white and scabbed, no, skinned in places by removed posters. One left behind, deserted, rejected for reasons unknown, of topless blonde, smeared overblown breasts cupped in her own hands, eyes closing in, begging, indoors, too fake. Pubescent bare-bulb tit. Curtains of mattress design, open, for it is the daytime, parted.

Window looks westerly. Below is a garden of surplus white goods, electrical items, gas cookers, bed bases, scaffolding, doors, rubbish bags the cats break open like crackers. Innards. Paper hats. Prophecies.

You will find your destiny in the eyes of a clown.

Every day Boyle sits on the bed and contemplates the houses, the new homes going up behind the razor-wire perimeter fence which begins after the garden. Psychotic dogs having fits when a door is slammed in a radius of two miles. Or a child cries. The city growing. He has counted twenty-eight of these three- and four-bedroom family units in this superb new development, Hazelwood Manor, arranged in groups of four which will have their own garages. There must be a hundred men working on the site. With the window open some days he has heard the Northern accents of some of them, down for the weekdays in a B-and-B or that caravan park he read about in the paper, the fight that broke out over a card game, fires started, travellers involved and men from the North, labourers, sparkies, roofers. Back up the road on the bus on a Friday night to the wife and the wains. Family men. Fathers of the next generation.

Twenty-eight homes in stages of incompleteness he can see without leaving his position on the bed, the pillow at his back, but he knows there are more, perhaps as many as fifty, and occasionally he countenances the desire to find out exactly, to make a count, a natural desire, good, about control, mental stability, and each time he promises himself the satisfaction of standing at the window later in the day and establishing the definitive amount, some essential fact about Hazelwood Manor. At some point every day he makes this promise to himself and yet so far he has failed to honour it. The question is whether this is an act of pleasure deferral or self-denial? Or is it a sign of something else, an inability, a deterioration; that he hasn't done it is a bad sign, a failure to use his mind, a typical laziness. It should be one of the tasks he forces himself to complete, the only way to beat time, like getting up at a particular time each morning, like having a wash, like doing some push-ups, putting structure on the vacant hours. Tasks and rewards.

He should know all about that. He should be a fucken expert at it.

Barely seven days in and he is slipping already. Lack of discipline. Remember those surveillance-force soldiers who can stand for three days without moving in a hedge shitting into plastic bags all for a car registration. There's discipline.

And they're the types who are looking for him now.

Again.

Buried in haystacks. Lurking curled in cement mixers.

Burn all hedges.

Burn all the rooms where men lie solitary and hunted. Huffing and grovelling in their own stupidity. Men who bring it all down on their own heads, persistently, every roof, every summer sky, and mope in the rubble looking bewildered. Irredeemable.

Smoke them out.

Say there is a week's worth of newspapers spread on the floor. Like a paint job in progress. Refuse of a desperate mind. The attempt to make sense. Victor brings them or a few Boyle found in the toilet across the hall and removed, no, confiscated, no . . . Violent paramilitary exposed by Russians improving their English while having a shit. Ah, that face is familiar to me I think yes. Did I not meet him on the stairs one night and he would not look me in my sorrowful Russian eyes? Victor says most of them are too stupid to notice. They watch Russian TV on cable all day in the living room, ten of them or more he has determined from the voices. The woman lies silently on the sofa in a soiled dressing-gown. Victor says he mustn't leave the room. Victor who was the only person he could think of when he awoke one morning and realised what he had done by the river and who he had done it in front of, the only witness, Fada, a man who would try to convince you he was sexually abused by a swan.

Fada has been singing his infested heart out to the newspapermen and the song he has been singing has no end, endless.

A household name of vileness.

Sang that once Boyle had shown him a gun.

Sang that Boyle had made sexual slaves out of impressionable humanities students.

Dear Dove, You've probably read a lot about me over the last week. The Guards have probably interviewed you as well. I'm sorry about that. Most of what has happened I've had no control over. I can hear you saying I use that excuse too much. Just don't believe everything you read. I talked to you honestly. You were right: you should have stayed away from me. I should have been stronger. I'm a walking disaster. Fada has been saying a lot of things about a lot of people and very little of it is true. But who am I telling? That story he made up about you and him in the toilet should prove to you what he's doing. Don't let it embarrass you. You're bigger than that. People will have forgotten all about it in another week's time. I never did half those things with him. I should have seen through him long ago. You tried to warn me. I hope when the Guards called your father wasn't too . . .

He tears the page out of the file pad, balls it, and throws it on the floor where a few seconds later it attracts attention with its crackling and blooming and stretching among the hopeless paper-flowers garland.

Make my wreath from these abandoned letters.

Dear Eleanor, I can't keep up . . .

Dear Mammy . . .

Dear Fada, You fucken conniving sick fucken . . .

That last night they had walked back together in silence to the flat, the two of them, side by side up the dry hill streets, beardy Boyle and shirtless Fada. Taxi-drivers might have noticed them but none came forward to help with enquiries. Nor the couple kissing on the wall that asked for a smoke – Boyle grabbed Fada by the arm when he stopped to oblige, pulled him the rest of the way. Indoors tea was made and a tape set in motion and then stopped mid-song. Fada fiddled with the makings of a joint, the hands shaking. Boyle sat on the floor and began to wait: for what was to come, for Fada to find the courage to speak to him, the right words, for the world to respond to what he had done, no, there were certain things that had to occur before it could be called a deed, the finding of the body for example, no, the world was extinguished, he was locked up within himself for ever, he would be denied the consolation of others and their community of deeds and praise, no . . .

It was like waiting, settling down in a corner for some bit of yourself to come back that was away on a circumnavigation of infinity, the good bit.

No, it was like a stone in mid-flight.

Fada braved it finally: So what are you going to do?

Boyle looked at him and saw only that stinking hovering treason word – you. He smirked at it and felt a fissure open in himself and the badness leak out. A cold bitter root.

He said: What you do is deny everything. You were drunk. You don't remember. You hear me? There're no witnesses.

What about the other guy?

He was out cold. He didn't see anything. He didn't see what happened.

You can say they started it.

And they'll send us straight home and say forget all about it then lads eh?

I just thought –

Don't think. You know nothing about this. Even being within eyeshot of this gets me in deep trouble. There was a fight. Ok. But you saw both of them lying on the ground when we walked away. Ok?

So I remember that? Fada handed across the joint.

Boyle turned it down. You remember us walking away and the two of them on the ground and you saw them moving. Somebody else must have come along and . . . Did you know the other fella?

Don't think so. But he might have known me.

Who the fuck doesn't?

It's not my fault.

You were there too remember. Do you know what that means?

But it was you who –

Who fucken what? That face was going to cost him, a year for every time he had laughed along with it, every look in the eyes.

Why? it said next.

Boyle shut his eyes to restrain himself: there was only a blackness that wouldn't have him. Excluded. Cast out.

You didn't have to, Fada said.

Have to what?

Fada shrank back, hung his head, smoked.

You didn't have to fucken get up on that car and start another one of your performances either. You were happy enough to see me going into them weren't you? You didn't have to piss on him did you?

Fada rose off the sofa and scuttled away across the room. Don't shout at me. You're making me nervous. I can't think.

Boyle laughed at that one. Think?

Is there any chance he could have swum to safety?

Swum to fucken safety?

Is there?

Listen; there was a fight and they went down and we walked away and left them on the street.

Maybe we should go to the Guards first.

No.

Why not?

Why?

Make a complaint about them attacking us.

No chance. We'll have to risk it. Maybe we might get lucky and the other fella doesn't know who we were. Think about it: he was plastered himself. He might be still lying there now. When he wakes up he's going to look around and go home and think the other one fucked off and left him. It's two of us against him. He was knocked out so he can't be a witness. Not a word to the cops right until we know.

Boyle got up and approached Fada. The hands were raised in protection, no, supplication. Don't hurt me mister.

Not a word to the cops. Right? They'll fucken hang me.

Fada nodded, eyes shifty. Glands that oozed his doom.

Why did you go to prison? Fada asked suddenly. It was a demand, an accusation.

Boyle fell for it. Face to face, he told Fada straight, the bare facts of it, told simply, tone sharp, fierce, about Sock, the van, the road-block, running away, end of fucken story, happy now?

The ghost of a grin on Fada's face.

To calm down the situation, to instil some degree of ordinariness, the sense that things were under control, Boyle decided to say he was going to bed. He lay down; he listened; his head was empty. He saw his own heart in a dream, pumping red. Then the woman showed up with her dog and he followed her through the market places. I'm bleeding to death, he said to the dog. I can't go on any further. The dog laughed at him. Boyle was filled with a horror that it was all a trick. I'm not moving any further, he said. The woman pointed ahead. Boyle saw an enormous curtain, scarlet, heavy like old velvet, stretching away into the distance. The dog sat down and scratched itself. He went towards it, the curtain, some hint of a crack in it, an opening, the big curtain.

He woke like he was about to vomit. He rushed into the other room. Fada was gone. Of course he fucken was. The sofa hadn't been slept on. The wee shite couldn't be trusted.

This was a fucken serious stupid mess.

He switched on the radio, waited through the talking for the news. A body had been found. Foul play suspected and all that.

He thought he'd better get out of the flat. Take a walk in the park and clear the head. There was time. Don't panic. He didn't know anything for sure. But what if Fada came back, wanting to talk about it more, needing reassurance?

It was afternoon before he chanced a move. He nipped out to buy some tobacco and a newspaper and waited for a sound that might be Victor coming in.

Some time during that wait he must have gone out to the yard, broken the window to get out there, and smashed the chair into pieces, that's what one of the papers said.

You stupid fucken wanker. Look at the fucken mess you've made of everything now. Your new happy life.

You're fucked, totally fucked.

At last at last, why is that singing refrain in your head you useless cunt . . .?

Dear Ma, I'm a . . .

To whom it may concern, I am guilty of murder. I came down here hoping to change myself, no, not even that, to alter the things around me, a change of scenery. I was resigned to myself. I wasn't looking for happiness or anything extravagant like that. Not much, more air, more room to breathe maybe, to think. I was suffocated by myself. I thought some kind of clarity was possible. I don't know any more. It seems now like the stupidest thing I've ever done. That might just be twisted thinking who knows? I arrived anyway and I toed the line. I rented a flat and found a job. I went to the lectures in the university. I walked about the streets of Dublin and saw the quiet nameless faces and wanted to be lost among them. I did everything by the book. I bit my lip and tried to make friends. I managed to forget myself some days. I did not judge. A girl rained oblivion down on me from the branch of a tree. Then one night I . . .

Say this page fell among the other crass lilies of the bedroom floor. Boyle quit the bed and went to stand by the window. There were men hammering on the clean blond roof beams in the wind. Who was he writing to with these letters? He wanted to make somebody understand something he didn't know himself. Definitely not his innocence. So he wanted to confirm his guilt maybe. Killing a person wasn't enough, wasn't real enough any more. Was that it? You have to convince them these days or they won't believe you.

No, that was fucked-up thinking. He wanted to tell the people he knew that it wasn't his intention to murder, his bidding, his desire. Hello, I am Mr Fucken Accidental. Out there men digging and laying pipes, fitting window frames, wiring, double glazing, insulation, sewerage. There was deliberateness. It seemed like the purest kind of freedom he had ever imagined. Years ago, he had worked on sites in Derry, on house jobs mainly, gutting a place, kitchen extensions. In one house he had found an old German Luger and a bag of bullets; he passed them on. Wasn't there the time working on some house when they had got the word to block the Duncreggan Road with the digger and Phil Healy stood in the way with his arms out and Pontious drove it straight at him, was there the time? And it was only a dry run. And Healy got a word in the ear one morning after it and lost his sense of humour for good.

A dry run.

My life is a dry run for an abandoned job. Security breach. Target unidentifiable. Unjustifiable risk to passers-by. Suicide mission. Abort.

Dear Eleanor, Take me with you . . .

The clarity at long last. Hugeness of each breath. The man who stands here before this window is somehow more than what he has done and said and felt. At last he has shed the burden of himself. He is cleansed. Each moment is vast and untainted. He could talk wisely and eloquently to his jailer. Things can be known. Everything is achieved at a price. This bright empty calm. Then the sudden surge of dread like there are wings sprouting through the flesh from your backbone. Littler ones higher up at the neck a-flutter.

Some people go to hell and come back having learned nothing, without even a memento or a good story. Empty handed.

What did he mean by thinking that exactly? Something to do with your man who flew towards the sun. Or was it swans? With loose tongues and big dicks. That fucken head-case has grassed on people he barely knows. Poisonous Paraclete. Lies and fantasies. Boyle in the park with three girls feeding them coke and stripping them at gunpoint was one story. Boyle persecuting the old woman was another. Tanya shagging every man she sold flowers to. Some alcoholic girl who worked in an art gallery who gave him money for sex. Con buying drugs off the Guards. Fiacra's girlfriend. The Dove . . .

Fada told the cops he fucked Eleanor, no, sucked shit out of her arse during the wake. That Boyle went mad when he found out.

Terrorist sex fiend on loose in capital.

Young artist brutally murdered by drug-crazed paramilitary.

Monster of the North.

Ex-IRA prisoner sought in Liffey slaying.

The blonde imprisoned on the wall gropes herself desperately as if she is begging for something that Boyle can't find a name for. Taking the pad and pen, he sits with his back to the door.

Dear Dainty, I've tried writing to you a few times and keep tearing it up. So you'll have heard all about it. I'm not going to waste your time trying to explain myself. I made a fucken stupid mistake, lost my head for a split second and that's me finished. I saw somebody dancing on a car and then it was already done. Most of the stuff that was said in the papers is pure rubbish which I'm sure you're bloody well aware of knowing me. Can you see me doing half those things? I only wish I could. I've been hiding out for the last week but I'm going to have to make a move soon. It's what I deserve but I can't go back to jail Dainty. There's only one way out that I can see. If it comes off you probably won't hear from me for a while. Maybe never I don't know. I'm sure you'll get over it anyway. I just wanted to tell you thanks for everything and I'll never . . .

Say it was evening when Victor arrived. He hadn't shown the night before which could have many explanations. Boyle listened for his voice below in the living room: there was another argument going on. They always turned up the volume on the television. When the knock came on the bedroom door and the grunt, Boyle worked free the stiff new bolt. A plate of chips and a burger in the big man's hands and then up at the face, emblazoned with bruises.

So the holiday's over then? Boyle took the plate and sat on the floor against the radiator. Victor shut the door quietly and stood in the centre of the room.

They say to me you go down, Victor said and pointed at the floor.

Did she tell you that? I wasn't even sure she was aware of me.

You must stay in room, this room.

I was starving Victor. Very hungry. I was looking for a slice of bread or something. Does she lie on that sofa all day and night?

It's not your business. You stay in this room. They don't want to see you. Then they want to know who you are.

I just sat and watched TV with her for about ten minutes and came back up. I didn't speak to her.

You stay in this room or they can't be trusted.

Wearily, Victor dropped a newspaper and a pouch of tobacco on the bed. He had taken a fair few punches to the face; he was moving slowly as if the movement of blood caused him pain. There must have been a crowd of them to hold him down.

So tell me Victor. I can see by your face there's been some new developments. Should I just clean this plate and skedaddle – just go I mean?

It's not important.

Police?

It's not important.

So it's worse than I thought then. Let me guess. Do you want a chip? In an attempt to find out something about me the police have been interviewing yourself and all the neighbours and uncovering a network of black-market activity and illegal immigrants. Neighbour has turned against neighbour. Cold or warm?

Hunger makes you mad.

Does it Victor? So does being kept in the dark. I need you to be honest with me. I'm stuck here all day not knowing a thing. Tell me what the fuck is going on. Who did your face for a start?

Victor had moved in front of the poster, the broad silent back

249

to Boyle who was chewing a mouthful of burger on the floor.

So come on Victor. What's the big mystery then? There's something not right here I've been thinking. I asked you if you knew a place I could lie low. Not to be a fucken prisoner. What do they know about me downstairs? Are they illegals? Go on answer me.

They are not your business.

Victor if the cops were outside the house right now I wouldn't blame you. I wouldn't. Do you hear me? I don't want anybody else getting into trouble. Just tell me to go and I will. I'm going to have to go anyway because I can't keep this up. But you have to be straight with me.

You must stay in the room, Victor turned and said, a cold ferment far back in the eyes.

Boyle swallowed another mouthful and decided to push it further. I'm going tomorrow Victor. Thanks for everything but I'm away.

Victor sighed. He sat down on the bed and leaned on his knees, tapping his fresh white trainers on the carpet.

I've one other way out Victor.

They released him.

Boyle thought for a minute.

Fada? You think I'll go looking for him? That's not what I mean. I'm not fucken interested in revenge. He'll destroy himself without my help. Or somebody else will get him. He's hurt too many people. But you haven't answered me. What did the police say to you?

Neighbours told we drank vodka together on the steps.

And what did you say?

Victor shrugged.

Boyle laughed. You didn't say enough by the looks of it.

They showed me a photograph, Victor said, sadly, perplexed.

Who?

From the newspaper. The woman who drowned. In the river.

Boyle put the plate aside and stood up. He went over to the window. A pillage, a city silently sacked and looted and smoking was the sunset beyond the wired-off compound of domestic bliss to be. Each house wore a miniskirt frill of plastic. Death smelled like vinegar. Eleanor had licked the grease off his lips on a park bench. When is it best to hire guard dogs as opposed to a nightwatchman? What are the pros and cons? This site is protected by Hamilton Security.

He said to Victor, They're just trying their luck. They don't even know who she is for fuck's sake.

They told me she is from Turkey.

Victor I have this bad feeling you're not telling me something.

She comes from Turkey. Victor shrugged.

So they're keeping it secret? They're looking for somebody then. They're waiting aren't they?

Boyle took the steps across the newspaper and paper flowers that would bring him nearer to the bed. Man walks on water, he thought. Last night in a bedroom in north suburban Dublin a man was seen to . . .

That woman's face has caused me more bad luck than anything. Pure jinx. You open the paper one morning and . . . Do you believe in that kind of thing Victor? Jinx. Bad luck.

I believe in everything, Victor said firmly.

You know what? This has just occurred to me so let me run it by you. I bet you that wee fucker has told them I had something to do with her death.

Victor nodded.

Don't just fucken nod. You're not a nodder and you're not a fucken shrugger either. Is that what they told you? Be fucken straight with me for fuck's sake.

Yes.

What? That I killed that woman and then attacked the other fella for doing the mask of her. What am I? A fucken obsessive lunatic. What else aren't you telling me? What's going on out there? What did you tell them?

I said you talked to me about her.

All I did was fucken ask you if you knew who she was or anything that's all.

You were angry, Victor said, almost irritable.

It was a lack of respect I thought. The woman didn't have a say. They were selling her face on bloody stalls. Do you not think that's a bit sick?

Boyle hesitated for a moment at the height of Victor when he stood up from the bed.

I have to go now, he said.

Do you think I did it too then?

Victor shook his head. No I didn't think you did.

So why are you throwing them the rope then? Unless you fucken want them to think I did it don't you? Am I getting warmer here Victor? Am I seeing the light?

I told them you were angry. I didn't tell them I thought you had murdered her. You are not thinking clearly.

Maybe I am thinking clearly, too clearly for some people.

I have to go now. Try to keep calm.

Fuck off Victor.

I'll try to come tomorrow.

And do you think I'm going to hang around here waiting for you and the mafia boys to come and take me away somewhere. Is that some of them downstairs? Would I get beyond the door Victor if I tried to leave? Would I? You've fucken set me up here haven't you? You sly cunt.

Victor closed the door without a word.

Dear Dainty, I'm being set up here big time. I know it sounds mad but there's more going on than meets the eye, the sane eye anyway, the good healthy eye. It's only become clear to me tonight. I'm going to have to make a run for it. I've been lying low in a house full of Russians. I think they're trying to pin another murder on me to get themselves off the hook. That woman who drowned in the Liffey. Did I mention that to you? I promise you I'm not being paranoid. They see an

opportunity to make the cops think I did it. I'm fucked anyway so why not be double fucked. There's this fella Victor
who I thought was helping me and I'm not so sure now. If I
turn up in a suitcase in the Liffey then you'll know it was him
or somebody to do with it. He used to live downstairs from
me in the house in the North Circular. I'm just thinking that I
gave him two letters to post the other day as well. I don't
know who to fucken trust. Nobody. I'm in this house and it
could be all Russian mafia. I don't know if they'll actually let
me go out of the front door. But I'm going to try later. And I'll
have to find a stamp for this somewhere. Jesus Dainty this is
some mess. Before, there was always a group of us. You knew
what you had done and even if you hadn't done it it didn't
matter. Everybody was in the same boat. I was an arrogant
bastard I've been thinking the last few days. The way I wanted the transfer out of the Blocks to cut off all links. Fucken
books and big ideas. Look where they've got me. I should
have stayed among my own. I've been out of my depth down
here all along. I thought I could just saunter down to Dublin
and start a new life. I wasn't up to it. I didn't have the
strength for it. Call it whatever you want but I fucked it up
like everything else I've ever done. And then I went and
threw somebody into the Liffey. I just lost it for a split second.
There was stuff building up in me, frustrations and anger.
That girl Eleanor just vanished without a word. She probably
guessed I was a waste of space. I saw that fucker Fada dancing on the bonnet of the car and it was like I was in a dream
and anything could happen. No, that doesn't get anywhere
near to describing it. I remember doing it. I remember the
way I had his ankle in one hand and the bottom of his
trousers in the other when I tipped him over. It was just a
fight that got out of hand. I'd had a run-in with him before.
He was the one who made the mask of that woman. Fuck it I
don't know what happened. I lost it. Lost the calm. All the
years sitting on my arse with my head up the divine
Buddha's arse and when I need him all I get is a djinn danc-

ing on a car bonnet telling me that death is not what we think it is, that everything actually means something else, something completely different, that this is death and there's no such thing as living, that it's all a dream and . . .

No, I'm not going to tear this up again. I'm going to put this in an envelope and get it to you somehow. I'm breaking out of here tonight. There's only one option left open to me if I want to stay out of jail or a shallow grave. They'll rub my nose in it for a while but I've no choice.

I hope everything works out for you.

That sounds ridiculous. But I have to say it. You stuck with me down the years. I'll never forget that. I've been a selfish bastard to you. What have I ever done for you? When have you ever come to me and said you can't take any more? I've been a fucken burden to you for as long as I can remember, trying to pretend I was a big guerrilla warrior or a fucken philosopher. I should have stayed at home with my feet in front of the fire or gone out dancing with my ma and da. Jesus I wonder what they're thinking about all of this. Do me a favour and try to tell them that all the stuff in the papers is lies.

Right I'm going to make a move. I think they're all in their beds now. Thanks Dainty. I mean it. Hopefully some day you'll walk into a bar somewhere and there'll be a face over in the corner you were glad once to see the back of. Did you really dump the sticks in the Foyle?

Don't let the bastards get you down.

Say he went across the landing into the bathroom, filled a sink with warm water and began to shave off his beard.

Say when he was done and he thought he looked exactly the same, he collected the paper flowers from the bedroom floor and returned to the sink with them in his arms, dropped them in and set a light to them. While they burned away he opened a window and looked down on the night in the street, the front gardens, the parked cars, the ownerless silence. A man passed under a street light and knocked on the door of a darkened house. The door was opened and a softer light showed in the hall and at the front window but only for a second or two, just long enough for the door to be shut again, hardly enough time even to get out of your coat.

Say Boyle returned again to the bedroom and put what clothes he had into his rucksack, bought in Derry with Dainty the day before the big move to Dublin. Followed by a night in the pub and Dainty coaxing all the women to give him a kiss goodbye. Walking up the Strand Road with Dainty singing and a rucksack full of tins.

Dear Derry . . .

He was ready now. Smoking a farewell fag, he sat on the bed and thought about going out of the window and down the pipes. Jump over the fence, tame the dogs, and curl up for the night in one of those beehives of plastic sewerage pipe.

He could hear the television through the floor.

Why was that blonde left behind on the wall? She was telling you in the way she squeezed her breasts that she knew how to take a man, that she would do things most women don't or can't. She had lost count of the number of men that had been inside her and it wasn't enough for her, it was beyond her control. She wanted mercy from her craving or final satisfaction. The whole world right up inside her.

Say he went back into the bathroom and burned Dainty's letter in the sink. He checked out the window again; a man, he couldn't be sure if it was the same one, was leaving the house he had seen the lights come on and go out in earlier. The man got into one of the cars and drove off but not before he had glanced up towards the window at Boyle.

Downstairs, the woman was lying in the same position on the sofa as the night before, wrapped in a shabby white dressing-gown, her greying unwashed hair tangled across a cushion. She could have been either thirty or fifty. Boyle lowered himself into an armchair not far from her head, settling his bag between his feet. A Russian voice talked on the television over pictures of an island in a vast butter-yellow lake where people were dressed in furs.

Is it a commune? Boyle asked her, to see what would happen. Her eyes were open but he couldn't make out the colour. The woman stayed silent.

Do you speak any English?

Again there was nothing.

Boyle forced a laugh out of himself, a snort.

You know I was going to climb out of the back window there but I wanted to come down and see you before I left. What do you think of that? I don't know why myself. I just wanted to sit here with you for a few minutes before I headed off. Into what I don't know. I wasn't even planning on trying to talk to you. I just saw you lying there and . . . I don't even know if you have a room or you just lie here or what you're doing here in this house.

The furs had come off on the TV and the people were walking about nude.

It must be some kind of colony, Boyle went on. The escape from the modern world. Some people can't get their foot in the door and others want to give up everything and get out. Back to the wild. Did you ever hear of those children found in the wild that were reared by animals? Wasn't one of them Russian?

The woman moved; she lifted her head slightly off the cushion and flattened out her hair across her ear. Boyle noticed that her hand was young, slender, long fingers with many rings that she returned to the refuge of the other in her lap.

I don't know why myself. I just wanted to sit here for a while with you before I go. I don't know what's outside that door you see. Maybe nothing. But I can't stay up in that room any longer. So tell me about Victor then? Good guy or bad guy? Big Victor.

He thought he saw the eyes glance in his direction but it was hard to be sure with the television and no lights on.

Big Victor, he said again. I don't know what he's up to. For a while there I thought he was setting me up for something I didn't do. I'm not sure any more. The head's going a bit crazy up there. I can't think straight. My head's in such a mess that it wouldn't surprise me if I wasn't actually sitting here talking to you and I was lying in some psychiatric hospital somewhere and the year is 1912, no, 2043. Do thoughts like that ever bother you?

It occurred to him then that the woman might be drugged. He wanted to touch her; her head was in reach. He couldn't take the risk: what if she started screaming and the boys came piling down the stairs, or worse, he reached out his arm and his hand went through thin electrostatic air.

Boyle rolled himself a smoke and watched the naked children playing on the shore of the yellow lake.

Listen, he said, just in case you can understand me and you need any help then this is your chance. I'm going now. If they're keeping you here against your will or anything or you want me to get a message to somebody or . . .

The woman's arm came out towards him and she nodded her head eagerly.

What? Boyle asked. You have to help me understand.

Her arms were a long pale good shape.

She kept nodding.

Boyle got down on his knees. What? Are you drugged?

The woman made a frowning face and then mimed inhaling a cigarette and blowing out a silent sensual fan of smoke around the room. She laughed but not for long and her face returned to its ghostly weariness.

Say Boyle lit the cigarette for her and went out of the front door to the street without any hindrance.

When he breathed in the night air and lifted his face to the sky he was struck by how much he had forgotten about his life. A sky fit to be called a heaven, a new kind of luxury that had just been born, the first silence, under it Boyle with everything he had left in a bag over his shoulder.

A memory arrived to fill in the void but was memory the right word? It was about him and his mother one day, a Saturday it would have been because they were in the town together. No she wasn't there in fact. It was about his father. Boyle, a boy of about eleven, was by himself: he entered the department store in the Diamond area of Derry. He had never been inside the building before. It was a female place, secretive, hushed, too expensive. Women moved seriously about with clothes over their arms or shoes and hats like they were all getting ready for some big show, a severe and mysterious performance. He was trying to be brave. Like quicksand the carpets were soft and deep under his feet as he went up the staircase to the perfume floor.

Perhaps the sense that this scene was unconnected with what he was doing at that moment, or about to do, on a street he didn't know the name of in Dublin made him wonder if the incident, no, event, the moment had ever actually happened. True, he seemed to remember having thought about it down the years but that might be wrong too. He would have to ask one of them some time, the parents, if he ever had the chance again. The past was consensual, the property of no man. It had to be negotiated. The pragmatists had taken over. No right or wrong. But you can't negotiate from a position of indifference. You have to believe in something. The day might come you open your front door one morning and see tanks in the street and you know you're going to have to fight for it or face elimination, extermination. They teach you how to remember. If it doesn't look like TV no one will believe you. They teach you how to talk about it and who to speak to. If you forget what happened you can always ask the cops.

The perfume department with its glass boxes looked like a museum, he thought, although he had never been in a museum.

Some women, the helpers, wore white clip-on gowns and lots of make-up. They were elegant and kind.

One of them with more buttons open than the rest, sprayed scent on to the end of slim pieces of card and floated them under his nose, one after another, until he was choking in a swarm of giant butterflies and must have fainted. A little later, young Boyle opened his eyes and saw the hats then the faces of two cops and the beautician smiling over their shoulders.

He refused to give his name like he knew was right.

They're just trying to find your mammy or daddy to take you home, the beautician said and stroked his brow.

He thought of his father who had sent him out to buy a present for his mother. No, his father had given him the money for a birthday present and it was young Boyle's own idea to buy her some perfume because he had heard his mother complaining that she was bored with the same bottle of perfume year after year.

He fixed his gaze on a cardboard cut-out of a beautiful woman in a cat mask and a black dress and determined they were never going to get a word out of him, the bastard cops.

How did it end? Did the cops give up and leave him in the care of the shop assistant? How did the little boy get home?

Had he cracked? Was that shame in his heart? Or anger?

Boyle couldn't remember.

Since then the smell of perfume could give him cramps in the guts like he was about to tell what should never be told.

It was to time to move on. Grandiosely to set in motion whatever was going to be. Give the two blind donkeys of cause and effect a good slap on their way. Tied tail to tail. Follow the stars to the crib of his future. At the gate outside the house, there was nothing to choose between left or right, uphill or gradually down, so he closed his eyes and went with the view that seemed strongest, the most vivid. A parody of instinct mixed up with Cartesian notions of truth, no, pretentious shite just. The victor was the right-hand way, the gentle downhill. Cars parked on one side, single blinking thinking red eyes in the alarmed interiors. Regulating, monitoring the owners' dreams in their housebeds. Gates and garden walls. Would he ever have his own front door?

The street was currently unused by any other citizen. He had it all to himself free of charge. It had been more than a week since he was last outside and the sense of moving was exhilarating. Things might just work out. There was a chance. He had a new face. Believing that it would be ok was the only way to make it happen. No different to magic. Maybe he should have taken the poster of the Madame with her hands full as a memento. To help him remember the low point.

The houses were mainly identical in shape but they each had their own individual touches – the curtains, front-door styles, some with an added porch: all that struggle to make a mark of difference under a cloistered suburban sky. Soon another choice presented itself in the shape of a brightly lit minor crossroads. Huntington Drive upper and lower. Again he shut his eyes. On down the hill was the true shining path.

Say another memory hit him at this stage. He had started to whistle, a leisure activity he seldom practised, not any tune in particular, maybe not even notes, and he found himself thinking about jail, and some of the men he'd known in there, and then a bomb-maker, a man called Talc, another whistler. Talc was placid but had a sharp dry wit. He also had a wife and five children, a day job and an underground room he had built himself. His eldest son grassed him up on a trip to the States where he found God and joined some cult. Talc went on the run for two years. The Brits when they caught him kept him for two months. He was tortured in ways that had become legendary. But he wouldn't give it to them. He had been inside for five years when the son showed up and asked for a visit. He had left all the cult stuff behind him: he wanted forgiveness from his father. Talc gave it without any qualms. A short while later news came in that the son was dead, shot ten times by another of Talc's boys who waited at the scene for the cops to arrest him.

And that was it.

Talc went on doing his days, whistling, playing cards, taking the visits from his wife and the other children and leaving a cloud of white dust in the air after he had his shower. Surviving. Both of them out now, father and son, free men, keys and money in their pockets. Real life not a story, Sartre said. The mind tries to make connections, explanations. Other people ask you questions and force you to make a yarn out of it to make it believable. I exist therefore – what? Start with the big We instead. We exist therefore I have a chance. No way to move from each instant of self-awareness to the next. I now to me now. Memory test.

But the heart keeps on pounding oblivious in the chest. And the television sets get bigger and bigger.

All this after being out in the open air for just fucken ten minutes.

The street, no, it was a road, was a long one and brought him to a junction, a baleful grove of traffic lights and signposts and safety railings around a white-striped confluence of tarmac. A sign told him he was in Blanchardstown. The cottages in front of him were the remnants of an old village on the city perimeter. This is what he was looking for. Everything had a centre, even the huge semi-detached estates had a nucleus of shops, banks and a school or a shopping centre these days. Social cohesion. While he was deciding again on left or right, a van stopped at a red light. Two men in the shadowy front. The road was empty. Cameras watched them, kept them in check. Boyle crossed the road and went right. The van revved up and passed him at speed.

It didn't take long before he could see different lights up ahead, more traffic lights and other colours that would have to be a parade of shops. A man was reading a newspaper behind the window slot in a garage, no, a service station. Further along, past the empty chip shop which Victor probably bought his food in, he was coming near a group of lads gathered around a bench at a bus stop. Boyle straightened up: he counted five of them, one directly in his path who was telling the rest of them some story of a fight from the gestures he was using. It was crucial to avoid all trouble. If they went at him he would have to run no matter what. Stave off the paranoia with action. Don't hesitate, don't give them a chance to think. He quickened his pace and made straight for them. They were silent and watchful, eyes to the leader, the one up telling the story.

Boyle turned to him: Would you have a light?

He had to say it again before another one of them produced a light. They had cans stowed under the bench. Smoking joints.

Boyle quickly made a roll-up and asked if there was a public phone anywhere near. For the first time in months he was aware of his accent. He handed back the lighter and looked at the faces. One of them might have shrugged.

Forget it, he said and moved on.

A woman was getting out of a taxi up the street and he ran for it. The taxi man was talking to him before he had the door closed. First there was a story he'd heard on the radio about a woman who waved down a cab in the centre and put a syringe to the driver's throat. She named a street. There a man was waiting who opened the driver's door and threw a Rottweiler in on top of him. The driver trapped in a seat-belt behind the wheel had the face torn off him. All for the few quid the driver might have on him. This was then followed by another story of more interest to Boyle. It seemed that the night before in St Stephen's Green there had been some kind of vicious attack on the swans by a gang who the Guards suspected used the park to sleep in.

Boyle laughed when he heard that.

I don't see the funny side of it.

You're right. It just reminded me of something.

We've lost our way as a people when we start harming animals, said the driver, a man named Mark O' Brien, and about the same age as himself, Boyle could see from the identification details stuck to the dashboard.

Where to anyway?

Boyle said he needed to find a telephone first. They were on a motorway. The driver offered the use of his mobile if the call was local. Boyle thought he couldn't refuse. Privacy was a rare commodity these days. He had looked at the number so many times in the past weeks he had it memorised. The driver pressed in the digits and handed the phone back over his shoulder. It was ringing.

Hello?

Is that Snowy?

Who's this?

Is that Snowy?

Macker don't annoy my head. I was nearly asleep there.

Think Buddhism.

What?

Buddhism.

Who the fuck is . . .

Long silence. The driver glanced in the mirror at him.

You're having me on.

Nope. You know how it is. It's tricky. You said to call if I needed anything Snowy.

You're a hot potato.

I need a favour.

A miracle more like.

Half of it is fucken lies.

What about the other half?

Silence.

I have to be quick here. I need a favour.

This is my home phone.

I get you.

I can't do anything for you. Do you hear me? You're on your own. The only thing I can suggest is you call Henry. Do you have the number?

Think so.

Well that's the best I can do. Call Henry. Best of luck.

Boyle handed back the phone.

Sorted? Where to?

Henry was old code for call back in an hour. The phone would ring out and there would be a message on the machine about where to go.

I've an hour to kill, Boyle said. Any ideas?

Depends what you want to spend bud know what I mean? I had four lovely birds in the back before you and dropped them off at a party in Glasnevin. I was tempted to go in after them myself. You could try your luck.

The wife wouldn't like that, Boyle said.

How much do you want to spend?

Money's not a problem, Boyle surprised himself by saying. He would have to be careful: he was beginning to enjoy himself. Playing the role of the good-hearted gangster.

He took it back and said he had a bit, but not much, just enough for a few days' holiday.

If you have the money you can do what you like in this town. You just come down from the North?

Not at all. I'm over from London.

You're well out of it if you ask me.

Boyle struggled with a long-lost urge to defend the place. Too right, he ended up saying. Been over in London years now. This mate of mine was supposed to meet me at the airport. Can't get him. Don't know what's going on.

Is it Blanchardstown he lives in?

Boyle had to think fast. That's another mate. I just thought I'd give it a go. He must have moved or something.

So where's the other one live?

Phibsborough was the first place to come into Boyle's head.

Well that's handy. We'll get you sorted out no bother. I know a pub there that's open late. You'll be grand there for an hour or so. Has a few of those dancing girls if you know what I mean. How does that sound?

The car stopped off the main street outside a door between

264

two shops. The driver told Boyle to ring the buzzer and a bouncer would answer.

Point over at the car and I'll give the horn a blast. He'll know the story then.

This man gets a bloody commission for every stray he drops at the door, Boyle thought to himself as he waited for the metal door to be answered. Another ridiculous situation. He gets into a taxi with one problem and gets out with a different one. When he had agreed to the driver's proposal he thought he'd be able to shut the door and walk away.

The horn went twice and the bouncer waved to the car. He was a big bastard with that inscrutable weary Slavic pallor and bright blue eyes. Boyle was frisked, his bag taken away, and then he was pointed down the stairs to the basement.

Say he found himself in a bar area. Some of the lights were too strong so it was hard to see how big the place was. There was a huddle of men at the far end. The tables and the dance platform with the pole were empty. He waited at the copper bar. Things hadn't started yet which was a lucky break. He'd have one drink not to attract attention and get out of there.

The woman who came to serve him was friendly and asked if he was on his own. She was a Dublin woman: the skin on her face was just starting to sag but her eyes were stunning, happy and green. Boyle told her he was supposed to meet somebody. He made up a name. The woman wanted a description. She laughed at his efforts to describe Fada.

He sounds like a cross between a tramp and a rat, she said.

You're not far wrong.

And he comes in here?

That's what he told me. Boyle shrugged.

Wait there a minute, she said and Boyle's heart sank to see her striding up to the other end of the bar and start asking the men. She pointed down towards him. Two of them came across the floor with her towards him.

I hear you're looking for somebody.

It's not important, Boyle said. He told me the other night he might be in here so I was just dropping in to see if he was about. No problem.

As if she were repeating what Boyle had said, the woman began to give the description again but the words were completely different. The three of them were racking their brains.

How often does he come in here do you know?

Boyle said he didn't.

If he's been in more than once then I'd know him.

And he's got bucked teeth?

Ask Dimitri up at the door.

The woman went through the description again, adding more new words while one of the men went upstairs to question the bouncer.

It doesn't matter, Boyle said. I'm going to head on now anyway.

As if he she could sense the isolation in him, the loneliness, the nameless need, the woman didn't want to let him go off on his own disappointed. She was mothering him. She brought him a stool to the bar and put another bottle down in front of him.

You sit there love and maybe he'll be in shortly. The place doesn't usually fill up until later. You all right? You need anything?

Boyle was left to reflect on the sorrows of the vacant stage, the rolling lashes of the disco lights, the naked punishment pole.

By the time he finally got out of there, he had been introduced and his sorry tale presented and embellished to at least twenty different sympathetic men. He didn't even get to watch a dancer in action around the pole: the first one was announced as soon as he said his goodbyes and was on his way up the stairs. Dimitri opened the door for him and said nothing. Five minutes later Boyle had to buzz again for the bag he had forgotten.

He was well over the hour when he dialled Snowy's number in a phone box outside a bowling alley. He thought it was typical, no, right, aesthetically pleasing, that a Guard car should stop at the lights and the two of them stare in at him as he listened to a voice, not Snowy's, a muffled male Southern voice, tell him to go to a house in Rathgar which was on the other side of the city.

Say Boyle stood out on the road waiting for a cab and the nerves started.

At that moment, nobody in the world knew where he was.

He tried to hold on to the thought but it kept losing its shape and dissolving. Or was it him dissolving?

Nobody knew where he was. Nobody might ever be sure again where he was if he went through with this and put his life in Snowy's hands. He would always be on the run. The lies he would have to tell would grow and grow with the years. An outcast, trusting nobody, turning away at the last moment from every tender or angry eye. An exile within himself. Murderer and absconder. He who evades retribution wanders in the desert for ever. In dread of the faces in the sand who know the truth. Intelligence reports tell us Boyle is living somewhere in Latin America. More likely packed off to outer London or Birmingham or Swindon where Maxy and that lot were stuck for years, shifting boxes around in a factory, a button factory, never able to come home, no, go home. Home? The word will never be spoken. Home will be the gap between himself and the world, between the word and the thing, the void separating his tongue from words, his fingertips from the touch of the tarmac. He squatted down and scoured his knuckles against the road surface until he saw blood.

I have spilled my blood on this spot. Like a ghost I will come back and haunt this street crying for my bones.

The purpose of a street is the lesson that it is not possible to look both ways at the same time. Man does not exist while on the edge of the road before he chances to look one way or the other. Act and be born.

Nobody in the sleeping city, in the world of hope and

shame, knew where he was. He alone carried the weight of these seconds, the tonnage of every impression, the sole witness and shoulderer. Would it all be the same after this? The store of solitude increasing until it can no longer be kept out of sight. People will see it on his face. Marked, branded. That man is lost. He cannot endure himself. He sits all day in a room with the windows painted black. The street between the two ridges of shut-up shops and pubs, even the names, Mc Cann's, Trudy's Florist, the Handsome Stranger, Byrne's Family Butcher's, Mahon and Sons, the ugly light dancing in the phone box, the sore knuckles, the mapped and measured firmament, a guilty heart, a dry throat – too much, too much.

The net was going to burst.

What if he turned himself in?

He ran back to the phone box and hit the numbers for Dainty's. The ring tones sounded loud, urgent, close just like they should but the answer machine clicked on and Boyle listened to Dainty's voice playing the Yank and saying he was not in at present with music in the background, leave your name and number and I'll be sure to call you right back just as soon as I get a chance, and the front doorbell going and Dainty muttering and sighing before it went off. Boyle rang three more times in case he could entice Dainty out of the bed if that's where he was, groping some drunken student under the covers, no, he had a new woman. Boyle left a message: Dainty where the fuck are you? Get up out of your bed. I don't know what to say now. This is some fucken mess. I'm still in Dublin. I'm out on a street. I was hiding there but I have to make a move. I was going to ask you about it but you're in your bloody scratcher. I've no idea how much you know about it all. Most of it is rubbish. I couldn't even tell you how it all happened. But I'm hung if I go near the police. I was trying to write to you. I don't know what to fucken say.

The time was up. Boyle counted two minutes out and rang again.

Me again. I was hoping you'd have picked it up. I'm in

Dublin. But I'm probably going to disappear for a while. You can guess what I mean. Fuck knows what's going to happen. I have to face it. There was a whole pile of stuff I wanted to say. You're the only friend I've got. I'm just fucken sorry for what's happened. You're the only friend I've got Dainty. I –

He hung up. He felt worse now, more stranded, more uncertain. He shouldn't have bothered trying to speak. It always came out wrong and left you dissatisfied and angry, and deeply fearful. He pushed open the door roughly and stood in the street with a desire to shout, to roar.

Say he began to run then.

It had first to do with the thought that the cops had all these phones bugged and might be on their way already – Don't risk it, don't risk it – but as the speed increased to a sprint, and the noise of his steps echoed around the streets so that he could have been ten men running, he found a spot in himself, it opened up in him, flowered, a place inside his breathing and the momentum of his legs, this buoyant place which wasn't his heart either where he was, no, where everything was hoarded, the bounty of his life, the bright cache, everything was remembered perfectly, and there was plenty more room, it could never be filled, the abundance, that savage generosity he had felt with Eleanor, jubilance, insatiable . . . and there she was now in her granny's armchair reading the poems, those fucken poems, gnawing on her own smile, and Dainty taking him on the boat ride up the Foyle to Greencastle to celebrate his first full day of freedom, or the time he locked Boyle out of the flat to force him to go to the shop – Come back when you've successfully reintegrated – and the Dove turning to look up at him in the lecture hall with the mineral-blue eyes that were a challenge to all philosophy, the feet he had grabbed and somersaulted into the river, and his ma and da dancing, dancing, dancing in the kitchen late at night, and Fada's sneering grin at the existence of every object in his path and the final salute to his last cell and spitting on the floor . . .

Say he had to stop because the hunger for more was . . .
Say he had to stop because there was nothing to . . .
Because it was too big, no, too . . .
It could never be completed.
Only destroyed.
No, because it was irresistible.

A taxi stopped immediately. Boyle got in the back behind the driver's seat to avoid conversation. Without comment, the driver waited for him to get his breath back and give the address. Then the car took off at speed as if the driver smelled trouble. He turned up a talk show louder on the radio: the people were screaming at each other down the phones from their houses in the drug-related violent working-class estates. But it was all staged. Fada had once told him he used to phone in for a laugh some nights. The car ran a red light and turned down towards Parnell Square.

The driver was right; Boyle wanted to get there quick, to have this thing over with, this journey, whatever it might be called. On O'Connell Street the mourners were gathered outside the nightclubs. Wouldn't it be appropriate, he thought, no, a perverse coincidence, the hideous golden mean, if he saw Fada scampering through the streets on this his last passage through Dublin, transit, conveyance, passage, how do you describe a movement towards something that is out of your control?

All these words were a method of not thinking. The tactical trigger to avoid the muscular void in the stomach. The heart fluttering like a flag over the abyss. In the winds of a foul anticipation. Something about the beast stalking towards Bethlehem. The car took him across the black river and the vista of bridges with their three green eyes. The countless cell lights of the stars gathered around the bull-beam spotlight moon. That disgusting suffocating rightness showed itself again in the Guards pulling their truncheons on a crowd outside a late-night shop, the bouncer down covering his face.

The car took him past the locked gates of Trinity where he had been fool enough to believe he could smell the wind from down a new road.

He stepped out of the taxi into a quiet street where the lamps glowed like fruit overhead in lavish foliage. The air was thick and spicy and alive with insects. Palm trees grew in the front garden of the house he was after. It was painted yellow, the next one blue, another one red. A set of stone steps went up to the dark front door and two shuttered windows: more of the house seemed to be below street level. This was money territory. The habitations of the gentle far from outrage. Book-lined living rooms, dusty pianos and velvet pillows. The fruit-bowl shield on the kitchen table. The paintings in the hall. The barefooted children. Here dwell the disciples of order, the mask lovers, the carnage dreamers.

A ripple of joy passed through him that it was not the right address. Was this salvation? But like all ripples it died and left no trace. He could not escape his destiny on the wrong street. He would be made to wander for ever from door to door. Is this the place? Do you know my face? The shadows trapped in the jungle foliage picked at the luscious locks.

The door opened at the top of the steps and a figure came forward, a man. He looked both ways but he couldn't have seen much for the trees. An army could be hidden in those branches. A horde of naked women.

Boyle waited. He was waved forward.

He halted at the bottom step.

Nice night for it, the other said. Dublin.

Where's Snowy?

Inside.

Tell him I want him.

Get off the street.

Tell Snowy I want him.

Boyle heard himself called an arsehole and the man went inside. Snowy put his head out and waved to him to come up.

Boyle took his time. A few steps into the ascent Snowy disappeared. One man still in front of the door.

Come on to fuck.

How's it going? Boyle said at the top. He stepped in close. Have I come to the right place?

It's in there. He smelled of fresh putty and whiskey. Shapeless face, moustache.

It?

The man blinked, flexed his shoulders. Then he glanced over Boyle's shoulder as if he had heard something suspicious. Pretence already.

Some house, Boyle said.

Fucken taxi.

What about it?

You took a fucken taxi. To the door.

Would have got lost otherwise.

Is that right?

You wouldn't want me to get lost would you?

The man sucked in his mouth like he was about to spit and looked Boyle in the face. He shook his head in disgust.

Boyle knew he was winding him up. He couldn't help a laugh.

The man's response was to hit him in the stomach, catch him and throw him back against the wall.

Quit it, Snowy said. Then to Boyle: What the fuck do you think you're dealing with here? Some wee fucken art student. Get fucken in.

The other one squared up now for a bout of thumping, the fists held at his chest.

Boyle said, I think maybe I've come to the wrong house. Sorry for the disturbance.

This is what I mean about you Buddha, Snowy sighed but he didn't elaborate. In now come on.

Thanks anyway but I'll head on. This is a very clean living area. Don't want to wake people up or anything you know Snowy.

Boyle saw the next punch about to come but Snowy caught the fist in mid-flight. He moved in nose to nose with Boyle and said, Don't wind me up Buddha. You've an opportunity inside to explain yourself. Otherwise you won't fucken know what hit you. Do you hear me?

I'm not here to explain myself Snowy. I've no fucken confession to make. I wanted a favour.

Snowy laughed: Every fucken breath you're taking is my favour to you. In there now or it's out of my hands.

Let me walk Snowy.

No chance. You called me.

Let me walk. You'll never hear a word from me again.

Like you walked on Sock Mc Kinney? And where would you go this time? Back up to Derry? Hide out in your da's shed for the next ten years? Buddha of the backyards.

People know where I am.

The Russians?

Boyle tensed the muscles in his face to control the fear. People know where I am, he said again.

The whole fucken world knows where you are Buddha that's the fucken problem.

Let me walk Snowy.

Get him in, the other one hissed. The name Gibbsey was called into the house. Moving car lights illuminated the ragged palm trees. Boyle nutted Snowy and swung for the other one. He started shouting. Something hit him on the back of the head. He was grabbed by the hair. Three of them had a go at him. He was pounded backwards into the hall, down on to the floor. A pistol was shoved into his mouth. The front door slammed shut, no, worse than that, much worse.

PART THREE

For the third time that day Dainty nods to the doorman on the steps of the hotel. He goes in through the open side door instead of the revolving ones. A woman is polishing a statue among the plants. At the desk the same girl who checked them in the day before is laughing on the telephone and touching her hair. She has a very long plait of black hair. The public bar is down a corridor to the left. They give you a bowl of olives with every pint. The chandeliers are from another century. He walks across the stone floor to the silver doors of the lift and presses the button. Before it has arrived, he crosses back through the lobby and out to the front steps again.

I'm a resident, he says.

The doorman puts on the face that he is happy to be of service. This man wears a top hat and tails for a living. He bows and carries suitcases and waves down taxis. He must be near retirement age.

I'm a resident, Dainty says again, so quit looking down your nose at me.

The doorman does shock now, stammers, clears his throat, blinks.

Dainty puts up his hand to stop any discussion: I'm not interested in an argument. I'm a resident, that's all I'm saying. But one other thing. You're working here a long while I take it?

A bus pulls in at the kerb from the airport. Dainty stands in front of him, a step lower.

How long, that's all I'm asking?

Forty-five years, the man surrenders eventually.

Dainty gives a whistle of appreciation and steps out of the way. He passes through the lobby again and calls another lift. It's empty when the doors open, golden and empty, like a chalice, like a spotless tabernacle. Then he sees himself in the mirror, big sweaty Dainty from the waist up.

Reeling away from the sight, he turns and almost collides with a man and a woman hurrying for the lift. There are apologies and smiles and Dainty finds himself forced into the lift with them. The fact that they are going to the same floor causes more smiling. Dainty stands with his back to the mirror. The couple take up positions against the other shining walls, getting their breaths back. He keeps his eye low on the carpet which is pale yellow and tries to think about something. His mother used to work in the sacristy of the Creggan chapel, cleaning. She brought priests' clothes home to wash now and again. Some mornings when he checked out of the window on the weather he saw priests' vestments or whatever they're called hanging on the line in the yard. The last time he was in chapel must have been Fergal's First Communion. Did they have a good day? What was Fergal wearing? They must have done the tour of the family houses but nothing of it would come back to him as they went up floor by floor. Forty-five years of being a doorman of a hotel, the man must have some great stories.

Are you enjoying your holiday?

The woman is talking to him. She might be Australian.

The words won't come so Dainty makes a face to show that things aren't too bad.

We have to leave tomorrow, the woman sighs, and I don't want to go. We've had such a good time. I could easily stay another week.

Life goes on, the man reminds her. He sounds more American.

Back to reality eh?

He looks to Dainty for confirmation. Dainty struggles to make some face but isn't sure how it came off.

We've just been to the modern art gallery, the woman continues. I thought it was very impressive. And the gardens are lovely. Have you been?

Dainty shakes his head, tutts, lifts his shoulders. His shirt is sticking to the mirror with sweat. They can probably smell him. He sees the woman do that smile with the raised eyebrows to her husband. He tells himself to keep thinking about something: There is a person whose job it is to clean this lift every morning. To erase the smudges the drunks like him leave on the gold and the glass. He couldn't find the room the night before and wandered the corridors. The Americans call these things elevators. What about those years in Boston, where had they gone? And when he came back he found out Boyle was hanging about with the hard men.

Well, enjoy the rest of your holiday, the woman says in the corridor. Maybe we'll see you in the bar later; you never know. Can't go home without a final stout can we?

Dainty tries to laugh. He catches sight of the greasy stain he left on the mirror as the doors close silently. The couple give a last wave from the door to their room. Alone in that corridor, just for a second, he feels a kind of violence which starts pains in his stomach. There are too many people, too many rooms, too many doors. The blue carpet is neatly tacked to the walls and the skirting board is well fitted. The neatly spaced lights are hidden in plastic clam shells. There is too much to take in. His guts are boiling. All these useless things must be destroyed. For a terrible moment he believes all these things want to be destroyed.

The swipe-card effort at his own door takes a few tries. Inside there's Maureen on the bed. The woman of his dreams whom he has treated unfairly. He wants past her to the toilet where he can kneel down over the bowl. Something tells him kneeling down would help. What about you Maureen? Any bars? Haven't seen you in ages. Legs looking great as usual, trim and smooth and polished. Maureen Donaghy on the bed reclined against a stack of pillows, reading her interesting book, the wee half-rimmed glasses on that he's always breaking with his rough sweaty fingers. Good legs for a woman her age. Two teenage boys over in Manchester. This woman who now on a hotel bed in Dublin turns the page of her book as if she is still alone and unwatched.

Kneel down beside her Dainty. He is stopped in his tracks by the flutter of a page. Throw yourself on the bed on top of her and make a foamy bouncy wave that would flip her into the air, books flying. Skirts ripping. Bra snapping. It would have been a good way to break the huff. Maureen is sulking. Dainty you are a man in a state of being punished. Chastisement is what you have on your plate for the next few hours and you know why big man. Out there all day on the streets and last night as well leaving her here alone in a strange room, Maureen angrily reading, legs crossed at the ankles, trapped and bored and seething among the furniture, the same as a hundred other rooms in this building. Ignored, standing just inside the door, he is a ghost that haunts the hotel, the victim of a murder from years ago who can't find rest until a mortal woman takes him in her arms. Last night in some pub he heard some ghost story but the details have gone blurred like so many other things, like the day he was married, like the first time he drove a car, like the birth of his first son.

Maureen, he says.

Come to me my love, she doesn't say.

Maureen what the fuck are you doing with that book?

That wasn't the right way to go about it, appeasing her. The words just came out. She flicks on to another page in defiance and it turns his stomach like a near miss by something fatal.

Maureen. We'll go back up in the morning. Ok? I'm sorry.

His voice is not his own. A man not sure of his ground. Out of ideas. A man who wants simply to lie on a bed beside a woman and tell her about an anger that wants to wipe out the whole show.

We'll go back up in the morning.

She takes off her glasses and rubs her dark brown eyes. She sighs, folds her arms and turns her face towards the window. Dainty lets his own eyes lean that way too, the thin white curtain stirring, puffing, twisting, wanting to forgive.

Long minutes later she says, You're full. I can smell the drink from here.

Looking at him now, she will be telling herself that he is as pathetic as her first husband when it comes to a crisis. She will be asking herself if this man is really worth her time, if all men are the same, blunted by their mothers. Or she might be searching his face for some clue how to help him.

I'm not. Dainty frowns at the idea that he's drunk. His arms hang sunburned and lifeless at his sides; he couldn't move them if he tried.

This patient brown-eyed woman with her girl's ankles makes another stab: Why do you want to shut me out? I know how you must be feeling but what is it you are trying to achieve? I'm left sitting here worried sick and too afraid to leave the hotel in case you come back and need me. Or there's a call from the police. Think about me for a second please.

These words have been prepared and arranged for their best effect. She is much better with the words than he is. She often sits him down and gives him a good talking to about things, about his behaviour or his temper or his drinking and somehow she does it in such a way that he believes she is right and means only the best for him. The book is snapped shut in the lap of her denim skirt; there's a fraction of a second when she struggles against the impulse to throw it at him, struggles and wins. I would not have moved Maureen, not flinched a muscle. Throw the bed at me. Pull out the sink. Throw it hard. Or push me out of the window. Run down and drive a bus over me. Nothing would hurt enough Maureen. No amount of pain would do.

We'll go back up in the morning.

Will we? What are we doing here in the first place? What exactly are you looking for? Do you even know?

Now his head is taken by the same heavy numbness that controls his arms. It won't shake or move or do anything. As soon as the neck goes he'll be standing there like a man in a noose.

Do you even know?

Leave it Maureen.

She reacts instantly, sits up on the bed, legs folded under her, Boyle style: Oh excuse me if I'm bothering you. You answer me now what you've been doing. Or I'm out of this room in two minutes flat.

She means it too; she has done it before. That trip to Cork when she stormed out of the B-and-B in the middle of the night and took the car.

Tell me you're not looking for anybody? Tell me you're not going to do anything stupid. It's not your fault you know. Just talk to me.

Ah Maureen all this man wants is to lie down on that bed there and put your nipple in his ear. Stop him turning into a ghost. Your heartbeat to calm his brain. His big fingers tied up in your hair. Close those curtains and undo your skirt. I see a rainbow stick floating on the waves. Green white and orange and silver painted ends. Broken once in a fight and repaired with plumber's tape. Scarred by tar and flame and dog tooth and floating lost in the ocean.

I can see the state you're in, she goes on, softening for some reason known only to her. I can see the way it's affecting you. Don't shut me out. Why do you think I made such a fuss about coming with you? I wanted to be here if you needed me. I wanted to go through this with you. And I get left sitting here. Just please tell me you're not going to do anything stupid.

Boyle and her would have got on. Maybe too well. A woman who has rediscovered herself she says. That revelation of hers out walking in the Lake District in the mist. You are living a lie, a tree told her. She went home and changed her life. Two teenage boys over in Manchester and their baldy da who waits for his wife to come home. Go find yourself, he told her in his house slippers. But she won't be back sunshine, not if I can help it, she won't be there to switch off your electric blanket or boil your eggs in her underwear or shout at the boys for taking the piss when you fall down the stairs, sober

as well. She tells Dainty these things you see. She hasn't
talked as much to a man in her life she has said. She tells him
everything. That fantasy of hers with the apples for instance.
Dainty had sipped his beer and nodded like he had heard this
type of thing every day of the week. Apple peels and a knife.
Tell me one of yours now, she had asked. This all happening
on bar stools at a Sandinista fundraiser in Derry. Tell me one
of yours. I've never really thought about it Maureen. That's a
shame, she said and her and the drink he'd bought her wig-
gled off to another table. He thought hard to come up with
one. He went to the local library. Fear nothing, especially
your own thoughts, Boyle said in a letter from jail.

Dainty? Answer me.

I was just out walking around.

Show me you're thinking straight. I know what you're like.
You're still upset about your brother as well aren't you? This
isn't the way to deal with it all. You've had a bad shock.

She crosses the room towards him through the space
between the end of the bed and the table thing with the TV on
it. Behind her, she leaves a trail of footprints in the soft carpet.
In a moment she will have her arms around his neck. Big
Cowboy Dainty rides into town to save the day. Seeking the
truth and justice and answers to how his best friend ended up
with bullets in his brain and dumped on a country road in the
hills, Wicklow, wherever the fuck it is. The wick is low. The
wick will never be dipped again. Donkeying about the
streets, wheezing, sweating, pissing in strange bogs. He saw
Trinity College with its quads and cobbles. He walked up and
down Grafton Street in search of a bad sneaky face. He took a
taxi to the North Circular Road and got a sight of the house.
He kicked bits of plaster-cast masks in the gutter running
with milk of magnesia. He stared into the river for hints.

Maureen takes his hands. It's not your fault my sweet.

I was just out in a few pubs.

How about you take me out to one now then? I'm sick of
this room.

Ok. I'll be back in a minute.

Why?

I'll be back in a minute. I have to go down to the lobby. You get your shoes on.

Out into the corridor before she can argue. He takes the stairs to avoid delays. Five flights, going slowly round and round. The exercise will do him good. Dainty you're a man fleeing the scene but you don't know why. Holed up in a pub with Maureen it suddenly seemed the whole thing was too final and done with and nothing left to do but throw in the sprinkle of dirt. Out into the lobby where a gangload of Japs have arrived. Hope you brought the geishas with you boys. Would you look at the face on that sour bastard of a doorman with the truckload of luggage he's got to bring in? Do you want a hand? Away and fuck yourself. Forgive me Maureen. I've had a bit of a shock and I'm not myself today. Or any day to come.

Dainty makes his way through the crowds on O' Connell Street. There are so many faces that after a few minutes he gives up looking. Anybody would think there's something going on, a meeting, a big assembly somewhere. It's just bodies moving by him, bits of colour. The street is some breadth, and high. The only person standing still is some poor lost nervous fucker holding a sign for a fortune-teller. Madame Miriam will reveal the secrets of your fate. He gives the man a nod and gets a dopey look back. Alco, he thinks, drank it all away, if he ever had anything. If you asked him he probably couldn't even tell you what happened to him. Nobody gives a fuck anyway and why should they? He stops at a crossroads, black and white like a stick he once had. The build-up of people behind him forces him into the road. A bike courier swerves out of the way. Dublin where there's no room left on the streets. There's another lot waiting to cross the opposite way. The GPO in the background with a big new freshly ironed tricolour against the sky. It wasn't that long ago when he made a decision to call the cops and let them in on the whereabouts of a wee meeting of incarcerated minds down in a caravan site over the border. The guns have turned into syringes. There's Jim Larkin now up on his pedestal, the voice of the worker with the giant hands held high. Who the fuck listens to you now? The great seem great because we are on our knees. It all changes Jim, you can't stop it. Maureen I wish I had hands the size of Jim's.

The last time in Dublin he was with the wife and she was pregnant near Christmas and wouldn't touch a drop for the whole weekend but didn't mind queuing for hours in shops with the stress levels going through the roof. That was Fergal curled up in her then. Eleven years old now. Took him out to see a film a few weeks past and they go in for a burger afterwards and Fergal asks him, What happened to my uncle in the cemetery Daddy? Never you mind wee lad. Those days are gone. It's all in the past. What's the past Daddy? Eat your fucken burger. And Fergal tells him there's this lad in his class who keeps getting picked on because his da used to be in jail and they're all slagging him that he looks like the milkman. Changing times. The young ones wouldn't be interested in a gun unless it had a brand name on it and went with their trainers. And fair fucken play to them. What's the past Fergal? The past is the way me and your mother felt when you were born. That's all you need to fucken know about it. The rest of it is some cunt with a big wallet.

Jammed in by the crowd on the bridge, he goes between two jewellery stalls to the stone rail. There's the Liffey, brown and dead. Hills away in the distance where they drove him in the boot. Typical the stupid fucker didn't even pick a river deep enough. A few of those philosophy books in the pocket to weigh it down. Spur of the moment the papers said. The first time you ever act spontaneously in your life and you throw some half-arsed student into a puddle of water and run away and ask the big men to save your bacon and sort it all out for you. I bet you got some surprise when you realised what they had in mind. The new protectors of the status quo. The proud new dispensation. You stupid fucker Boyle; you stupid arsehole.

When he heard on the TV that a body had been found professionally dead and identified, Dainty went straight round to the house of Boyle's parents. There were journalists sitting in their cars up and down the street out of the rain and two police Land-Rovers. The downstairs front window was boarded up. Wee Jack from next door whose wife had died the month before answered when he flipped the letter box. He had two sons out the back on watch. We'll have to board up the fireplace as well in case they send down one of those cameras they use for looking down your throat, Wee Jack was joking.

What happened to the window?

Last week it came in when it was all in the papers sure. A brick.

I should have dropped in sooner. Tommy and Mary probably haven't spent as much time in the house since they were married.

Jesus, are those two married? Wee Jack blessed himself.

Tommy was mopping the kitchen floor. He got Dainty a can.

You all right?

Can't take it in Tommy. The fuckers –

Tommy put up his hand to stop.

Dainty couldn't: Fucken trial without jury. And them up on their high horses about Diplock courts for fucken years.

And isn't there another family in Dublin who've lost a young son? Tommy wielded the dripping mop at him.

He left me a message on the phone. Dainty hadn't planned to give out this information. Boyle always said he couldn't hold his tongue. Tommy was squeezing out the mop. They were preparing the house for the corpse. More than likely Mary was upstairs in Boyle's old room making space for a coffin. In that same room one night it had dawned on him and

Boyle that they could do whatever they wanted with their lives, go anywhere, taste anything, grope women with sun-licked breasts. They turned the music up and jumped around to hurry on the future. Then they heard voices in the street. From the window they watched Tommy being beaten to the ground by soldiers and thrown into the back of a Saracen. Mary ran drunkenly after it up the street until she fell over and lay there screaming and shouting. Boyle wouldn't go out to her. Why wouldn't you fucken go out to her? I was picking her up before I even realised you weren't there. I couldn't make you out so much of the time.

He was wondering if I'd seen you Tommy. He was in a tight corner Tommy. He was saying to send the two of you his best.

Tommy put his hand down on the tablecloth as if it were a child's head. I don't want to know, he said, softly, firm. It turns my stomach the whole lot of it.

Come on now Tommy.

You've two of your own am I wrong? What do you want for them? This kind of carry on? I don't want to hear another word about it. We'll give him his funeral and that's it finished. And we can all get on with our own lives.

Dainty goes into a pub and orders a pint. The barman is chewing a sandwich. Dainty hasn't eaten since that lunch with Maureen on the way down yesterday. The pub has one of those old snugs but he's the only one in. He knocks it back quick and leaves, still thirsty.

The street with all the people scurrying and carrying and nibbling like they're all insects at a carcass. Buddha Boyle where are you now? Sailing about like a turd in the mystic. Back in line with you mucker and I'll promise to keep an eye out the next morning I'm eating a tin of pilchards or skinning an orange. Or digging for worms to take the boys fishing out on the Line. Or maybe you'll come back as a colour. Fucken yellow.

Or the next time I'm hunting giraffes on the savannahs.

At that moment Dainty realises he has never seen a giraffe, not in real life. He sets his mind to remember the last time he had been in a zoo. He can't be sure if he ever was. And the boys? Shocked, he gazes around him at the busy wobbly humans. That's one thing he's going to put right when he gets home. There'll be one good thing coming out of this stunt. He'll take the boys by the hand and take them to the zoo. Show them the polar bears and the spiders. Maybe ask Maureen. See the looks on their faces. It'll be a moment to remember when he's pissing himself in some nursing home, sniffing the air-freshener nozzle for a taste of glory.

Trinity to his left where he was that morning and saw nobody with an intelligent face. Heard somewhere the Guards can't arrest you in the university grounds. Place built to educate the aristocratic youth of the day. Somebody needs to tell them they didn't do a very good job. The art of high-minded butchery the exception. A young woman sat high on a flight of steps and Dainty approached, shuffling, hands in his pockets to show he meant no harm. He thought he'd chance it: I'm looking for a friend of mine. Noel Boyle. Did you ever hear of him? The girl put her hand flat on her head and had a good honest think. She was lovely. Kind eyes. Her disappointment that she couldn't help him was so touching that he made up another name, Gregory Hillsmith, just to delay.

Dainty stops suddenly on the street. He has no idea where he is going, what's the fuck he's doing. The people passing don't even notice the state he's in, the total absence of anywhere to go. He can't breathe properly. And his woman blaspheming against him back in the hotel because he's a danger to himself and others and she feels left out and wants to be needed. I need you now Maureen. I'm going to collapse. She's heard me talking about him, she even spoke to you on the phone one night, and now she's reading things in the newspapers that would disgust her and send her packing, not right away, but slowly, week after week, a few months down the line she'll be thinking I'm only as good as my friends.

Every time I let her down, I will, I will, it's impossible not to let a woman down eventually, I'll do something or other and she'll link it to that pervy hoodlum murdering friend of mine who was put out of his misery in dirty Dublin she nods away sympathetically about as I tell her it's all lies Maureen, it is, Boyle wasn't like that, I knew him, that other wanker made it up for some reason beyond the scope of my imagination. Even so, she'll have that suspicion in her head, somewhere in that sharp determined mind of hers, like a leaf among the thorns, or the other way round, thorn in the leaves, that I'm no better. The ramifications go on and on, rippling out.

He makes it into another pub. This one is better, bigger, music on and a big TV screen showing the horseracing. He gets a table all to himself with a comfortable armchair facing away from the window. He thought he was going to die out there. He's shaking, wheezing. Settle the nerves, watch the horses and take a taxi back to the hotel in a while. It'll be all right. He'll talk Maureen round. At the bar there's a crowd of lads who look like they've been drinking for a couple of days. It'll be all right. The race on is being led by a horse with pink and white colours called Hullabaloo. Three-to-one on it is and well clear of the rest. Somehow watching it cross the line and the jockey not even putting a fist in the air is relaxing to watch. Settle the nerves. Have a few pints and calm this whole thing down.

Da what did you see in Dublin?

A lot of people. The crowds on Henry Street. An old river.

Da, Da what did you see in Dublin?

Tricolours fresh out of the laundry. Unarmed policemen on horseback.

What else Daddy?

I talked to this young girl not much older than you Fergal and she has nowhere to go and no money. She sleeps on the streets at night.

Was she funny?

Eh?

Did she tell you a joke?

You watch your lip wee lad. Money she was after.

What else Daddy? Something good?

I saw the swans in Stephen's Green. All the tourists.

Is that all?

Well I saw a street cleaner and he was sweeping the gutters clean of all these broken bits of plaster. And I stopped to talk to him and he told me they were bits of these masks of a dead woman.

Aw Daddy. Something better. That's scary.

I talked to a woman on Grafton Street who'd been selling flowers there for the last thirty years and her mother before her.

What are you, another reporter or what? she said to Dainty when he asked about her daughter. Her weathered face reminded him of woodworm. Dainty came straight out with it and told her he was a friend of Boyle's.

Well you can take your custom some place else, she said and turned her back on him.

He had a bunch of flowers in his hand, roses for Maureen.

I don't want your money. Take them. Go on now.

Your daughter was slandered and so was my friend.

She reared round at him, finger in his face: Slander is hardly the word for it. That one said we were dealing drugs off this stall. And prostitution. People believe these things. There's no smoke without fire, they think. I've been here more than thirty years on this street. I know more about this street than any of them put together. Don't come round here trying to use your bully tactics on me. My daughter had nothing to do with nothing. So go back and tell that to your vigilantes or whatever you are. You lay one finger on my daughter and you'll hear me and mine shouting about it until there's no tomorrow hear?

I've fucken nothing to do with that lot missus, Dainty said, holding up his hands.

Well whoever you are you were brought up without manners. If you want to talk to me you can control your tongue.

Dainty apologised. A customer was waiting: Dainty watched the mother show the flowers for approval and wrap them up.

Have you seen him? he asked next.

That one? She blessed herself. He won't come near me if he knows what's good for him. I was never fond of the sight of him at the best of times. Sick in the head that's my opinion. And people are worse for minding him. I don't want any more trouble hear? I've seen too many men with that look in their eye.

How do you mean?

Who you talking to love? I can tell by looking at you. And the smell of drink off you. I don't want any more trouble or I'll be starting a bit myself do you understand me love? I can make plenty of trouble too hear? Don't bring your troubles down here to my door. Take my advice and go back to your wife. You married?

Dainty decided to keep it simple and nodded.

She doesn't know where you are does she? No, I can see by your face she doesn't. Your friend, if that's what he was, I'm sorry for him and we'll never know the full story but he didn't know right from wrong when the moment came. My daughter has learned that lesson well now and I thank God for that. It'll put a head on her shoulders now I hope. Take my advice love and go back up home where you come from and give those flowers to your wife from me.

He had done what she told him and set his nose for the hotel. I'm going to lie down beside you Maureen and tell you everything. Stroke you and talk my heart out to you. All the woes and curses. Only along the way he had stopped for a quick drink and set out for the daylight once more without the bouquet. He had tried to find the bar again and then there's a blank and he's standing in the hotel room staring at Maureen reading on the bed, at her legs, knowing he isn't ready, there's more to do, it's not time, he's searching for

something, wishing she would say the right words to keep
him there and let him off the hook.

This next pub looks familiar. High bronze-topped horseshoe.
Gas lamps still functioning and stained glass. Crumbling mirrors of snakeskin glass to create space. Magic in the smoky
folky air. Take a stool there Dainty mucker. What have you
been doing with yourself? I was with these Swedes in one bar
talking about the horses and I went off to find a phone and
here I am. Who's round is it anyway? Listen to the tinkling
and the voices murmuring. I remember a time when I was far
away in America in the back of a car and a girl put her hand
down my trousers, this older blondey one, and offered the
hand round to be smelled by the lot of them. The pints wait
swirling settling blackening on their golden dais like verdicts
for us all. I see you in ten years' time in a castle in Corsica.
Maureen sweeping, clapping the birds out of the bedroom
before our afternoon siesta. Or one of the times up in the jail
and Boyle had made you a kite for the boys and you stopped
the car in the snow on the Glenshane Pass and let it blow
away, that fucken sad thing, you couldn't give it to your sons,
a prisoner's fucken kite.

And how's the head today?

And who the fuck is asking?

No need for that now. You got home ok so?

This wee man is nodding at Dainty. This gormless face.
Tufts of sandy hair. Plain man's suit. These pointy shoes. And
a wrinkly suitcase.

Do I know you? Do I need to know you like? 'Cause this
isn't a good fucken time for polite conversation you get me?

The wee man decides it's a joke and laughs like an out-of-
work shoemaker. He unfolds an ironed handkerchief from
the breast pocket and wipes his wee man's brow. A tartan
hanky for dabbing at sweat.

No luck with the hunt so? And a wee wink accompanies it.
Will you have a drink with me so?

Some wee fucken country Irishman with a suitcase and a tartan hanky and a buck-toothed barman in a black velvet bowtie.

I've been keeping an eye out myself around the town, he goes. No sign as yet but never give up that's my motto.

Your motto?

Never give up. He winks again.

Well I'll have a double whiskey then.

And sure why not? It's a bad story that, a bad thing to happen. It would take the wind out of your sails.

So where you going with the suitcase? You're not leaving us I hope.

I'm only arriving sure aren't I? Weren't we talking about it last night? You were saying you could fix me up somewhere. Where's that lovely woman you mentioned? Maddy was it?

He doesn't give the name. He keeps it secret, waits. Wee Tartan is already scanning the bar, a bland banal smile, like he would never dare expect to find anything. A sipper.

Maureen my hope come here on your smooth trim legs and save me. I don't trust this man. I'm surrounded here by things that bear no resemblance to life as we know it. This stool is not safe. My eyes are cheating, deceiving me. Give me a smile like that one at the bottom of the Academy Road. Our first night remember after that party? Wee Tartan here is telling me he's a free agent, the last of the wains are reared so he's packed his bag and walked out of the back door. I did my duty, he says, and no man can deny it. Who does he think he's kidding with his wrinkly wizened suitcase?

That was a very interesting conversation last night, he goes on, very interesting indeed. It's good to stretch the mind like that even if it couldn't be true. Did it just come to you there and then or have you been thinking about it for a long time? The phantom-limb idea. Remember you were telling the group of us your theory? If the body can have a phantom limb then why can't a city? Phantom places you said. Buildings, ghost streets. Whole people. Phantom pubs. I was laughing at

293

that one as I fell asleep and the black man in the bunk below me complained. Phantom pubs – that's a good one.

Who the fuck are you? Dainty sticks in.

Wee Tartan puts down his glass. Gives Dainty a look, a new look, a bit serious now, which says: You know the answer to that inside you.

Don't fucken look at me like that. I don't even know you.

Wee Tartan nods like this is always what happens to him.

What do you want? Dainty says.

Whole people was what you said. If a limb can do the haunting then why can't the whole person, the whole body.

Dainty shakes his head in admiration. You're fucking with my head here wee man.

We had a great night of talking. I learned a lot. The silver lining so I suppose.

The silver lining? What you on about?

The story of your friend there and what happened to him. I seem to remember reading about those masks in the newspapers. It must be hard on you. Especially after what happened to your brother.

Boyle you fucker. I'm on a stool here and I don't know where I am any more or who it is who's talking to me. I don't know where I am. People get what they deserve, that's the issue at stake. Trouble attracts trouble. No matter what the accident is people say they feel guilty about it, watched it once on the TV. Even after a robbery. They brought it on themselves somehow. The man hit by the blast bomb sucked the pieces towards himself. He chose to take the long way to work because of the woman he wanted to avoid. The city ruined by an earthquake gets down on its knees to pray for forgiveness. The woman mugged at the bus stop. Shame of the victim, guilt of the survivor or something. Have you ever heard such a pile of shite? Middle-class fuckers wanting to keep us down in the dirt teaching us to feel ashamed because they're fucken terrified we'll catch ourselves on and go out of our heads with our new-found peace and freedom and come after them and their fucken houses and their fucken wives and wipe out the whole lot of them. Divide and conquer.

It must be hard on you, Wee Tartan sighs again.

You seem to know a bit too much about me for my liking, Dainty says, trying to hold himself together. Don't fucken mention my brother again.

Wee Tartan dips his crafty head, a wee bow of shifty sickening acquiescence. He's after something.

Maureen he's after something in me. Acting all innocent but he'll leave a mark on you. I can see him climbing out of a grave with that fucken suitcase and dusting down his clothes with his tartan rag. He'll follow you down the hill under the flags and you'll never get rid of him. That hanky of his is to cover up his mouth watering.

Here now and listen to me whoever you are or I'll pan you. Boyle was always the fucken same, always trouble humming around him. Some people attract it no matter what they do. Even as wains he brought every fucken fiasco down on our heads. Crashing cars, breaking things, getting caught all the time like he fucken wanted it. Ask any girl he ever went out with. Which wouldn't take you too long. He doesn't know he is, he thinks he's acting for the best, but he always manages to land himself in shit. All those years in prison because he couldn't say no to people. That carry-on with the mobile library sure. It was a total disaster. No plan. Nothing. Same with the job before that when they tried to take over the house. Some wee lad runs straight out through the back door as they come in. They're in there an hour watching the TV before they realise and the phone's ringing and it's the cousins telling them to get out or they'll call the cops. A farce. The fact is he could never get laid so he turns into a gunman instead, makes a balls of that and decides he's a philosopher. I want to go to Dublin to change my life Dainty. I need new experience Dainty. I need my fill of something new. New everything. To lose myself. He needed a good fuck that's all Tartan. Or whoever the fuck you are. I doubt you've ever tried it but it's more physical when you lie beside a woman and she starts to wriggle around under you. The women of his own town weren't good enough for him but. He came out of jail like some paranoid guru returning from years of meditation in the East. Without the suntan. Call it what you want, education or finding yourself or freedom or losing yourself, or escape, whatever's your pleasure, simple or vulgar but the man was looking to get his end away and fucks some half-arsed student into the river instead and the new city fathers try to wash the blood off their own hands by dipping them in his and dumping him at the side of some mountain road. Executed by the IRA. Rogue elements my arse. By the new protectors of the status quo. Antisocial and criminal behaviour. Don't get me started Tartan or I'll fucken explode here you know what I mean. The whole fucken lot of it is a joke. Divide and conquer that's all it's about and the stupid cunts never see it.

Dainty propels himself into the company of two stiff-backed middle-aged women, stylish business-suit types, big knees, sham blondes and the make-up paste to cover the lines. Discontent is bad for the skin ladies.

Listen to me, he says, don't be alarmed. Just let me sit here in your company for five minutes until I get my head in order. You don't have to talk to me or anything. Carry on with what you were saying and I'll just sit here quietly. My head's in a bit of a mess. For a minute I thought I was standing over there talking to – you don't want to know. You'd run away screaming. I'll be grand in a minute. Had a bit of bad news the other day. About a friend of mine. But don't worry I won't bother you with it. Carry on with your conversation. What was it about? Husbands was it? You should hear my ex-wife on the subject.

We were talking about you, one of them says, and puts her hand on his knee.

Think Dainty: this is not the way things happen. Think you stupid fucker. Where are you?

He gets to his feet and does a survey of the entire room. It's busy, it's noisy, it all looks real enough. He takes a slug.

How many are there of you fuckers? How many? Show yourselves. Now listen to me those of you who don't know what I'm talking about. You might not be aware of it but there are some . . . He pauses and looks at the two women who now are pretending to be afraid, affronted, outraged. I don't know what they call themselves but they creep up on you. Like these two. They try to mess with your head. They take advantage of you when you're not at your best. I'm a man plagued by guilty thoughts I admit it and I'm down here in this city because my best friend died. He was murdered here in this town. So I had to come down. For a look? I don't have a clue what for. I just had to. Maybe he used to come in here. Noel Boyle. Any of you ever come across Noel Boyle? It was in all the papers. And there was this other character by the name of Fada. A right wee conniving fucker he was too. And the two of them seem . . .

The buck-toothed barman approaches with his hands in the air like a man under arrest, a man with a sad smile, like he's almost glad to be caught, it was great while it lasted, we had a good run.

Dainty manages to wangle another drink out of him before he makes his exit, keeping it dignified, apologising to the ladies for disturbing them. No bother at all, look after yourself. Good night now. Same to you both. Lovely charming people one and all. You can't hide from decay in the prim and tidy bushes of the ordinary, remember that ladies, my parting word. Outside, it is a revelation to find he is crying, big Dainty. Sneaking out of him craftily without warning. The laughter he hears must be his own too. Where to now then? It's hardly fair that a man in distress has to make all these decisions by himself. Who makes the rules in this bloody town?

He is in a street and the street is deserted and dark and all there is. The hotel is in another place altogether having a party with yesterday and next week and always. The street might be his very own because of its perfect emptiness. The Dainty Highway name it. Full to the brim with darkness like a dirty sheet stuffed down the side of the bed. There's fucken poetry for you now. Jammed down the side just in the nick of time before the door opens and in comes Lady Number Two for the night shift. You've a sick mind Dainty Gorman. Never thought you had it in you. They try to beat it out of you with the wage stick. Get you up in the morning for work, scare you you'll feel isolated and useless. I'll be a happy man on my sofa with a few cans and the sound of my woman humming to herself in the shower. Let them all whinge. All the whiners and mopers and gripers and sniffers. This is you here and now and there are worse places, far worse, you never forget that boyo, never. Smell that richness on the air like the room after an afternoon session with Maureen when she nips round between her lectures. The poetry's pouring out of you tonight buckeroo.

On his own street he stumbles back against a wall, calls out the name of his beloved and sinks down to his arse and thinks he'll sit there for a while. Maureen throw in the books and the Peace Studies degree and we'll go begging. All I need is a tin cup. Or a hat. Drop me a few quid and I'll tell you a great wee yarn about what happens when you take yourself too seriously. Here we are in the here and now. But what's this? He's sitting on something. Reaching behind him, he finds a lump of white rock. Or is it chalk? He closes one eye, holds it up in front of him for inspection. It's a nose, one off those death masks. He kisses the tip of it. She was some beauty all right. Could you ever have imagined the trouble you'd cause? Opens his legs, presses the snout into his groin: have a sniff of that my girl. He does a laugh of wickedness at himself: Dainty the Coarse. Maureen likes it though. She likes him to talk dirty. What he wants to do to her. She has a wicked side she kept to herself down the mothering years. I'll try Maureen but I'm no good at it. And there she is herself in all

298

her glory under the old-fashioned street light, one leg up like a grammar-school girl. Maureen I'm sorry. Are you waiting on me? I'll be back shortly and you can be as angry with me as you want. Don't look the other way. It's ok now. Why are you crying?

But Dainty O that's not her.

Another fucken stand in replica. He throws the nose in the direction of the street light, missing by a long way and thumping, shattering against a shop shutter. A different face turns towards him startled.

Fuck off Boylo I'm warning you. We've nothing to say. Did Buddha kick you out? Keep it to yourself whatever it is. I've fucken enough to be getting on with. You were always too fucken wrapped up in yourself to see that anyway. All your fucken questions. Some of us just have to get on with it. When's the last time you even sent a birthday card to one of my wee boys eh?

Holes in his face, Boyle points up the empty street.

Dainty sees nothing at first: then he hears feet like somebody running, scampering in bursts. Under a dread that it might be one of his sons he tries to get back on his feet: Can't have them seeing you down on your arse whether this is all a dream or not, or worse, deeper down than dreams. He flounders back again to the ground. Whoever it is he can see now is moving from wall to wall at a run, then waiting, listening. Maybe it's Wee Tartan who's been mugged and stripped of his suitcase and the grave filled in and he has to wander the world with all the other soulless forgeries. Soulless forgeries? Not bad Dainty. Pass me that guitar. There's a song in my heart. Seems Boyle is backing off but he continues to point. You see if this is fucken Death come to get me I'm going to beat your head in Boyle do you hear me? Warn me or something; don't just point.

The figure crosses the street, stops, then crosses again at a diagonal, soldier style.

Hi you, Dainty shouts. What are you up to?

Barefooted, the figure cuts over the street again and back and drops down beside Dainty on his knees. The eyes are petrified, half up into his skull, checking all around him. There's a rough beard but it's a youngish man. He's wearing an old granda shirt and trousers but the dirt is thick on the hand he lets lie on Dainty's knee, panting heavily.

You all right?

Do you want to see my cock?

Maybe later.

Do you know this? You'll find the key under the doorstep. For though she gives me up her breast, its panting tenant is not mine.

No idea. Is it code? Sit down there. Have a rest.

I can't, he says. His eyes are looking everywhere at once, starving.

You're having a bit of a bad night by the looks of it.

Did you see anybody coming this way?

This is my street you know.

Do you know this? I sought the hall, and behold – a change from light to darkness. The wind-chimes in the ditch.

Told you. I don't. You the hunter or the hunted?

The fella is now nervously examining the sky. Strong smell of flea powder off him. They flew up from the lake, he says. I saw them gathering last night. Forty, fifty of them. A shudder in the loins. Their hearts don't grow old.

Sounds bad. They after you?

Now from inside his shirt, he takes out a feather, a long white mouldy greasy one, and offers it in both of his hands for respectful inspection.

Is that what they're after?

Dainty gets the top-secret nod. He leans in closer and immediately starts to choke, like the thing has sucked all the air from his body. Gasping, he rolls over on the ground.

The fucker is straight up and sniggering at him. The fucker is dancing around him, wee hopping steps, wagging that feather wand or fuck knows its name, taunting him with it, snorting, wheezing. Any time Dainty moves he gets a lash of it and the thing drinks the breath out of him. Do you know this one . . . do you know this one? the fucker's chanting and bits of songs or fucken poems. Or pure mad nonsense. The filthy bare seaweedy feet jiving around his head are all he can see. And the useless street light lighting nobody's way between the skinny legs and proud of it. He makes feeble grabs for them, the hairy ankles. The fucker rain dances over them. He isn't letting up either Maureen. He's not getting bored of it. The feather tickles against his knees now and the suction is pulling his eyes out, in, out, there's no difference. Stuck spew. Dainty can't imagine the end point: the opposite of exploding, the magnetic opposite. Just let me up and I'll blow town, no delays, no questions. It's like he's being strangled from inside. Or dry vomiting pure tasteless darkness out of himself. This is my street, he wants to shout for his head is clear while he's gagging but when the breath comes there is a severe pain in his temples and he doesn't know which is worse. The fucker isn't going to stop. These are your last thoughts Dainty. Hairy cha-cha-ing feet and cold balls of light. Hissing and chants and the power hoover stroke of that feather down his body. Boyle could have warned him to run. This fucker is too much for me boys. Skipping around me singing. These are the last squashed thoughts boys. Mouth gulping like a fish, he's going to wedge it in and ram the feather down my gullet. Maureen?

Maureen?

Yes? I'm here.

Where are we?

Dublin. The hotel bar.

I was choking. That fucker Fada was choking me with a feather.

It was a dream.

Your man Fada was fucken choking me with this feather.

You've been asleep.

No Maureen. He fucken had me.

301

(Very long pause.)

Come on. They rang the room for me to come down and get you. The place is empty.

I called your name.

I heard you. Come on. Bedtime.

I have to tell you about Boyle. He's not what they say he is.

I know. I'm just glad you're safe.

I promise I won't leave you like that again. And I've got this great dirty line for you.

Do you?

I mean it. A class one.

It's about time lover boy.